The Legacy of Armstrong House

A. O'CONNOR

POOLBEG

Published 2017
by Poolbeg Press Ltd
123 Grange Hill, Baldoyle
Dublin 13, Ireland
E-mail: poolbeg@poolbeg.com
www.poolbeg.com

1

A catalogue record for this book is available from the British Library.

ISBN 978-1-78199-853-3

Typeset in Sabon 11pt on 15pt by Poolbeg Press Ltd
Printed and bound by CPI Group (UK) Ltd, Croydon, CR0 4YY

www.poolbeg.com

About the author

A graduate of the National University of Ireland Maynooth and Trinity College Dublin, A. O'Connor is the bestselling author of twelve novels, including *The House, The Secrets of Armstrong House, The Footman, The Left-Handed Marriage* and *On Sackville Street*. He has written one children's book on Irish patriot Michael Davitt, also published by Poolbeg.

Also by A. O'Connor

This Model Life

Exclusive

Property

Ambition

Full Circle

Talk Show

The House

The Secrets of Armstrong House

The Left-Handed Marriage

The Footman

On Sackville Street

Published by Poolbeg

Acknowledgements

A big thank-you to Paula, Kieran, David, Caroline and all at Poolbeg and to my editor Gaye Shortland. And thank you to the readers who have followed the story of Armstrong House and the people who lived there through to this third chronicle in the series.

For Jan

PROLOGUE

1853

Christmas at Armstrong House was always Lady Anna's favourite time of the year. She loved the period leading up to Christmas Day. She loved putting up the magnificent tree in the drawing room. She loved the giddiness that seemed to overtake the servants as they decorated the house. She loved how her husband, Edward, became relaxed and distracted from the usual strains of running the vast Armstrong estate. But most of all she loved the pure excitement that took hold of their seven-year-old son, Lawrence. Anna had known many children, but she didn't believe she ever saw one who got so much pleasure from Christmas as he did.

How different it had been before Lawrence was born! She used to dread the approach of Christmas. When she had married Edward twelve years ago and they had come to live in the sprawling Armstrong House in the west of Ireland, she had at first missed her family in Dublin and this longing seemed to become more acute at Christmas time, regardless of how much she loved Edward. But, as time went by, there was another reason why Christmas had filled her with dread and sorrow. Their marriage had remained childless for some years. And each Christmas the absence of toys under the tree had hurt more and more, and the echoes of an imagined child's laughter had sounded through the house even louder than before and had become unbearable. Each Christmas Day, the tradition had always been that their friends and neighbours would come for dinner and spend the day at Armstrong House. And each year the pitying looks of their friends and neighbours, as she sat at the top of the dinner table, became less disguised and more hurtful to behold. Each year the look of frustration on her husband's face as he jealously viewed their friends' and neighbours' children enjoying the festive season became more unbearable and she had secretly begun to fear she was infertile. All that had changed when Anna eventually became pregnant and Lawrence was born. At last they had their child, their very own child, and finally Edward had his heir.

This Christmas Eve she watched nervously as Edward lifted Lawrence high to light the topmost candle on the Christmas tree.

"*Be careful, Edward!*" she said for what must have been the twentieth time as the little boy, armed with the lit taper in its long brass holder, swayed close to the already lit candles on the tree.

Edward rolled his eyes and Lawrence squealed in delight as the candle began to glow.

"What a clever little man you are!" Edward gushed as he put the boy safely back on the floor. He stepped back and admired his son, Lawrence's slightly curled blonde hair lit up by the candlelight and his happy blue eyes smiling up at him.

"*Again! Again!*" cried Lawrence excitedly.

"There isn't a candle left unlit!" Edward said, taking the taper from Lawrence's hand and blowing it out. "You've lit them all!"

Lawrence stood back and admired the tree with the candles twinkling. "I think it's the best tree in Ireland! If not the whole empire!"

"I daresay you might be right!" smiled Anna. "I don't think even Queen Victoria's tree could compete with yours. Now, it's nine o'clock, Lawrence, and high time you were in bed."

"Just half an hour more!" pleaded Lawrence. "Papa promised he would read me a story first."

"It *is* Christmas Eve," said Edward, winking at Anna. "Just one story and then it's straight off to bed for him so he can be up early in the morning to open all his presents."

Anna smiled and raised her eyes to heaven. "All right! One story and then to bed! I know I never have a chance when the two of you unite against me!"

Anna pretended to be irritated but, in reality, was delighted at the closeness between her husband and son. Often she had felt, during the long years of childlessness, that it had affected Edward even more than her. Not having an heir.

She looked on fondly as Edward led Lawrence to the sofa in front of the huge roaring fire where the boy had already hung his stocking on the mantelpiece.

Lawrence cuddled up to his father who opened a book and began to read "A Visit from Saint Nicholas".

"*'Twas the night before Christmas, when all thro' the house
Not a creature was stirring, not even a mouse . . .*"

They say you can never miss what you never had, Anna thought, but Anna and Edward had missed Lawrence so much before he was born. She studied Edward. Now in his forties, Edward had the physique of a much younger man. She studied his kind face, his once chocolate-brown hair now greying at the sides. People always told her how lucky she had been to marry him. As she looked at her happy family, she didn't need to be told. She knew it herself.

The next morning Anna came down the staircase and could hear that the house was buzzing with excitement. The servants were rushing around, preparing the house for the guests who would be arriving that afternoon.

"Merry Christmas, my lady," said their butler, Barton, as she reached the bottom of the stairs.

"And a very happy Christmas to you, Barton. Where are Lord Edward and Master Lawrence?"

"They are in the drawing room, my lady, where there appears to be much merriment already," said Barton with a smile as he left her to continue his duties.

Anna smiled as she heard Lawrence's shrieks of delight coming from the drawing room. She made her way across the hallway and into the room where she saw Lawrence furiously rocking on a large new dappled-grey rocking horse with a long white mane, as Edward happily looked on.

"Lawrence! Stop that at once! You're ruining the rug and no

doubt the floorboards beneath it! You must ride him in the nursery not here!" said Anna.

"Oh, let him alone, Anna!" said Edward. "A rug is replaceable but a childhood memory is forever, especially a Christmas one."

"Oh, Mama, isn't he beautiful? What will I call him?" shouted an excited Lawrence.

"Let's give it some thought," said Anna. "Such a handsome horse must have *just* the right name."

"My old horse will be so happy to have his company!"

Anna looked over at the Christmas tree where Lawrence's already opened presents now lay scattered around.

"I thought you were supposed to leave the opening of your presents until after church, Lawrence," scolded Anna, pretending annoyance.

"I couldn't wait, Mama! I would have exploded with excitement if I left it any longer!"

"Hmmm, and I am certain your father didn't try too hard to stop you either," said Anna, smiling at a guilty Edward.

"I take all the blame," said Edward as he approached his wife, hugged her and kissed her, before whispering "Happy Christmas, my love."

She hugged him before turning her attention back to Lawrence.

"Now, Lawrence, go at once to Nanny and change quickly for church – otherwise we will be late. And tell Nanny to have a footman put the old toys you have chosen in the carriage and you can give them to the village children after church. I'll tell Barton to take the basket of oranges and sweets for the children out to the carriage . . . and, Edward, get the footman to carry that rocking horse up to the nursery before Lawrence completely ruins that priceless carpet!"

"Any more orders, my lady?" Edward said mockingly.

"I'll let you know if there are!"

Lawrence jumped off his rocking horse, ran to Anna and hugged her. "Yes, Mama. And thank you for all my presents!"

"Do you like them, my pet?" she asked, kissing his head.

"I love them!" he said before running out of the room.

"You really are going to spoil that child, Edward," scolded Anna.

"Isn't that what he's there for? Besides, I've never seen such an unspoilt child, despite everything he is given."

"He is," sighed Anna happily as she held her husband tightly, hardly believing that after all their years of longing and despair all their dreams had come true.

Anna and Edward, with Lawrence, proudly took their pew at the front of the church for the Christmas morning service. The church was on the green of the village that Edward had built on the estate for the estate workers.

Afterwards, they took their time speaking to their workers and tenants while Lawrence excitedly went to join the children, a footman carrying a huge box of toys with him.

The vicar approached Anna and Edward.

"Thank you for a lovely service," said Edward.

"And the choir was delightful," added Anna.

"I'm glad you enjoyed it. I do try to make the Christmas service something special. We have a lot to be grateful for, since the Famine." The vicar's face clouded over at the memory. "Every day is a blessing after the horror we all witnessed."

"Indeed," nodded Edward, hoping the vicar would not dwell on the subject as he knew Anna would become distressed. He could see that Anna's eyes were welling up at the very mention of the word 'famine' and the terrible memories it stirred up in her.

Although the Famine had affected everybody desperately, Anna had seemed to see it as her personal crusade to work endlessly to alleviate the suffering of the victims. She had run herself into the ground going from workhouse to workhouse, helping the peasants. In the end Edward had feared for her health and sanity and banned her from continuing with her good work, pleading with her to put her duty to their baby before her need to help others. He had begged her to stay at home before she caught typhus or one of the other terrible illnesses in the workhouses and brought it back to Armstrong House and infected their child. She had eventually, very reluctantly, obeyed her husband's pleadings and stayed at home. But a terrible depression seemed to come over her after that. People said it was because of the sights she saw doing her good works for the famine victims. It had taken a long time for her depression to lift. Gradually, with Edward's love and support and with her devotion to their son, she had recovered and seemed to become again the carefree happy woman he had married.

"My, my! But isn't Master Lawrence getting bigger by the day, bless him!" declared the vicar to Edward's relief at the change of subject.

"Isn't he?" smiled Edward, looking at his son who was handing out presents to the village children.

"And such a jolly little fellow!" said the vicar.

"He has his father's disposition!" mocked Anna.

"Ah! Isn't it a grace to see toys being handed out to children again," sighed the vicar. "Unlike during the Famine when if they were lucky enough to be handed a potato –"

"Yes, well, we had better be getting back to Armstrong House, vicar – we have guests arriving shortly." Edward cut the vicar off quickly before he began a tirade of misery and, taking Anna's arm, began to lead her over to Lawrence and the children.

"Your traditional Christmas dinner?" called the vicar after them.

"That's right," Edward said over his shoulder. "Good day, vicar, and a Merry Christmas!"

"Have a lovely Christmas, vicar!" Anna called. "That was a little rude!" she scolded Edward under her breath. "We should at least have invited him to drop by Armstrong House later."

"And bore and distress our guests with tales of the Famine for the day? I think not, my dear. Some of us try to forget the past."

"And some of us can never erase it," said Anna as her eyes became glazed over.

Edward looked at her for a moment before quickly saying, "Besides, the vicar will be quite busy with his own wife and children, I daresay. And lest we forget, his wife is even more morbid company than the vicar! Come, let us give the oranges and sweets to the village children before setting off for home."

Anna slowly walked down the path to the carriage after her husband. The vicar looked on from the church door as Edward handed out coins to the village children and Anna gave them oranges and sweets. They were such a generous couple, the vicar thought. Though not without their troubles over the years. As he studied Anna, her smiling face didn't deceive him. She had never lost the sadness in her eyes since the Famine. He remembered her when she had come to live at Armstrong House as a young girl. She had been very pretty and lively. He remembered her shining brown hair and delicate features. As he watched her now getting into the carriage, helped by Edward, he thought she had grown out of her prettiness and turned into a beautiful woman. She had matured into a serious Lady of the Manor, but the vicar missed that young fresh-eyed girl she used to be.

On the journey back to Armstrong House, Anna seemed lost in her thoughts as she gazed out at the passing countryside. In a way, it was good to hear the vicar talk about the Famine. Nobody ever talked about it at Armstrong House. Anna was sure that Edward had instructed everybody not to mention it there for fear of upsetting her. And she never mentioned it herself – though it was never far from her thoughts. She could never forget the dreadful things she saw as she travelled the countryside carrying out her good works, and all the time searching . . . searching.

She glanced down at Lawrence's happy face and smiled at him. She refused to ruin his Christmas Day by her brooding about a time he was too young to even remember.

The carriage continued down one of the many country roads that criss-crossed the vast Armstrong Estate. They passed by Hunter's Farm, a small manor house set off the road surrounded by sycamore trees, which was home to Edward's cousin Sinclair and his family. Although Hunter's Farm was their nearest neighbour, Anna never visited there. Sinclair was Edward's estate manager. She remembered how, when she had first come to live at Armstrong House as Edward's bride, she took an instant dislike to Sinclair. The dislike was mutual. When Sinclair had married the young widow Diana Hunter who lived at Hunter's Farm and had given the house its name, the dislike soon turned to hatred. Within months of Sinclair and Diana's marriage, they had produced a son, Harry. And as the years went by and Anna and Edward remained childless, it was presumed that Sinclair and Harry would become Edward's heirs. Anna clearly remembered the disdain and disrespect Sinclair and Diana had shown her during those years. Almost openly mocking her for not producing an heir as they arrogantly acted as the natural successors to Armstrong House. Edward, in his naiveté and worship of his cousin, could see none of it. The birth of Lawrence had changed all that as he rightfully supplanted Sinclair and Harry as the heirs to Armstrong House. Strange, Anna thought, how when she was childless Sinclair and Diana had upset her so, and now they were thankfully insignificant to her. She had to put up with them at family occasions – they would be guests at Armstrong House for Christmas Day. But other than that, thankfully, she had little to do with them. Edward still worshipped his cousin and, to her irritation, Lawrence had a strong friendship with Harry, despite being four years his junior. But to Anna, Sinclair, Diana and Harry were now irrelevant.

Edward looked up at the house as he stepped down from the carriage. Along with his family, it was his pride and joy. He had overseen every detail during the design and building of the house, ensuring it was the perfect home for his new bride Anna.

The house was baronial and granite stone, three storeys high with the third storey windows pitched under the black tile roof. The windows were tall and Gothic.

As he and Anna walked up the flight of steps to the front door, he paused and looked back at the view. It always took his breath away. At the end of the forecourt was a path that led to manicured gardens with fountains where Anna loved to stroll. Across the forecourt to the front of the house was a balustrade, in the middle of which was a flight of steps that led down to a terraced garden. There were two more balustrades and flights of steps, each leading down to a garden. From the bottom garden, steps and a path led onto the lakeshore. The view of the lake from the house stretched for miles. And on the far side of it was a series of hills and mountains, forever changing colour depending on the weather, clouds and sun.

They walked through the front door arm in arm, into a giant hallway with a spectacular staircase at the end. The large drawing room was immediately to the right, while a smaller parlour was to the left. Behind the parlour was the ornate dining room with its immense table and behind that was the library where Edward spent much of his time conducting the estate's affairs. On the other side of the hallway was the entrance to the ballroom, the scene of so many joyous parties and events over the years.

Coming home to this house never failed to lift Edward's heart. He glanced at his wife, to find her smiling back at him, and he knew she felt the same.

At one o'clock the guests began to arrive. The house quickly filled with people, with Barton and his footmen showing the arriving guests through to the front drawing room where they were cheerily greeted by Anna and Edward.

They were gentry and aristocracy from across the county whose highlight of the social year was Christmas Day at Armstrong House. The house's staff circulated amongst the guests with trays of hot port, whiskey toddies and mulled wine.

"At least the snow held off this year, Anna," said Lady Fitzherbert. "Do you remember last year? I thought we'd never get here the snow was so deep."

"I remember it well, Lady Fitzherbert. And the snow continued falling all day. You and Lord Fitzherbert had to stay the night here."

"As did many of your guests, as I recall. With the mild weather this year, at least we will not have to impose further on your hospitality tonight!"

"It is no harm if you do – there's always a room for you at Armstrong House – at any time," said Anna with a warm smile.

"Bless you, my dear!" Lady Fitzherbert reached forward and grasped Anna's hand affectionately.

As Lady Fitzherbert chatted away idly, Anna spotted Barton showing Sinclair and Diana into the drawing room, followed by their son Harry. She braced herself for the false greeting they would give each other. She watched as Edward swept over to them and embraced Sinclair in a hug before embracing Diana and kissing her cheek and then tousling Harry's hair affectionately. She watched as they joked and chatted together. Sinclair was still the huge giant of a man he had been when she had first arrived at Armstrong House, though his once jet-black hair was now peppered with grey. Diana, once a great beauty, had weathered somewhat with age but she still had a presence about her, and was beautifully presented with her immaculate blonde hair swept up in a bun. Her reputation as the best horsewoman in the county still maintained, her figure was no doubt kept by the endless riding she did every day. Harry, now aged nearly twelve, was a curious mix of both his parents. He had Diana's colouring and build, but his father's face.

"Anna! Look who has arrived!" called Edward as he led Sinclair and family over to her.

"Cousin Anna, Merry Christmas," said Sinclair as he bent forward and kissed her cheek.

"Same to you, Sinclair."

"Happy Christmas, Cousin Anna," said Diana as she kissed Anna's other cheek.

Anna nodded at her and smiled. Anna hated how they always called her cousin. She was only a cousin of Sinclair's by marriage, and certainly not a cousin of Diana's.

"I am so glad you could make it," said Anna.

"How could we not?" asked Sinclair.

"Indeed – how could we not?" repeated Diana.

"Dinner is not until three, so please do avail of the canapés – and we have mulled wine, whiskey toddies and hot port," urged Anna. "And indeed, if you prefer, less seasonal drinks which are being served from the sideboard." She remembered when Sinclair and Diana used to just walk into Armstrong House's kitchen and take whatever they fancied back to Hunter's Farm. That was when they felt entitled as Edward's heirs. She could tell by Diana's sly eyes that the memory must be passing through her mind as well.

"Most kind," said Sinclair as he took a hot whiskey from a passing footman's tray.

"Harry!" cried Lawrence, seeing his friend and rushing over. "What did you get for Christmas?"

"A pony," answered Harry.

Anna discreetly raised her eyes to heaven. They gave the child a pony every Christmas and then expected Harry to care for it and rear it during the year before they sold it at a profit at the mart each December, just in time for them to buy another pony for him to do the same with. She wished just once they would give Harry something that they didn't make a profit from. And what the process was doing to the child's emotional development didn't bear thinking about.

"What did you get?" asked Harry.

"I got a new rocking horse – a huge one – and a spinning wheel, and a jack-in-the box, and toy soldiers, and a train, and a –"

"Yes, yes, Lawrence, that will do," said Anna, becoming embarrassed.

"Mama made me take all my presents up to the nursery in case they got in the way," said Lawrence. "Mama, may I take Harry up to the nursery to show him everything and so we can play?"

Anna smiled. "Very well. But please remain calm, Lawrence – you are getting too excited."

"Yes, Mama," said Lawrence. He grabbed Harry's hand and they rushed out of the drawing room.

"I believe Christmas presents are an opportunity to teach children responsibility not frivolity," said Diana.

"Indeed, you are correct, as always," said Anna. "If you will excuse me . . . ." And she made her way to chat to other guests.

A while later Diana was perched on a couch in the drawing room beside Mrs. Foxe, a matronly woman with an honest loyal face, a glass of wine in her hand. The Foxes owned the neighbouring estate and were good friends of Edward's and Anna's.

Looking around the crowded room, she saw Sinclair deep in conversation with Edward at the fireplace while Anna circulated chatting to the guests.

"Edward and Anna always put on such a lovely Christmas Day for us all," said Mrs. Foxe.

"*Hmmm* . . . there's something a little distasteful about the abundance of it all though – so soon after the Famine," said Diana. "As for the money wasted on the child, with all those presents they continue to inundate him with! He'll be ruined!"

Mrs. Foxe looked surprised. "I think little Lawrence comes across as anything but ruined. Most pleasant child I've ever met – and I don't like them as a rule!"

"Still distasteful – so soon after the Famine."

"Well, I doubt Anna or Edward could reproach themselves with anything concerning the Famine. Edward made sure that not one tenant was evicted or starved on the Armstrong Estate. And I'm sure it was not easy for him to do so financially. As for Anna – well, what can I say about Anna? While every other lady in the country dared not stir from the drawing room for fear of being robbed by a desperate mob or catching typhus from some poor unfortunate creature, Anna was out distributing food parcels and visiting the workhouses. She worked tirelessly to help the desperate. Why, she nearly killed herself along the way, she worked so hard!"

"Oh, don't we know!" said Diana, raising her glass of wine to her lips and taking a sip. "Haven't we all heard of all she did over and over again!"

Mrs. Foxe looked at Diana, not at all pleased with her tone.

Just then Barton came in and rang a bell, causing a silence to fall on the room.

"Ladies and gentlemen, Christmas dinner is served!" he announced.

Anna quickly made her way to the door where she turned to address her guests. "Let us make haste to the dining room where a feast awaits!"

Suddenly a high-pitched scream ripped through the house, followed by a loud thud.

Anna's heart stopped for a second and her face creased in shock as she swung around.

"Lawrence!" she whispered. "*Lawrence!*"

She pushed past a stunned Barton and raced out into the hallway.

"*Lawrence!*" she screamed as she saw her child's body lying at the foot of the staircase, blood pouring from his head. She ran to him and sank to her knees beside him.

"Lawrence, my baby, my baby!" she cried frantically as she cradled him.

As the other guests began to file out of the drawing room, Edward burst into the hall.

"What on earth is going on?" he demanded and then he went white as a ghost as he saw Anna with Lawrence at the foot of the stairs.

Edward raced to them and fell to his knees beside them.

"Lawrence – can you hear me? *Can you hear me*?" demanded Edward as he attempted to take the boy out of Anna's arms.

As Edward saw how still Lawrence was, he turned to the crowd gathered around them and roared, "*Get a doctor! Get a damned doctor now!*"

Anna looked on in shock as Edward tried to shake Lawrence awake.

"He must have fallen down the stairs," she heard a voice say.

Anna looked up the stairs and saw Harry standing at the top of the stairs, his face unconcerned. As she stared at him in shock, he turned and walked away.

CHAPTER 1

Present Day

The tourist bus pulled into the forecourt in front of Armstrong House. Kate Collins was waiting for them, with a big smile pasted on her face.

The tour operator got off first and Kate stepped forward to greet her.

"Helga?"

"Yes – you must be Kate?" said Helga.

They shook hands.

"I'm afraid we are running late," said Helga impatiently. "We should have been here half an hour ago."

"That's fine, there's no rush," Kate assured her.

"Fine for you maybe, but we're supposed to be at Westport House in three hours exactly!" said Helga.

"Well, I'm sure you will make it on time," said Kate.

The German tourists were descending from the bus and filling up the forecourt. Their cameras at the ready, they already were taking photos of the views across the lake and the front of the house.

"Good afternoon, everybody, and welcome to Armstrong House!" said Kate loudly. "We welcome you most warmly to our home and we hope you enjoy your visit."

"Where was he shot?" asked an enthusiastic woman, making a beeline for Kate.

"Eh, Lord Charles Armstrong was shot at the gateway into the house – the main gate that you drove through on the way in," said Kate.

"Oh, if I had known that I would have got the driver to stop! I wanted a photo of the spot!" said the woman irritably.

"I'm sure the driver will stop for you on your way out," said Kate.

She smiled to herself. It was the question all the tourists asked. Where was Lord Charles Armstrong shot? It had been four years since Kate had co-produced the docudrama *The Secrets of Armstrong House*. She had often thought the film would never be finished. It had been about life at Armstrong House at the turn of the century in the Edwardian era, and focused on the shooting of Lord Charles Armstrong, who had been her husband Nico's great-grandfather. Kate had been in her glory making the film. A former actress who had been obsessed with Armstrong House and the Armstrong family since she had first arrived there to live ten years before, she had taken great joy from uncovering the mystery of the shooting of Charles and bringing it to the world's attention through the film. She remembered Nico had been vehemently against the making of the film, as he had not wanted his family's dirty laundry aired in public. How they had fought during the filming as she uncovered the truth behind the shooting! But he had come round eventually to the idea and actually praised her when the film got rave reviews. She remembered how she had found out she was pregnant during the filming – something she had never bargained for when she had started with the film. Their son Cian had been born just after filming had wrapped. Nico also did not object to the money made from the film which had proved to be not only welcome, but essential for the continuing running of Armstrong House. Kate and Nico had discovered since they married and moved back into the renovated Armstrong House that a manor of that size was incredibly expensive to run. It had been built by Nico's ancestors in the 1840s when the house was the epicentre of a vast estate that had thousands of acres to support it financially. Kate, since retiring as an actress had no regular work, and Nico as an architect did not bring home nearly enough money to keep the house running as it should be.

"Shall we start the tour?" called Kate to the tourists. "We can begin inside the house and then you are very welcome to tour the gardens at your leisure. They have been restored to how they were during the nineteenth century. I think you'll find the terraced gardens in front of the house with their spectacular views particularly interesting."

Kate walked up the steps and into the giant hallway, followed by the tourists.

"Armstrong House is a wonderful example of early Victorian architecture. Although the house was damaged by fire during the Irish War of Independence, photographs and paintings were studied painstakingly to restore the main part of the house to its original state. And so, as you stand here in the great hall of Armstrong House, you see it as the original occupants did in the early Victorian age."

The previous year, Kate had had a brainwave. The docudrama had attracted so much interest and there had been so many enquiries that it occurred to her that it would be a wonderful idea to open the house to the public, concentrating on tours. Nico had of course hated the idea, and again fought her vehemently on it.

"I don't want to live in a shop window!" he had objected. "I don't want our house to become a Disneyland full of people gawping at our lives!"

"It's an excellent idea, Nico," she had said. "It will bring in needed revenue for us to continue running the place to the standard it needs. Armstrong House isn't just our home, Nico, it's of historical interest, and we are the keepers of it for future generations."

Kate always found that the best way to bring Nico around to her way of thinking was to play on his humanitarian side. He was always too proud to admit to doing anything for purely financial gain, but if he felt it was doing something for posterity he felt better about himself. Kate, who had been brought up in New York, felt no need to apologise for doing something for financial gain. However, she did genuinely love sharing the history of Armstrong House. She always felt incredibly lucky to live there, and enjoyed letting other people experience the place.

As Kate talked the tourists through the different portraits hanging on the wall, she stopped at the portrait of a man and a woman.

"This is Lord Edward Armstrong and his wife Lady Anna," said Kate. "They were the first inhabitants of Armstrong House. In fact, Edward built the house for Anna on their marriage as a gesture of his love for her."

There was a chorus of '*aahs*' from the women in the audience.

"At the time, Armstrong House was the epicentre of a huge estate that stretched to thousands of acres. It was home to thousands of tenant farmers. Of course, the Great Famine in the mid-19th century affected the estate greatly. But Edward was known for his kindness, unlike many other landlords during that terrible era. No tenants were evicted for non-payment of rent and no family starved or had to emigrate. And Anna was very much before her time as a crusader, tirelessly fighting for the rights of the tenants and starting charities to assist the afflicted around the country."

Kate moved on down the hallway and into the drawing room.

"This is the original oak carved fireplace which thankfully was spared in the fire during the Irish War of Independence. The French window at the end of the room was not an original feature of the house, but was added during the Edwardian era . . ."

As Kate continued to go through the minutiae of the room, she didn't observe that there was a man standing at the back of the tourist group who was staring at her intently, listening to her every word and observing her every movement.

Nico Collins sat at the island in the kitchen of Armstrong House, working on his laptop while his four-year-old son Cian played on the kitchen floor beside him. The kitchen was in a semi-basement at the back of the house and Nico had begun to refer to it as "the trenches" as he retreated to the safety of it when Kate was showing her tourists around the rest of the house. It was the only place he could get on with his work as an architect in peace while noise and disruption took over the rest of the house. As he tried to concentrate on his work he heard footsteps coming down the corridor. He looked up, expecting to see Kate, but instead saw a matronly woman standing there.

"Hello – can I help you?" he asked.

"No, I am just taking a look around," said the woman in a heavy German accent, as she began to walk further into the kitchen, examining the fixtures and fittings.

Nico realised she was part of the tourist group.

"Are you lost?" he asked.

The woman turned around and looked at the man seated at the island as if she felt he had no right to be there. He was a tall man with fair hair who was now taking his reading glasses off to get a better look at her.

"No, I am not lost," she said. "I read that the servants' quarters of the house used to be downstairs so I came down to take a look." With that, she continued her investigation.

Nico managed to hide his irritation with the woman who had obviously ignored the sign at the top of the stairs leading down to the basement, asking tourists not to go beyond that point.

"I have to say, it is not what I expected," said the woman, looking annoyed.

"Sorry?"

She waved her hand around the expansive kitchen which was chic and modern, with no signs of any original features. When the house had been restored, the basement was the only part of the house that had been modernised.

"This!" she said, pointed angrily to the cream porcelain tiles and the inbuilt microwaves and oven. "That is not what Lord Edward and Lady Anna's servants were working with, is it?"

Nico fought back the temptation to give her a sarcastic reply. Kate had him well warned to always be polite to the tourists if they crossed his path.

"Eh, no. The house is also a family home, *our* family home, so the kitchen is designed for *our* needs rather than those of the Victorian servants."

"All in such bad taste," said the woman. "A modern kitchen in a period house! That is a disgrace."

Nico watched in amazement as she turned and left. He shook his head in irritation and tried to concentrate on his work again.

Then the phone rang. He got off his stool and went over to answer it.

"Armstrong House," he said.

"Hi, is Kate there?" came a woman's voice.

"She's not available at the moment – can I take a message?"

"For goodness' sake! It's Fidelma O'Brien at the *Daily Mail*. I arranged to do a phone interview with her at three o'clock. She said to ring this number."

"Well, I'm afraid she's tied up with a tourist party which arrived late."

"Well, can't you go and fetch her? I have to have this interview done and written in two hours – otherwise it'll miss going to print!"

"Look, I don't even know where she is. Best I just get her to ring you back?"

Fidelma sighed loudly. "Tell her not to bother if it's later than half an hour!" she said quite rudely. "Honestly! Kate's been badgering me for weeks to do an interview on this new project she's working on and then, when I finally agree, she's entertaining tourists!"

Nico tried to keep his patience. "I'll let her know – thank you," he said quickly and hung up the phone.

He shook his head and went to squat down beside Cian and his toy trucks.

"I don't know what your mother is up to half the time!" he said, smiling, as he tousled the boy's hair.

The train pulled into the station at Castlewest and Valerie Donovan stepped off. She quickly looked up and down the platform but there was no porter in sight.

Just then a middle-aged man wearing a tweed jacket walked past her.

"Excuse me!" she called to him.

He turned and looked at her questioningly.

She smiled sweetly. "I wonder if I could ask your assistance?"

"Yes?" asked the man, smiling warmly at her American accent.

"I simply can't manage all my luggage on my own!" she said, pointing to her five suitcases which were still on the train.

"Oh, it will be my pleasure!" said the man as he cast an appreciative eye over the very pretty blonde with the American accent.

Valerie stepped aside and let him move the luggage onto the platform.

"Just don't know what I'd have done if you hadn't come along!" she said.

"No problem at all!" said the man and made to walk on.

"Sorry!" said Valerie, halting his progress. "If you could just watch my cases for two minutes while I get a porter?"

"Oh, eh . . ." said the man.

"Thanks!" said Valerie and she left him with the cases while she walked down the platform and into the station building.

The minutes ticked by as the man stood there, staring down the platform and then at his watch. He was now late for an appointment.

Valerie then emerged onto the platform with a man but no luggage trolley.

"Oh thanks!" said Valerie. "No porter, can you imagine? But, luckily, I found this taxi driver. If you wouldn't mind giving him a hand with my luggage I'd be eternally grateful!"

The man managed to smile through gritted teeth as he began to haul two of the large suitcases down the platform. Valerie and the taxi driver followed with the rest of the luggage.

"People are always so helpful in Ireland!" said Valerie, safely ensconced in the back of the taxi.

"Where to?" said the taxi driver as he sat into the front.

"Armstrong House," said Valerie as she gaily waved goodbye to her irritated helper.

The tour had finished inside the house and now the guests were wandering through the terraced gardens to the front of the house and the garden to its side.

Kate stood at the balustrade at the edge of the forecourt, looking down at the garden below as the guests sauntered around.

"Excuse me, would you mind if I take some photos of the house," asked a voice to her left.

She turned around to see a man in his late thirties, dressed casually in jeans and shirt. He was a handsome, dark-haired man with sallow skin.

"Be my guest," said Kate with a smile. "I always love when people take photos as I think it's a record being held for the future in unknown places."

"Yes?"

"Well, you never know what the future might bring and where records can be found. When we were restoring the house ten years ago there wasn't much to go on. A lot of the house had been fire-damaged for years and so we had to search the most unlikely of archives to find old photos and even film reels to show us what the original house looked like."

The man started to take photos. "I never thought of it like that," he said in a southside Dublin accent. "Well, let's hope that the house will never again suffer a catastrophe that obliges anyone to go searching again."

"Let's hope so!" agreed Kate.

"You did an amazing job on the restoration. It's like stepping back into another world when you go through the front door."

"Thank you," said Kate.

The man stopped taking photos and put out his hand. "If I could introduce myself – I'm Doctor Daniel Byrne."

"Kate Collins." She shook his hand and smiled.

"I watched your film with great interest," said Daniel. "It was a fascinating piece of history and, as I'm stationed down here for the next six months, it gave me a useful insight into the area."

"Oh?" asked Kate. "You're not with the group of tourists?"

"No, I just booked a place on the tour here for the visit today." He gave a short laugh. "Sorry, I'm not explaining myself properly – I'm overseeing the excavation of the famine mass grave in Castlewest."

22

"Oh!" said Kate, her interest piqued. "How exciting! I've been hearing all about that. Have you started work there yet?"

"Just this week," said Daniel.

"You're an archaeologist?"

"Yes, a bio-archaeologist. So, we will be studying the bodies that are buried there. We are hoping to discover a lot during the excavation. Everything from their age groups to what their actual causes of death were. It's not enough to know they died of starvation – as you no doubt know, many died of other illnesses brought on by starvation. It should really give us a picture of what life was like for these unfortunates during the Famine."

Kate's mobile started to ring. She quickly took her phone from her pocket and saw it was Nico phoning her. She put the phone on silent to concentrate on her new acquaintance.

"I've been absolutely fascinated by the plans for this excavation since I heard about it first, and was delighted it got the go-ahead eventually," she said.

"Well, yes, it took a lot of time for the government funding to come through. But I'm hoping we can make a real scientific breakthrough."

Kate became animated as she spoke. "Lady Anna Armstrong, who was the first inhabitant of this house with her husband Edward, was a tireless crusader during the Famine on behalf of the victims. She probably met and tried to help some of the people who ended up in the famine grave. I'm actually working on a new film about her life, and would be keenly interested in paying a visit to the excavation site to see your work."

Kate had become so engrossed in her conversation with Daniel that she didn't even notice the taxi pull into the forecourt and Valerie get out from the back of the car.

"*Sis!*" Valerie called loudly, causing Kate to jolt and turn around.

"Valerie!" exclaimed Kate, shocked at seeing her sister standing there.

Valerie swept forward and embraced Kate in a massive hug. "It's so good to see you!"

"Where did you come from?" asked Kate.

"New York. I just flew in this morning."

"But – but you never said you were coming!"

"I thought it would be a nice surprise for you."

"Well, yes, of course it is. But what a surprise!" Kate hadn't seen her sister in three years.

Helga, the tour operator, was at the door of the bus and busy counting heads as the tourists got back on.

"*We are about to leave! Could everybody get back onto the bus who should be on the bus!*" Helga shouted.

"That's my call," said Daniel to Kate. "Lovely to meet you. Please do drop by the excavation site."

"Oh, yes, I most certainly will," said Kate, shaking his hand. "Very nice to meet you too."

Daniel headed quickly back to the bus.

"He's attractive, isn't he? Who is he?" asked Valerie, looking after the bus as it headed off.

"Oh, just an archaeologist working in Castlewest," said Kate absentmindedly, still astonished to find her sister arriving on top of them, unexpected and unannounced.

"Well, where is that husband of yours and my wonderful nephew?" asked Valerie.

"They're inside. Nico will be as shocked to see you as I am," said Kate.

Valerie linked her arm through Kate's and, ignoring her luggage which the taxi driver had left in the forecourt, led her up to the house.

"My gosh, Kate! Is this where you live?" she said, taking in the splendour of the building. "It's truly amazing! How lucky you are! But then – I guess you're used to living in stunning houses. Remember that house you lived in with Tony? My gosh – I remember staying there with you and just being blown away."

Kate felt awkward at the mention of Tony, her first husband. It was strange but since she married Nico and moved into Armstrong House with him, it was like she didn't give her life before that much thought. It had at times been a very glamorous life with her being an actress married to a very rich man like Tony. But it had also

24

sometimes been a tragic existence for her with a lot of sadness. She had only ever found real happiness with Nico. To such an extent that she tried not to think about her life before then. And much as she loved her sister, Valerie was from that previous life and it felt somehow out of place that she was here now.

They entered the house and Valerie was even more impressed. She dropped Kate's arm and began to wander around the hall, looking at the family portraits.

"*Kate!*" Nico was calling loudly as he came up the stairs at the back of the hall with Cian by the hand. "Kate! I've been trying to ring you this past half hour! There's a journalist from the *Mail* who has rung three times trying to do some interview with you."

"Oh no! Fidelma, I completely forgot!" said Kate. "Why didn't you give her my mobile number?"

"I did after she rang me the second time! She couldn't get through to you either," said Nico, suddenly spotting the woman looking at the Lord Edward portrait.

"I must have put my phone on silent by mistake," said Kate, taking out her phone and seeing all the missed calls.

"Hi, Nico!" said the woman as she turned around.

He blinked a few times, failing to recognise her at first. Then he realised it was Kate's sister! He had only met her once before, three years ago when they were visiting New York.

"Valerie?" he said.

"So good to see you again!" said Valerie, rushing forward and giving him a kiss on the cheek and then turning her attention to Cian. "Oh, my gosh – last time I saw you, Cian, you were just a baby! You've grown so much!"

"I have," he said, nodding.

"I'm your Aunty Valerie, you know."

"I didn't know," said Cian.

"Well, now you do and we're going to have fun together!"

Nico was still taken aback at her presence. "Nice to see you again, Valerie. We weren't expecting you." He turned quickly to Kate for clarification. "Were we, Kate?"

"No, we weren't," confirmed Kate, preoccupied with her

mobile. "I'm really going to have to phone Fidelma back straight away, otherwise I'll miss doing the interview."

"You go and phone her, Kate, don't worry about me," urged Valerie. "I'll just stay here and get to know my nephew."

Kate threw an apologetic look at Nico and then rushed into the drawing room to make her call.

"Nico, be a darling – my suitcases are out in the forecourt. Would you mind bringing them up to my room?" said Valerie.

"Eh, sure," said Nico.

When he walked out the front door he looked at the five huge suitcases sitting on the forecourt and scratched his head.

"I put her in the Green Room," said Nico who was making dinner when Kate finally got off the phone from Fidelma and came down to the kitchen. "This spaghetti is nearly done – I made the sauce earlier so it just needed reheating."

"Okay," said Kate. "Cian, put away those toys now. Dinner is almost ready."

"My fav'rit! Spaghetti!" he said as he rushed to put the plastic dinosaurs he was playing with into a toybox.

"What's Valerie doing now?" Kate asked.

"She said she was going to have a shower," said Nico. "Why didn't she tell you she was coming?"

Kate raised her eyes to heaven as she fetched Cian's bowl and cutlery. "Why doesn't Valerie ever do anything that other people normally do?"

"When did you hear from her last?"

"An email at Christmas. She never made any mention of even thinking of coming to Ireland."

"She's got enough luggage to last her a year! Did she say how long she was staying?"

"I know as much as you do, Nico," said Kate, becoming irritated. "Cian, sit up to the table now." She fetched him a drink from the fridge as he clambered up and knelt on his chair.

"I haven't managed to do a thing all afternoon with work," Nico complained. "Between a German tourist wandering down and telling me the kitchen was in bad taste, to that journalist ringing me incessantly looking for you, to heaving your sister's cases upstairs for her, at her behest, while listening to her bang on about the nightclub scene in New York having had its day!"

Kate tried not to giggle. She did find Nico funny when he got worked up over things. However, the German tourist and Fidelma being a nuisance was one thing. Her sister Valerie arriving in on top of them without an explanation was quite another. History had taught Kate that, wherever Valerie went, trouble was sure soon to follow.

"I want my dinner!" said Cian, banging with his fork on the table.

"Hush, Cian," said Kate. "It's coming now."

"Hello!" came Valerie's voice as she walked down the basement corridor to the kitchen.

"In here!" Kate called.

"Oh, I feel like a new woman after that bath," said Valerie. "I am starving – the food they serve on the transatlantic flights these days wouldn't feed a cat! What's for dinner?"

"Nothing fancy, just meatballs," said Nico as he drained the spaghetti.

"My favourite, how did you know?"

"Mine too!" said Cian.

Valerie smiled at him as she went to the wine rack.

As she selected a bottle of Merlot Nico gave Kate an amused look.

Valerie opened the bottle and proceeded to take three glasses and fill them.

Then she sat down at the table next to Cian.

"It really is so good to see you, Kate, and this little man," she said, taking a good swig from her glass. "I'm sorry I haven't been better at keeping in touch, but – you know how it is."

"I'm as guilty as you are on that front," said Kate, taking a seat across from her. "But I wish you had said you were coming, Valerie. I would have collected you from the airport and at least done a shop to get something special in for you."

"Oh Kate, you know I hate a fuss!"

"We might have been away on holiday – you took a chance that we were even here," said Nico as he put out plates and cutlery.

"Where's my dinner?" Cian demanded. "I'm hungry!"

"It's coming, Cian," said Nico. "Behave."

"Oh, no, it wasn't a risk," said Valerie. "I checked your website beforehand and saw you were open for tours, so I knew you'd have to be here."

"Clever of you," said Kate.

"And how clever are you? Opening this place to tourists after the film was made – you must be making a mint?"

"Hardly a mint – but a house of this size takes a lot of money to run and maintain and the tours certainly help, as did the film of course," said Kate.

"The architecture business not making enough dough, huh, Nico?" smirked Valerie.

"As Kate said, it takes a lot to run Armstrong House," said Nico, wondering if he had been insulted. He began to serve up the spaghetti.

"Well, I'd never have had you down as a tour guide, Kate!" said Valerie. "Bit of a comedown for an award-winning actress!"

Now it was Kate's turn to feel she was being insulted.

"I actually enjoy showing the house to people and telling its history. People are genuinely interested, especially after the docudrama," she said.

"Oh, I'm not judging you, Kate. I admire anybody who can turn their hand at anything to earn a crust," said Valerie.

Nico put a large serving dish on the table. "Help yourselves to meatballs, ladies." He spooned some sauce and meatballs on top of Cian's spaghetti, then sat down. "How is your own career going, Valerie? Still singing?"

Valerie rolled her eyes. "Don't mention the war! I'm still getting lots of gigs but, you know, everybody wants to be a singer these days! They all think they're going to be the next Lady Gaga and, well, let's face it, I'm not getting any younger. But I still have my regular clubs that retain me."

"The entertainment business is such a ruthless one," said Kate with a shudder, thinking back to her acting days. She felt a degree of sympathy with Valerie. At least she herself had managed to reach a certain level with her acting and had starring roles in mainstream movies in her day. But Valerie had been doing the club circuit in New York for years and never got a break.

"It's really strange being back in Castlewest," said Valerie. "How long is it since Mum and Dad left here, Kate?"

"Well over thirty years," said Kate, remembering the small house they had lived in before emigrating to New York.

"First time I've been back since. I visited you and Tony when you lived in your house in Dublin but you didn't have this place then. Strange how you ended up back here, wasn't it, Kate? Strange how things turn out."

Both Kate and Nico cringed at the mention of Tony's name.

"I think I never really left here in my heart – and I always loved Armstrong House." Kate was thinking fondly back to her childhood. "Remember when we used to come here and play as children?"

"I do. But it was all shut up then and fire-damaged," said Valerie.

"I think I loved it even back then," said Kate with a far-off look in her eyes.

"How's your daughter, Nico?" asked Valerie. "You had a daughter from your previous marriage, didn't you?"

"Yes – Alex – she's very well. She's at university now."

"Look at the two of you!" said Valerie, filling up her glass with wine again. "Both of you on your second marriage and here's me without chick nor child!"

Nico glanced over at Kate, feeling uncomfortable at his sister-in-law dragging up the past. She seemed quite insensitive and he hoped she wouldn't say anything about Tony that would upset Kate.

Right on cue, Valerie went on: "Speaking of how decrepit this place used to be, it was Tony's money that did the joint up when you were married to him, wasn't it, Kate?"

"How long are you actually planning on staying here?" asked Nico, quickly changing the subject.

"Well, I actually haven't decided yet. Not sure! It's not a problem, is it?" asked Valerie.

"No, of course not," said Kate, feeling overwhelmed at the thought of her sister staying more than a couple of days.

"So, Kate, tell me more about that attractive man you were chatting up outside when I arrived. An archaeologist, you said?" said Valerie.

Nico looked at Kate as she turned to address him rather than Valerie.

"Yes, a man called Doctor Daniel Byrne – he came up with today's tour. He's the archaeologist in charge of the excavation of the famine grave that has started in Castlewest."

"Oh?" said Nico. "What was he doing here?"

"He was just interested in seeing the place. I was thinking it might be a good idea to tie in the excavation with my new film? If they find anything interesting in relation to the Armstrong Estate and any of the tenants from here."

"What new film is this?" asked Valerie.

"It's at the very early stages, but I'm hoping to put together a documentary about the builder and first inhabitant of Armstrong House, Lord Edward, and his wife Anna."

"Oh, any takers for the project yet? Any film companies interested?" said Valerie.

"As I said, it's at its very early stages, so no," she said as she leant forward to wipe Cian's sauce-smeared mouth with a paper napkin. "But I expect to find takers. Anna was a fascinating woman – a tireless worker on behalf of famine relief."

Valerie made a disinterested face. "Can't see much interest in that. I mean, at least the last film you made was about the shooting of Nico's great-grandfather. People love that kind of thing. But a tireless charity worker – it's not singing to me, Kate."

"Well, not everyone is interested in sensationalism like you, Valerie," said Kate abruptly. "Anyway, Daniel invited me to visit the excavation site."

"How interesting! I might tag along. I didn't get a proper chance to speak to Daniel earlier," said Valerie.

"Eh, no, you won't," snapped Kate, dismissing the idea outright. The last thing she wanted on a fact-finding mission was Valerie trying to flirt with the archaeologist in charge.

Valerie rolled her eyes at Nico.

"That was delicious," she said, pushing away her plate. "What's for dessert?"

"My fav'rit!" said Cian. "Ice cream!"

"Mine too," said Valerie.

CHAPTER 2

1859

Diana Hunter turned her stallion into the gateway of Hunter's Farm. She trotted the horse up the driveway and brought him to a halt outside the house. As she dismounted a stable boy rushed over and took the reins from her.

"Did you have a good ride, Mrs. Armstrong?" he asked.

Diana didn't deign to answer. "Take her to the end stable and make sure she is watered and well groomed. I will be checking her myself later."

She walked towards the house. Hunter's Farm was a small manor house. It had been Diana's home for eighteen years. When she had first come to live there as a young widow she had been looking for a small farm to lease to breed her horses. The farm and house had been part of the Armstrong Estate. She had been Diana Hunter then and renamed the farm after she had moved in. It had not taken her long, using her beauty and excellent horsemanship, to ingratiate herself with the local gentry and she was often invited up to Armstrong House when there were social events there. It hadn't taken her long to captivate Lord Edward's cousin Sinclair and they were married. Of course, she had moved things along more quickly by becoming pregnant and putting Sinclair in a position that he had to marry her. Nobody knew that Harry had been conceived before their quickly arranged marriage, the birth being explained as premature when he arrived early. She sometimes wondered whether their courtship would have ended in marriage if she hadn't trapped Sinclair. Looking back, she wondered whether a young widow who leased a farm from his cousin would have been enough to capture a man as ambitious as Sinclair, even with her beauty and brilliant horsemanship.

Diana walked through the front door and looked down at the row of riding boots that were standing unpolished by the door and raised her eyes to heaven. She continued down the long narrow corridor, past the dining room and into the parlour where Sinclair was sitting at a desk reading through accounts. Their now sixteen-year-old son Harry was sitting beside him as Sinclair impatiently explained to him how the accounts were done.

"Harry, did I not tell you this morning to polish those riding boots before I set off on my ride?" said Diana.

"I haven't had time as Father has been showing me accounts all afternoon," answered Harry.

"Well, go and do them now before dinner and put them in the tack room when you have finished them," ordered Diana.

"Why can't one of the stable boys do that?" said Harry.

"Because I am telling *you* to do it!" snapped Diana. "If you are to be the best horseman in the county then you need to have a love of everything to do with horses, starting with polishing riding boots!"

"Go and do what your mother tells you," said Sinclair. "I've wasted enough of my time today trying to explain once again how accounts work to you!"

Harry got up from his chair and left the room.

Diana went to the drinks cabinet and took off her riding hat before pouring two tumblers of whiskey. Sinclair rose from the desk and took one of the glasses from her. He sat down on an armchair while she sat across from him on the couch.

"Did he learn anything you were teaching him this time?" asked Diana.

"Doubtful!" said Sinclair, taking a slug of the whiskey. "He still comes across as thick as a plank half the time."

"Perhaps you might not be the best teacher of such matters?" suggested Diana.

"Well, I can only do my best with what I am given!" said

33

Sinclair. "We are unable to send him to an expensive school in the way Edward and Anna will be sending their son. I'm always surprised that Edward didn't offer to pay to send Harry to a school."

It was an old theme of Sinclair's and one that Diana encouraged at every opportunity. He usually just brooded on these old grievances but occasionally he needed to talk.

"I'm sure he would have, and I'm sure it was *she* who stopped him from doing so," said Diana, knowing that this would add fuel to the fire.

"Anna . . . the cause of all our problems," sighed Sinclair. "I know Edward still adores me, but she has tried to poison him against us over the years. He is fearful of doing anything in our favour for fear of upsetting her."

"What grieves me most is how we have been robbed of everything – *everything* – by her and that spoilt brat of a son of hers," said Diana, deliberately proceeding to go over old ground. "It was *all* in our grasp, the title, the thousands of acres, Armstrong House – and then after years of us thinking she was barren she produces Lawrence – and displaces our son as the rightful heir of the Armstrong legacy. Our son ends up polishing riding boots while theirs is sent off to expensive schools. Sometimes I can hardly bear it. So near and yet so far." She punctuated this by taking a big gulp of her drink.

"My grandfather paid for me to go to the same school and university as Edward – you would think Edward would do the same for Harry."

"But you were still an earl's grandson, albeit by his second son, whereas Harry is merely a second cousin to the present earl. The legacy becomes less with each generation. By the time Harry has children, they will only be distant cousins."

Sinclair became even more agitated. "If this estate had been left to Edward to run, it would have been destroyed years ago. It has always depended on my abilities and effort. All Edward does is wander around the estate passing the time with the tenant farmers. It is up to me to make sure they pay their rent and keep Edward and

Anna living in luxury up at the house. Without me, they would be nothing."

Diana nodded in agreement. "Not that they ever give you credit for it. And now you are training Harry to be the estate manager for the future, and it will be he who will run the estate while Lawrence swans around as Lord of the Manor. The unfairness is incredible. And to think if Anna had remained barren and Lawrence was never born, Harry would have inherited everything. Armstrong House should be his legacy."

Sinclair finished his drink and stood up and went to tug the bell-pull. "Where *is* that bloody lazy cook of ours? I'm starving!"

Outside in the hallway, Harry sat on the bottom step of the stairs while he polished riding boots, listening to every word.

The next day, at Armstrong House, Anna sat in the small front parlour which was across the hallway from the drawing room, reading a letter from her brother. She always had her post delivered to her in the parlour when it arrived and she would then spend a pleasant interlude reading through the letters she'd received. An avid letter-writer herself, she loved receiving correspondence from her family with all the latest news and gossip from home. All her family lived in Dublin, so far from where she was in the west of Ireland. Her brother John was now Lord Stratton, inheriting the title when their father passed away a few years before. He lived with his wife in Fitzwilliam Square in the house where Anna had grown up, and of which she had such happy memories. With Lawrence being an only child, she went out of her way to make sure he visited her brother and sister's homes in Dublin as much as possible, so that he would be friends with their children, and she regularly had them down to stay at Armstrong House. She often worried about Lawrence being an only child and that was why she went out of her way to make sure he knew his cousins. Similarly, she pursued and made friendships with the other aristocratic families who had children around the country so that Lawrence had a good network of friends and was never lonely.

The only child close by, other than the peasant children, was

Sinclair's son Harry. As much as she had tried to steer Lawrence away from Harry, it was inevitable they had become close friends growing up, despite the difference in age of nearly four years. She could have accepted that, but she hadn't expected that Lawrence would worship Harry in the same way that Edward had always worshipped Sinclair. For such a wealthy and influential family, the Armstrongs were a very small one, with Edward being an only child and having only one cousin, Sinclair, who had been an only child as well.

As she read through her brother's letter, she saw that his youngest son was starting at Eton in the autumn and he was strongly urging her to enrol Lawrence there at the same time so that they could be together.

Edward walked into the room and came over to kiss her.

"A letter from John," she said, folding over the letter and putting it on the table in front of her.

"What news from Dublin?"

"He was just writing that Jeffrey is starting at Eton in September, and suggesting it might be nice if Lawrence went there as well."

Edward's face clouded over and he opened his mouth to speak – but Anna hurried on.

"The two boys would be together, and of course John's two other sons are already there. He's saying there would be a great network waiting for Lawrence when he arrived and –"

"I thought we had already discussed this," Edward interrupted, "and that everything was decided. Come September, when it is time for Lawrence to go to school he will go to Galway, where there's an excellent school. He will be not too far from us and come home every weekend and we can visit him whenever we want during the week."

Anna frowned. She knew Edward couldn't bear the thought of Lawrence leaving for boarding school, as indeed neither could she. But he would soon be thirteen, his time with governesses was over and they both knew it would be good for him to be surrounded with children of his own age.

"Well, I know all that, dear, and fully agree," she said. "But I just wonder if we are doing the right thing. Most of the aristocracy in Ireland are now sending their sons to England for school. I don't want Lawrence to miss out, or to be looked down upon in the future because he didn't go to the right school."

"No one will ever look down on a Lord Armstrong, Anna, that I can assure you. I really don't want to talk about it any more. I know your brother means well, and cares for Lawrence, but I could not bear for him to be so far away from home. Why, we would only see him at Christmas and summer! That would never do!"

Anna nodded. The thought of seeing Lawrence so seldom would cause her despair as well.

"Well, I shall write back to John and thank him for his kind suggestion and thoughts, but politely decline," said Anna.

Edward smiled and nodded.

"Where is Lawrence?" she asked then.

"Oh, he's gone off with Harry for the afternoon," said Edward.

Anna's heart filled with dread. "Doing what exactly?"

"I don't know – whatever young boys do presumably!"

Anna sighed. "One good thing about Lawrence going away to school is that he won't be so reliant on Harry for company."

"Harry's a very nice young chap. I see no problem with the friendship."

He looked at her challengingly. This was an old dispute between them.

"So you keep telling me!" said Anna. "*I* think the boy is reckless, and leads Lawrence astray. Things always happen when Harry is left in charge, and not good things – surely you have to admit that?"

"You are just prejudiced against the boy because you dislike his parents."

"*Despise* is the word I would use, not *dislike*. I'll never forgive them for the way they treated me all those years before Lawrence was born. Why, they made me feel like an unwelcome stranger in my own house!"

Edward raised his eyes to heaven. "Not all that again – please spare me! Have they in any way been rude or disrespectful to you since then?"

"They wouldn't dare – now! I know I'm wasting my breath talking about them to you, but I do not want Lawrence coming under Harry's influence the way you were under Sinclair's for years. I want him to be his own man. Harry is so much older than him and Lawrence naturally admires and idolises him. That gap in age between them is unsuitable in all sorts of ways. Besides, Lawrence is to be an Earl and Harry is at best gentry. Our son should be keeping better company."

"And now you are being a snob, as well as everything else!"

"Only in regard to them. Now, where did you say Lawrence and Harry were going to?"

Edward ignored her as he looked through the bookcase for a book.

"*Edward*!" Anna cried, giving him a fright.

"Whatever is the matter with you?" snapped Edward.

"Where has Lawrence gone to with Harry? I want to know. I do not want any more accidents – I could not bear it!"

"They have gone down to the lakeshore to do some fishing, that is all. I told them not to stray further from the house, and to be back before afternoon tea. Is that all right?" Edward sounded annoyed.

"And not to go riding without you present?"

"Yes, and not to go riding. My lord, Anna, you do fuss so sometimes!"

"Can you possibly blame me with Lawrence's history of accidents? Heavens, we waited long enough for him! We don't want anything to happen to him!"

"Nothing will happen to him! He's got Harry with him to look after him – and he's older and more mature than Lawrence."

"That's what I'm afraid of," Anna whispered to herself.

CHAPTER 3

Lawrence was waiting patiently, holding his fishing rod, on the forecourt in front of Armstrong House for Harry to arrive.

When he at last saw Harry arrive into the forecourt with his fishing rod he jumped off the balustrade where he had been seated.

"You took your time," said Lawrence as the older boy approached him.

"I had to muck out stables and then polish saddles," explained Harry irritably.

"Don't you have a stable boy to do all that?" asked Lawrence.

"He's already overworked, so Mother says I need to work too. She says if I'm to be the best horseman in the county I need to be in the stables as much as possible."

"Gosh, sounds like a bore. Why would you want to be the best horseman in the county anyway?" Lawrence was curious.

"Because I am not going to be Lord Armstrong one day and I need to actually have talents and ability to make my way in the world – that's what my parents say," said Harry bitterly.

"Oh, I wouldn't worry about all that. When I am Lord Armstrong, I'll make sure you want for nothing," said Lawrence cheerily as they headed down the first flight of steps towards the lakeshore.

"In the way your father makes sure my father wants for nothing?" Harry said sarcastically.

"Well . . . yes," said Lawrence innocently.

"My father wants for a lot. He runs the whole of Armstrong

Estate for your father and gets none of the profit. It's not fair that your grandfather inherited the whole estate and my grandfather got nothing. There were only two sons in the family – it should have been divided up." Harry sounded very bitter.

Lawrence shrugged. "I don't know how these things work. But the eldest son always inherits the title and estate, that's what Mama says."

"And *she* would know, of course," spat Harry.

They reached the lakeshore and began to fish, casting their lines far out into the lake. Lawrence could tell that Harry was in bad form and so didn't push the conversation too much.

As hour passed by but they had no luck in catching a fish.

"This is a waste of time," said Harry. "There are no fish near the shore today to catch anything."

"They'll come soon," said Lawrence.

Harry looked along the shore and saw that the usual couple of small rowboats were moored near the boathouse. He thought for a while.

"Come on," he said, reeling in his fishing line. "We'll go out in one of those boats and we'll be able to catch fish from there."

"I don't think that's a good idea," said Lawrence.

"Why not? We're bound to catch plenty of fish if we're out on the lake."

"Mama says I mustn't go on a boat without an adult being present," said Lawrence.

Harry's face became mocking. "Mama says! Mama says! You are such a Mama's boy! You can't ride a horse unless your father is with you, you can't climb trees unless a servant is with you, you can't do *anything* without your mama giving you permission!"

Lawrence flushed and hung his head. "There probably aren't any oars anyway," he mumbled.

"There will be. I often take one of the boats out. That's why they're there – so anyone from the house can go out on the lake anytime they please."

"I don't want to go. My parents would be angry."

"Oh, I don't know why I bother being friends with you! You are so dull and boring! I can't have any fun because you're not allowed to do anything!"

Harry grabbed his fishing rod and began to head back to the steps leading up to the gardens.

"Where are you going?" asked Lawrence.

"Home! There's no point staying here with you, not catching any fish because you're too scared to go out in a boat."

Lawrence thought for a moment. "All right! Let's go out in a boat – you're right – we'll catch plenty of fish then."

"Are you sure you don't want to check with your mama first?" mocked Harry.

"Of course not, come on," said Lawrence, reeling in his own fishing rod.

He headed over to the boats.

Smiling, Harry followed him. They reached one of the boats and jumped in. Then Harry began to row out onto the lake.

"Don't go too far, Harry, I'm not as good a swimmer as you," said Lawrence.

"We're not going swimming, we're going fishing!" sneered Harry.

"I know that, but just in case anything happens," said Lawrence, becoming nervous as he saw the shoreline get further and further away.

"Nervous Nelly!" mocked Harry.

A while later, Harry looked around and stopped rowing.

"This should be far enough now," he said. "Plenty of fish here, I'd say."

They cast their lines out into the water and waited. Time seemed to go by endlessly and still they didn't catch anything.

Harry jumped up and sighed loudly, then peered down into the water over the side of the boat.

"Lawrence, look! There's a school of fish just at the side of the boat!" he cried excitedly.

"Show me!" said Lawrence, getting up quickly and going to look where Harry was pointing.

"Look!" said Harry.

"I can't see anything," said Lawrence.

"There, you fool! Just there!" said Harry, pointing further over the edge of the boat.

"Where?" asked Lawrence in confusion as he could see nothing.

"Lean further out and you'll see them!" urged Harry. "Put your hands on the gunwale and lean right out."

Lawrence put his two hands on the rim of the boat and leaned as far out as he could. Harry leaned back and then suddenly threw his full bodyweight against the edge of the boat where Lawrence was leaning. The boat swayed dangerously and Lawrence screamed in fright. Then Harry threw his weight against the side again and the boat capsized, throwing both boys into the water.

Harry surfaced and clung to the boat. He scanned the water behind him.

Then Lawrence came to the surface, coughing and choking and heaving for breath. He floundered in the water then swam a few strokes splashily and grabbed onto the side of the boat.

When Lawrence had got his breath back he looked over the boat to the shoreline and panicked.

"What will we do?" he cried, shaking with fright.

"The boat will sink soon," said Harry. "We'll have to swim ashore!"

"I'll never make it!" panted Lawrence, gripping onto the boat for dear life. "*You* will but not me."

"You have no choice! Otherwise you'll go down with the boat!"

Lawrence's eyes frantically searched the shoreline and gardens leading up to the house but he could see nobody.

"*Help! Help!*" he screamed at the top of his voice.

"It's no good, they won't hear us from here – we'll have to swim for it," insisted Harry. Lawrence was filled with terror as he gazed at the distant shore.

Anna was upstairs in her bedroom which was at the front of the house. She crossed over to the mirror over the fireplace and undid the collar around her neck. She had decided to take an afternoon nap and looked over to the huge four-poster bed that looked really welcoming. She thought of her discussion with Edward. He was probably right. She did fuss too much over Lawrence. She should give him some independence. She wandered over to one of the windows that faced out to the front of the house. No matter how many times she looked out at the view, it still managed to take her breath away.

She scanned the lake to see if there were many fishermen out that day. It was a lovely day for fishing. She spotted one small boat a good distance from the shore and wondered whether someone from the estate had taken it out. She squinted to try and see it better. Her heart filled with dread as she realised the boat had capsized and there was someone waving in the air for help. She opened the window quickly and she could hear very distant cries.

"Lawrence," she whispered before suddenly screaming *"Lawrence!"*

She turned and raced from the bedroom out to the corridor. She ran to the staircase and rushed down it, screaming at the top of her voice *"Edward! Edward!"*

Edward came out of the library where he had been working and hurried along the hall, catching his wife in his arms as she reached the bottom of the stairs.

Barton and two of the footmen came rushing into the hall as well.

"Whatever is the matter with you?" asked Edward in alarm, seeing Anna was as pale as a ghost.

"It's Lawrence! He's out in the lake! *He's in trouble*!" wailed Anna as she pushed him away and rushed to the open front door. She raced down the steps and across the forecourt.

Edward followed her with Barton and the footmen. As Edward saw what was happening out on the lake, his eyes widened in terror, and he quickly overtook Anna and began bounding down the steps and through the gardens to get to the lake. The footmen raced along with him.

Anna fell as she tried to make her way down the steps, her crinoline dress tripping her up. A gardener came to help her to her feet and then tore off after the other men. Anna lifted her crinoline to her knees, and continued to race across the garden and down the next flight of steps.

Out on the lake Lawrence was frozen with fear.

"*Come on!*" shouted Harry as he began to swim back to shore. "*The boat is sinking! You'll drown!*"

"*Don't leave me, Harry!*" pleaded Lawrence.

Then, as he saw Harry swim powerfully away, he forced himself to let go of the boat and follow.

He was soon exhausted. The shore seemed to be getting further and further away as his body ached and he began to flounder, taking in mouthfuls of water and choking on it.

Edward reached the shore and waded out before diving in and swimming frantically in Lawrence's direction.

One of the footmen dived in and followed him, but the gardener, just then arriving, called out to the other footman and pointed at a boat moored near the boathouse further along the shore. He and the footman raced towards it.

Anna reached the water's edge, her heart pounding as if it might burst. Sweat and tears filled her eyes and she could hardly see. She wiped her eyes with the sleeve of her dress and then could see her son in the distance, helpless, his arms flailing in the air.

She ran into the water and began to wade out, but Barton ran in after her and, grabbing her around the waist, pulled her back to the strand.

"Let me go, Barton, I command you!" gasped Anna as she struggled to free herself, but Barton would not release his grip of her.

"My lady, you can't even swim! And that gown will sink you as soon as you get out of your depth!" said Barton. "And, look, there's a boat going out to rescue them."

Anna saw Lawrence sink under the water as Edward tried to get to him. At the same time, Harry reached the shore and crawled onto the shingle where he collapsed. Barton left Anna and went to attend to Harry.

Edward had been only yards from his son when the boy

disappeared under the water. Taking a deep breath, he dived under and looking around frantically saw Lawrence floating beneath the surface. He reached forward and grabbed the boy by the hair, pulling him up to the surface and holding him tightly.

The men in the boat now reached them. They hauled Lawrence up and into the boat then pulled Edward on board as well. Seeing that, the other footman turned and swam for shore.

"Out of my way!" said Edward as he knelt beside his son. "*Lawrence! Lawrence!*" he cried, but the boy's body was lifeless.

"He's not breathing!" said the footman.

Edward began to pummel Lawrence's chest and then in turn breathe air into his mouth. He kept repeating this, until Lawrence suddenly started to splutter and cough up water. Then he opened his eyes.

"Papa," whispered Lawrence before he closed his eyes again.

"*Row ashore – quickly!*" shouted Edward and the men began to row.

They reached the shore and Edward carried Lawrence out of the boat.

"Is he all right?" asked Anna, nearly terrified to ask.

"He needs a doctor quickly – he stopped breathing for a while," said Edward.

One of the young footmen took Lawrence from Edward's arms and quickly carried him up the steps back to Armstrong House, Edward hurrying behind.

Anna felt her body fill with relief and she shook uncontrollably. She had thought they had lost him. She collapsed on her knees in the grass, her sodden crinoline bunched around her.

She felt her eyes fill with tears and looked over to Harry who was now sitting up on the strand, drenched, but looking unemotional. Barton had put his own jacket around him to keep him warm.

"You! *You!*" accused Anna as she pushed herself to her feet and marched over to him.

Then, to Barton's shock, she reached down and pulled Harry up by the arms and then proceeded to shake him violently and slap him across the face.

"*You nearly killed him!*" she screamed.

Barton stood back stunned for a moment and then quickly intervened.

"My lady!" pleaded Barton. "My lady, please!"

As she was showing no sign of stopping her assault on Harry, Barton grabbed the boy and pulled him away from her, shielding him from any further abuse.

"My lady – please remember yourself!" begged Barton before he turned to Harry and said, "Come along, sir, and I'll take you back to Hunter's Farm."

Anna stood alone on the strand, shaking with anger, her eyes fixed on Harry as Barton escorted him away.

CHAPTER 4

That night, Anna sat beside Lawrence's bed as he drifted in and out of sleep. She looked at the clock on the wall and saw it was nearly ten o'clock. The doctor had said that, all going well, Lawrence would be fine after a few days' rest in bed, but there was a risk he might get pneumonia and so the room needed to be kept warm at all times. The scullery maid had loaded the fireplace with logs which burned brightly.

Anna stood up and went and kissed Lawrence's forehead. He opened his eyes.

"Are you leaving, Mama?"

"Just for a short while – I'll be back soon."

"Papa?"

"He will be up to you very shortly." She smiled at him and kissed him again before leaving the room. She closed the door after her and took a deep breath before continuing down the corridor and down the stairs.

As she reached the bottom she heard the drawing room door open. She saw Sinclair and Diana emerge with Edward. Sinclair glared angrily over at her, and Diana stared at her in disgust. Then Diana made a move to walk towards Anna, her mouth open ready to say something, but Sinclair grabbed her arm and directed her to the front door where Barton let them out.

"We'll speak tomorrow!" Edward called after Sinclair as he left and he nodded back.

Anna continued over to the drawing room and Edward followed

her inside, closing the door behind them.

Edward walked over the couch and sat down, burying his face into his hands.

"What did they want?" asked Anna.

Edward looked up abruptly at her and repeated incredulously, "What did they *want*?"

"Yes, that's what I asked."

"You *attacked* their son! You shook him, and slapped him, and hit him – just after he had nearly been drowned! That's what they wanted! An explanation! Which is exactly what I want from you as well. And before you try to deny it, I've checked with Barton, who confirms what you did!"

"I don't deny it, not one bit of it!" answered Anna. "Any mother would do the same in my situation, a lioness protecting her cub."

"And what about *their* cub? Harry doesn't matter? He can be beaten around like a rag doll by you?"

Anna's eyes widened in astonishment. "Are you so blind that you cannot see what happened here today? Lawrence nearly died! You said yourself he had stopped breathing when you pulled him out of the water."

"And Harry nearly died too!" said Edward.

"Ha! No, he didn't. He was never in danger, not for a second. He's four years older than Lawrence, powerfully built, and a very strong swimmer. Lawrence is just a child."

"There is still no reason to take it out on Harry."

"Do you know, Edward, the reasons why I love you are sometimes the same reasons why I hate you. Your naiveté, your kindness, your insistence upon putting others first, the need to always do the right thing, even putting Sinclair and Diana's feelings before the life of your son!"

"That's not true!"

Anna sank to her knees in front of him in despair. "Do you understand we nearly lost our precious Lawrence today? That he could be dead?"

Edward's eyes filled with tears. "Of course I realise that. I held his lifeless body in my arms."

"Then we could have lost the most important thing in our lives – and it is all down to Harry!"

"How can you just blame Harry for this terrible accident? And that is all it was – an accident, Anna."

She stood up. "Lawrence told me it was Harry who insisted they go out on the boat. He told me it was he who pointed out a school of fish and told Lawrence to lean far out over the gunwale though there were no fish to be seen. Then he rocked the boat so it would turn over."

Edward looked shocked. "It's still an accident, Anna. And Lawrence should have known better than to go out in the boat – we have warned him often enough. I love Lawrence to distraction, but he has to take some responsibility here as well. He disobeyed orders."

"Oh, so I'm not being a fusspot now then, am I?" she mocked.

Edward sighed and said, "Clearly not. Lawrence does seem to be accident prone. I do finally concede that to you."

Anna began to walk up and down the room. "Lawrence is only accident prone when Harry is around him."

"What are you talking about?"

"Think about it, Edward. Think of the last few years. It started that Christmas Day when Lawrence fell down the stairs and nearly got killed. Who was at the top of the stairs with him – Harry! Then the time when Lawrence was on the hunt and the gun had been 'accidentally' loaded and backfired and nearly killed him – who gave him the gun, only Harry! Then last year when the horse threw Lawrence and he hit his head against the wall – who was he riding with – only Harry! Who suggested Lawrence ride that unbroken horse – only Harry! The tree! When Lawrence fell from the tree and broke his arm – who was he up the tree with – was it not again Harry?"

Edward stood up abruptly. "I can scarcely comprehend what you are suggesting."

"I'm not suggesting anything, Edward, I'm stating it! Usually in the past, Lawrence has covered up for Harry, saying it was his fault. But not today. The poor child got such a shock, he told me Harry caused what happened. Ask him yourself, if you don't believe me. I

think this is the first time that Harry has not covered himself –
because he swam off and left Lawrence to his fate. Hence Lawrence
is not covering for him. Even worse, he repeatedly told Lawrence
he must swim for shore – though he knew Lawrence didn't have the
strength for it – and told him that the boat was sinking! Tell me,
Edward, was that boat sinking? Did it sink? No, it did not!"

"Well, so Harry in his panic thought it was sinking! And what
could he have done but swim ashore to save himself?" said Edward.

"He could have tried to help Lawrence, instead of just –
abandoning him."

"But why would Harry do such things? Why would Harry want
to cause Lawrence harm?"

"Not just cause him harm." She said the next words quietly: "To
finish him off."

Edward's mouth dropped open. "Finish him off? As in *kill* him?"

Anna nodded gravely.

"Have you lost your mind? You are accusing Harry of trying to
murder Lawrence?"

Anna nodded assuredly. "For Lawrence to be killed, and for it to
be seen as an accident."

"An accident orchestrated by Harry?"

"Yes," said Anna.

Edward's face was a mixture of disbelief and anger. "And you
still have not said for what purpose?"

Anna threw her hands in the air. "For everything, you fool! With
Lawrence out of the way, Sinclair and his son Harry become your
heirs . . . as it was before Lawrence was born!"

He stared at her for a while and then turned to walk out of the
room. "I'm not listening to any more of this rubbish. You've always
tried to turn me against Sinclair and his family, but I never thought
you would stoop to such a level. To accuse Harry of such dreadful
deeds! Will you stop at nothing to get rid of Sinclair?"

Anna ran after him and, grabbing his arm, turned him around
and held him tightly. "Oh Edward, it gives me no joy to be saying
these things. But I beg you to open your eyes before it's too late.
Don't rely on my word – ask Lawrence tomorrow what happened with

the boat. The facts speak for themselves. Harry abandoned Lawrence in the lake, didn't even try to help him though he is four years older and a powerful swimmer. Look at all the incidents that have nearly killed our precious child. Never mind your love for me, but if you have the love you claim to have for our son, I am begging you to act now. Next time, it will be too late, and Lawrence will not survive."

Edward stared down at his wife's distraught face. How he had always loved her, worshipped her even. When he had met her first he fell head over heels in love with the bright, clever, carefree girl, the eldest daughter of Lord Stratton, the respected MP. He had watched her change over the years, her carefree nature lost. First during the hopeless years of desperately wanting a child and then through what she witnessed during the Famine. Her cleverness had grown to wisdom through the years, but sometimes her wisdom seemed more like paranoia to him. And yet, the facts that she was stating were true. Lawrence had had many near-misses with death, the worst being that day, and Harry was certainly always at the scene. But he could not believe what she was accusing to be true.

But she was his wife, and Lawrence was his son, and he must do everything to protect them if they felt they were in danger.

"And what do you suggest I do?" he asked eventually.

Her face lit up in hope and she spoke quickly. "Get rid of them! Finally remove Sinclair and Diana and their murderous son from Hunter's Farm and the estate. Let us be free of them and our son out of danger."

"You know I can't do that. Who would run the estate?"

"Get another estate manager," said Anna.

"Nobody could step into Sinclair's shoes. He's irreplaceable."

Anna let her husband go and stepped back from him. "I see. I asked you years ago, before Lawrence was born, to get rid of Sinclair and his family, and you refused to do it then, putting them above me. Now, you are putting them above your son, the one you claim to love so much. Be it on your head if anything further happens to Lawrence. I will hold you responsible. And you will not be able to live with yourself."

She turned from him and walked out of the room.

CHAPTER 5

The next day Edward walked into Lawrence's bedroom where the governess was sitting beside the bed reading him a story.

"Good morning, my lord," she said, standing up.

"Good morning. If you wouldn't mind leaving us, Mrs. Culver?"

"Certainly, my lord. He's much better today, I'm glad to report." The governess smiled and left the room, closing the door behind her.

Edward bent down and kissed Lawrence's forehead. "*Are* you much better today?"

"Oh, yes, Papa, but I'm still very cold," said Lawrence.

Edward looked at the fireplace where there was a roaring fire. He hoped the child wasn't coming down with pneumonia.

"Well, I shall ask the maids to bring up some extra blankets for you," said Edward, sitting in the chair beside the bed that Mrs. Culver had vacated. "Well, you gave us all quite a fright yesterday, young man."

"Yes, I'm sorry, Papa. But not half as much a fright as I gave myself!"

Lawrence smiled at him. "I can imagine. Whatever possessed you to go out in the boat when you had been told so many times not to do so without an adult?"

Lawrence remained silent as he stared out a window.

"Speak the truth, Lawrence. I want to hear the truth from you."

Lawrence took a deep breath before speaking. "Harry suggested it."

"But did you not tell him you were not allowed?"

"Yes, Papa, but he said he would go home and leave me if I didn't go and started teasing me that I was a Mama's boy."

"You must never allow yourself to be pressurised into doing something that you know you are not supposed to do again, Lawrence. Do you understand me?"

"Yes, Papa."

"And – and how did the boat come to overturn?"

"Harry said there was a school of fish and told me to look over the side at them. I couldn't see any fish and so he told me to put my hands on the rim of the boat and lean out further. And then he threw himself against the side of the boat and it started rocking horribly and he did it again and the boat capsized, and then – and then we were in the water!" Lawrence burst out crying.

Edward got up and sat on the bed, holding the child.

When Lawrence calmed a little, he said, "Then we clung on to the boat but Harry said it was sinking and we had to swim for shore."

"And did you not ask Harry for help?"

"I begged him, but he swam off," said Lawrence. "It wasn't his fault, Papa – he thought I could swim to the shore like he could though I told him I couldn't. I really couldn't, Papa!"

Edward sighed as he patted Lawrence's head.

Edward sat at his desk in the library pondering the whole situation and wondering how best to handle it. He didn't know what to believe. He had to admit that at best Harry was unreliable, careless, reckless and uncaring. At worst he was an attempted murderer! It was all horrendous. He knew he could not broach the subject with Sinclair and Diana and accuse their son of any of these things. Nor could he exile Sinclair and his family from Hunter's Farm. Firstly, they were his only relatives in the whole world apart from Anna and Lawrence. He couldn't fall out with them. Secondly, on a more selfish note, he knew the Armstrong Estate could not function without Sinclair. Sinclair had been running it for over twenty years and was irreplaceable. The estate itself was still financially shaken from the Famine and now only recovering. And what if Harry really wasn't the cause of all these accidents with Lawrence, but Lawrence himself was genuinely accident prone?

But Anna's words had chilled him, and Lawrence's account had disturbed him. Lawrence's safety was paramount. As he thought, an idea formed in his mind.

Anna was seated on the couch in the small parlour, reading her daily post, when Edward came in.

She barely looked up at him.

"Lawrence seems much better today," he commented as he went to sit beside her.

"I know, I was in with him earlier," she said, still sifting through her post.

"I have been thinking of everything we discussed, and decided that the best thing for Lawrence is to go to Eton," said Edward.

Anna dropped her post and stared at him. "Really?"

"Yes. He will be well supervised there, and your brother's three children will be there to mind him. And, as you said, a lot of the Anglo-Irish aristocracy are sending their children there and so he will make good contacts and we will already know a lot of the families who are already there."

"But that means we will hardly ever see him," said Anna. "Can we bear that?"

"I've also decided that we should buy a house in London and live there while Lawrence is at school in England. Then we can see him frequently."

Anna was overcome with excitement and worry all at once. "But that would mean your leaving Armstrong House for long periods of time."

"Which I am quite willing to do until Lawrence has left school and is old enough to come back to learn the running of the estate himself – and – and old enough to look after himself without us worrying about his safety all the time."

"Oh, Edward, I love you so much!" she said, throwing her arms around him and kissing him.

"I think it might be good for all of us to get away from Armstrong House for a while. I think there are too many memories here for you from the Famine years which you have never recovered from. Most of our friends have acquired houses in London and spend part of the year there and so we shall not be short of company."

"But I thought you always said you didn't want to be an absentee landlord like they are?" said Anna.

"I am willing to make this compromise to make you happy and for Lawrence to get the best in life," said Edward.

"I do love you," she said, kissing him again. "What about the house here?"

"Barton can oversee it, and I shall be returning regularly for business."

"And what about the running of the estate?"

"That will be left in the hands of Sinclair, as it always has been."

"But –" began Anna.

"Don't push me any further, Anna!" warned Edward. "I'm giving you what you wanted and putting Lawrence's safety and your concerns first. Sinclair remains – that is non-negotiable."

Anna saw the stern look on her husband's face and nodded. "Thank you, Edward."

He reached for her and took her in his arms. The last thing he wanted was to leave Armstrong House and go to live in London, even if it was just temporarily. But he did need to put his son's safety first. The memory of Lawrence's lifeless body as he dragged him into the boat made him shiver. If Lawrence was indeed in some danger while at Armstrong House then he needed to get him away for now.

Also, Anna did not seem to understand the seriousness of what she had done in attacking Harry in the way she had, if the boy was innocent. He knew the story would soon spread around the parlours of the stately homes of Ireland, how Lady Armstrong had viciously attacked his cousin's son, for no apparent reason other than he had nearly drowned along with Lawrence. If they didn't leave quickly, there would be a scandal. Edward knew that people already whispered about Anna. They whispered about the bouts of depression she had suffered after what she had witnessed during the Famine. He did not want those whispers to develop, on the foot of her attacking Harry, into a rumour that she was now developing some kind of mental illness. And Sinclair and Diana, never fans of Anna, would be only too happy to spread those rumours after what had happened with Harry.

They had to leave Armstrong House, to escape a scandal engulfing them.

CHAPTER 6

Present Day

Valerie had kept Kate up talking until two o'clock the previous night. Once Kate had got over the initial shock of her sister arriving out of the blue she thoroughly enjoyed catching up with her, talking about old times, and telling stories about their childhood. They had grown apart when they reached adulthood as their lives had taken very different paths. And since Kate had lived in Ireland for the past fifteen years, they had grown even further apart. They had sat in the drawing room chatting. Kate had forgotten how much Valerie could actually talk and also how much wine she could consume.

Valerie then, of course, slept the morning away and only got up in time for lunch, while Kate was woken by a lively Cian at eight.

"I kept getting the creeps last night every time I filled another glass of wine," said Valerie as they sat down to lunch.

"Why?" asked Nico.

"Well, I kept seeing your ancestors' disapproving looks from their portraits. They look quite an austere bunch!"

Kate laughed as she gave Nico a mocking look. "I shouldn't worry too much about Nico's ancestors, Valerie – they were quite a bawdy bunch from what I've learned."

"Wherever did they get you come from then, Nico?" asked Valerie. "Couldn't imagine you've ever been bawdy."

Nico smiled briefly at her. "I have my moments."

Kate leaned over and kissed her husband. "Oh, yes, Nico has even been known to have two glasses of wine at dinner on occasion."

"Two! Take a walk on the wild side, Nico!" taunted Valerie.

Nico really didn't know how to take Valerie. Clearly, he had nothing in common with her – surely she could see and accept that? But she seemed to be unable to stop deriding him.

"Any bus tours today?" asked Valerie.

"Not today," said Kate. "I was actually going to take the opportunity to go and pay a visit to the excavation site in town. I can't wait to see what they're doing."

"I have to go to Galway for a meeting for the day, did you forget?" said Nico quickly.

"No," Kate told him.

"Well, who's going to mind Cian?" asked Nico, gesturing to his son who was busy cramming his mouth full of chicken nuggets.

"I'll take him along to the site with me," explained Kate.

"You're not taking a four-year-old to an excavation site, Kate," objected Nico.

"Why not?"

"I want to go with Mummy," declared Cian.

"See!" said Kate.

"No! Because there will be dead bodies there and stuff," said Nico.

At this, Cian stopped chewing and stared at his father.

"Oh, don't be silly. They've only started the dig so I doubt they'll have found anything yet, and besides what harm would it do him?" said Kate.

"I still don't want him going down there, Kate – he should be playing not visiting a burial site," said Nico.

"For goodness' sake, Nico, I'm not spending hours there! I'll be just dropping in."

"I know your 'dropping in' and, yes, you will be hours there. You'll get side-tracked by something and forget what time it is. It's not fair on Cian."

"I'll look after him," volunteered Valerie, causing all three at the table to stare at her. "We can spend the time playing here. Give me an opportunity to get to know my nephew better."

"No – he might make strange with you," said Nico.

Valerie ruffled Cian's hair as he laughed up at her. "Of course he won't make strange with me. I'm not a stranger, I'm his aunt."

"No, he'll start missing us and then he'll throw a tantrum," said Nico.

Kate looked at him and raised her eyebrows. Normally neither of them would refer to Cian's tantrums in his hearing.

"Well, if he does, I'll phone Kate and she'll come straight back," said Valerie.

"If you're sure, Valerie?" said Kate, warming to the idea greatly.

"Of course!" smiled Valerie.

"But –" began Nico.

"You'll be late for your meeting, Nico," snapped Kate, closing down any further discussion.

Nico nodded and stood up. "I'll see you tonight." He kissed Kate and Cian and gave a polite nod to Valerie before making for the door.

"Hope you get some big deals done in Galway today!" Valerie called after him. Then turning to her sister, said, "Is he always so – sombre?"

"Nico's not sombre. He takes things a bit seriously, but he has the best sense of humour you could imagine," Kate defended him.

"I'll just *have* to imagine it because I've seen no sign of it yet!" said Valerie. "He's so different from Tony."

"I wish you'd stop mentioning Tony!" Kate snapped at her.

"Sorry!" Valerie made a face at her.

Kate took a quick mouthful of her coffee and then smiled. "No, it's me who's sorry. Sorry for snapping – it's the alcohol from last night. I'm not used to drinking mid-week."

"Clearly!" said Valerie as she reached over to her handbag. Taking a packet of cigarettes out, she went to light one up.

"Oh, Valerie, if you wouldn't mind going outside to smoke? It's just we don't like smoke in the house with Cian," said Kate.

"But you used to smoke like a trooper! You even used to smoke cigars, as I remember it?"

"Yes, well, I haven't smoked in years, not since I became pregnant with Cian," said Kate.

Valerie huffed as she threw her cigarette packet back into the bag. "I don't want one that much that I have to stand out in the cold!"

As Kate drove her Land Cruiser to Castlewest she felt guilty at snapping at Valerie. She had very much enjoyed the previous night with her. She had forgotten what fun she could be. And she imagined that, looking on, her life with Nico might look a little regimented. But she was sure, once Nico warmed up and Valerie calmed down, they would get on and be great friends. She wasn't sure exactly how long Valerie was intending to stay, but she was determined to make the most of her visit and take the opportunity to become friends again with her sister.

She drove up to the excavation site and parked. She took out her mobile phone and called her friend Brian Pullman. Brian had been the director and producer of the previous docudrama she had made – *The Secrets of Armstrong House*. She had discussed the new film she was planning with him and he had been enthusiastic. He said he wanted to be on board for the production and would try to raise finance for it.

"Hi, Brian, any news?" she asked.

"I'm afraid I don't have any news for you, Kate – no good news anyway."

Kate felt her heart sink. "What do you mean?"

"Well, I've been touting the idea to different people in the industry and nobody seems enthused about the project."

"How can that be? After the success of the last film?" Kate was astonished.

"Well, this new film is a different kind of concept, Kate. The last once was about the shooting of Lord Charles Armstrong. It had all the ingredients investors think audiences want – sex, violence and a mystery. Whereas your new proposal doesn't have those ingredients."

"Did you try the investors who made a packet from our last film?"

"Of course – they were the first people I brought the project to. But they feel there isn't enough to warrant a film on Lady Anna.

She's just too – virtuous!"

"Well, it's a sorry world we live in when that isn't of interest!" said Kate.

"You know the industry as much as anybody, Kate."

"Sadly, I do."

Kate realised she must appear to be confident. She knew that if Brian got any sign of her belief in the project waning, then whatever interest he had would evaporate and it would be dead in the water.

"On the positive side, I gave an interview to the *Mail* yesterday about Lady Anna and the film and I've doing another for the *Independent* next week."

"Well, perhaps that may arouse more interest than I'm getting," said Brian.

"And I'm not even finished doing my research and putting together my full proposal."

"Well, let me know when you are. But it needs to be a lot stronger than what you've given me already. In the meantime, I'll keep mooting the film to potential investors."

"Thanks, Brian, I'll talk to you later."

"See you, Kate."

Kate sat for a minute after she hung up. She couldn't believe there was no interest in a new project, especially as the last one had been so successful. She knew Lady Anna's life needed to be told in film – she just needed to approach it from the right angle.

She got out of the Land Cruiser and made her way to the excavation site which had barricades erected all around it.

Its site was beside a huge Victorian building, part of which had housed the town library for years. But it had formerly been the local workhouse. Now it had a new function as Daniel and his team were working from there and she had heard that some of the rooms had been converted into offices and labs for them.

She went to the site entrance and, pushing open the heavy gate, walked in and saw a series of tents there and a team of archaeologists at work. She walked around, observing the careful digging that was in progress. She spotted Daniel instructing some younger men. She waved and walked over to him.

"Oh, hello, Mrs. Collins – how good to see you again!" said Daniel, shaking her hand.

"Please, call me Kate. I couldn't wait to see what was going on," she said.

"Would you like the tour?"

"Yes, please!"

They began to stroll around, with Daniel commenting on the work and procedures.

"Why was this place chosen as the burial site?" asked Kate.

"Because at the time this was outside the main town, and it was also annexed to the workhouse," said Daniel, gesturing to the building.

"Oh, I see," said Kate, looking up at the Gothic building.

"Unfortunately, the fatality rate in the workhouse was very high and so when people and infants died they were just thrown in here," said Daniel.

"Then going into the workhouse didn't save them from death," said Kate.

"Far from it. That's why what we are doing here is so important – we need to discover the exact nature of the people's deaths – what illnesses befell them in that workhouse." He looked at Kate, his expression sombre. "And the field also became a dumping ground for other victims of the Famine – there were victims lying dead on roads and in ditches. And then they were just left here where they were eventually buried by the authorities."

Kate looked back at the old building and tried to imagine what it was like when it operated as a workhouse.

"My husband's great-great-great-grandmother, Lady Anna Armstrong, would have been a regular visitor here, given the work she did for famine relief. She was a patron of the workhouse here, among many others. Hard to imagine that she ever recovered from what she would have seen here. It must have had such a dreadful impact on her life."

"I imagine it could not have been any other way. In fact, as part of my research I found many references to Lady Anna in regard to her work here."

Kate's eyes lit up. "Did you keep notes and records of the

references? I'd love to compare them to what I already have. As I told you, I'm working on a project about her life at the moment."

Daniel smiled at her. "That was actually why I stole myself onto that tour bus yesterday. I'd read about the new film you're planning and was hoping to meet you."

"You should have just rung and asked to speak to me!" said Kate.

"I did. But a man said you weren't there and didn't ask to take a message," said Daniel.

Kate cringed at Nico's lack of social graces.

"I do apologise – I can't imagine who that was," she said.

"Would you like to come into my office and I'll show you what I've found on Lady Anna so far?"

"I'd love to!" answered Kate enthusiastically.

She followed him away from the main excavation site and through a side door leading into the building. As she walked through the corridors she tried to imagine what the place was like in the 1840s. She imagined it looked very different from the sterile government building it was now.

She followed Daniel into his office and sat as he began to take down files that were stacked on shelves.

She lost track of time as he showed her copies of old documents relating to Lady Anna.

"Where did you get all these?" she asked, amazed.

"From government archives," he said.

She flicked through the documents – everything from letters that had been written to the board of governors, complaining about conditions at the workhouse, to receipts of money donated and collected by Anna.

"One notable thing – the Armstrong Estate had a policy of not evicting," said Daniel.

"Well, yes, Lady Anna could hardly campaign for famine relief while she threw her own tenants from the estate!"

"Think about it – as the Armstrong Estate was one of the biggest estates in the county, the mass grave out there might have been much bigger but for that. But that didn't stop the estate from having a lot of serious trouble during the Famine which caused a huge amount of agrarian unrest. People thought there might be a revolution. People were so desperate that crime shot through the roof – there were robberies, theft of cattle and sheep. The Irish Constabulary had to draft in a huge amount of extra police to keep social order. In fact, there was an armed guard at the gates of the Armstrong Estate to stop the starving masses from storming the estate and plundering it."

"How do you know all this?"

"From the police records at the time. It's very strange, but as people were dying in their thousands, police still had to file all the reports of crime and incidents."

"How cruel! There was money for bureaucracy but not for food," said Kate.

"Hasn't that always been the way?"

"I wonder could I get my hands on those police files?" she said eagerly. "I think it would really show what life at Armstrong House was like at the time and also show the other side of Anna's life."

"I can certainly put you in contact with the right people," promised Daniel, "but I did make some copies – I can photocopy them for you."

"Oh, that would be great!" she said, beaming.

"Kate!" called Nico as he came into the kitchen.

To his surprise he found Valerie there cooking dinner while Cian sprawled on the couch which was positioned under the window, watching a cartoon on the wall-mounted television.

"Did you have a good day?" asked Valerie as she continued stirring a saucepan of gravy.

"Yes – eh, where's Kate?"

"She's not back yet," said Valerie.

"Not back!"

"She rang twenty minutes ago – she'll be here soon," said Valerie. "She was just leaving the excavation site."

Nico raised his eyes to heaven. "I knew that would happen, that she would lose track of time."

"Why did you ask where she was then?" Valerie shot back.

He took off his jacket and sat down at the table.

"I've done roast lamb," she said, pouring the gravy into a sauce boat. "Much better than plain old meatballs, don't you think?"

As Valerie took the roast from the oven and began to carve it she chattered away about different restaurants in New York which were her favourites.

Nico, who had poured them glasses of red wine, just sipped at his and listened as he set the table.

"I'm so sorry I'm late!" said Kate, rushing in carrying a large file which she carefully placed on a side table. "I didn't realise what time it was!"

"You never do!" said Nico as she leaned forward and gave him a kiss.

"Sorry, Valerie, for lumbering you for so long with Cian," she said, going over to the couch to give the little boy a hug.

"Oh, no need to apologise," said Valerie as she walked past, carrying the lamb on a serving plate. "We had a great time, didn't we, Cian?"

"Yes! Aunty Valerie let me have chocolate all day!"

"Not too much, I hope – he'll be sick," said Nico.

"Oh, Nico! Don't be such a fusspot!" said Valerie as she forked out the lamb onto the plates. "Hey, can you bring the other serving dishes over to the table?"

"You won't have to mop up when he gets sick," said Nico as he began to ferry a number of dishes to the table.

"Everything in moderation – including moderation – that's always been my motto," said Valerie.

"Valerie, when did you learn to cook?" asked Kate, amazed at the feast Valerie had produced. "Beans on toast used to be your limit!"

"I learned to cook when I was dating this head chef who worked in a Michelin-starred restaurant in Manhattan. He was Italian, very emotional." Sitting down, Valerie reached for the bottle of wine and topped up their glasses.

"And what became of him?" asked Kate, bemused, as she helped Cian up onto his chair.

"He threw one frying pan too many in a hissy fit, and out the door I ran," said Valerie. "I learned a valuable lesson – not to date anybody with Latin blood in them."

Kate rolled her eyes as she sat down.

"So how was your day at the excavation site?" asked Nico, anxious to talk about something grown-up.

"Absolutely fascinating," said Kate, helping herself and Cian to mashed potato. "They are doing remarkable work there. Really going to demonstrate what people went through during the Famine. And, most importantly for me, Daniel had lots of documents with references to Lady Anna and her work at the workhouse there."

"Really?" Nico was genuinely interested.

"Daniel made me copies of everything relating to Anna," said Kate, nodding over to the file on the side table. "It will be a real help in putting my film together."

"Was it my imagination yesterday – or is Daniel a very attractive man?" asked Valerie.

"Yes, he certainly could be considered an attractive man," said Kate, frowning and wondering if her sister was making mischief. "He's coming to the house tomorrow, by the way."

"What?" asked Nico.

"I said I would let him see the correspondence and documents I have from Lady Anna, in case it might help him with his work."

"A case of 'I'll show you mine if you show me yours'?" giggled Valerie.

"But, Kate, you know I have to go back to Galway tomorrow for a further meeting," said Nico.

"Yes, and why is that a problem?"

"Again – who is going to mind Cian?"

"For goodness' sake, Nico, you make Cian sound as if he's hyperactive and can't be in people's company. He'll be fine playing while I go through things with Daniel."

"Well, that's going to be a great day for him! Sitting in, listening to you and this archaeologist talk about the Famine!"

"We'll only be an hour or so!"

"Sure you will!" said Nico.

"Look, it's no problem," said Valerie. "I'll look after Cian while Kate is busy with yer man. Problem solved!"

"That's very kind of you, Valerie, but we can't impose on you again," said Nico.

"My gosh – we're family! How could it possibly be imposing?" said Valerie as she reached for the bottle and filled the glasses again to the brim.

Nico stirred in his sleep and woke. Turning over, he saw that Kate wasn't there in the bed. He sat up, put on the bedside light and looked at his watch. It was three in the morning. Concerned, he got out of bed. He had left Kate drinking with Valerie in the drawing room long before midnight. As the conversation had turned to Valerie's different hairstyles over the years, he really couldn't listen to any more and had bailed to bed.

He put on his dressing gown and walked down the corridor to the stairs. He could see the main light was still on in the hallway below. As he walked down the stairs he could hear singing. He stopped to listen and realised it was Kate and Valerie singing Carly Simon's *Coming Around Again* at the top of their drunken voices in the drawing room. He raised his eyes to heaven, turned and went back to bed.

CHAPTER 7

Kate opened her eyes and blinked a few times. She turned over in the bed and saw that Nico wasn't there. She tried to think what time she had gone to bed the previous night but couldn't recall. In fact, she couldn't even remember going to bed. She sat up, looked at her watch and panicked when she saw it was just after noon. Remembering that Nico had been due to go to a meeting early that morning, she jumped out of bed, put on her dressing gown and slippers and raced out of the room and down the stairs.

"*Nico!*" she called but there was no answer. "*Cian!*" she called in a panic.

She frantically ran down to the kitchen but could see no sign of life there either. She raced back upstairs, calling for Cian, but as she looked in all the rooms she saw that there was nobody there. She buried her face in her hands. Cian was missing and there was no sign of Valerie. What was she doing drinking all night? Valerie was probably in a drunken stupor somewhere.

She raced out the front door and into the forecourt, looking anxiously around. Then she heard somebody speaking, raced over to the balustrade and looked down on the first terraced garden. She was filled with relief when she saw Valerie sitting on the grass playing dinosaurs with Cian. She went to the steps and quickly ran down them.

"Oh, hello, how are you?" asked Valerie cheerily.

"I didn't know where you were!" Kate sat on the grass and hugged Cian closely.

"Too nice a day to be cooped up indoors, especially when you have all these beautiful gardens," said Valerie.

"I feel dreadful. I can't remember going to bed," said Kate.

"You've become a lightweight, Kate. I remember a time when you could drink me under the table."

"Well, that was a very long time ago," said Kate, marvelling at the fact that Valerie looked refreshed and bright as a daisy.

"Where's Nico?"

"He left for his meeting early."

"You saw him?"

"Of course. He was hardly going to leave Cian unsupervised with you passed out in bed," said Valerie.

"How was he?" asked Kate, filled with embarrassment at the thought.

"He didn't say much, but then he never really does anyway, does he?" said Valerie.

"Oh, I feel so irresponsible," Kate said, rubbing her forehead.

Valerie got up from the grass. "Oh, what's wrong with you, Kate? You had a couple of drinks and had a good time. Not much chance for you to do much of that around here these days!"

"Oh . . ." Kate made a face, remembering, "I've got Daniel coming at two and I'm supposed to be going through a load of documents with him. I won't even be able to see straight."

"You'll be fine! Just go and have a long hot soak in a bath and you'll feel like a new woman. Here, take one of these." Valerie reached into her bag which was lying on the lawn. Taking out a bottle, she shook out a pill and handed it to Kate.

"What is it?" asked Kate suspiciously, pushing it away.

"It's just a vitamin, Kate! Hardly speed!"

Kate looked at the pill and then put it in her mouth and gulped it down.

"Now off you go and have a hot bath," said Valerie. "You want to look nice for Daniel!"

Kate did feel better after a bath so she had something to eat. When she went into the drawing room she cringed when she saw the empty bottles of wine lying around from the previous night and to her horror saw red wine spilled on the Persian carpet. She quickly took the bottles of wine and the two glasses down to the kitchen. She was rubbing at the wine stain with a wet cloth when the doorbell rang.

She went out to the hallway and hid the cloth behind a large potted plant. Then she opened the front door and found Daniel standing there, carrying a briefcase.

"Hi, Daniel," she said, beckoning him in.

"Ready for an afternoon of historical research?" he asked with a smile.

She grimaced. "I'm afraid my sister is staying with us from New York, so I ended up having a very late night. I've had a clearer head for historical research."

"Ah, I see," he said, following her in. "Would you prefer to leave it till another time?"

"Oh no, I'll be fine. I'm just explaining why I'm not at my best and brightest. I'm looking forward to showing you what I have about Anna."

As she led him down the hall to the library, she saw him looking at the portraits on the wall and staring at the ornate ceilings.

"I really feel as if I'm stepping back in history when I'm here," he said. "It was the same when I was on the tour the other day. Such an ambiance."

"Thank you. That was what I was trying to achieve when restoring the house."

In the library, he took his time looking at the room as it was not open to the public and he had not seen it when he was on the tour. He saw it had been restored too but could also see that the Collinses used it as their office. There were architect drawing boards on one desk and on the main desk were files and papers.

"I managed to put together some really interesting items that were connected with Anna and her work during the Famine," said Kate, gesturing to him to take a seat beside her at the desk.

She put on white cotton gloves and he put on the gloves that had been left there for him.

70

She began to hand him documents. "These are original newspaper cuttings from the 1840s – letters sent to them by Anna. You'll see from the letters she sent to the *London Times* that she was desperately trying to appeal for people to put pressure on the parliament to give aid."

Daniel started to read through the letters in the newspaper cuttings. He saw all the letters were signed off by Lady Anna Armstrong, Armstrong House, County Mayo.

"This is brilliant. She goes into great detail about the suffering she is witnessing," he said.

"When you think about it, this was the only way the people in Britain could get a sense of what was happening in Ireland, a century before film footage became the norm," said Kate.

"Her descriptions are so graphic," he commented. "And, of course, her being the wife of an important aristocrat gave them so much more clout."

"These here are letters to her father, again from the 1840s. He was a Member of Parliament in Westminster and again she describes what is happening here in Mayo and urging him to use his position to bring more aid."

"How did these letters come back to Armstrong House if they were posted to her father in Dublin?"

Kate shrugged. "That I don't know. But I presume she found them there after her father died and brought them back."

Daniel nodded. "That would make sense. And where were all these items for all this time?"

"Armstrong House was left abandoned and locked up since it was set on fire during the War of Independence. The fire mainly affected the front downstairs of the house and they managed to put it out before it destroyed the upstairs, though of course the whole place was ruined with smoke pollution. So there was a huge amount of stuff that survived the fire and was just left here for decades untouched. It had been stored in boxes and old-fashioned trunks. A lot of Anna and Edward's stuff had been stored in the attic rooms by the generations that came after them and so they escaped the worst of the fire."

"And you went through it all and sorted it out?" he asked, impressed.

"Yes."

"It must have been an excruciating task."

"I loved every moment of it. I felt I was putting together the history of the house," she said. She handed over some leather-bound books. "These are diaries kept by Anna."

He could see that some of the covers had been singed by fire, but the leather covers had protected the pages inside.

"She doesn't write about anything personal. Again, they are her thoughts and sights of the Famine, often quite heart-breaking. Others are her writing about the daily running of Armstrong House and the estate, which is really important to me for the film I'm going to make about life during her time here."

"Ah!" said Daniel, reaching for his briefcase. He pulled out a file and handed it to her. "And this is how I can help you. It's the police file for the Barony of Armstrong from the nineteenth century, which you were asking for."

Kate's eyes lit up on seeing it and she quickly riffled through it.

"As you'll see when you study it, you get a sense of the siege mentality that was here at Armstrong House during the Famine. There are letters from Lord Edward asking for police protection on the estate. Another one asking for a police escort for Anna as she goes about her work at the workhouses. And then just countless and countless reports of theft and robberies from the estate."

"The desperate people trying to feed themselves," said Anna.

"And the Armstrongs trying to protect themselves and their assets," said Daniel.

"May I keep this?"

"Of course," said Daniel, taking a camera from his briefcase. "And if I could take photos of the documents you have for my files?"

Kate nodded. "Of course."

The afternoon seemed to fly as Kate led Daniel through all her documents and he photographed what he felt was important and continued to make notes.

When at last the door opened and Nico walked in, he seemed surprised to see Daniel there.

"Oh hi," said Kate. "Nico, this is Daniel who I was telling you about. Daniel, this is my husband Nico."

Nico shook Daniel's hand.

"It's a real pleasure to meet you," said Daniel, studying him intently.

"Likewise."

"Your wife has been kind enough to help me with the research I'm doing," said Daniel.

"Yes, Kate loves to do research," Nico said, giving her a look with an arched eyebrow.

"It must be an amazing feeling to be descended from such an illustrious line of people," said Daniel.

"I'm not sure it's that illustrious. Did you not see Kate's film on my great-grandfather Charles and his decadent life before he got shot?"

"I did have the pleasure of seeing it, yes," chuckled Daniel. "But Lord Edward and Lady Anna – you must be proud of them and all they did from building this house to their charity work."

"I suppose," said Nico. "To be honest, I don't know much about them, strange as that might sound. It's Kate who has the obsession with my family's past, not I. I prefer to look to the future."

"Well, the past is more comforting, isn't it?" said Daniel. "We know what happened in the past, so it's much safer than the future."

"One way of looking at it, I suppose," said Nico before turning to Kate. "Where's Cian?"

"He's with Valerie," said Kate.

Kate could sense the disapproval from Nico, though he was obviously determined not to show it in front of a stranger.

"I'd better go find them. He's probably driven her demented by now, or vice versa," said Nico as he started to go but then, to Kate's surprise, he turned and said to Daniel, "You'll join us for dinner?"

"Oh, I wouldn't want to impose?" said Daniel.

"Believe me you'll not be imposing. You'll be saving me from an evening of listening to my wife discussing shopping and hairstyles with her sister. They may even treat you to a rendition of Carly Simon if you're lucky."

Nico's tone was sarcastic rather than humorous and Daniel threw a quizzical look at Kate, but she didn't meet his gaze.

She turned her attention back to the documents immediately.

To Nico's surprise, when he went down to the kitchen he found Valerie had once again been busy preparing their dinner for the night. Now a very contented Cian sat on the couch being read to by his aunt.

"Valerie!" Nico said as he sniffed at the chicken dish that was on the stove. "You should have stuck with that Michelin-starred chef you were seeing for longer. You would have ended up with a Michelin star yourself!"

She laughed. "Is Kate still with that man?" she asked.

"Yes, engrossed in history," said Nico. "He's staying for dinner."

"Oh?" She looked happy at the thought. "That should liven things up for a bit."

Nico and Kate rarely ate in the dining room, but Kate suggested it as she knew Daniel would love to eat in the old-fashioned splendour of that room rather than downstairs in the ultra-modern kitchen. Nico didn't object.

"At least it's a farther journey to the wine rack for Valerie – rather than just reaching across to the counter and grabbing another bottle!" he said to Kate as they loaded up the dumbwaiter. It was operated by an old-fashioned pulley – a feature Kate had insisted they retain and which now delighted visiting tourists. Nico never stopped protesting that it should be replaced by an electric one.

Upstairs, they found Daniel already seated at the long table while Valerie arranged cushions on a chair for Cian.

"We only met briefly – I'm Valerie Donovan, Kate's sister," Valerie was saying as Nico and Kate began to unload the dumbwaiter.

Soon they were all seated and handing around the beautiful old serving dishes.

"I believe it's you I have to thank for this wonderful dinner?" said Daniel to Valerie.

"Oh, yes, cooking is just one of my many talents," she said, winking at him as she filled his wineglass. She went to fill Kate's glass but Kate put out a hand and stopped her.

"Not for me," she said.

"Oh, don't be so silly, Kate," said Valerie, pushing Kate's hand out of the way and filling her glass. "So, tell me all about this wonderful excavation work you're doing, Daniel."

"I'm sure Kate doesn't want to talk about it again – she's heard it all afternoon," said Daniel with a smile.

"Oh, I'm sure Kate could never tire of the subject," said Nico, giving her a sarcastic look.

Looking very irritated, she took up her glass of wine and took a large gulp.

As Daniel chatted away to Valerie about his work, Nico murmured to Kate, "Do you really think you should drink again tonight? I thought you had a bus tour in the morning?"

"Actually, Nico, I do not need you to monitor how much I drink," she muttered back.

"Really? You fell in the door of the room last night – you didn't even know where you were!"

"Oh, shut up!" Kate hissed at him, before turning her attention back to Daniel.

"So we're asking people who live in and around Castlewest to give a voluntary DNA sample," said Daniel.

"Why?" asked Valerie.

"To see if we can match the bodies in the famine grave with families who live here today. I think there's a very good chance that relatives of those people are alive in Castlewest now."

"How fascinating!" said Kate. "My family lived here for generations before we emigrated to the States in the eighties. I'd very much like to take part."

"Of course you would!" said Nico under his breath.

Valerie made a face. "I don't think I'd want to know! I wouldn't want to know if an ancestor of mine was buried there. Let sleeping dogs lie, that's always been my motto!"

"I think at last I actually agree with you on something, Valerie," said Nico.

"Well, we'd love you to be involved, Kate," said Daniel.

"Perhaps you can tie it in with your new docudrama," said Nico cynically.

"Perhaps I can," Kate shot back. "Of course, Daniel, there is no point in Nico taking part in the DNA experiment. His ancestors were living in safety at Armstrong House. No chance they would have ever been thrown into a famine grave!"

Nico looked at her defiantly. "Well, if everyone else in the area is taking part, then I don't see why I should not."

"Well, you're more than welcome to participate, Nico," said Daniel. "Although I've never met anybody who can trace their relatives back so assuredly as you can."

"It's the benefit of aristocracy," said Kate sarcastically.

"Oh, Kate, be quiet. You know I'm not an aristocrat in any shape or form," said Nico.

"When did the title die out?" asked Daniel.

"My grandfather, Pierce Armstrong, was the last earl. He only had a daughter, my mother, so the title did not pass to her as it could only pass to a male heir, and there was no close male heir as Pierce had only one sister who had no children. Any male cousins had titles of their own so never claimed the Armstrong title. Which I'm very much glad of, because there is no place for such antiquities in a modern republic like Ireland."

"Hear hear!" Valerie banged her fork on the table and laughed. "Although it is a bit of a pity all the same – a title would suit you, Kate!"

"I think Kate doesn't need a title for everyone to see she's a lady," said Daniel with a smile at Kate.

"Thank you, Daniel!" Kate smiled warmly at him at the compliment.

"Well, many thanks for your hospitality," said Daniel as Kate showed him to the front door much later. "Not to mention all the information you gave me regarding Lady Anna for the work we're doing."

"It's I who should be thanking you for the police file. I can't wait to get into it."

"Well, don't get too excited about it – when you wade through it you'll probably see it mainly concerns poaching!"

"Have a safe trip back to Castlewest. Where are you staying?"

Daniel pulled a face. "I'm booked into the Castlewest Arms Hotel. Not the nicest place I've stayed in."

"I can imagine. I think the wallpaper is the only thing keeping up the walls at this stage!"

"I need a place to rent. But I can't find anywhere. All the houses are booked up by tourists as it's peak season."

"Yes, of course," said Kate, an idea forming in her head. "Listen, we have an old lodge house – Hunter's Farm. It's the small manor house you passed on the way up here?"

"Yes, I saw it."

"Well, Nico's family used to use it as a holiday home when they were living in Dublin and this place was uninhabitable because of the fire. It's not in great nick. It needs a lot of work done on it and we're hoping to raise the money one of these days to do it. But if you're stuck and looking for a cheap place to rent until you find something better?"

Daniel's face lit up at the idea. "Very much interested, I have to say!"

"I'll ring you tomorrow and whenever you're free I'll show you around it, if you like?"

"Great, thanks!" said Daniel and gave her a small wave as he walked down the steps to his car.

"Goodnight!" called Kate and she watched as he drove away.

Valerie appeared, leaning against the drawing-room door.

"One for the road?" she asked as she swung a bottle of red in Kate's direction.

"No, Valerie! I just can't have a late one again like last night. You may have heard Nico say that I have a bus tour in the morning to show around."

"Oh, I heard Nico all right!" said Valerie sarcastically.

"I'll see you in the morning," said Kate as she headed up the stairs.

Nico was already in bed when she went into the room, reading through some papers connected to his work.

"Is he gone?" asked Nico.

"Yes," said Kate.

"Seems a nice enough kind of fellow."

"Yes, very interesting man," she said. "I've offered him Hunter's Farm to rent until he finds something else."

"*What?*" said Nico, throwing down his papers and taking off his reading glasses. "Whatever did you do that for?"

"Because he needs a place to stay and we could do with the money," explained Kate.

"But Hunter's Farm is in a shambles, Kate. The plumbing is fucked and the electricity is dodgy. And it's a mess. We haven't used it for years!"

"Oh, it will only take us an afternoon to clear it out," said Kate.

"I have too much work at the moment to be clearing anything out."

"Well, Valerie will help me then in that case."

"The multi-talented Valerie! Of course she will! Just keep feeding her wine and she can do anything!"

"Oh, don't be so ungenerous, Nico. I quite like having her here. I had forgotten what fun she could be."

"Yes, a little too much fun, perhaps? You were so drunk last night you could barely make it from the door to the bed without me helping you."

Kate was becoming angry. "You know I work around the clock trying to keep this place going from making films to showing German tourists around to grabbing an opportunity of making a little extra by renting out Hunter's Farm – and then you attack me for having a couple of nights of fun with my sister!"

Nico flushed with annoyance. "I know how much you do, Kate. But what upsets me is that you never discuss your plans with me. You just decide to do something and go ahead and do it without ever asking my opinion. From tour buses to film documentaries to renting out Hunter's Farm to having your hyperactive sister land in on top of us! I don't like living in what you have turned our home into. I feel as if I'm living in a train station half the time! I like peace and privacy. But you turn everything from our home to my family's history into a commercial enterprise!"

"Well, perhaps if you earned enough then maybe I wouldn't have to do all these things!" she spat.

"Well, thank you very much!" he said, hurt flying across his face. "I'm sorry that I'm not a multimillionaire like your last husband so you could still be the lady of leisure that you were!"

"*Fuck you, Nico!*" she said, her eyes stinging with tears. Turning around, she walked out of the room.

"Where are you going?" he asked.

"Down to join Valerie for a drink!" she declared, slamming the door after her.

"*Kate!*" he called after her, but she didn't come back and he hurled his papers on the floor with frustration.

Kate stormed down the stairs and across the hall into the drawing room, expecting to find Valerie there. But the room was empty except for a half bottle of wine and an empty glass on the coffee table. Kate realised that Valerie must have gone to bed already. Kate went over and filled the empty glass. She took a swig of wine from it and sat down on the couch. She was infuriated after her argument with Nico. Infuriated that he had thrown all her hard work back in her face. And most infuriated that he had brought Tony into the argument. Tony was completely off limits and he knew that.

As she took another swig from the glass she realised she had played dirty in the argument as well by saying he didn't earn enough money. She knew how hard he worked. She admitted to herself that Nico was correct when he said that she rarely consulted him on any plans she made for the house or for them. But she had found through her years with Nico that his first reaction was to shoot down anything she suggested. He was a natural conservative who didn't like change or new ideas. Whereas Kate loved new challenges and ideas and bringing them to fruition. Experience had taught her not to bother telling Nico about things she put in motion until after they were in motion, and then eventually he came round to the idea and agreed with her. Wasn't that how all marriages worked? Somebody led and somebody followed. If nobody led then nothing would get done.

She looked at her watch and saw it was just past eleven. After her run-in with Nico she didn't feel in the least tired and now she didn't even have Valerie to while away the time with. She stood up abruptly and, taking the bottle of wine and the glass, left the drawing room and walked across the hallway and into the library. Closing the door and turning on the light, she walked across to the Chesterfield desk and sat down, placing the bottle of wine and glass beside her. She took the file that Daniel had given her, opened it and began to read through it.

Kate didn't notice the time slipping away as she became engrossed in the file. Daniel had been correct – it was a fascinating angle on life on the Armstrong Estate at the time, and she wondered if this was the angle she should use for her film. She took her time reading all the poaching and burglary reports on the estate during the famine years. As Daniel had said, there were letters from Lord Edward to the Sergeant in Castlewest demanding police protection.

There was a very long and passionate letter from Lady Anna to the Sergeant, complaining about police brutality that had occurred when a riot broke out in Castlewest in 1848, as the police tried to retain control as the starving masses attacked shops in the town to get food supplies.

"*Is it not horrific enough,*" she read, "*that these poor unfortunate creatures have nowhere to lay their heads at night and no food for their children, but they then suffer at the hands of your police force. All humans deserve respect and the afflicted do not warrant the rough treatment they are receiving from your officers, merely because they are being forced to beg to stay alive. I urge you and your men to show at least some kindness.*"

Kate put the letter to one side and continued reading through the file as she poured herself another glass of wine. She found a lot of correspondence from a Sinclair Armstrong to the police. She wondered who this man was. He signed the letters as the estate manager. She knew that Edward had been an only child but because of Sinclair's surname he must have been somehow related to him. She found the tone in Sinclair's correspondence to be totally different from Edward and Anna's.

She turned to her computer and went onto the peerage website and did a search on the Earl of Armstrong's family. She scrolled down the long line of lords, ladies and Right Honourables until she found Sinclair Armstrong's name. She saw that he was the son of the Right Honourable Jamie Armstrong, second son of Lord Robert Armstrong. As she studied the period Kate realised that this made Sinclair Edward's first cousin. Intrigued, she read the rest of the entry on Sinclair and saw that he was married to a Diana Hunter from Yorkshire and their address was Hunter's Farm, the Armstrong Estate.

Kate looked up, surprised. "Diana Hunter," she said out aloud, realising that Sinclair's wife had given the small manor house the name that had stuck through the centuries. Kate had always imagined Hunter's Farm had been named after guests who had stayed there during the hunting season.

There were no more entries about the couple and it didn't show if they had children. But Kate realised that Sinclair was the last connection with aristocracy, and the privilege of being included in the peerage wouldn't have been extended to his children. Kate imagined it must have been hard for Sinclair. By just an accident of birth, with his father being born second, he was being excluded from the vast wealth of the Armstrong Estate that through the system of primogeniture has passed through his uncle to his cousin.

With renewed interest, Kate continued to study Sinclair's correspondence to the police. His letters were rude and demanding. What's more, instead of trying to evoke any sympathy from the police towards the victims of the Famine, Sinclair was demanding they take brutal action. And to Kate's surprise she read Sinclair was requesting police presence at evictions on the Armstrong Estate. Kate was shocked as she had always understood that there had been a policy of non-eviction on the estate and yet here was evidence that Sinclair was carrying them out. Was this with the knowledge of Edward? As she continued through the file into the 1850s, she was surprised to see that instead of things calming down after the Famine, crime in the Barony of Armstrong seemed to escalate. Reports of poaching and burglaries on the estate seemed to grow. Kate realised that this was the beginning of agrarian aggression in Ireland. That the Famine had led to a great hatred of the landlords, even ones who had been relatively kind like the Armstrongs. Kate understood that the Armstrongs had moved from a golden age of unassailable prominence before the Famine to a period of shaky politics for their class. A period that would eventually lead to total peasant unrest and rebellion as the century progressed and eventually lead to the aristocracy's downfall. She kept on reading through the file into the 1860s and suddenly came to an abrupt halt when she spotted a police report. She picked it up and studied it.

August 15th, 1865

A footman arrived at the police station at ten o'clock tonight to report a serious incident at Armstrong House. I went to Armstrong House, accompanied by Officer Grady. At the house, we met with Lord Edward Armstrong who informed us that a woman had been victim of a serious assault of a sexual nature at the house. Lord Armstrong said the woman in question was being attended to by the doctor. He did not reveal who the victim was and was unsure or did not want to say who the culprit was. Lord Armstrong appeared to be very shaken and was acting peculiarly. We asked permission for the victim to be interviewed. Lord Armstrong left us for a period of time and then on his return informed us that no charges were being pressed and that he would deal with the matter himself.

No follow up.

Sergeant Bourke

Castletown Police Station

Kate stared at the report and then read it again. She felt at once horrified and enthralled.

She had often in the past got strange feelings in the house. Feelings she could not explain. She loved the house so much. But because of how old and big it was, she expected that it would have a variable past. Life was variable so why should a house's history not be? As she discovered any unhappiness or shocking events that had happened to the previous occupants through the centuries before, it would at first unnerve her. Nobody likes to think of their house and home ever having bad things happen there. But then she accepted the house's history as she would accept a person's life – often uneven, sometimes happy and sometimes sad. But as she looked around the huge library her nerves got the better of her. Who had this woman been who had been attacked in such an awful way and who had been the attacker?

She stood up and closed over the file, and then quickly left the room and raced upstairs to bed and to Nico.

CHAPTER 8

1865

The drawing room of Marlborough House, the home of the Prince and Princess of Wales, was filled with the aristocracy of London as the young couple hosted one of their famous social nights. In the five years since Anna and Edward moved to London they had attended numerous events where they met the Royal family, eventually becoming favourites of the Prince and Princess.

As Edward stood beside Anna in the glorious drawing room where the Prince and Princess circulated among their guests, he reflected on their lives since they had left Armstrong House. They had bought a four-storey townhouse in Regent Park and were quickly absorbed into the city's social life. They had many friends amongst the Anglo-Irish who lived in London or kept houses there. Anna, particularly, seemed to thrive in the city. After all, she had been brought up and lived all her life until her marriage in Dublin and fitted back into city life as if she had never left it. Their life was so different now. They went to the theatre or dinner parties most nights. They regularly attended balls and decided to eat out in a restaurant for lunch or dinner at a moment's notice. Their social life at Armstrong House had always been busy, but the difference was their diary had to be planned weeks and sometimes months in advance. When they had guests or social events at Armstrong House or attended events at the other stately houses in Ireland, everything needed to be planned due to the distances that needed to be travelled. In London, they were only a hansom cab away from the next event. Yes, Anna had thrived in London and it had been the best thing for her to leave Armstrong House. Looking back, Edward thought, she seemed haunted in the years before they left Ireland. Now she seemed like the girl he had married, not the woman who had been changed by the Famine. Lawrence too had thrived at school in Eton and it was hard to believe he was now nineteen and leaving school.

As happy as everyone seemed, Edward pined for his native Mayo all the time. He missed it desperately. He had never lived in a city, except for when he had been at university, and was at his absolute happiest in the beautiful countryside he had grown up in. He travelled home as much as possible for business. Anna rarely accompanied him, even though the advance of the train network to the west of Ireland now made the travel there so much quicker, comfortable and convenient. They had not gone home for the past three summers of Lawrence's summer holidays. Instead they had taken the opportunity to travel. The first summer they had travelled the Continent, the second the United States and last summer they had travelled through South America. Anna insisted they should take the opportunity to travel while they could. It was Anna who seemed to come up with the excuses for them not to go home to Ireland, for Lawrence seemed as enthusiastic and eager to go home as Edward was. It was strange that Anna seemed not to want to see the home he had built for her as his bride and which she had claimed to love for so many years. He wondered if she still thought Lawrence was in danger from Harry? Had what happened with the near-drowning frightened her so? There was so much he wanted to ask Anna, and yet life had taught Edward that it was easier not to try and delve into her mind – it only led to denial and confrontation with her. As a rule, they were as much in love as ever and extremely happy in their marriage, but Edward was fully aware after a quarter of a century that when problems appeared in their lives it never brought them closer together, but pushed them apart. It was much easier to brush problems under the carpet.

The Prince and Princess of Wales reached Edward and Anna.

"Your Royal Highnesses," greeted Edward as he bowed while Anna sank into a deep curtsy.

"Lord Armstrong, so nice to see you again – and Lady Armstrong, you are looking very beautiful tonight," said the Prince.

"Thank you, your Royal Highness, for an undeserved compliment," said Anna.

"What is this we hear? That you are leaving us?" asked a concerned Princess Alexandra.

"You have heard correctly, ma'am, we are returning to live on the family estate in Ireland," said Edward.

"And what prompts this move?" asked the Prince.

"Our son, Lawrence, is graduating from Eton next month, sir, and so it is time for him to learn to take over the running of our estate."

"Is he not going up to Oxford or Cambridge?" asked the Princess.

"He has chosen not to, ma'am," said Anna, trying to not look as displeased as she felt about this.

"And a career in the army does not beckon?" questioned the Prince.

"He is definitely not militarily minded," said Edward. "Lawrence is the same as I, and his dearest wish is to live the life of a country gentleman."

Alexandra nodded. She was fully aware that the Armstrong Estate was one of the largest in Ireland, and she could understand the practical knowledge Edward wished to bestow on his son to manage that responsibility.

"Well, we shall certainly miss your faces here on the social scene, won't we, my dear?" said the Prince.

"We most certainly will," agreed the Princess.

"We hope to come back for the Season each year," said Anna earnestly.

"And perhaps the next time Your Royal Highnesses are in Ireland, you might consider staying at Armstrong House?" suggested Edward. "We have the train all the way to Mayo, so the journey is not so cumbersome."

"Ah yes, Ireland! My mother loved Killarney," said the Prince.

"Yes, Her Majesty's visit to Killarney was an outstanding

success," said Anna. "And weren't you stationed in the army for a time in Kildare yourself, sir?"

As soon as Anna said this, she felt a sharp pinch on her arm from Edward that startled her. She also saw the Prince look uncomfortable and the Princess's face turn sour.

"Indeed, wonderful place, Ireland," nodded the Prince as he moved on to talk to his next guests.

"We hope to see you again before you return to Armstrong House," said the Princess with a forced smile as she too moved on.

"Did I say something wrong?" whispered Anna to Edward.

"*Yes!*" hissed Edward. "Before the Prince was married, when he was stationed at the Curragh Camp in Kildare with the Grenadier Guards, he had an affair with a woman who was supposed to be an actress, but rumoured to be a prostitute! His parents were outraged and it is believed Queen Victoria thought the scandal killed her husband!"

"Oh!" Anna was shocked. "I knew he had a reputation, but I never guessed . . ."

"That he would keep such company!" said Edward, his eyes dancing with mirth.

Edward had his arm around his wife as they drove home to Regent Park.

"Edward?"

"Yes, my love?"

"I wonder – I wonder if we are doing the right thing? Going back to Armstrong House after all this time?"

"Yes, we are, Anna." Edward's voice was determined.

"But, will we not miss all this?" she said, looking out the window at the fine Georgian buildings.

"You might, but I won't. I hate being an absentee landlord. London is full of them. And what is more important, Lawrence has expressly stated that neither does *he* want to be an absentee landlord. In fact, he refuses to be one, and I am very proud of him for that. Armstrong House is his legacy, and it is a legacy he wants. He misses it as much as I do."

"But –"

"But nothing, Anna! We made a pact that we would stay in London until Lawrence left school. He is now six-foot-two and built like an ox. He is in no danger from anybody at Armstrong House any more. He is well able to defend himself from Harry or anybody else you conjure up in your head as a danger to him. You are being selfish if you try to keep him away from his legacy at this stage, Anna. We've lived our lives your way for the past five years. Now it's time for you to step back and let Lawrence live the life he was born for."

Anna looked out the window. She knew she couldn't fight Edward on this any further. She knew she couldn't fight Lawrence either, who was insistent on returning home. She dreaded returning to Armstrong House. She dreaded returning to the memories. And she had a terrible feeling of dread for the future that she could not comprehend or understand.

The carriage pulled up outside their house and the driver got down and opened the carriage door for them. Edward got out and held his hand out to Anna. She glanced at him as she stepped out and managed to smile as they walked up the steps into the house.

Anna sat at her dressing table as she removed her jewellery. Edward came back from the bathroom, already changed into his dressing gown.

"Whatever were you thinking suggesting the Prince and Princess should come and stay with us at Armstrong House?" questioned Anna as she removed her necklace. "Have you any idea what a royal visit would cost? We would have to prepare the house for months in advance."

Edward laughed lightly. "I shouldn't worry, Anna. I doubt their Royal Highnesses would ever take up our invitation. It's rarely they go to Ireland and, if they do, they stay at the Viceregal Lodge in Dublin."

"They are probably wise to stay away from Ireland with the nationalism and anti-royal sentiment growing there since the Famine," said Anna. "It is hard to hear the Prince declare Ireland a wonderful place when one million of his mother's subjects were allowed to perish needlessly there not twenty years ago – and one million forced to emigrate."

"*Hmmm*," said Edward, not wishing to enter into a conversation on the subject.

Anna swung around on her stool to look at Edward.

"Was that true what you told me about the Prince's affair while stationed in Kildare?"

"Absolutely true, unfortunately. It was the talk of the gentlemen's clubs at the time and many a parlour as well. Did you never hear of it before?"

"No, I certainly didn't. It's not the kind of gossip that would reach my ears," she said dismissively. "Well, pray continue – what happened?"

"Nothing much more than I already said. The young prince got mixed up with a woman while in Kildare with the Grenadier Guards. What was the woman's name . . . Nellie . . . eh . . . Nellie Clifden, if my memory serves me right."

"And who was she?" Anna's curiosity was on fire.

"They said she was an actress, but the truth as I was told it was that she was a prostitute. She was brought to the young Prince by friends when he was stationed in Kildare and they had a brief liaison. Apparently the Prince was a – a novice in such affairs until he met Nellie."

Anna shuddered. "Those poor wretched women. Driven to sell themselves. But why – *why* – would the Prince of Wales want to be with a woman like that when he could have had his pick of aristocratic women in Europe?"

Edward shrugged. "People do things for many reasons, often incomprehensible to others. It was certainly incomprehensible to Queen Victoria and his late father who, when they heard of their son's dalliance, sent for him at once and had him married off to Princess Alexandra before he destroyed the royal family with his shenanigans with an Irish harlot."

Anna's face filled with concern. "And what became of this Nellie Clifden after the Prince was done with her?"

Edward shrugged. "Who knows? She disappeared and that was the last anyone heard of her. There were rumours the Royal family paid her to go away and be quiet, but I imagine she just drifted back into the life she knew and wasn't missed by anyone. Let's face it, ever since the Famine, thousands upon thousands of people have disappeared through death or emigration. As if they were never here."

Anna's face was overcome with sadness and she quickly turned back to face the mirror and grabbed a handkerchief to wipe away a threatening tear.

"On the other hand," said Edward, "it's also quite possible that Nellie did very well out of the situation – if the Royal Family paid for her silence. She may have had the funds to emigrate to America and start a new life there – hence was never heard of again."

Anna swung around on her stool again. "I think it was absolutely disgusting of the Prince to use a poor girl from a different world and then just cast her away after he had finished with her. She might have been a loose woman, but how dare he treat her like that!"

"Well, I think the girl posed a much bigger threat to the Prince, if the affair had ever become public, than he ever did to the girl," said Edward as he took off his dressing gown and got into bed. "What if she had become pregnant? It would have brought down the monarchy."

CHAPTER 9

There was much to do in London as the Armstrongs prepared to leave, such as packing trunks of their personal items to be taken back to Ireland, and reducing the staff at Regent Park to just caretaker level.

"I wonder should we close up the house altogether until we use it again?" suggested Edward.

"No, Edward!" said Anna. "We need to keep a presence in the house, to keep it heated, aired and maintained, and the garden from going wild. We're only keeping three servants here, so the expense will not be great."

"It just seems a waste, when we could just lock the house up," said Edward.

"It would look bad for us to lock the house up. Also, I was not lying to the Prince of Wales – I very much intend for us to return here each year for the Season once we have settled back into Armstrong House." Anna knew the reason Edward wanted to get rid of all the servants and lock the house up was not down to being thrifty. She knew, if the house was not kept up with the presence of a caretaking staff, then the likelihood of them being able to return to live there easily would be diminished.

"Oh, yes, the Season, I forgot," said Edward dismissively, looking as if once they got back to Armstrong House he never had any intention of being in London for the Season again.

"We *shall* be attending the Season, Edward. If for no other reason than that in the future Lawrence will need to select a suitable wife, and will need to be familiar with the Season in order to choose wisely."

"I chose you without either of us ever having done the Season," Edward pointed out.

"Times have changed for the aristocracy in Ireland since we were courting, Edward. In our day, the social scene in Ireland for our class was centred on Dublin, but since the Famine London has taken over in prominence."

Edward had to admit that was true. The Anglo-Irish did see London as their capital now. A lot of them who owned vast estates now kept homes in London rather than Dublin and marriages with the English aristocracy were commonplace. It was a sad reflection that since the Famine their class was now resented and the general population often showed hostility to them. This made them look to England for their identity more than before. When Edward was growing up it would have been unthinkable that he would have gone to school or university anywhere else than in Dublin. Now the norm was London. That was why he felt it was so important for them to return to Armstrong House and lead the charge to rebuke this trend.

Anna walked around the drawing room, checking that she hadn't missed anything that needed to be packed. They were leaving at the weekend. Lawrence was staying with friends in the country and due to return to London the following day. Then he would stay in London at the house for a month on his own before joining them in Ireland.

Anna became a little panicked at the thought. "Edward, I wonder if we are wise to leave Lawrence on his own here?"

"He won't be on his own – Keating will be here," said Edward, referring to the butler who they were retaining.

"I know that. But he's never been on his own before unsupervised," said Anna.

"It will do him a world of good. He's left school now, Anna, and needs to learn responsibility. The best way for somebody to *learn* responsibility is to *give* them responsibility. If he had opted to go to Oxford or Cambridge he would have been unsupervised there.

Unless you had planned on going to university with him?" Edward raised an eyebrow mockingly.

"I just worry," she said.

Edward came over and embraced her. "As I keep saying, Lawrence is now well capable of looking after himself. You need to loosen the apron strings a little. You worried about him when he was at Armstrong House and you worry about him now that he is in London. And it's not as if he's a tearaway – in which case I should worry myself. But he's the most sensible of young fellows."

Anna sighed. "I know you're right. Maybe it's just because we only have the one child."

CHAPTER 10

The train swept through the Irish countryside towards Mayo. Anna and Edward were in a private carriage and as Edward read the newspaper Anna was deep in thought. Soon the train would arrive back in Castletown, the nearest town to the Armstrong estate. Last time Anna had been home, three years before, the train station hadn't been opened or the track laid to Mayo. She remembered the long journey by road from Dublin to Mayo, often staying overnight at one of their friend's homes to break the journey. The country had certainly changed for the better. She wondered what other changes there were. Their long-serving and trusted butler Barton at Armstrong House had retired two years previously and Edward had hired a new one, who was called Taylor, through an agency in Dublin. Edward sang Taylor's praises and Anna knew her husband had always been good at hiring staff and spotting potential. Her thoughts drifted back to when she had first come to live at Armstrong House. With Barton's departure, Anna knew that there was now nobody left working at the house who had been there when she had first arrived there. All the previous staff at the house and the gardeners, stables boys, groomsmen and drivers had now long since left or retired or were dead. This gave Anna a strange kind of relief. Returning to Armstrong House now was a fresh start, a new start, with nobody there who knew her from before.

Anna wondered how Lawrence was doing in London on his own. She hoped that, now he had finished his exams at Eton, he was enjoying his time in the city with his friends before he came back to Armstrong House to assume the mantle that Edward was preparing to hand over to him. As she thought of the Prince of Wales' antics in Kildare when he was left for the first time unsupervised, she was filled with a dread, despite Edward's assurances. But she knew Lawrence was a very different character from the Prince of Wales. He was a sensible, caring young man whom they trusted implicitly. Anna knew Edward was right, but she would be glad when Lawrence arrived safe and sound at Armstrong House.

The train's whistle blew loudly as it slowed down and pulled into the station.

"*Castletown*!" called the stationmaster loudly as the train pulled to a halt.

"Ah, here we are!" said Edward, standing up, pulling down the window of the carriage door and popping his head out.

"Can you see Taylor?" asked Anna, standing up and collecting her bag, coat and scarf.

Edward had arranged for the butler to accompany a driver to meet them off the train.

"No," said Edward, straining to look up the and down the platform which was now busy with people getting off and on the train. He reached out the window and opened the carriage door from outside.

Collecting his belongings, he stepped out onto the platform and gave his hand to Anna to assist her out.

"Where is Taylor?" he said irritably.

"Perhaps he just sent a driver instead of coming himself?" suggested Anna.

"Perhaps. Though I specifically told them in my letter to send Taylor as I hardly know what any of the drivers or stable boys at Armstrong House look like any more! Where is the damned man?"

The platform cleared and the stationmaster came walking quickly down the train, closing the doors before the train continued on its journey.

"Oh, hello, Lord Armstrong, welcome home, sir," he said when he reached Edward and Anna.

"Good afternoon, Reilly. Have you by chance seen anybody

from Armstrong House? We were supposed to be collected by our butler, Taylor," said Edward.

"Indeed I didn't, your lordship."

"Could he be outside?"

"He might be, sir – I haven't looked outside."

"Though why he'd wait there I cannot imagine," said Edward.

"Well, as I said, they may have sent some young lad without Taylor," said Anna, "and he might not understand what needs to be done."

"True," said Edwards. "Could you check, Reilly?"

"I will indeed but give me a minute – the train is due to leave now," said Reilly.

"But all our trunks are still on the train!" said Edward. "In the goods carriage."

"Oh!" said Reilly. "I'll call the porter. We must hurry, sir – the train needs to leave."

Reilly rushed off while Edward strode after him to check if Taylor had arrived outside.

There was no carriage in sight.

Edward strode furiously back to Anna. Then Reilly came hurrying down the platform with a porter and luggage trolley.

"Come along, Lord Armstrong!" said Reilly, beckoning to him as he headed to the goods carriage. "The train needs to leave!"

Edward looked perplexed at being given instructions by the stationmaster, then he hastily followed him and joined the other men in the struggle to get the trunks out of the carriage in double-quick time.

Anna looked on in horror as her beautiful travel trunks, bought in Harrods, were thrown unceremoniously onto the platform.

As soon as the last piece of luggage was removed and the men jumped out, Reilly slammed the door of the goods carriage shut and the blast of his whistle pierced the air.

Puffing and panting, Edward sat down on one of the trunks to regain his breath as the train moved off, gathering momentum as it went.

"That's the most exercise you've done in five years!" said Anna, laughing to herself.

"Bugger!" said Edward, catching his breath. "I'll kill that damned Taylor!"

"If you'll excuse me, I'll be getting back to my work. I'm sure somebody from Armstrong House will be along to collect you shortly," said Reilly. With a smile he ambled back to his office.

Anna had noticed something odd in the station master's manner. In all her time living at Armstrong House the locals and townspeople nearly bowed down to the Armstrongs and the other aristocracy. And yet Reilly, although very pleasant, didn't show that reverence that had always been there before. Anna hoped it wasn't a sign of the times, of the growing republicanism and nationalism that had been sweeping through Ireland since the Famine.

Anna went and sat down on a trunk beside her husband and said, "Welcome back to Ireland!"

Two hours later and Anna and Edward were still sitting on their trunks on the platform, afraid to leave them unguarded.

"This is ridiculous!" said Anna. "Are we to sleep on the platform tonight? Are you sure you told them to collect us?"

"Yes, I tell you!" answered Edward, equally annoyed. "I wrote to Sinclair more than two weeks ago saying to have Taylor meet us at the station at four o'clock on June 4th. Could I be any more exact than that?"

"Sinclair!" said Anna, raising her eyes upwards as it all made sense to her now. "You didn't tell me it was Sinclair you wrote to! I thought it was Taylor. Did he reply?"

"Well, no."

"Oh, Edward!"

Anna stood up and walked over to the stationmaster's office and knocked on the window. She could see Reilly half asleep inside. A few moments later Reilly emerged.

"Still no luck, your ladyship?"

"Unfortunately no, Mr. Reilly. There appears to have been some kind of mix-up. Could I trouble you to organise a lift for us back to Armstrong House?"

"Oh, let me think, who can I get? It's not like London here, you know – there aren't any hansom cabs."

"I am fully aware of that, Mr. Reilly, but I would be most grateful if you could arrange a carriage for us," smiled Anna.

"Leave it with me," said Reilly as he sauntered off.

Half an hour later, Anna and Edward were sitting in the back of a cart borrowed by Reilly from a local farmer. Reilly's son Tim was driving them back. Their trunks had been left in Reilly's care – they would send someone from the house to collect them.

Of course, when Reilly had arrived back with the donkey and cart, Edward had protested.

"Good lord, man, surely you could have found a proper trap suitable for Lady Anna to ride in? Do you really expect her to sit on the floor?"

"I'm sorry, your lordship, but there was nothing else available anywhere nearby."

"Never mind, Edward," said Anna. "Let's just go. I don't want to wait around here any longer." She might have imagined it but she thought Reilly looked as if he was trying to keep a straight face. She wondered how hard he had actually tried to find a suitable vehicle.

"I'll find something for you and Her Ladyship to sit on," said Reilly.

Seated on a tartan shawl, they set out to endure an uncomfortable jolting ride to the Armstrong Estate.

"Thank heaven!" said Anna as the gates at last came in sight.

"Well, this is an auspicious arrival back!" said Edward.

Anna suddenly started laughing as they turned in through the gateway and began the journey up the long driveway that led around the lake up to the manor.

"What's so funny?" asked Edward.

"I'm just thinking – if the Prince of Wales could see us now!"

Tim pulled up in the forecourt outside Armstrong House and Edward helped Anna down.

Then, rather dishevelled, he and Anna made their way up the

steps to the front door. Tim followed, carrying the personal luggage they had brought with them.

"Thank you, Tim – we'll send someone in the morning to the station to collect the trunks," said Edward, handing him a coin. He had already paid Reilly fairly handsomely for his help such as it was.

"Thank you, sir," said Tim with a grin and, tipping his hat, he left.

Edward knocked loudly on the door.

A minute later the new butler Taylor opened the door and looked shocked to see them there.

"Where the blazes were you?" demanded Edward. "We've been waiting for hours for you to collect us, you stupid man!"

"I – I – we weren't expecting you!" said Taylor as Edward pushed past him into the hallway.

"I'm Lady Armstrong, Taylor," Anna introduced herself, realising Edward was in too much of a bad mood to do it. She quickly took Taylor's appearance in and saw he looked like a perfect butler – honest, diligent with slicked-back black hair.

"Welcome, my lady," said Taylor, still bemused.

Anna followed Edward across the hallway to the drawing room where, she had no doubt, he was going to pour himself a stiff drink.

"We should never have let Barton retire!" said Edward as he stormed in.

"He *was* eighty-three!" reminded Anna him.

Then they both stood stock still as they beheld Sinclair and Diana sitting there on sofas, being served drinks by a footman.

"Edward!" said Sinclair, standing up, looking shocked. "We weren't expecting you!"

"Well, that is clear!" said Anna, amazed at seeing her arch enemies sitting in her drawing room as if they lived there.

"Sinclair!" Edward protested. "We have been waiting *hours* at the train station to be collected! Why didn't you send Taylor to collect us?"

"Because you never asked me to!" Sinclair defended himself.

"Of course I did! I sent you a letter two weeks ago with all the details of our arrival!" Edward all but shouted.

"Well, if you did, I never received it!" said Sinclair.

"Never received it?"

"It's the post!" said Diana, placing her glass delicately down on the table beside her. "The postman has been falling down on his duties for some time now."

"Of course he has!" said Anna sarcastically under her breath.

"I'll be having strong words with that postman tomorrow," said Sinclair. "This must be the tenth letter he has failed to deliver to me."

"I think he's drunk half the time," said Diana. "But you're here now, that is the main thing!"

Getting up, she walked over to Edward and kissed his cheek before turning to Anna and kissing hers, declaring, "It is so good to see you again, Cousin Anna. And you look so well. Please do sit down."

Somewhat bemused, Anna sat on the sofa and Diana stood smiling at her.

Sinclair shook Edward's hand before bending to kiss Anna's cheek.

"It looks like you could do with a drink, Cousin Edward," said Diana, walking to the drinks table and pouring him a large whiskey. "Hours at the train station, you say? At least it wasn't raining."

She handed Edward the glass, and he took a big gulp from it.

"Well, we knew you were due to return home – but we didn't know when," said Sinclair, seating himself on the sofa again. "How did you get here anyway?"

"The stationmaster eventually arranged some transport," said Edward, not wanting to mention the cart. "But our trunks are still at the station."

"Is Lawrence not with you?"

"No, if you had got my letter you would know that he will be returning in a couple of weeks," said Edward.

"Well, we must make sure we don't leave him stranded at the train station and make the arrangements properly next time!" said

Diana. She went over to the bell-pull and tugged it.

Anna was trying to decipher what was going on. What were Diana and Sinclair doing in their drawing room, having drinks as if they lived there? They hadn't been expecting them so they weren't there to welcome them.

A few moments later and Taylor arrived in, looking flustered.

"You rang, Mrs. Armstrong?"

"Taylor, we shall be having two extra for dinner tonight," said Diana. "Please inform Cook – I do hope she has prepared enough – perhaps she could add some side dishes? And have the footmen make the extra settings at the dining table."

"Very good, Mrs. Armstrong," nodded Taylor, who then hastily left the room.

"Anna, do have a drink. Or would you prefer a cup of tea to revive you after your ordeal?" said Diana. "Yes, a cup of tea would be best."

Before Anna could respond Diana pulled the bell-pull twice.

"I tug the bell-pull once for Taylor or a footman, and twice for a parlourmaid," explained Diana, retaking her seat beside Anna. "It saves confusion."

A few moments later a flustered parlourmaid arrived in.

"Bring Lady Armstrong a cup of hot sweet tea, and then arrange to have their bedroom made up for the night," said Diana.

"Yes, Mrs. Armstrong." The parlourmaid then made a hasty retreat.

"So what news from London?" asked Diana.

Anna looked at Edward, her face masked in confusion.

"Forgive me if I appear rude," she said, forcing her voice to remain calm and casual, "but do you often have dinner at Armstrong House?"

"Well, yes," said Diana, looking perplexed. She gave a little laugh. "Where else would we have it?"

Anna gave a little laugh back. "Why, at home in Hunter's Farm."

Diana looked at Edward in surprise. "But – but – we haven't lived in Hunter's Farm for three years, my dear."

"I beg your pardon?" asked Anna.

"Not since we moved into Armstrong House," said Sinclair.

"*Moved in?*" cried Anna, looking at Edward for some explanation.

"Yes, Edward suggested, nay insisted, that we move into Armstrong House this past three years. And that is what we did," said Sinclair.

"Rather than let the servants go wild and have nobody to answer to after Barton left," said Diana. "Don't worry, we have left your bedroom as it was and we don't sleep there. We stay in the Blue Room."

"*The Blue Room!*" squealed Anna.

"And Harry is in the Green Room," said Sinclair.

"*The Green Room!*" Anna cried. "But that used to be Lawrence's room!"

Edward looked embarrassed as his face went red and he refused to look at Anna who was staring at him angrily.

"Edward said you would be fine with the arrangement," said Diana.

"Did he now?" said Anna, glaring at her husband.

Edward mustered the courage to look at his wife and she could see his eyes were appealing to her not to make a scene.

She managed to calm down as she really didn't want to make a complete show of him in front of his cousin and wife.

"And what are your plans now that we are back at Armstrong House?" asked Anna, whose first concern was to get them out of her home as quickly as possible.

"Well, naturally, we'll move back to Hunter's Farm," said Sinclair.

"Naturally," replied Anna.

The door of the room opened and a young man sauntered in. Anna at first didn't recognise him and then realised it was Harry.

"Harry!" Edward, glad of the distraction, went over to shake his hand. "How good to see you again. And how are you, my dear fellow?"

Harry looked a little dazed at seeing Edward and Anna there.

"Just fine, Uncle Edward," said Harry, shaking his hand.

"Anna, look who it is – it's Harry," said Edward, propelling Harry in Anna's direction.

"So I see," said Anna.

"Hello again, Cousin Anna," said Harry and bent down to give her a kiss on the cheek.

Anna hated how they called her cousin when she was no blood relative of theirs, nor was Edward Harry's uncle. They did everything to try to appear to have close ties with them and the aristocratic title.

"And what have you been doing with yourself, Harry?" she said, trying to appear interested as she studied the young man.

"I help Father run the estate here," said Harry. "Did you not know?"

"No, I'm afraid I'm out of tune as to what has been happening here," said Anna.

"He also came first at the Horse Show in Dublin last year. We're all very proud of him. He's the finest horseman in the county," smiled Diana.

"Ah, then he takes after his mother," said Anna, realising that looks-wise at least he very much took after Sinclair. She wondered what his personality was like now? She remembered him as a child, always there watching. She managed to hide a shiver as she remembered all the near-fatal accidents Lawrence had in his company growing up. She cringed with embarrassment as she remembered how she had hit him and attacked him down on the lakeshore after Lawrence had nearly drowned and she held him accountable. She was sure the memory of what she had done was passing through Harry's mind as well as he smiled pleasantly at her. And now he had been staying in Lawrence's bedroom while they had been away. How could Edward have permitted that?

CHAPTER 11

Anna endured the rest of the evening and night in Diana and Sinclair's company. Harry had not joined them for dinner, saying he had estate business to attend to. Diana's conversation revolved mainly around horses, and Anna had to stifle her yawns on more than one occasion. She thought the evening would never end as Edward and Sinclair chatted away warmly as they always had before. Finally she took the opportunity to declare she was exhausted from all the travel and needed to retire to bed. She grabbed Edward's arm, not giving him the chance to stay down talking and drinking with Sinclair, and bid them goodnight.

Anna waited until they climbed the stairs and made the safety of their bedroom before she rounded on her husband.

"Whatever were you thinking of allowing those three to live at Armstrong House?" she demanded, the anger she had been hiding for the evening now at last being allowed to explode.

"It made total sense, Anna. There was no point in having a full staff of servants here at Armstrong House and nobody for them to cater to. It made sense for Sinclair, Diana and Harry to live here and make sure the house was run properly, especially after Barton retired. They have done us a huge favour!"

"How is getting free food and accommodation and a fleet of servants for three years doing *us* a huge favour? Are you out of your mind?"

"You see, *this* is why I didn't tell you they were moving in. Because I knew you would overreact!" said Edward.

"You never even discussed it with me, let alone told me. You've hidden this from me for three years!"

"I didn't discuss it with you because I knew you would forbid me to do it!"

"And yet you still went on and let them move in here regardless of how you knew I would react?" She was outraged.

"They were supposed to have moved back to Hunter's Farm by now. You weren't supposed to see them living here."

"Oh, so I was to be duped? The lie was to be permanent!"

"Of course not! How could it when everybody in the area, to say nothing of the servants, knew they were living here? But I wanted to spare you the shock of seeing them here. I told Sinclair in my letter to be moved out by the time we got back."

"Oh yes, the famous letter that mysteriously disappeared. How convenient for Sinclair and Diana that it did!" spat Anna.

Edward buried his face in his hands. "Oh, Anna, don't start this paranoia again! Are you now accusing Sinclair of lying that he never got the letter?"

"Of course I am!"

"Oh, Anna, I really don't think I can cope if you start all of *that* again! You can't let your paranoia take over our lives like you did before. We did what you wanted and moved away from Armstrong House while Lawrence was at school. We made a pact that we would then return home and live our lives as *normal*!"

"How can we live our lives as normal when I have a husband who blatantly keeps the truth from me! Who lies to me, in effect! Who moves his cousin and wife, whom I despise, into our home for three years and deliberately doesn't tell me!"

"Yes, Anna – *our home*. Armstrong House, where we should have been all this time, but were forced to move out of because of your wild imaginings. If it wasn't for Sinclair and Diana minding our home and our estate for all these years, then goodness knows what a state it and we would be in by now!"

"You have let them take over! They have been living here as if *they* were Lord and Lady Armstrong for the past three years. I would never have agreed to that! You handed them on a plate what they have so desperately wanted for years."

"It was you that handed it on a plate to them, by not staying here and fulfilling your responsibilities as Lady Armstrong," Edward accused her.

Outside the room, Sinclair and Diana had reached the top of the stairs on their way to bed. They had stood rigid as they heard the shouting coming from Edward and Anna's room. As the shouting became angrier and more intense, Sinclair and Diana smiled at each other.

Harry waited until he was sure everyone had gone to bed and then he came out of his room and looked up and down the corridor to make sure the coast was clear. Then he tip-toed to the far end of the corridor to the servants' stairs and made his way down through the house to the kitchen.

The kitchen was in darkness.

"*Gertie!*" Harry whispered into the darkness.

A moment later a figure in a white nightdress stepped out of the shadows.

"I thought you weren't going to come!" said a young woman's voice.

"I said I would, didn't I?"

"I can't stay long," she said. "I'll be missed."

"They're all asleep upstairs, they won't miss you," Harry assured her, then he grabbed the young maid and kissed her passionately.

"I can only stay a short while," she insisted as he kissed her neck and groped her body. "Mr. Taylor is a light sleeper and he'll surely sack me on the spot if he catches me out of my room at this time of the night."

"Don't be so ridiculous – I'll have Taylor fired if he says anything to you," said Harry.

"Oh, Harry!" she said, kissing him. "But, sure, you won't be able to fire anybody now His Lordship and Her Ladyship are back."

Harry pulled back from her, his face angry, and then he smiled and started fondling her again.

"Don't, Harry!" she said as he went to lift her nightdress. Gertie knew she was playing with fire meeting Harry as she did. She knew she was risking her job and position if it ever got out. But she couldn't help herself. From the time she had started working in the house, Harry had begun to flirt with her and she found the attention irresistible. That an Armstrong would be interested in *her*, a girl from nowhere! And he had told her he loved her. He had told her the previous week. There was no denying he had said the words to her.

"Harry, *no!*" she insisted, pushing his probing hands away.

"Why not?" he demanded.

"Because it's not right!"

"What's not right about it? I told you I loved you, didn't I?"

"I still can't, Harry. Doesn't matter how much we love each other. I'd face eternal damnation if we ever did!"

"It would be worth it," he said, nuzzling her neck.

"I'd better get back to my room," she said.

"No!" he insisted. "I won't be here for much longer."

"What do you mean?" she asked, horrified.

"Now that Edward and Anna are back, my parents and I have to move back to Hunter's Farm, so it will be much harder to meet you. This could be our last opportunity."

"No!" She was despairing at the thought of him leaving the house. She had never known such happiness as she felt during the snatched time she had with Harry. She didn't think such happiness could exist for the likes of her.

"So – we – really – have – so – little – time," Harry said between kisses as they fell to the floor.

CHAPTER 12

Anna pretended to still be asleep the next morning as she heard Edward get up and prepare himself for the day. Only when he left the room did she open her eyes and get out of bed. She walked languidly over to the window. Looking out, she saw the morning was a beautiful one with the lake pure blue as it stretched out into the distance. Such a beautiful lake – a lake that was so nearly the scene of tragedy. She sighed deeply as she remembered.

She and Edward had argued into the night and she couldn't remember what time it was that they had finally gone to bed. She went and tugged the bell-pull and a few minutes later a maid knocked and came into the room.

"Good morning, my lady."

"Good morning. Could you bring my breakfast up here, please?" said Anna.

"Yes, my lady," nodded the girl. She left, closing the door after her.

Anna had no desire to have breakfast with Sinclair and Diana looking at her from across the table. They had said they would be leaving Armstrong House that morning.

After Anna had eaten her breakfast, she called the maid to run her bath. But bathed and dressed for the day, she still did not venture from the bedroom. She kept a close eye out the window and at noon she saw activity out in the forecourt. Diana and Sinclair were getting into a carriage while their luggage was being loaded on the back by footmen. As Anna watched them drive off

from the forecourt and disappear down the long driveway, she was
sure they must be furious at having to leave Armstrong House. By
the look of them they had made themselves very much at home
there in Edward's and her absence. For all purposes, they had acted
as if they were Lord and Lady Armstrong and must be resentful at
having to relinquish that role.

Taking her shawl, she turned and left the bedroom. Continuing
down the corridor, she walked down the flight of stairs where she
found a maid polishing a mirror.

"What is your name?" asked Anna.

"Gertie, my lady," said the maid with a quick curtsy.

There was so many new staff at Armstrong House that Anna
realised it would take her a while to get to know them all. She
quickly looked Gertie up and down and saw she was a voluptuous
girl with slightly unruly curly hair pulled back in a bun. There was
something about the girl's face that Anna couldn't quite decipher. A
cheekiness, a defiance. This was a girl, Anna imagined, who needed
to be well supervised to keep her out of trouble.

"Where is Lord Armstrong, Gertie?" questioned Anna.

"In the library, my lady," answered Gertie.

Anna nodded and continued past her and out the front door. It
was obvious that all her servants were looking at her with
trepidation and curiosity. She imagined it was hard for them to now
get used to a new mistress, after Diana being there for so long.
Anna was also sure that they would be very grateful that she was
the lady of the manor once they got to know her. Diana's
mistreatment of servants had always been well known.

Anna breathed in the fresh air and decided to go for a walk. The
last thing she needed was another argument with Edward and so
she decided it was a good idea to stay out of his way for the day.
First, she went into the gardens that led off to the side of the house.
They had been kept immaculately since she had been last there. She
remembered how, when she had first come to live at Armstrong
House, she had helped set out those gardens, directing the
gardeners where to plant trees and shrubberies and where to build
fountains. It was gratifying to see her work now in full bloom after

all these years. She came back into the forecourt and then made her way down the steps that led to the first garden terrace. Memories flooded back of all the garden parties they had there over the years. She continued down the flight of steps to the next terraced garden and then continued down to the lakeshore, where she stood and looked out at the tranquil lake. It was so quiet and peaceful that it seemed a million miles from the hustle and bustle of London. And also a million years since the day Lawrence nearly drowned there.

She walked along the shoreline, deep in thought. She knew what a terrible wrench it had been for Edward to leave Armstrong House for the past few years. And he had done it because of his love and concern for her. As she thought of all the husbands who were in the London set they had known, she remembered all the vices their wives had to put up with. The affairs, the drinking, the gambling. And it was all just accepted as the way husbands behave. Edward had been so different from most of them. He had never even looked at another woman in all their years of marriage. He adored her, that she knew. Perhaps she took him for granted sometimes but maybe it was a natural thing to do after so many years of marriage. The previous night, the coming home to Armstrong House, should have been a joyous occasion for him. Coming back to his home, and getting it ready for their son to come home and take it over. As she walked along, she realised Armstrong House was her home too. And she had let them be driven out of it and even tried to persuade Lawrence not to return there but to choose a life in London.

Edward had banned Anna from ever mentioning how Lawrence had nearly drowned in the lake that day. He had said he didn't want Lawrence to be upset by being reminded of it. Anna knew he hoped their son would forget the facts of the day – and, most of all, Harry's involvement. Oh, what it was to have a husband who swept everything under the carpet and pretended nothing unpleasant ever happened!

She walked on. As she reflected on their desperation to have a child, she knew it wasn't just their need to be parents that had caused that desperation. It was also to provide an heir for the Armstrong Estate. And when Lawrence had been born there was such celebration that an heir had finally been born. And here she was all these years later trying to dissuade and discourage Lawrence from taking the legacy he had been born into.

She stopped walking and stared out at the lake, realising what a fool she had been.

Diana and Sinclair were in the drawing room at Hunter's Farm, drinking whiskey.

"Well, here we are – back again!" said Diana.

"It seems so small compared to Armstrong House," commented Sinclair.

"That's because it is small compared to Armstrong House. It's going to take a long time to get used to living back here after being Lord and Lady of the Manor."

"I never thought she would come back here. From what Edward said she was gloriously happy in London. She's a city girl at heart, never fitted in here," observed Sinclair.

"She's come back to protect her son's inheritance. Pure and simple. I'm sure she doesn't want to be back here but is doing it for Edward and Lawrence," mused Diana.

"I doubt they will stay long. Lawrence hasn't been here in three years – he's used to a different life now. He'll never settle back."

"Oh, they will stay . . . unless they are driven away," said Diana.

Harry walked into the room. "Dempsey says there is trouble over at Toormore. Two of the tenant farmers have been having a feud and it's broken out into violence."

Sinclair looked at Harry irritably. "Well, go and sort it out! Must I do everything around here?"

Harry nodded and left his parents alone.

Anna opened the library door and saw Edward seated at his desk going through some paperwork. He looked up at her warily, obviously in no mood for a continuation of the argument from the previous night. Anna walked straight over to him and around his desk. Putting her arms around him, she bent down and kissed his mouth.

"What was that for?" he asked, looking surprised.

"For everything," she said, smiling at him. "I don't know how you put up with me. I can only apologise for my behaviour last night. You are, of course, as ever, right. How can I insist we leave Armstrong House for years and then complain of how it has been run in my absence?"

Edward's face softened. "I should have told you Sinclair and Diana had moved in."

"Well, they have moved out now!" she said cheerily. "And it is our house again, I am very happy to say."

He smiled broadly at her, delighted that she seemed to show the first sign of happiness to be back at Armstrong House.

"I was just in the ballroom before I came in to you," she said. "Can you remember the last ball we had here?"

"No, I can't."

"We used to have such parties here, do you remember?"

"How could I forget?" he said with a smile. "But it seemed in bad taste during and after the Famine to host a ball."

"When you designed and built this house for me before we were married, you had a ballroom included because this was what this house was meant for – joy and celebration – and that is what we are going to have. I've been thinking that we should host a ball for Lawrence's return next month. We can invite all our old friends, and the aristocracy from around Ireland. It would be so lovely to see people like the Earl of Galway and Earl of Arran again, don't you think?"

"I think that's a wonderful idea!" He was thrilled.

"And a wonderful opportunity to introduce our now adult son to them. After all, this is going to be his home for the rest of his life. Lawrence needs to become friends with all our friends."

Edward stood up and took her in his arms and kissed her.

CHAPTER 13

Anna was run off her feet over the next weeks, rushing around organising the ball for Lawrence's return. She made sure all the invitations went out in plenty of time and was delighted to see they were all accepted. She found herself getting excited at seeing all their old friends, who would be travelling from their stately homes around the country for the ball. She was busy organising with Taylor all the bedrooms to be prepared. As the house could not accommodate all the guests due to attend, she arranged for the guest houses on the estate to be opened and prepared. She spent hours going through the menus with the cook to make sure the food would be perfect on the night.

"We need to open all the French windows," she said as she inspected the ballroom, which was situated at the back of the house behind the drawing room. Even though the ballroom had not been used in years, it had always been Anna's favourite room in the house. On the far side of the room was a row of French windows that led out to a terrace that looked out on the parkland leading up to the house. The rest of the walls in the room were covered in rich velvet wallpaper, gold-leafed mirrors and portraits. But it was the ceiling that most inspired Anna. It was intricately designed and carved by a craftsman Edward had brought from Paris and was embellished with gold. In its centre was a magnificent chandelier, with smaller chandeliers at intervals the length of the room. People said, when Edward was building the house, that a ballroom was an extravagance not shared by many other of the great houses in

Ireland. But Anna realised this room set Armstrong House apart. If the Prince and Princess of Wales ever did accept their invitation to stay, she knew the ballroom would ensure they could entertain the Royal couple in style without any embarrassment.

"So, Taylor, on the night of the ball this room will be furnished with long tables during the banquet. Afterwards, the tables will be removed by the footmen and the dancing will commence here."

She saw the look of concern and anxiety on Taylor's face. She smiled reassuringly at him.

"Do not worry, Taylor. I know you might not have entertained on this scale before. But I have every faith that you and the staff will perform the task magnificently."

"Thank you, my lady," nodded Taylor.

He had come to like Lady Anna very much in the short time she had been there. He had heard a lot about her over the years, and had been nervous about working for her. But after three years of working for Diana Hunter Armstrong, she was an absolute pleasure. It was hard to forget the arrogance, rudeness and sometimes cruelty with which Diana and Sinclair had treated the staff while they were living there. The staff had all been terrified of them. They had acted as if they were Lord and Lady Armstrong and their arrogance had been hard to bear at times. But he found Anna to be kind and patient, sometimes a little fussy, and often lost in her own thoughts.

He, like everyone else, was very much looking forward to the arrival of Lawrence. Taylor hoped Lawrence would share the same temperament and values as his parents. If he did, then working at Armstrong House would be a pleasure from now on.

CHAPTER 14

Present Day

The next morning Nico and Kate were cold with each other. It was always that way when they'd had an argument, neither of them wanting to be the first to make a move to make amends. And both had said some harsh words to each other the previous night.

"Have a good day, I'll see you later," said Nico as he left the breakfast table.

Kate was busy fixing breakfast for Cian and didn't bother to say goodbye.

"Can I feel some agitation in the air?" asked Valerie.

"He's supposed to be working from home today and minding Cian while I show a bus tour around," snapped Kate. "Selfish bastard!"

Valerie giggled. "It's not a problem Kate. I'll mind Cian."

"Well, that's why he's gone off! He knows you'll step in."

"As I keep saying – I don't mind!"

"But I do! He can't just swan off and break our routine. He minds Cian when I show the tours."

"I want to play with Aunty Valerie!" demanded Cian, pushing his breakfast bowl away from him.

"See! I win the vote!" said Valerie.

"Okay," said Kate with a sigh, not altogether pleased at Cian's enthusiasm for his aunt.

Cian grinned and went back to devouring his cereal.

"Have you had an argument?" Valerie asked.

Kate nodded.

"Not over me?" Valerie didn't look too concerned.

"No, of course not! I told Daniel he could rent Hunter's Farm – that small manor house down the road – and Nico went mad."

"He's probably just jealous. Daniel is very attractive so maybe Nico's nose was out of joint when you got on so well with him and now he's moving just down the road?"

Kate scoffed. "Nico is not the type to get jealous. I could move Brad Pitt down the road and his nose wouldn't be out of joint!"

"Well, then – what's the problem?" said Valerie.

"Oh, everything! He thinks I take control and don't consult him on things."

"I see," said Valerie pensively.

Kate suddenly felt she had to get a grip on things. She hadn't seen Valerie in years and she really didn't want to be discussing her marital problems with her.

She gave a little laugh. "Oh, don't mind me, Valerie. Nico and I are like two squabbling kids at times, nothing serious." Kate swept Cian up and hugged him tightly as he laughed.

Valerie lifted her coffee and sipped it, nodding while smiling.

Kate led the group of American tourists around Armstrong House, following her usual routine.

"And this is Lord Edward Armstrong and his wife Lady Anna," said Kate, stopping at the portrait on the wall in the hallway. "Lord Edward built this house for his bride Anna when he married her. During the Famine Anna worked tirelessly for famine relief and Lord Edward did not allow any tenants to be evicted from the Armstrong Estate as was happening around the country."

As Kate looked up at the portrait and studied Lord Edward she realised, having read through the police file on the Armstrong Estate, that this simply was not true. There had actually been evictions on the Armstrong Estate, overseen by this Sinclair Armstrong, the estate manager. Had Edward known of these evictions? Had he consented to them or just turned a blind eye? In the same way that he seemed to have turned a blind eye to this assault on a woman in 1865. Or had he another reason not to have allowed the police to press charges? Was he protecting somebody? The report from Sergeant Bourke had said that a footman called to the station but when the police had arrived a shaken Edward had dismissed them. What had been his involvement in this assault on this poor unfortunate woman in this house? As she stared at the portrait of Edward she now saw him in a completely different light. Before she had seen him as kind and benevolent, but now there seemed to be so much more.

"Kate?" said a voice, jolting her out of her thoughts.

It was the tour guide and when Kate looked around she saw thirty-three expectant American faces wondering why she had halted for so long, standing silently before this portrait.

"Oh, sorry – this portrait fascinates me!" she said with a little laugh. "If you follow me now I'll show you the ballroom which was the setting for many glamorous events . . ."

Kate was due to show Daniel Hunter's Farm that afternoon but, excited about what she had found on the police file, she quickly rang Brian before she met Daniel.

"Hi, Brian, listen – I think I might have found something of interest for the new film."

"What new film? We have no backers yet," said Brian.

"I found something on a police file from 1865. Lady Anna and Lord Edward were still at Armstrong House then, very much in charge."

"What is it?"

"The police report says there was a sexual assault on a woman at the house in August of that year," said Kate.

"Okay – and?"

"And I think there is a story here, one that will interest the backers to come in and finance the film," said Kate, trying to hide her exasperation.

"I mean – and who was attacked?" he asked.

"I don't know yet."

"And who did the attacking?"

"I don't know that yet either."

"*Kate!*" he groaned.

"Look, just trust me on this. See what I can come up with, okay?"

"Well, it had better be enough to make this film – its chances are not looking good right now," said Brian.

His word panicked her. She took a deep breath and made herself speak confidently. "I'll be back to you shortly with a story so good that you'll be fighting away the investors – they will all want a piece of it."

He gave a laugh. "Okay – let's keep in touch!"

"Talk to you soon," she said. She hated it when a director said, 'Let's keep in touch'. It usually was a polite way of saying 'fuck off!'. She looked at her watch and realised she was late for her meeting with Daniel.

Grabbing her car keys, she raced out the door.

"Oh, this is perfect, absolutely perfect!" declared Daniel as Kate showed him around Hunter's Farm that afternoon.

"Are you sure? It's a bit topsy-turvy," she said, looking around. Everything was in disarray and there were boxes everywhere. "I can get it cleaned up for you."

"Don't bother, I'll do it myself," said Daniel.

"The heating isn't working, the plumbing is dodgy and the roof needs to be replaced at this stage," she said, a little embarrassed.

"It's summer, I won't need the heating and I'm archaeologist don't forget. I once lived in a tent in Egypt for two months. A bit of dodgy plumbing will be a luxury compared to that!"

"Well, if you're sure?"

"I am, thank you. Just give me your bank-account details and I'll pay the rent directly in. It should only be for a while, so you won't be stuck with me forever."

"You sound like an ideal tenant – stay as long as you want!" she said with a laugh. She hesitated, biting her lower lip. "Daniel, I want to show you something that I found on the file you gave me last night."

"Yes?"

She handed over the report from Sergeant Bourke about the woman's assault.

"It's not in connection with your own work at the site," she said. "It's fifteen years after the Famine ended. But it could be very important to my film."

He read the report and then looked at her.

"How awful, I wonder what happened?"

"Well, that's what I'd love to find out. Who was assaulted and why weren't charges pressed. Could you put me in contact with the person at the police museum who gave you a copy of this file?"

"Of course. He's a bit hard to get, so I'll give him your number and he can phone you, if that's all right?"

"Of course. That would be great."

CHAPTER 15

Taking advantage of Valerie's seemingly endless offers of babysitting, Kate drove to the office of the *Connaught Telegraph*. She had found them remarkably helpful before in her research. As a newspaper that went back to the 1820s, it was great record of events in the county through the centuries.

"I'm looking for the copy of the newspaper of August 15th, 1865," she said.

She was shown down to the library where she found the newspaper of that week. She was wondering if there had been any report of the assault in the local newspaper.

She looked through the newspaper. It was filled with topics as diverse as religious services to the price of heifers that went to market. There were reports of evictions on some estates and then she stopped abruptly when she saw an article about the Armstrong Estate. But to her surprise it was in relation to a sporting event.

The Glorious 12th – Shooting Season Starts

The Shooting Season commenced this week on the 12th with the shooting of red grouse. Reports are that grouse-shooting around the county has been brisk and the first day of shooting promises a record season.

A hunting party at the Armstrong Estate set off in the morning, heading over to the Knockmore part of the estate. The party was led by Lord Edward Armstrong and included Lord

and Lady Fitzherbert, the Foxes of the Foxe Estate and the visiting Earl and Countess of Mountdare. The young Viscount Armstrong was also present on the shoot after recently returning to live on the estate from London. The weather was good, leading to excellent shooting conditions which, it is believed, has led to a record shoot for a single day on the estate.

Kate thought hard as she wrote down the date – the 12th of August. She quickly checked the internet on her phone to find what the Glorious 12th was and read that it was the official start of the grouse-shooting season.

"A day of marked celebration throughout the United Kingdom of Great Britain and Ireland as the law permits the shooting season to begin with grouse-hunting," Kate read from her internet search.

So this was not a normal week on the Armstrong Estate, but akin to Christmas at the time, she thought. And there would have been many guests staying at Armstrong House to go on the shoot.

She continued her search but found nothing about the alleged assault.

As Kate pulled into the forecourt of Armstrong House her mobile rang.

"Kate Collins," she answered.

"Hello, Mrs. Collins. It's Tommy Daley here from the Garda Press Office. Daniel Byrne asked me to give you a call?"

"Oh, yes, thank you for getting back to me," she said, feeling excited.

"Daniel explained that you were looking for information regarding the alleged assault at Armstrong House in 1865 as material for your film."

"Yes?" Kate held her breath.

"I looked through the database and, no, there is no further information. To be honest, the copy of the file that Daniel has is everything that relates to the incident that we have."

"Oh." Kate was deflated. "No reports were given to the head office in Dublin?"

"Nothing at all. Sorry about that," said Tommy.

"No problem, thanks for trying," said Kate.

After she hung up, she got out of the car, feeling disappointed.

Just then Nico pulled into the forecourt. He got out and, carrying his briefcase, crossed over to her.

"Well, thanks for just swanning off this morning and leaving me with Cian. You knew I had a bus tour," she said.

"I figured Valerie would help."

"That's not the point, Nico. We have a routine and you shouldn't change our arrangements just because you were sulking after our argument last night."

"I wasn't sulking," he said hotly. "But I didn't fancy tripping over you and your sister for the day either. I wouldn't have got any work done with her yapping all the time."

"Let's face it, Nico, the house is big enough. I'm sure you could have found a quiet corner if she is that much of an irritant to you. Besides, your irritation with Valerie doesn't stop you taking advantage of her looking after Cian or cooking dinner!"

"And where have you just come back from? Doesn't look like you mind taking advantage of Valerie either," he said.

"I just popped into Castlewest to the shops, that's all," she lied. "Anyway, I would like and appreciate it if you could show Valerie a little more courtesy and friendliness tonight. She won't be staying that long and I'd like her to leave with a good impression of us."

"I will be charm itself! And have you found out how long she *is* staying – exactly?"

"Oh, give me a break!" she said and stalked off indoors.

Nico did his best to be charming to Valerie over dinner. But he really did find her incessant talk about the most trivial matters extremely irritating.

He was delighted to take Cian off to bed afterwards but Valerie was still in full flow, in regard to both talking and drinking, when he got back after the whole undressing, washing and story-reading routine.

With an almost audible sigh, he joined her and Kate at the table.

"So there I was, singing 'Caught in a Bad Romance' in this club in Lower Manhattan and this man came up to me afterwards and said I had the most beautiful singing voice he had ever heard!"

"That's quite a compliment," Nico said.

"He said he was a producer from EMI records," said Valerie.

"*Said* he was?" asked Kate.

"Three dates later and I find out he's an accountant from Connecticut – *with* a wife and three children! Two boys and a girl!" Valerie took a gulp of her wine.

"Did he even work for EMI records?" asked Nico, wondering how gullible Valerie was.

"No! He worked for Proctor & Gamble! The nearest he'd ever been to the music industry was inside a record store!" said Valerie.

"What a shithead!" said Kate.

"I called him a few other choice words when I found out, I can tell you," said Valerie.

The doorbell suddenly rang.

"Who's that? Are we expecting anybody?" Nico asked Kate.

"No." Kate shrugged as she went to stand up.

"I'll get it," said Valerie. "If they're not good-looking I'll send them away!"

Valerie trotted out of the room.

"How many boyfriends has she actually had?" asked Nico.

"*Sssh!*" Kate hissed.

The door opened and in came Valerie, accompanied by Daniel.

"Look who it is!" she said.

"Oh, hello, Daniel!" said Kate.

"I just wanted to give you this," said Daniel, handing her a bottle of champagne. "Just to say thank you for rescuing me from the Castlewest Arms Hotel!"

"Oh, you shouldn't have!" said Kate, smiling.

"Sit down, sit down," said Valerie.

Daniel took a seat at the table.

"So, have you settled into Hunter's Farm all right?" asked Nico.

"Like a dream. It's such beautiful house."

"Well, it was in its day," said Nico.

"It's just perfect for me to stay in while I'm working at the excavation site. A house that was there during the Famine – it gives me a real connection with the past."

"Well, while you're here, why don't I open this and we can celebrate your moving in!" said Valerie as she wrestled the champagne bottle from Kate. Then she went and took down some champagne glasses from the top shelf of the dresser.

"Eh, those are antiques, Valerie. We usually don't drink from them," said Nico, alarmed. "There are some others in that cupboard next to the dresser."

Valerie ignored him as she picked up all four glasses in one hand and set them down unsteadily on the table. Nico's hands shot out to hold them upright.

"Honestly, Nico!" she scoffed. "We're hardly going to break them!" She popped open the bottle of champagne and began to pour the champagne.

"I wouldn't be too sure of that judging by the red-wine stain on the Persian rug," said Nico.

Kate felt uncomfortable. Much as she found Daniel's company fascinating, she felt awkward as Valerie was yet again taking over and, given the argument she had with Nico the previous night, she figured Nico was not in the mood to entertain again.

"Cheers!" said Valerie, clinking her glass against Daniel's and sitting down next to him.

The others clinked and they all drank.

"Oh, did Tommy from the police phone you, Kate?" Daniel asked.

"Eh, yes."

"Did he have any further information on the assault?"

"What assault?" asked Nico, alarmed.

She cringed. "Oh, it's nothing, Nico. It's just something in connection with my film."

"Something to do with Lady Anna?" asked Nico, looking at her in concern.

Kate turned to Nico. "I read in the police file that Daniel gave me that there was an assault in the house here in 1865, that's all."

"What kind of an assault?" asked Nico.

Daniel became animated. "It was sexual assault on a woman. The police were called but no charges were pressed."

"In 1865?" said Valerie, looking around the room and giving a shiver.

"And you're making this part of your film?" said Nico.

"It would be an interesting angle, don't you think?" said Daniel.

"Not really," said Nico. "I thought after the last film Kate made about my family, the next one was going to be all about their charity work and good deeds."

"Probably nothing will come of it. There's no information for me to follow up," said Kate.

"When did that ever stop you before?" said Nico under his breath as he took a sip of his champagne.

"Maybe it was Jack the Ripper!" said Valerie excitedly.

"Oh, don't be so silly, Valerie," said Kate. "It was two decades before those murders and the west of Ireland is a long way from the East End of London!" She was hoping the conversation would move on quickly as it was just another excuse for Nico to claim that she kept things away from him.

"Well, that may very well be," said Valerie, "but I saw this programme once that said Jack the Ripper was an aristocrat and, if he was, who's to say he mightn't have been staying here at one of those fancy parties they used to have?"

"Don't be so daft, Valerie," said Kate.

"I really don't like the direction you're taking with this film, Kate," said Nico. "I don't want this kind of thing associated with our home."

Kate fixed Nico with a steely look. "We'll talk about it later," she said and turned her attention back to Daniel. "How did the dig go today?"

"Oh, very well. In fact . . . ." Daniel turned to a bag he had brought in with him, "I actually brought those DNA tests to take samples from you all if you could spare the time. Saves you the bother of coming down to the offices at the site. It might be wise to do them now before we have any more champagne?"

"What do we have to do?" asked Kate, intrigued.

"Oh, I just take a swab of saliva from your mouth and then put it in the sample bottles and label it with your names."

"Let's do it!" said Valerie.

"Do you want to go first, Kate?" he said, opening the kit.

"I'll go first!" said Valerie, seductively opening her mouth to Daniel.

"Well, there's no point in both of us doing it, Valerie," said Kate. "We have the same DNA presumably and so Daniel will only need one sample to trace if we have any ancestors in the famine grave."

"Well, no, Kate – surprising as it seems, the way DNA is passed on is complex and siblings won't necessarily have the same results," said Daniel.

"Oh!" said Kate.

"There you are!" Valerie crowed, smirking at Kate.

"Anyway, I brought three kits for samples in case anyone felt they were being left out!" said Daniel.

"Nico, are you still interested in doing it?" Kate asked, hardly able to believe he wanted to participate.

"Yes, I am. It would be nice to be included in something around here for a change!"

"Excellent!" said Daniel.

That night as they prepared for bed, Nico asked, "And when were you thinking of telling me about this assault that allegedly took place here?"

"I only found out about it last night – I didn't get chance to tell you."

"Were you ever going to tell me? Or were you just going to make it the centrepiece of your film and I'd find out about it after it was made?"

"Of course I'd have told you."

"I wonder? I just don't like the route you're trying to take for this film, Kate. Can I remind you that these are my ancestors, my family, my home? I wish you'd treat them with respect."

"I am treating them with respect, Nico. But if something

happened here I would like to discover the facts."

"And then present them to the public like you did with the shooting of my great-grandfather! By the time you're finished Armstrong House's reputation will be destroyed!"

"Aren't you interested in what happened here? Aren't you interested that something as awful as that could have happened here? And what the circumstances were?"

"Not really, no. I'd much prefer not to know."

"Head in the sand," she said, getting into bed beside him.

"Kate," he said, taking her hand, "this house is over one hundred and seventy years old. Many, many things happened here, some we could never guess. Why not leave it all in the past?"

"Because – because I can't," she said. "I feel tied to this house like I'm tied to my body or mind. Ridiculous, I know, as it's not my ancestors who lived here. But I've always felt the bond. And I love the house so much that nothing could deter my love for it. And just when I thought I knew everything about the house, I learn something new. Isn't that some kind of fate? That I'm supposed to find out everything? That the house wants me to know everything that happened here?"

He looked at her, trying to understand her, and then just shrugged.

He let go of her hand, turned off his bedside light and settled down to sleep.

"Goodnight, Kate," he said, leaving her in darkness with her thoughts.

CHAPTER 16

1865

It was the day of the ball and Armstrong House was a flurry of activity. Taylor and the footmen were running around making sure everything was spick and span, while downstairs in the kitchen the cook and her staff were working round the clock to make sure everything would be perfect for the evening.

As Anna rushed around the house checking nothing had been missed, she was even more excited about seeing Lawrence who was due to arrive soon.

As she anxiously looked out the drawing-room window to see if the carriage that had been sent to the train station for Lawrence had arrived yet, Edward asked, "You did make sure to send an invitation to Sinclair and Diana?"

"Yes, I told you before I had," she said irritably.

"And Harry?"

"Yes – *and* Harry!"

"Good," he said. "I had said it to them anyway."

"I'm sure you had!" she said.

"They are quite excited about seeing Lawrence again."

"Really?" She sounded unconvinced. Then she saw a carriage arrive into the forecourt. "*Here he is!*"

She rushed from the drawing room and to the front door, quickly followed by Edward.

Anna raced down the steps and across to the carriage from which Lawrence was emerging.

"Lawrence!" she cried, throwing her arms around him and

hugging him tightly.

"Well, I must say this is a welcome!" said Lawrence as Edward pushed his wife out of the way and, clapping his son on the back, gave him a welcoming handshake.

"Oh, we missed you!" said Anna.

"It's only been a month!" laughed Lawrence.

"Did you enjoy your time in London with your friends?" asked Edward.

"Oh, I had a capital time!" said Lawrence.

"There's a good fellow," said Edward.

"Everyone can't wait to meet you tonight," said Anna.

"Well, I'm looking forward to meeting them too."

Lawrence moved away from his parents and walked to the end of the forecourt to look out at the view across the lake.

"Oh – I've missed this place!" he declared, taking in a deep breath of fresh air. He turned and looked up at the house. "It hasn't changed a bit."

"And it's missed you," said Edward.

"And to think I never have to leave again!"

"Except to attend the Season in London," Anna reminded him hastily.

"It's all yours – it's just waiting for you," smiled Edward, clapping his son on the back again.

"And more importantly – no more school! No more Eton!" Lawrence gave an exaggerated shiver. "Oh, I am glad to be rid of that place!"

"Best time of your life – your schooldays," mocked Edward.

"Really?" said Lawrence. "I sincerely hope that is not so as in that case I don't have much to look forward to."

Anna took his arm. "Come on in, Lawrence, you must be hungry. And we don't have much time to get ready for this evening. I have your new white-tie suit all waiting for you in your room. You'll look so handsome in it every girl will be after you!"

"Sounds good!" said Lawrence as Edward took his other arm and they led him inside.

Diana inspected Harry who was dressed in his white-tie outfit in the parlour at Hunter's Farm.

"Yes, you'll do," said Diana eventually. "In fact, you look very well."

"Thank you, Mother."

"Now, Harry, this is a wonderful opportunity for you tonight. There are going to be some of the wealthiest families in the country at the ball so it's a great opportunity for you to find yourself a wife with money, and more importantly land."

"Yes, Mother."

"Now that Anna and Edward and their brat are back, to marry well is your only chance of getting a position in life other than renting Hunter's Farm from your cousin for the rest of your life and having nothing of your own – as has been your father's lot in life."

"Yes, Mother."

"You have so much going for you – if you play your hand well you can make a canny match. Make sure to tell the girls that you are an Armstrong, grandson of a lord, and boast about your riding prowess and the awards you have won. And that you are an experienced estate manager. Even though you have no money of your own, a young woman of means could see you as an asset to manage her affairs and look after her land for her."

"Yes, Mother."

"And also, Harry, do not waste your time targeting any beautiful girls. Concentrate on the plain girls, as they will be more flattered by your attention, and more likely to be susceptible to your charms."

"Yes, Mother."

"And dance! Show off your dancing skills! I didn't spend all those hours teaching you to dance for no reason. It's to impress a potential wife!"

CHAPTER 17

At half past six that evening the carriages began to arrive in the forecourt. Edward, Anna and Lawrence stood in the hallway at the bottom of the stairs as the guests were announced by Taylor. Anna never felt so proud at seeing her old friends and introducing them to her son, now all grown up. Lawrence greeted them all with charm and good humour, and she could see they were all taken by him.

"The Earl and Countess of Mountdare, and their daughter Lady Margaret," announced Taylor.

"Lady Anna, Edward, so good to see you again and welcome back to Ireland," said the Countess as she kissed Anna and Edward on the cheek.

"You are looking well, Clementina," Edward complimented her.

"I'm wearing well, I'll give you that," said the Countess before turning her attention to Lawrence. "And Lawrence! Well, the last time I saw you, you were but a child. Whatever they fed you at Eton seemed to work – you are taller than your father!"

"They fed me a diet of the most dreadful porridge you could imagine, Countess, and a terrible concoction of apple and rhubarb crumble, not to be recommended!"

The Countess laughed lightly. "You poor boy, sounds like obscene cruelty to me! May I introduce my daughter, Margaret?"

Margaret stepped forward and curtsied slightly. "Good evening, Lord and Lady Armstrong. Thank you for the invitation."

Anna smiled at her. "You are very welcome, my dear. My, you

131

have grown too since we saw you last!"

Anna studied the girl and saw she had turned into a very pretty young woman with brown hair and green eyes. She noticed how she blushed as she shook Lawrence's hand and she saw Lawrence smiling and looking keenly at her.

Anna addressed one of the footmen. "Tom, do escort the Mountdares into the drawing room and make sure they are served champagne."

"I look forward to speaking with you later," said Lawrence to Margaret as they were led away and Margaret blushed even deeper.

"Mr. and Mrs. Sinclair Armstrong, and Mr. Harry Armstrong," announced Taylor.

"Dear Edward," said Diana, leaning forward and greeting Edward with a kiss before also kissing Anna, "and Cousin Anna."

"Good evening, Diana," said Anna.

"It feels strange being announced in a house that we have lived in for the past three years!" laughed Diana.

"Well, you deserve the same courtesy as the rest of our guests," said Anna, making the point that they were guests and were not to consider Armstrong House as their home any more.

"And this – this must be Lawrence!" exclaimed Diana. "My goodness, I genuinely would not recognise you! You've changed so much in the last three years."

"He has become a man!" laughed Edward.

"Indeed he has! Do you remember me at all, Lawrence?" asked Diana, smiling.

"Of course I do, Diana – how could I forget you?" asked Lawrence as he leaned forward and gave her a kiss on the cheek.

"I told you he was grown up, didn't I?" said Edward to Sinclair who had been hovering in the background.

Sinclair stepped forward, staring at Lawrence intently. "Indeed you did." Sinclair studied the tall well-built young man before him with his neat fair hair and light blue eyes.

"Hello again, Sinclair. I used to call you 'uncle', do you remember?" said Lawrence with a smile.

"Yes, an honorary title," said Anna.

"Well, it's good to see you again, Uncle Sinclair," smiled Lawrence as he held out his hand.

Sinclair reached out and shook it. "And you – welcome back to Armstrong House."

Lawrence looked over Sinclair's shoulder and exclaimed, "Harry!" Moving quickly to him, he clamped both of his hands on Harry's shoulders, smiling delightedly.

"Hello, Lawrence," said Harry.

"It *is* good to see you again!"

"And you."

"Well, we have so much to catch up on! I can't wait to hear all you've been up to."

"And you," said Harry again.

Anna became alarmed at seeing Lawrence so fondly greeting Harry. All her fears about Harry as a child came flooding back to her. And Lawrence seemed to have whitewashed the drowning incident from his mind!

"You're holding up the line, Lawrence!" Edward pointed out good-naturedly as he indicated the line of couples in the hallway waiting to be announced.

"The Earl and Countess of Galway!" announced Taylor much to Anna's relief.

"We shall chat later," Lawrence said to Harry.

"Come along, Harry!" said Diana and she led Sinclair and her son into the drawing room which was full of chattering people.

Diana took two glasses of champagne from a tray held by a passing footman.

She handed one to Sinclair and saw he was as white as a sheet.

"Whatever is the matter with you, Sinclair? You look like you've seen a ghost!"

Sinclair took a swig from his glass before saying, "I think I just might have."

The banquet was in full flight. Edward, Anna and Lawrence were sitting at the head table with some of the more important guests, including the Mountdares. By chance Lawrence had been seated beside Lady Margaret and Anna observed them surreptitiously. They seemed to be hitting it off.

Anna looked around the ballroom at all the happy faces and realised how good it was to be home, to see all their old friends and to have Armstrong House filled with joviality again.

As Taylor refilled her wineglass, she whispered, "You and the footmen are doing an excellent job, Taylor."

"Thank you, my lady!" said Taylor, brimming with pride.

As Anna continued to glance around the ballroom she spotted Sinclair and Diana who she had deliberately seated at the far end of the room near the door. Diana was busy chatting to the other guests at the table, but Anna became unnerved as she saw Sinclair staring up at the top table. No doubt he was resentful of not being seated with them.

"Do you like dancing?" Lawrence asked Margaret over their meal.

"I adore dancing. I never tire of it. I could dance all night every night!"

"Unfortunately, I've got two left feet!" said Lawrence.

"Oh!" said Margaret, looking disappointed. "That's a pity. Did you not go to dancing classes?"

"At Eton?" Lawrence looked at her and laughed.

Margaret blushed. "I wonder then how a young man learns to dance. We were taught at school."

"I don't know! From their sisters or mothers, I presume. I have no sisters and my mother is not a keen dancer either, I'm afraid."

"Poor you! Deprived! You'll never survive the social circuit if you can't dance properly. I shall teach you when the music starts."

"I don't want to make a spectacle of you in public," he said.

"Oh, I shouldn't mind, shouldn't mind in the least!" she said with a smile.

CHAPTER 18

After the meal was finished, the guests wandered out into the gardens or into the drawing room and parlour while the footmen removed the tables from the ballroom. Anna walked out one of the French windows onto the terrace with Mrs. Foxe. It was a beautiful summer's night and Anna looked on contentedly while the guests took in the night air.

Anna saw Lawrence walking Lady Margaret around the gardens, pointing out different things of interest to her.

"They could make a handsome couple, don't you think?" said Mrs. Foxe with a knowing smile.

"I suppose. But Lawrence is too young to even be thinking of marriage."

"Do you think so?" mused Mrs. Foxe. "I think Lawrence will be just like his father and will fall in love very quickly and have one true love all his life."

Anna smiled at her. "Perhaps. I really hadn't thought of Lawrence settling down before."

"Why ever not, dear? He is back home now and will be at Armstrong House for the rest of his life. Running the Armstrong Estate will be a huge responsibility for him. I think it would be very helpful for him to have a good woman at his side to help shoulder the responsibility from the earliest opportunity."

"I hadn't given it any thought."

"You have been such an asset to Edward after all."

"Have I?"

"He could have never managed without you, Anna. And that's what Lawrence needs as well – a good woman by his side. And Lady Margaret would be quite a catch. Lawrence could do a lot worse, and not much better!"

"Yes, she seems to be a very agreeable girl, from appearances," said Anna, giving the subject more thought.

"As well as having all the necessary requirements of being from an excellent background with excellent connections and having impeccable manners," Mrs. Foxe prompted. "There is many a suitor after her, I can tell you."

Anna was now deep in thought as she observed her son with Margaret. "And what of the family. Does she have many siblings?"

"She's one of six children – a middle child, I believe."

"Six children, that sounds promising. And her own parents – were they from large families?"

"The Earl is the eldest of seven children and the Countess one of eight!"

"That does sound like excellent breeding material!" said Anna, who knew only too cruelly the pressure on an earl's wife to produce heirs.

Lawrence walked around the gardens with Margaret, hands behind his back, passing other guests as they chatted and took in the air.

"So," said Lawrence, feeling slightly uneasy as he was not used to the company of young women, having no sisters or female friends and having been away at a boarding school. "How do you spend your time?"

"I beg your pardon?" she asked, confused.

"What do you do with your days without work or school?"

"Oh, I'm very busy all the time. I have piano lessons on Monday, singing lessons on Tuesday, Italian lessons on Wednesday, French lessons on Thursday –"

"Does that not – get a little boring?" he asked.

"Not at all. I enjoy it all and the lessons will equip me for life when I am married," said Margaret. "And, of course, the evenings and nights are never dull as my mother and father have a full social schedule which I attend with them."

Lawrence nodded, realising that Margaret was being presented as a potential wife at all these social events, and he found himself becoming jealous.

"Hence why you are a good dancer? You must have had plenty of practice," he said.

"I have indeed," said Margaret. "What about you? How will you spend your days now you are back in Ireland?"

"Well, I fully intend to learn the business of being an estate manager so I can run it as best I can in the future," he said.

"Will you not just hire an estate manager?" she asked.

"I want to be hands-on running the Armstrong Estate. I think too many of the estates in Ireland are left in the hands of hired managers instead of the owners being involved themselves."

"I see," she said, thinking of her own father's estate which had four managers, to whom he left the full running of the estate, rarely getting involved in the day-to-day details.

"There was so much damage done during the Famine and I think if our class does not act now to mend bridges and repair relations with the tenant farmers and native Irish, then there will be all sort of troubles ahead for our country."

"What kind of trouble?" she asked.

"Well, you must have heard of all the talk of revolution and Ireland breaking away from the United Kingdom?" said Lawrence.

"Not really – I pay no attention to politics," said Margaret. She had been trained never to discuss or express an interest in politics to a man, for fear it would scare him off. She had been told to always disguise her intelligence for the same reason. But as she looked at Lawrence, he seemed so natural and honest she felt she could let her guard down with him and just be herself. But she decided to keep her guard up for now, just in case.

Lawrence and Margaret were on the dance floor as the chamber orchestra filled the magnificent room with music.

Margaret quickly realised that Lawrence had not been lying when he said that he was a bad dancer.

"Try following me," said Margaret as he held her in his arms.

"*One*-two-three – *One*-two-three."

Lawrence tried to follow her instructions but was finding it hard. She noticed he was becoming embarrassed by his clumsiness and that it was drawing a little sniggering from passing couples as they whirled by.

"Would you prefer to sit this one out?" asked Margaret, offering him a way out.

He nodded. "I think it might be for the best."

She led him off the dance floor to the front of the ballroom which was filled with people standing and sitting, talking and laughing, being catered to by Taylor and the footmen who were constantly refilling their glasses.

"I do apologise," said Lawrence and Margaret's heart went out to him as she saw he was genuinely embarrassed.

"There's nothing to apologise for, Lawrence," she said. "Why don't you ask your mother to organise some dancing lessons for you? It would be a shame not to be able to dance properly when you have such a wonderful ballroom here at your house."

"I might do that," said Lawrence.

"Besides, you'll need to dance when you start courting. How else will you let a young woman know you are interested in her?"

He looked at her quizzically.

Suddenly, Lawrence felt a hand grab his shoulder and he turned around to see it was Harry.

"Harry!" he said, smiling broadly.

"Well, well, little cousin! Who might this be?" asked Harry, focusing his attention on Margaret.

"Eh, Harry, may I introduce Lady Margaret Mountdare. Lady Margaret, this is my cousin, well, he's actually my second cousin, Harry Armstrong," said Lawrence.

"I am pleased to meet you," said Margaret, giving a small curtsy.

"And I am *very* pleased to meet you," said Harry. "You are some swine, Lawrence. You are only back in the country for two minutes and you are hogging the prettiest girl all evening."

"Oh, eh, I'm not –" stuttered Lawrence.

"Relax, I'm only teasing you," said Harry, taking two glasses of champagne from a passing footman and handing them to Lawrence and Margaret before taking one for himself.

"Harry and I were like brothers growing up," said Lawrence. "We were always in each other's company."

"Indeed. I couldn't go anywhere without turning around and finding Lawrence there," said Harry as he slightly nudged Lawrence out of the way and moved closer to Margaret. "So, Lady Margaret, tell me all about yourself. I'm intrigued to know."

Anna was watching the trio. She had observed that her son hadn't been out of Margaret's company all evening. As she chatted with people, she did some subtle research on Margaret and found everyone sang the girl's praises. She became concerned as she saw Harry join them and begin to dominate the conversation with Margaret. She had hoped that Harry would have gone to university or joined the military, but from what she had found out he was very much following in his father's footsteps, with a career on the estate. She marvelled again that Lawrence seemed to have forgotten that Harry had tried to drown him. Perhaps he had forgiven rather than forgotten? Lawrence was so good-natured and big-hearted. He might have written it off as just a boyish misadventure that should be left in the past.

"Anna, would you honour me with a dance?" came a voice and when she turned she was surprised to see the speaker was Sinclair.

"Oh – why – yes, of course, Sinclair," said Anna, trying to disguise her horror at the thought of dancing with him.

He led her out to the centre of the ballroom and they began to waltz.

They danced in silence and she smiled awkwardly at him.

"I never knew you were such a good dancer, Sinclair," she said eventually.

"Am I? I seldom dance. Diana doesn't enjoy it – she's is at her happiest on a horse, not a dance floor."

"Well, no woman can compete with her at that," said Anna truthfully.

"I haven't seen any of your own family here tonight – the Strattons?"

"Unfortunately, none of them could make it. My brother is going into politics and so is very busy on the election campaign, contesting for the parliamentary seat that once was held by my father."

Sinclair nodded. "And your sisters?"

"They are all abroad on vacation at present."

"Bad timing, in that case," smiled Sinclair.

"Unfortunately so, in this case."

"And what of your cousins? None of them could make it either?"

"I'm afraid not," said Anna. "I'm not really in that much contact with my cousins any more."

"Really? Why?"

Anna shrugged. "No reason – life just takes people in different directions."

"But you used to have a cousin who used to come to Armstrong House and stay regularly when you first married Edward."

Anna shrugged. "Indeed many of my cousins stayed with us at that time."

"Not really. Just one. I can't remember her name, but she was here a lot of the time."

Anna looked perplexed. "Which one are you referring to?"

"Oh, come, come, Anna. You know who I'm talking about. The two of you were like sisters, you were as thick as thieves . . . *Georgina* – that was her name!"

"Oh, yes, Georgina!"

"Whatever became of Georgina?"

"I haven't been in contact with her for many a year. I believe she is alive and well."

"Where is she living now?"

"On my cousin's estate, I believe."

"What is the name of that estate again?"

Anna felt herself go red. "I don't know which one, Sinclair – my cousin has many estates. I never realised you carried a candle for her!"

Sinclair's black eyes clouded over. "I don't."

Anna was relieved that the music came to a halt.

"Thank you for the dance, Sinclair." She curtsied and quickly walked away from him before the orchestra started up again. She grabbed a glass of wine from a passing footman and took a gulp. Sinclair had unnerved her. What was he doing bringing up the subject of Georgina after all these years?

Taylor and his footmen were so run off their feet catering to the guests that he asked permission from Anna for a couple of the maids to come upstairs to assist collecting empty glasses from the guests. To her delight Gertie was told with another maid to go and work upstairs. She hadn't seen Harry since he had returned to Hunter's Farm with his parents, and she was desperate to see him.

"Do not speak to the guests," a flustered Taylor ordered Gertie and the other girl. "Just walk around with a tray and pick up the empty glasses and bring them straight down to the kitchen and then go back up again."

As Gertie crept into the ballroom she could hardly believe the sight before her eyes. She had never served at a ball before and could never have imagined such glamour existed. She was wide-eyed as she saw the women dressed in such glittering gowns and jewels and the men in white tie. She quietly went around the ballroom, collecting empty glasses that had been left down, or people placed their glasses on the tray as she walked by.

She anxiously searched through the crowd looking for Harry – she knew he had to be there. She got a thrill when she saw him but she was taken aback as he looked so distinguished in his white tie. She saw he was talking to a young man and a beautiful young woman.

"Who's that Master Harry's talking to?" she asked a footman.

"That's the young Viscount Lawrence, Lord Armstrong's son, our new and future Lord and Master," said the footman.

"And who's the woman?" asked Gertie.

"I think she's the Earl of Mountdare's daughter," said the footman as he marched off, holding aloft another tray of glasses of champagne to be served.

As Gertie circled the room, she couldn't take her eyes off Harry, hoping he would see her and smile over at her.

Then Harry took his eyes off Margaret for a moment and glanced around the room.

She smiled over at him warmly, but to her surprise he looked straight through her as if she wasn't there and turned his attention back to Margaret.

Confused, she ventured nearer to him, but he still paid no heed to her. Seeing that his glass and those of the other two were nearly empty, she took her opportunity to approach them.

She walked up to them.

"May I take your glasses, please?" she said though she had been told not to talk to the guests.

"Oh, yes, thank you," said Margaret, placing her glass on the tray.

Harry turned around and looked at Gertie as if he didn't know her.

He went to place his glass on her tray but purposefully missed it and it fell to the ground and smashed.

"You stupid girl!" barked Harry. "Look what you've done!"

Gertie was badly shocked. She had only been used to him speaking sweet nothings to her before. She blinked back tears.

"It's not the girl's fault," Margaret protested.

"Of course it's her fault! What is she doing upstairs anyway? This is a footman's job – clean up that mess at once!"

Gertie bent down quickly and put the broken pieces of glass onto the tray.

"What is the problem?" asked Taylor, arriving over to see what the fuss was.

"Keep her downstairs in future, will you, man?" said Harry to Taylor.

As Gertie stood up she looked in danger of bursting out crying any moment.

"Take that tray downstairs and there's no need for you to come back up," Taylor said to her and she hurried off out of the ballroom.

"Apologies, sir," said Taylor as he went off about his business.

"You just can't get good staff any more," complained Harry.

"It was only a broken glass!" said Lawrence.

"In any case, what were we speaking about?" said Margaret, who had been trained to always ignore any unpleasantness with servants in public.

"We were speaking about what an atrocious dancer dear Lawrence is. But, I am delighted to tell you, I am an excellent dancer. May I?" Harry held out his arm to her.

"Oh, eh, yes," said Margaret, taking his arm, and smiling at Lawrence as she was led out to the dance floor.

Lawrence grew deflated as Harry then monopolised Margaret, dancing on and on with her. As he chatted away to other guests, he kept one eye on Margaret.

"You really are a wonderful dancer," said Margaret to Harry. "But this really must be our last dance."

"But why?" he asked as he twirled her around.

"Because it's not fair on Lawrence, leaving him alone all this time," said Margaret.

"Oh, Lawrence is fine, don't worry about him. You know, you have the most beautiful green eyes I have ever seen."

She smiled awkwardly at him. "Thank you. Has Lawrence been courting anybody, do you know?"

"Lawrence? Courting? Ha!" scoffed Harry. "Lawrence is just a boy – he knows as much about courting as he does about dancing!"

"I imagine there will be many a girl interested in him," said Margaret.

"Well, he's not the brightest button in the box, you know. Thick as a plank, really. And he's very clumsy. I can't really see him making a success of his life here. It's my father who has run this estates for decades, not Lord Edward. The place would have fallen apart without him. And it will be myself who will be taking over the running of it in the future. The success of the Armstrong Estate is down to my father and me. I should like my own estate one day, to run it with the excellent skills I have developed."

"Really?" said Margaret, unimpressed by his boasting and how he was speaking about his relatives.

The music came to a halt and, before it started again, Margaret said, "Thank you for the dances, Harry."

As she went to move off, Harry grabbed her arm roughly. Startled, she looked down at his hand and up to his face for an explanation.

"I'm so sorry!" he said smiling, as he let go of her arm. "I was just going to ask you to stay for another dance."

She shook her head firmly. "No thank you. That's quite enough dancing for one night."

He watched as she walked off in the direction of Lawrence.

As Margaret passed through the crowd her she was suddenly confronted by her mother.

"Who is that man you are continually dancing with?" asked the Countess.

"He's a cousin of the Armstrongs," said Margaret.

"Well, stop wasting your time with the spare and start concentrating on the heir!" said the Countess as she pushed Margaret in the direction of Lawrence.

Anna made sure to steadfastly avoid Sinclair for the rest of the night. He always unnerved her but he was particularly unnerving that night. He usually showed no interest in her, and so she found it alarming that he had showed an interest in her now. Why was he enquiring after her family? She knew it wasn't out of polite conversation. She felt relieved as she saw Sinclair, Diana and Harry leave at one in the morning. The ball was still showing no sign of stopping, so she was determined to enjoy the rest of the night.

CHAPTER 19

Sinclair opened the front door of Hunter's Farm and walked in, followed by Diana. They made their way silently to the drawing room where Sinclair poured himself a large whiskey.

"Well, they certainly put on a good show," said Diana.

"*Hmmm*," said Sinclair.

"Lawrence seemed taken with that young twit of a girl. That's the last thing we need – him marrying and producing more heirs to distance us from the title," said Diana.

"*Hmmm*."

"You were less than cordial all night. Whatever was the matter with you? You should have at least pretended to be civil. They are back – we can at least disguise the fact we don't want them back."

Sinclair knocked back his drink and slammed the glass on the table before turning to Diana, his face a mixture of excitement and anger. "He's not Edward's son!"

"I beg your pardon?"

"Lawrence – he is not Edward's son." Sinclair spoke the words quietly and menacingly.

Diana laughed. "What in the world are you talking about?"

"Did you not see it? Did you not recognise him?"

"See what?" Diana was exasperated. "Recognise who?"

"When Anna married Edward and came to live at Armstrong House, she had a servant – do you remember him?"

"Which one! You are talking over twenty years ago and Anna has had many servants – how am I to know which one you're talking about, for God's sake?"

"Oh, I remember him – I remember him well," said Sinclair as he began to pace up and down. "I remember him because there was all that business about a locket."

"A locket?"

"Yes, a valuable locket of Anna's went missing, and she accused this servant of stealing it. I carried out a search of his cottage myself and found the locket hidden there. That's why I remember him so well. I arrested him and he was to stand trial and to be transported to Van Diemen's land for his crime."

Diana's face creased at the memory. "I remember something of the matter, now you mention it."

"We had the man locked in a stable for the night to be brought to the jail the next day, but then," Sinclair became more animated, "then *Anna* pleaded his case to Edward! I remember it well! When Anna realised that he was to stand trial and be deported, if not hanged, she pleaded his case! She pleaded with Edward that being evicted from his cottage, fired from his job and thrown off the estate was punishment enough. And Edward, the soft fool, went along with her and that's what happened. He was removed from the estate and that was the last we ever saw of hm."

"And what has all this to do with this wild accusation you are making about Lawrence?"

"We never saw him again – until tonight! Lawrence is the spitting image of the servant – *Seán*!" Sinclair's face lit up as he remembered the name. "The servant's name was Seán!"

Diana sat down as she stared at her husband. "You can't be suggesting . . . that Anna and this servant . . ."

"I am telling you that Lawrence is the spitting image of Seán. Lawrence is Seán's son, I tell you! He has to be."

"But – but why didn't you recognise the resemblance before?"

"Because it's three years since we have seen Seán. He's changed considerably and grown into manhood. He's approaching the same age that Seán was when he worked at Armstrong House."

"But surely Edward would see the resemblance between Lawrence and this servant?"

"I've always thought that Edward was quite thick! He could never see what was under his nose. And, besides, it's different for him. Edward has seen Lawrence all the time as he grew up – people often don't notice changes as they happen before them. It's like seeing someone for the first time in ten years and being shocked at how they have aged, but people living with them don't notice, because they see them all the time."

"But what you are suggesting is preposterous!" said Diana. "Anna! This is Anna we're talking about! She wouldn't even leave the piano legs undressed, let alone sleep with any man but her husband! Let alone a servant! Why would she ever do such a thing? She's never had a nuance of scandal even whispered about her in all these years. She's too respectable to do such a thing."

Sinclair's mind was whirling as he stopped pacing and stared at Diana. "She did it to beget an heir."

Diana's mouth fell open.

"Do you see?" he asked.

"Yes," she said faintly. "The barren years."

Sinclair nodded. "Exactly. She was desperate to produce an heir. We had written off her prospects of ever having a child and we and Harry were the heirs. And then she suddenly became pregnant. Well, it all makes absolute sense to me. Edward is infertile. She slept with Seán for the purpose of fathering a child and passing it off as Edward's, and so secure her position in life."

"And all that business with the locket, then, was it a false accusation? To discredit Seán and prevent him from revealing the truth and destroying her?" Diana was now becoming excited as the story was pieced together.

"Of course! It makes sense. She needed the man away from estate and so accused him of stealing a locket."

"But how did the locket then appear in his cottage?"

"Perhaps she gave it to him, or planted it there when she was on one of her love trysts," said Sinclair.

"I can scarcely believe it of her. It's just beyond belief."

"Do you think I could get this wrong?" he asked.

She studied her husband. She knew how cunning and clever he

was. If he said that Lawrence was the spitting image of the servant and they had to be related, then she knew he would not get that wrong.

"But do you understand what this means for us, for everybody? Lawrence is an imposter, a cuckoo, the son of a peasant. He is not an Armstrong, Edward has had no issue. With Edward childless, the correct lineage for the Armstrongs is through me to Harry."

"But how could we ever prove such a thing?" Diana asked.

"I don't know, but I will not rest until I do and have that cuckoo and his harlot of a mother thrown out of Armstrong House," vowed Sinclair.

"But that is an impossible task!"

"Nothing is impossible, Diana. Somebody other than Anna knows the truth. And I suspect her cousin Georgina does."

"Georgina? Why do you think that?"

"Cast your mind back to those early years, Diana. Anna had her cousin staying all the time. They were inseparable. I found the girl irritating and nosy, always poking her nose in where it wasn't wanted or needed. Anna relied a lot on her for strength in those days, before Lawrence was born. And then she disappeared and never came back to Armstrong House. She knows something, and Anna got rid of her, in the same way as she got rid of Seán."

"But you are suggesting Anna is a completely different person from the one everyone thinks she is. You are suggesting she is a ruthless bitch, using and casting aside people as she sees fit!" Diana was trying to marry this view of Anna with the one she had always had of her before.

"Well, that is obviously the real Anna. Let's face it – if she could sleep with a servant and pass the offspring off as Edward's all these years, then she is capable of anything." And Sinclair quickly poured himself another whiskey and knocked it back.

CHAPTER 20

Harry had hardly slept that night as he thought of Margaret Mountdare. He could tell she was impressed by him. If Lawrence hadn't kept getting in the way, he would have had her full attention for the night.

He presumed that the Mountdares with the other guests would leave that morning so he made sure to ride up to Armstrong House first thing.

He knocked on the front door and an exhausted Taylor answered it.

"Good morning, Master Harry," said Taylor as Harry strode into the hallway.

"Where's everybody?" asked Harry.

"Some guests are in the dining room, others still not awake, sir. It was a very late night."

"Where is Lady Margaret Mountdare? Is she up yet?"

"Yes, she is having breakfast in the dining room."

"Tell her I would like to see her – I'll be in the parlour," said Harry.

Taylor walked into the dining room which was full of guests having breakfast. He spotted Margaret who was seated between Lawrence and her mother. Her father was in his room, still intoxicated from the previous night.

Taylor went over to Margaret and bent to her ear.

"You have a visitor who wishes to see you in the parlour, Lady Margaret," whispered Taylor.

"Who wishes to see her?" demanded her mother whose keen ear had overheard.

"Em, Master Harry Armstrong," answered Taylor.

"Whatever does he want?" asked the Countess.

"Well, there is only one way of finding out," said Margaret.

She excused herself and got up from the table.

Lawrence had overheard as well and became crestfallen as he imagined the purpose of Harry's visit.

As Margaret walked away the Countess smiled brightly at Lawrence. "So, pray continue telling me about these wonderful plans you have for the Armstrong Estate."

Margaret opened the door to the parlour and walked in. Harry was at a window looking out, his hands clasped behind his back.

"Good morning, Harry," she said, closing the door behind her.

He swung around with a big grin on his face. "Good morning, Margaret!" He walked over to her rapidly. "How are you this morning?"

"Very well, thank you. You wished to speak to me?"

"Yes, I believe you are leaving for home today?" he asked.

"Indeed, yes," she said.

"I wanted to meet you first to ask if it would be permissible for me to write to you?"

Margaret was taken aback and felt awkward as she searched for the right words.

"Well?" he asked eventually.

"I – I am much flattered, Harry. But – I think I must decline your offer," she said.

Harry's mouth dropped open. "I see! May I ask why we cannot write to each other?"

"Well, it's just – it's just I don't think we have enough in common to warrant us sending letters to each other!"

Harry's face became so angry that she felt herself becoming frightened.

"I see!" Harry spat. "And what do we not have in common?"

She didn't want to incense him any further so searched for the right words. "I'm not that interested in your pursuits – horse-riding, hunting and so on."

"Perhaps if I had a title and a several-thousand-acre estate, you might deem we had something in common then!" he snarled, leaning angrily towards her.

Margaret smiled politely at him and turned to leave. "I had better return to the dining room, or my mother will be worried about where I have got to."

As she turned, Harry grabbed her arm roughly, stopping her progress.

Margaret looked back at him, alarmed and frightened.

Harry's angry expression suddenly evaporated and he smiled pleasantly at her as he released her arm. "Of course! I hope you have a pleasant journey home."

"Thank you," said Margaret and she hurried from the room.

Early that afternoon the Mountdares were leaving and Anna, Edward and Lawrence were in the forecourt to see them off.

"I've had the most pleasant time, thank you for all your hospitality," said the Countess.

"The pleasure was all ours, Clementina," said Edward as he reached forward and kissed her cheek before he turned his attention to the Earl who looked extremely fragile from a hangover. "And I hope to see you soon again, Grover."

"Indeed," muttered the Earl as he walked shakily to the carriage and climbed in.

Anna beckoned to Edward to follow her and with a final wave to their guests they went back inside, leaving the two young people to say their farewells.

"Well, it's been wonderful meeting you," said Lawrence.

"And I've very much enjoyed meeting you," said Margaret.

"I hope to organise those dance lessons so we can dance properly next time we meet," said Lawrence.

"I look forward to it," said Margaret, still not turning to join her parents who were peering out of the carriage, waiting for her.

Margaret stood waiting for Lawrence to say something else but he just looked awkward and uncomfortable.

"Margaret! We shall miss the train if you do not hurry!" called the Countess.

As Margaret still stood waiting for Lawrence to say something, her nerve and patience snapped.

"Lawrence!" she said.

"Yes?"

"The custom is that if you would like to keep in contact with me, then you ask for permission to write to me!"

"Oh, yes, of course."

Margaret became exasperated. "Well, do you want to write to me or not?"

"Yes, of course I do!" said Lawrence.

Margaret was relieved. "Good, because I would very much like to write to you as well and see you soon."

Lawrence beamed. "Nothing would please me more!"

"*Margaret! If we miss that train I'll kill you!*" the Countess shrieked from the carriage.

Margaret gave Lawrence a final smile and then hurried to the carriage and got in.

"For goodness sake, what kept you?" said the Countess. "Did he agree to make contact with you or not?"

"Yes, he's going to write to me," said Margaret with satisfaction as she looked at her father who had fallen asleep already.

"He looked as if he needed a little persuasion!" said the Countess.

"He's just a bit shy – I had to ask *him* – but he was very pleased," said Margaret.

"Thank goodness for that! I think I shall extend an invitation for Lawrence to visit us at Kilternan House," mused the Countess.

"Oh, that would be wonderful!"

"I'll organise a social event and have Lawrence invited, I think. It might be wise not to invite his parents as well. Lady Anna can be a little suspicious and obstinate at times. Best we don't have her along, in case she tries to interfere."

"Good idea."

"Whatever did that Harry Armstrong want this morning?"

"He asked permission to write to me," said Margaret, becoming uncomfortable at the memory.

"I hope you told him no in no uncertain terms?"

"I did decline his offer, yes," said Margaret.

"The cheek of him! Who does he think he is? He might be in some way related to Lord Armstrong, but it doesn't give him the right to set his sights on the Earl of Mountdare's daughter!"

"He is somewhat pushy and pig-headed – to say nothing of big-headed – qualities that would put me off him, regardless of who he is."

"You've only yourself to blame, Margaret! What were you thinking of dancing with him so much and giving him so much time last night?"

"It was hard to get away from him, and besides I didn't want to be rude."

"Margaret! When you are in the market for a husband there is no time to be either polite or rude! You do your window-shopping quickly, and if there's nothing there that meets your requirements then you move on quickly to the next shop! You don't linger in a shop where they have nothing you want to buy! The same rules apply when shopping for a husband as apply when shopping for a hat!"

"Yes, Mama," said Margaret as she sat back in her seat, thrilled that she was entering into correspondence with Lawrence.

In the courtyard at Hunter's Farm Harry was aggressively shoeing a horse as Diana looked on.

"Gently, Harry! You're frightening the horse!"

In frustration Harry stood up and threw the hammer across the yard.

"Whatever is the matter with you?" demanded Diana.

"Nothing!"

Diana observed her son. "I take it you got nowhere with that Lady Margaret you were all over last night?"

Harry said nothing but looked down at the ground in anger.

"You were wasting your time with her, Harry! I told you to aim for the plainest girls not the prettiest! Her family are too wealthy and she's too pretty – you didn't stand a chance! I told you to aim high, but not that high! You don't have anything to offer materially, so you need to get a girl who is weak and insecure and delighted to get a man!"

"Why should I have to settle for second best, while Lawrence gets first choice?" demanded Harry angrily.

"Because he's Edward's heir, not you," said Diana as she walked off.

CHAPTER 21

It was a few days after the ball and all the guests had returned to their homes. It was a sunny afternoon and Edward and Lawrence were riding through the estate.

"Your mother was very happy with the success of the ball," said Edward, smiling at Lawrence.

"She certainly was. She put a lot of work into the night."

"Between you and me, I was quite worried about her settling back here. But she seems to be fitting in just fine."

"Oh yes, she has certainly made no complaints to me yet. You know, I used to worry about her when I was growing up. She seemed so sad sometimes. It would last for days, and then she would be all right again."

As their horses trotted along Edward glanced at his son. He had always tried to protect him from things when he was growing up and it was hard for him to realise he was now an adult and didn't need such protection any more. That he could have adult conversations with him.

"Well, you were too young to remember the Famine, but it had a terrible impact on everybody. Your mother was not like the other ladies, or indeed the men of our class who shut themselves away from the horrors of the Famine and hid behind their high walls in their stately manors. No, your mother worked tirelessly in the workhouses and saw some terrible things. Things she will never be able to forget. That was what caused those sad periods she suffered from that you remember."

"She never talks about those times, and what she saw," said Lawrence.

"It's too painful for her. But we should be very proud of the work she did during those years. I know I am very proud of her."

"Oh, so am I! I just wish I knew more about her back then."

"She was amazing," said Edward.

They trotted on in silence for a while. Then, as they slowed to a walk, Edward spoke again.

"All this will be yours one day, Lawrence. And I want you to really enjoy it, to know the people and love the land, as I do."

Lawrence smiled over at his father. "I already do, Papa."

They passed a neat little thatched cottage which belonged to one of the tenant farmers.

"Good afternoon, your lordship!" said a woman and Edward pulled his horse to a halt.

"Good day to you, Mrs. Kelly, and how are you keeping? Well, I hope?"

"I am indeed, your lordship. And, sure, all the better for seeing you. You're as welcome as a pot of gold at the end of a rainbow!"

Edward smiled over at Lawrence. "You remember my son, Mrs. Kelly?"

"Sure, don't I remember him well as a child? And he's grown into a handsome man! It is wonderful to have ye back at the manor. We have missed ye all dearly."

As his father chatted away to Mrs. Kelly, Lawrence saw the rest of the Kelly family making hay in the fields around their farm.

"I have just made soda bread and some lovely blackberry jam. Will ye come in for some tea and bread?" asked Mrs. Kelly hopefully.

Lawrence looked at his father for approval. "May we?"

"Of course, very kind of you to ask, Mrs. Kelly," said Edward.

As Lawrence turned his horse into the farmyard, Edward spotted Sinclair at a neighbour's farm down the road.

"You go in and I'll join you in a few minutes," said Edward to Lawrence.

Lawrence nodded at his father, dismounted and went into the cottage after Mrs. Kelly.

Edward trotted quickly down the road where he saw Sinclair was in a confrontation with another tenant farmer.

Sinclair was shouting at the farmer who seemed to be pleading with him.

"What appears to be the problem?" asked Edward on reaching them.

"Nothing!" said Sinclair, throwing a look at the farmer who quickly turned and went back into his cottage.

"I wish you wouldn't speak to them like that, Sinclair," said Edward.

Sinclair raised his eyes to heaven. He and Edward had had countless arguments over the years with the different management styles they had. Sinclair had blissfully not missed those arguments while Edward was away and wasn't about to start on another round of them now.

"I am the estate manager, Edward, and I manage the estate as I see fit – that is our agreement," he said.

"I know that, Sinclair, but a little humanity wouldn't go amiss," urged Edward.

"Humanity doesn't pay your bills, rent does. I've told you over the years peasants only understand one thing – brute force! Why, if it was left to you, you would be going around having tea and scones with them all day, while they robbed you blind and poached from you!"

"Well, Lawrence and I are about to have tea at the Kellys', as you mention it. Would you care to join us? Mrs. Kelly has made fresh soda bread."

Sinclair rolled his eyes as he mounted his horse. "No, I would not care to join you! I need to get over to another of your tenants who is also in arrears. Really, Edward, I don't know how you can drink tea with peasants – they won't respect you for it and will only take advantage."

"I like to think if you treat people fair, they will be fair to you," said Edward.

"You can enjoy that philosophy, because I make sure the rents are paid and the estate is running efficiently. You can be all kind and benevolent as I take the brunt of their hatred."

"I have never doubted your efficiency as an estate manager, Sinclair. I am merely suggesting that there might be a middle ground to manage the farmers."

They rode together back up the road.

"Did you enjoy the ball?" asked Edward, anxious to change the subject.

"Very much so – it was a very interesting night," said Sinclair. "It's a pity none of Anna's family could make it down."

"Yes, her brother is running for parliament so they are all very busy."

"So she said . . . Is Anna's cousin helping with the election?"

"Which cousin?"

"Georgina? That was her name, wasn't it? The girl who used to visit here all the time?"

"I doubt it. Georgina is a cousin on Anna's mother side, there was no history of politics on that side of the family."

"Did she visit you much in London? Georgina?"

"No, we haven't seen Georgina in years. To be honest, that is the way I'd like it to remain."

"Why is that?"

"Well, Georgina became a very bitter and cynical person after her fiancé jilted her. I found her a negative presence around the place, so was glad when she stopped visiting."

"But Anna and she were good friends – have they not been in contact all these years?"

"No. I think Anna could no longer cope with Georgina's negativity either," said Edward.

"She never married?"

"Gosh, no, not after she had been jilted. She was seen as second-hand goods after that, and what man would marry her when she had already been abandoned by another?"

"And whatever became of her?"

"I believe she still lives on her brother's estate which he inherited from their father."

"Is the estate near Dublin?"

"Tullydere is in Westmeath," said Edward as he reached the

Kellys' gate and turned his horse in. "Are you sure you won't join us?"

"Quite sure," answered Sinclair as he turned and galloped off, whispering the word out loud. "*Tullydere*."

"Tullydere," announced Sinclair to Diana that evening. "That is the name of Anna's mother's ancestral home, and where Georgina is still apparently living, according to Edward."

"And what do you intend to do with this information?"

"I am going to pay her a visit."

"Visit Georgina? What do you hope to achieve by that?"

"I hope and intend for her to admit the truth to me. To admit that Anna had an affair with her servant and got pregnant."

"But she will never admit such a thing to you! Were you ever even friendly with Georgina?"

"Not in the least! As I remember we had a healthy dislike for each other," said Sinclair.

"Then why would she talk to you or confide in you?"

"Because I suspect she has been treated very badly by Anna over the years. There has been no contact between them. I suspect she is bitter with life, and very bitter with Anna, and maybe just waiting for an opportunity to get back at her."

"By destroying her reputation?"

"All I need is a witness to confirm what I know and then Anna and her bastard of a child will be destroyed forever."

CHAPTER 22

It was morning and Gertie was carrying a bucket of ashes out the back door from the kitchen and through the courtyard where they were left in a basin before they were taken away by a stable boy later on in the day. She tipped the ashes in and turned to go back to the house.

"*Gertie!*" hissed a voice and she turned around to see Harry standing at the gable end of one of the stables. She looked at him for a moment and then continued to walk back to the house. When she had got to her room the night of the ball she had cried her heart out after Harry's treatment of her.

"*Gertie!*" Harry hissed again.

She wanted to walk on and ignore him but she was unable to. She stopped and looked back at him. He was beckoning her over to him. She shook her head and went to walk on.

"*Gertie – please!*" cried Harry with a sad pitiful look on his face.

She looked at the house and there was no sign of Taylor or any of the other servants. She put down the bucket and walked quickly over to the gable of the stable.

"What do you want?" she asked coldly.

"I wanted to explain about the night of the ball," he said.

"There's nothing to explain. You're an Armstrong and you owe me no explanation," said Gertie and she turned to walk away, but he grabbed her arm and pulled her back.

"*Let me go!*" she insisted.

"I *had* to act the way I did to you at the ball," said Harry.

160

"What do you mean?"

"With Taylor and Lawrence and everyone there, if I showed you any attention they would have got suspicious. And you know what that would mean. If it were ever found out about us, you'd lose your position here."

"You didn't have to be so – cruel!" said Gertie, her eyes filling with tears. "You made me feel worthless."

"Oh, my darling, that's the last thing I ever want you to feel," he said, embracing her.

"Let me go," she said, fighting him away but he restrained her arms and kissed her.

She suddenly burst out crying.

"Oh, I'm so sorry I had to behave like that!" he said. "But I had to – can you see why now?"

"You really hurt me," she sobbed against his chest.

"Now, now, stop those tears," he said, lifting her face up and wiping away her tears.

"You know I love you, Gertie," he said. "I have to see you soon. Tonight!"

"But it's impossible with you not living in the house any more."

"You can take the key hung up at the back door and creep out and I'll meet you in the stable here at two in the morning."

"No, Harry! If Mr. Taylor caught me, I'd be finished for good!"

"He won't catch you. Just be careful. You'll be back in your bed before anyone notices."

"But –" she began but he silenced her by kissing her. "Don't you want to be with me? Don't you love me any more?" He managed to look hurt and upset.

"Of course I do! I just . . . all right . . . I'll be here at two o'clock."

"Good girl!" He kissed her again. "You'd better get back to work before they miss you."

Gertie nodded and hurried back to the house.

CHAPTER 23

Anna was sitting in the dining room with Edward and Lawrence, having breakfast, as Taylor stood by.

"Has the post arrived yet, Taylor?" asked Lawrence.

"Not yet, Master Lawrence."

"Do let me know when it arrives, there's a good chap," said Lawrence.

"Yes, sir."

"Expecting a letter from anyone important?" asked Edward knowingly.

"Not particularly," answered Lawrence.

"For goodness' sake," said Anna, "you only received a letter from Margaret yesterday. Surely another one wouldn't arrive so soon!"

"Perhaps not," said Lawrence. "Em, I understand her mother will be writing to you shortly."

"Oh?" asked Anna.

"Yes, to invite me to stay at their estate. They are having a ball seemingly."

"You? Are your father and I not to be invited to this ball?" asked Anna.

"I'm not sure, I don't think so . . . The Mountdares aren't just inviting me for the night of the ball but for a few days."

"Aren't you the special guest!" said Anna.

"Well, I think it will be very good for me to see how the Mountdares run their estate and see if I can pick up any methods

162

for here," said Lawrence. "Don't you think that a good idea, Papa?"

Edward tried not to laugh. "An excellent idea, Lawrence. I'm sure you will be most busy there viewing their latest agricultural machinery and prize heifers!"

"I still think it a little rude for Clementina not to invite us," said Anna, not pleased that she would not be there to oversee what was going on between Lawrence and Margaret. Knowing Clementina Mountdare, Anna suspected she was purposefully keeping her out of the way so she could manoeuvre the young couple closer together.

"I'm sure there is no intention of rudeness on Clementina's part," said Edward. "And Lawrence will enjoy himself immensely. From what I remember, Kilternan House is a beautiful place to stay."

"If you say so!" said Anna, not at all happy.

"Anyway, I must attend to my papers," said Edward, getting up from the table and kissing Anna before leaving.

Anna watched him leave and then turned to Lawrence.

"I know Margaret is very charming and attractive, Lawrence, but just bear in mind you have plenty of time to settle down. It's different for a man than for a woman. Margaret needs to make a match as quickly as possible and to make the best possible engagement while she is in her prime. *You*, on the other hand, have all the time in the world."

Lawrence became irritated. "I don't think Margaret has even thought along those lines yet, Mama."

"I think you'll find she probably has, and Clementina most certainly has," warned Anna. "Although I would certainly have liked more children, I suppose I have been spared the stress of trying to marry a daughter off to the most eligible bachelor. It's become such a ruthless affair these days." She sighed. "What are your plans for today, Lawrence?"

"I'm going out riding with Harry," said Lawrence.

Anna looked at him, alarmed. "Just the two of you?"

"Yes, he's going to show me over the Toormore part of the estate which I'm not that familiar with, and introduce me to some of the tenants there."

A. O'CONNOR

"Well, why don't you wait until your father is free and he can take you there instead?"

"No, I want to go with Harry. I've hardly had the opportunity to spend any time with him since I arrived back."

"Lawrence, there are certain friendships that need to be left in boyhood, and that with Harry is one of those. Harry is only a second cousin to you and really not of our class – the link is quite tenuous at this stage. His family are landless and his father a mere employee on the estate."

"I shouldn't let Papa hear you speak of Sinclair like that," warned Lawrence.

"It's just not a suitable friendship for you any more, Lawrence," she insisted. "There's going to be such a chasm between your wealth and lifestyles that you will have no common ground."

"Harry is still family in my eyes, and I will not abandon him because of your snobbery," said Lawrence.

"But –"

"Enough, Mama!" Lawrence became angry. "You cannot dictate who I see! You don't want me to correspond with Margaret, you don't want me to take a ride with Harry! What am I allowed to do? This is worse than school! I need to be allowed to live my own life and with the people that I choose."

Lawrence stood up abruptly and threw his napkin on the table before storming out past a passive-appearing Taylor.

Anna sat in thought. She was filled with fear of Harry still, and the memories of all the accidents Lawrence had in his company as a child. But how could she broach these fears with Lawrence, when she never had any proof, and Edward had never believed her suspicions? Especially as it was clear that Lawrence had simply forgotten the incident on the lake, or had chosen to forget. Besides, if she did broach the subject with Lawrence and Edward found out, he would be furious at her and accuse her of trying to prevent Lawrence from settling in back at Armstrong House.

Perhaps Harry had changed, she reasoned, maybe whatever had gone on with him as a child had passed. Although, observing him the night of the ball, he had seemed as cocksure and arrogant as he

164

had been as a child.

"May I take this, my lady?" asked Taylor, indicating her plate.

"Oh, yes, thank you, Taylor."

He removed her plate.

"Taylor?"

"Yes, my lady?"

"When his lordship and I were living in London and Mr. Sinclair and his family were in residence here at Armstrong House, how did you find Master Harry?"

Taylor looked surprised. "It really is not my place to comment, my lady."

"Of course, I apologise," said Anna, realising she was asking Taylor to break butler etiquette.

"But I will say, my lady, that I am very glad that you and Your Lordship are back in Armstrong House and that young man is no longer living under this roof." Taylor's eyes looked steely.

"Thank you, Taylor," said Anna, returning his steely expression, indicating she had appreciated his opinion.

Lawrence and Harry rode down a road that wound its way through Toormore.

"You have to be particularly careful of the peasants who rent in this area," said Harry.

"Why is that?"

"They can be a disruptive lot. They are always fighting with each other, and used to have faction fights back before they became outlawed."

Lawrence had heard all about faction fights. They were violent brawls that used to break out at fairs with two gangs viciously attacking each other. The rules of the faction fights were that there were no rules, and often people got badly hurt or killed. Sometimes hundreds of people were involved. The police before the famine years used to keep out of these brawls, believing one side was as bad as the next. But in the years since the Famine, the police had cracked down on them, and anyone caught risked imprisonment.

"It still doesn't stop them fighting, and we've had to call the police a few times in order to restore peace," said Harry. "They are thieves and vagabonds that live in this part of the estate. They'd cut your throat to get a shilling. And they only understand one thing – brute force! Which is how my father governs them."

"I sometimes feel a bit of a fraud as I listen to you speak as you do," said Lawrence, embarrassed. "You seem to know so much more about the estate than I do."

"That's because I was collecting your rents while you were at that posh school in England."

"Well, that's behind me now, and I really appreciate all you are telling me."

"Information is free, but experience is priceless," said Harry.

"Well, that's what I want now – experience of running this estate," said Lawrence.

"Well, experience can be gained, but talent you are born with," said Harry. anxious to undermine Lawrence as much as he could. "You either know how to deal with tenant farmers or you don't. That's why my father and I are so important to this estate."

"Of course," said Lawrence. "My father has always said how important Sinclair is in that respect."

"I'm glad he realises it."

They rode along in silence for a while.

"I think I'm to visit Kilternan House soon – the Mountdares are inviting me to a ball there," said Lawrence.

Harry found a rage rising in him at hearing this. "Why would you want to waste your time going there?" he asked.

"It wouldn't be wasting my time. I'd very much enjoy it."

"Well, you won't learn about running an estate attending balls at the other side of the country," said Harry.

"It's only for a few days, and I hope to learn how they are running their estate there from the Earl."

"Ha! From what I know the only thing you'll learn from the Earl of Mountdare is how to drink gin!" scoffed Harry. "He's intoxicated half the time and has no involvement in the running of his estate. I believe his wife does all the finances."

"Still, it will be interesting. And I shall get to meet Margaret again."

"Margaret?" said Harry, her rejection of him still wounding him greatly.

"Yes, we have been corresponding with each other since her visit here."

Harry looked sharply at Lawrence. This new-found knowledge infuriated him. Margaret had refused to correspond with him but she had agreed to with Lawrence. It all made sense to Harry now. She had rejected him because she had her eye on Lawrence. If it hadn't been for Lawrence interfering with them the night of the ball, then she would have been happy to correspond with him. He tried to wipe the anger from his face.

"I think she's quite amazing, Margaret, don't you?" asked Lawrence.

"She's no better or worse than any girl who was at the ball," said Harry. "You wouldn't want to give her the wrong impression though."

"What do you mean?"

"That you are in any way serious about her when you meet her next. I mean, there's so many girls to choose from, isn't there? Why take a bite out of the first apple you find when there's a full orchard to choose from? Have you tried it on with any of the maids yet?"

"Sorry?" asked Lawrence, looking over at him, confused.

"The maids at Armstrong House. Half of them are there for the taking. You wanted experience – you may as well start with them!"

"I wouldn't dream of – of – doing anything with a servant," said Lawrence, shocked.

"Why not? Why waste your time writing letters to Lady Margaret when you could be having real fun in the house with one of the girls? Just make sure you are never caught!"

"Have you been with any of them?" Lawrence asked, flabbergasted at the thought.

"Try Gertie! She's always game for anything!" Harry winked over at him.

"But that would be a disgrace if it were ever found out," said Lawrence.

"Then don't get found out!" said Harry. "Go on – I dare you! Just tell them they are beautiful and you love them – works every time."

"I think I'd rather not, Harry. I don't want to be with a servant girl."

"Coward!" goaded Harry.

Lawrence suddenly felt like he was back being a child with Harry – when Harry was always goading him and taunting him to do something. To go further, take a further risk, touch danger. Like the day he had nearly drowned on the lake.

"I think we should turn back," he said.

"No, we haven't reached the end of Toormore yet. I want to show you the waterfalls there," said Harry, riding on.

A troubled Lawrence continued to ride on beside him.

The next day Anna was in the drawing room doing tapestry when she heard a knock on the front door.

A few minutes later Taylor came in.

"Would you like tea, my lady?"

"No, thank you, Taylor. Who was at the front door?"

"It was young Master Harry, my lady – he's in the library seeing His Lordship on estate business," said Taylor.

After Taylor left, Anna sat in thought for a while then put aside her tapestry and went to the drawing-room door and held it ajar as she waited. Ten minutes later she heard the library door open and close and Harry stride through the hallway to the front door.

"Harry!" Anna called, stopping him in his tracks. "Could I have a word with you?"

Harry nodded and followed her into the drawing room and closed the door.

She stood there, smiling at him.

"You wanted a word, Cousin Anna?"

"Yes, Harry. I just wanted to apologise for the incident that happened many years ago. I've hardly seen you since, in order to do so."

"Incident?"

"On the lakeshore that day, when Lawrence nearly drowned and I attacked you," she said.

"Oh, yes, I remember," said Harry.

THE LEGACY OF ARMSTRONG HOUSE

"I don't know what came over me. Hitting a child like that, quite unforgiveable of me."

"It's forgotten, I accept your apology," he said, smiling.

"I know it's inevitable that you and Lawrence will be spending some time together now we are back at Armstrong House. I believe you went for a ride together to Toormore?"

"Yes, I was showing him that part of the estate," said Harry.

She smiled back and then the smile dropped off her face as she walked straight up to him.

"And I wanted to tell you, Harry, that I will be watching your every move. I do not want my son again to start suffering the litany of accidents he did when he was in your company as a child. I am putting you fully in charge of his wellbeing. If a hair of his head is damaged, a finger cut, a knee bruised, then I will hold you accountable. Do you understand me?"

"I don't know –"

"If anything happens to Lawrence you will be blamed and you will wish you were never born. You may just hope and pray that he doesn't have any accidents, for your own sake. Now – do you understand me?"

Harry nodded and quickly left the room.

Anna took a deep breath and sat down to continue her tapestry.

CHAPTER 24

Tullydere stood proud in the lush rolling midlands countryside as Sinclair rode up the long driveway. As he neared the sprawling building, he saw it was a mediaeval castle that had been modernised and built on to over the centuries. The latest addition was an early Victorian extension. He had travelled by train to Westmeath and then hired a horse for the final leg of his journey to Tullydere. He had thought about how to approach Georgina. He didn't want the rest of Anna's cousins to realise he had come to call at Tullydere, in case word got back to her. He had decided then that rather than arrive at the house and request to see Georgina, he would perhaps find a servant or a stable boy first to seek her out for him. He saw some farm labourers making hay in a nearby field.

"A fine day for making hay!" he called over to them.

"Indeed it is, sir, long may the weather last," said an older man who approached him. "Are you lost, sir?"

"No, I'm calling to a friend of mine who lives at the Big House – Miss Georgina?"

"Oh, yes, Miss Georgina." The man looked it at him curiously as hardly anybody called to see Georgina. "But sure, Miss Georgina hasn't lived at the Big House in I don't know how many years."

Sinclair felt his heart sink.

"She lives in a lodge on the estate, down by the river," said the man.

Sinclair was elated that she was nearby and that he did not have to call to the Big House.

"Could you tell me how I can find my way there, friend? I have a gift to deliver for her," he said.

Sinclair followed the man's directions and found the small two-storey thatched lodge overlooking a river. There was a rose garden in the front and he saw Georgina and a servant girl tending to the flowers. He pulled up by the garden and Georgina stopped pruning and looked at the stranger. Her mouth dropped open as she recognised Sinclair.

"Good day, Georgina," said Sinclair with a wide smile.

"Is everything all right, Miss Georgina?" asked the servant girl, seeing her mistress's expression. "Will I fetch one of the men from the Big House?"

"Eh, no, that won't be necessary, Molly. You can go in and start cooking supper for tonight," said Georgina.

Molly went inside and Georgina walked to the end of the garden towards Sinclair who had dismounted and tied his horse to the gatepost.

He smiled at her. "It's good to see you again, Georgina."

He tried to keep his face friendly and neutral, but he was shocked by her appearance. She was now quite grey and aged. But then he realised it had been nearly twenty years since he had seen her last.

She stared at him in silence, obviously shocked at seeing him again and filled with curiosity as to why he was there.

He looked up at the house and smiled. "What a pretty house you live in."

"My brother gave it to me when I moved out of the Big House," she said.

He smiled at her. "Yes, I know what it feels like to be the poor relation and made be grateful for the homes our rich relatives provide for us."

"Why are you here, Sinclair?" She was suddenly alarmed. "Has something happened to Anna?"

"No, nothing has happened to Anna. She is quite deliriously happy at Armstrong House with her husband and son. They have returned to live there from London, hadn't you heard?"

"No, I hadn't," said Georgina, and Sinclair noticed her voice had a tinge of bitterness and annoyance.

"Well – will you not invite me in?" asked Sinclair.

Georgina hesitated before nodding and he followed her up the garden path and into the house. Inside, she showed him down a narrow hallway and into a small parlour that had latticed windows and beams running across the ceiling.

"Most cosy!" he said, seating himself in an armchair.

"Can I offer you a drink? I only have sherry," she said.

"A sherry would be most welcome."

He watched her cross the room to a half-filled decanter on a side table. Taking two small glasses she began to fill them. As he studied her pouring the drinks, he noticed she had a tremor in her hands. He thought she was a woman who had suffered a lot of emotional hardship in her life and imagined she drank a lot of sherry.

She walked over to him and handed him a glass before sitting across from him on a sofa.

"How is your wife? And you had a son, as I remember?" she queried.

"Both doing splendidly. We are still at Hunter's Farm – you remember, the manor house on the estate?"

"I remember it."

"You – never married?"

She looked annoyed. "No, I didn't. How could I after . . ."

He nodded as she trailed off. "You should have sued that man for breach of promise."

"What good would that have done? Only disgraced myself further and shown myself up even more," she said, taking a sip of sherry.

He liked how her bitterness with life was making her so open. He hoped it would lead her to help him.

He nodded sympathetically. "I remember when he jilted you. You spent a lot of time at Armstrong House afterwards. Anna was very good to you, helping you recover."

Georgina's face became even more bitter. "Yes, she was good to me – then."

"But, I suppose, people run out of sympathy after a while. They can only offer so much support before they have to get on with their own lives. And after Lawrence was born, well, Anna had to put him and being a mother first."

"What makes you think we haven't been in contact all these years, even if I didn't visit Armstrong House?"

He looked at her. "I know you haven't been in contact with her."

Georgina took another quick drink from her glass and Sinclair could see that he had been correct in that Anna had abandoned her, and that it had affected Georgina very much.

"Well, it's as you say, she had other responsibilities. I couldn't expect her to continue nurse-maiding me," Georgina said.

Sinclair sat forward and spoke softly. "I know Anna treated you very badly, Georgina. Yes, she had become a mother, but she could have included you in her life, and in the child's life. I'm sure it would have been a kindness to you to at least make you his god-mother, considering how close you were. To give you a part in her child's life, considering you had none of your own."

Tears seemed to threaten to overcome Georgina but she managed to keep herself in check. "I – I don't blame her for getting on with her own life. She owed me nothing."

"I don't believe that. She owed you a great deal. You were like sisters! Why, when she came first to live at Armstrong House, she found it very hard to settle in. It was only your visits and encouragement that kept her going, especially during those long years before Lawrence was born."

"I tried to be as best a support as I could to her," said Georgina. "It wasn't easy sometimes, especially as Edward disapproved of me for some reason."

"He was just being selfish, if you ask me. He wanted Anna all to himself and no distractions. He told me himself he thought you were a bad influence on her."

Georgina's face flashed with anger. "He said that?"

Sinclair nodded. "And as for Anna, all these years she's lived the life of Riley. You know they were living in London this past five years?"

"I had heard."

"As part of the Marlborough set by the end, no less, keeping company with the Prince of Wales every night. While you –" he gestured to the small room, "were left to a life of insignificance. The spinster aunt only allowed up to Tullydere at family events like Christmas and Easter."

"It is not the destiny I wished for myself," she acknowledged.

"Or deserved. And Anna could have made all the difference to your life, if she had just *included* you in hers," sighed Sinclair.

Georgina finished off her sherry before quickly going to the decanter and refilling her glass. She stood there for a while looking out the window at her rose garden, deep in thought. She turned around to Sinclair.

"Sinclair, what are you doing here? Why have you come to find me, of all people, after so many years? Surely not to offer me a sympathetic ear? Unless your personality has changed completely. You never struck me as a bleeding heart."

He sat forward earnestly. "But I think you misunderstood me back then, Georgina. Or was poisoned against me by Anna."

From Georgina's expression he judged his observation had hit home.

"I never got on with Anna, that I do not deny," he said. "But perhaps now, after all these years of coldness from Anna, you might understand why I disliked her so."

"Perhaps," said Georgina.

"I wanted to see you to – to apologise for any insensitivity you might have suffered from me back then, or any vulgarity I might have displayed," he said earnestly.

She looked into his eyes and seemed moved by his words. Clearly, it had been a long since anyone had shown her any kindness.

"I am touched that you thought to come all this way to do that – but," she shook her head in realisation, "in reality, you're quite correct, Sinclair. You never behaved badly to me directly – it was Anna's descriptions of you and her relaying back alleged behaviour by you that coloured my opinion of you."

"She is very manipulative," said Sinclair.

Georgina sighed. "Perhaps she is."

"And that is why it is breaking my heart to see how she is manipulating my adored cousin Edward to such an extent."

Her interest was piqued. "How so?"

"By continuing to pass off Lawrence as his son, when we both know that he isn't."

Georgina dropped her glass on the floor and stared at him in horror.

"Whatever are you saying?"

"We both know it, Georgina. Lawrence is not Edward's son. He is a result of a filthy liaison she had with her servant Seán."

"Have you lost your mind, man? Do you realise what you are saying?"

"I fully realise the truth. And you know the truth as well, Georgina – you know she had an affair with that peasant."

"I know nothing of such nonsense!"

"Do you know she had the man arrested after the birth of Lawrence? She accused him of stealing a locket and had him arrested. He was about to be sent to the other side of the world, destined for a life of hard labour, when the poor bastard managed to escape."

"Well, I'm sure if Anna said he stole a locket then stole a locket he did!"

Sinclair shook his head. "I don't believe it for a second now. Not since I saw Lawrence, now grown into a man, since coming back from London."

"What do you mean?"

"Lawrence is the spitting image of his father – and I mean his *real* father – Seán! You can't escape your genes, and Lawrence has certainly not escaped his!"

"We see what we want to see, and you clearly want to see that Lawrence is not Edward's son, for whatever reason you have," said Georgina.

"Come to Armstrong House and see him for yourself, if you don't believe me."

"I am not welcome at Armstrong House to see anybody, let alone to see Lawrence."

"And why is that, Georgina? Why? Because you know the truth and Anna saw you as a threat just because you had that knowledge and cut you out of her life the same way she cut Seán out. There are only three people in this world who can confirm that Anna had sexual congress with that servant – Anna, Seán and *you*!"

"I believe you to be quite insane!"

"Why are you still protecting her? After the way she treated you? You owe her nothing and I am giving you the opportunity for revenge."

"How?"

"By telling the truth. By confirming she had sexual relations with that servant and that Lawrence is the offspring!" spat Sinclair.

Georgina jumped to her feet and ran to the door, calling, "Molly!"

Sinclair ran after her and grabbed her by the arms. "*Tell the truth!*"

"You're mad, let me go! You are going to destroy the house of Armstrong if you continue with this – this – folly!"

He shook her. "Better to destroy it than it to be taken by the bastard son of peasant!"

Georgina cried out in shock as Molly arrived at the door.

"Miss Georgina? Will I fetch one of the men from the Big House?" gasped Molly.

"*No! Just show this – gentleman – out – now!*" demanded Georgina as she pulled away from Sinclair.

"I'll be back," promised Sinclair. "I won't give up until I expose the truth."

Sinclair marched out of the room, quickly followed by Molly.

Georgina raced to the table and with shaking hands poured herself a sherry and gulped it back in one go.

The following night Diana waited anxiously at Hunter's Farm. At eight o'clock she heard a carriage pull into the driveway and jumped from her armchair to look out the window. She saw Sinclair get out of the carriage and pay the driver before it turned and drove away. A few moments later she heard the front door open and slam and Sinclair came down the corridor and into the parlour. He threw his bag down on the floor.

"Well, did you find her?" asked Diana anxiously.

"Yes, I did, living in a cottage on the estate and drinking sherry to get her through life by the look of her."

"And did she talk? Did you find anything out?"

"It's as I said. Anna dropped her after Lawrence was born and they haven't seen each other since. She knows the truth, I could tell from her reaction. But when I challenged her, she went into shock and demanded I leave the house."

Diana was crestfallen. "Then she won't cooperate with us and expose Anna?"

"I thought she would be thrilled at the idea of getting revenge on Anna after the way she's treated her. But I think blood is thicker than water, and she won't betray Anna to such an extent – for now anyway."

"So what do we do now?"

"I think we need to find out for sure if Lawrence can be disinherited if the truth comes out. There is a barrister is Dublin called Jeffrey Fetherston –"

"No, Sinclair! You will be risking our position here on the estate if Edward finds out what you are doing!"

"I know Fetherston to have handled many a separation and scandal and is known to be confidential and discreet beyond compare. I think it is imperative that I meet with him as soon as possible and get his opinion on the matter."

"But you must not mention who is involved! You can't mention Edward and Anna's name!"

"I won't. I shall merely say I am inquiring on behalf of a friend. Anyway, Fetherston can be trusted in a brief. As I said, I am told that if Fetherston ever spoke of all he knows, then three quarters of the aristocracy of Ireland would be destroyed."

Diana nodded. "I suppose there is no point in continuing with this unless we are sure that Lawrence can be disinherited."

CHAPTER 25

Anna had spent the morning in Castlewest visiting the drapery shops as she was having some new gowns made for herself. It was just after lunch and she was back at Armstrong House in the drawing room, sitting at the desk writing letters. She had been so busy recently that she had been falling behind in her correspondence and was trying to catch up. They had been at the Fitzherberts' estate the previous night for dinner and had a delightful time. She had received an invitation from the Countess of Mountdare, inviting Lawrence to a ball they were having the following month. Lawrence had been very enthusiastic about the idea and Anna was writing back to the Countess, accepting the invitation on his behalf. She knew the reason Lawrence was so enthusiastic was altogether to do with Margaret. She also knew the Countess's invitation was an attempt to engineer a meeting between the youngsters again, and that the Mountdares clearly approved of Lawrence as a prospective suitor for their daughter.

There was a knock on the door and Taylor entered.

"Sorry to disturb, my lady, but there is a lady here to see you."

"Who is it, Taylor?"

"She would not give her name, but insisted she should see you and that she is a friend of yours."

"I'm not in the habit of receiving guests who will not announce themselves, Taylor."

Suddenly the door pushed open behind Taylor and a woman walked in.

178

"Hello, Anna," said the woman.

"Georgina!" exclaimed Anna, dropping her pen.

"I beg your pardon, ma'am, but I asked you to wait in the parlour," snapped Taylor.

Anna slowly rose from her chair. "It's all right, Taylor . . . you may leave us."

Taylor nodded and left the room, closing the door behind him.

The two women stared at each other for a while. Then Anna smiled, quickly crossed the room and gave Georgina a kiss on the cheek.

"Georgina, it's good to see you again."

"You're looking well, Anna. You've hardly changed."

"Nor have you," lied Anna, who was shocked at how Georgina had aged.

Georgina stepped away from Anna and wandered around the room, looking about her.

"And the place hasn't changed. How long has it been since I was here? Eighteen years?"

"I – I can't remember, Georgina."

"It was at Lawrence's christening party, that was the last time I was at Armstrong House."

"Was it?"

Georgina turned and studied Anna intently.

"How did you get here?" Anna asked.

"I got the train and then managed to get a carriage to bring me here from Castlewest."

"But you should have told us you were coming – I would have sent a carriage to collect you from the station."

"Would you have?"

"Of course! Why didn't you write and tell me you were visiting?"

"Because I doubted you would have replied," said Georgina.

Anna smiled uncomfortably. "Hardly!"

Anna's mind was racing. What was Georgina doing here after so many years? Why hadn't she said she was coming? And what would Edward say when he saw her?

Luckily, he and Lawrence were out riding on the estate and weren't expected back until early evening.

"Are you staying the night?" she asked.

Georgina smiled cynically. "There was a time you wouldn't even had to ask me that. It would have gone without saying that I would stay. And not just a night but sometimes weeks – remember? This was like a second home to me."

"Well, you are still welcome here, Georgina, you always have been."

"Really?" Georgina sounded unconvinced. "No, I am not staying the night. I have booked into an inn for tonight and shall be returning to Tullydere in the morning on the first train."

Anna felt relieved as she said, "But there really is no need . . ."

She trailed off as she saw Georgina's dubious expression.

"Are you hungry? We've just had lunch, but I can order you food." Anna made her way to the bell pull.

"I am not hungry, Anna. As my visit is to be short I won't waste time eating."

Anna became even more scared about the purpose of Georgina's visit.

"Is all well at Tullydere?" she asked, suddenly concerned. "Richard is not ill, or Joanna?"

"All are very well at Tullydere. My brother and his wife and their five brats are all doing exceptionally well," said Georgina.

"That is good. It must be a little uncomfortable for you now with the children getting bigger?"

"I'm rarely at the main house. I was sent to live in a cottage on the estate many years ago. Joanna always despised me, and it became impossible for us to live under the same roof, even a roof as big as the one at Tullydere."

"Well, at least you have your own place now," Anna said, always aware of the festering hatred between Georgina and her sister-in-law and not surprised that it had become unbearable. Towards the end of their friendship, Anna had felt quite sorry for Joanna when she realised how bitter and negative Georgina had become.

"Yes, I have my own place. Barely big enough to swing a cat in and they allow me one maid, who can't even boil an egg correctly."

Anna nodded sympathetically, realising Georgina's bitterness had not softened over the years.

"Shall we walk?" asked Georgina suddenly.

"Oh, yes, if you wish – it is a lovely day," said Anna who was grateful for the suggestion. She didn't know what Georgina was there for, but would prefer to be away from any of the servants who might be listening in the house.

Anna took her shawl and they made their way to the front door and walked outside.

"I think we might walk in the side garden?" suggested Anna.

"As you wish," said Georgina and they walked through the forecourt to the garden at the side of the house.

"The gardeners do a wonderful job," said Georgina.

They walked along the paths that criss-crossed the garden, past the fountains and manicured hedges and trees.

Anna said nothing as they walked along.

Georgina suddenly spoke. "I waited for weeks, then months, for you to write to me but when it went to years, I just gave up."

Anna felt extremely awkward as she struggled with what to say. "I am sorry, but time just moved on and I was so busy. I was doing a lot of work for the Famine at the time."

"I heard all about your work – who didn't?"

"I became immersed in trying to help the people, and afterwards – well, it affected me very badly."

"So you are blaming the Famine for your cutting me out of your life?"

"No, of course not! Well, perhaps it played a part."

"And was there any other reason?" asked Georgina.

"No."

Georgina looked at her cynically.

"Well, if the truth be known," Anna said hesitantly, "you had become difficult to be around, Georgina. I know being jilted affected you very badly and living at Tullydere with your brother's family was difficult for you, and so – and so I suppose I could not cope with who you had become."

"Oh, so it was *my* fault? Shall we blame the Crimean war while we are at it?" said Georgina sarcastically.

"Things change, Georgina. We all change, and sometimes we just have to move on with those changes."

"But we were like sisters! You told me everything! You confided in me about everything. You told me things . . . that only I know."

"Things change, people change."

"No they don't, not really, not deep down. I think the problem was you told me too much, confided too much in me. And then because I knew too much, you needed me out of your life, because you perceived me as being a threat."

"That's nonsense."

"The fact that you suspected, after your own doctor's investigations confirming there was probably no problem with you, that Edward was infertile."

Anna ground to a halt and stared at Georgina's face which had seemed to become twisted in a joyous anger.

"The fact that you were terrified you would not produce an heir, and Sinclair and his son would inherit everything."

"*Stop*!" demanded Anna.

"The fact that I told you that you needed to become pregnant by somebody else and pass the child off as Edward's or else you would end up as desolate as I was."

"*Georgina!*"

"And the truth that that was exactly what you did."

"I am not listening to any more of this! *This* is the reason why I broke off all contact with you," said Anna furiously. "Because you had become clearly insane!"

"Oh, you are denying it all now, are you? The conversations we had, the plans that we laid?"

Anna turned to walk away. "Thank you for the visit, Georgina – it has been very nice to see you, but perhaps you might leave it a further eighteen years before you visit again! I shall ask Taylor to get one of the stable boys to drop you back to town. You might be in time to catch the evening train back to Tullydere and have no need to stay in that inn you booked into."

"You are in danger, Anna!" Georgina called after her.

Anna ignored her and continued to walk quickly away.

"Sinclair visited me at Tullydere!" Georgina called.

Anna stopped in her tracks and felt herself go cold.

"Sinclair visited me last week. He knows, Anna, he knows Seán is Lawrence's father."

Anna turned and stared at Georgina and then quickly marched back to her and slapped her hard across the face.

"Get out! Get away from me and never return! I never want to see your miserable face again!" cried Anna.

"I have come here today to warn you, Anna. You must listen to me or you will be destroyed. Sinclair knows."

"And why would he go to you if he ever suspected such a ridiculous thing?"

"He knows how close we were. He knew I'd know. And he was right."

Anna laughed out loudly. "And what makes Sinclair even think such a ridiculous thing?"

"He told me that Lawrence was the image of Seán. He said there was no doubt in his mind because of the strong similarity."

"His mind! His twisted stupid mind! How dare he! How dare he even think such a thing! Such a lie!"

"You can keep denying the truth to me, Anna. But he's not going to stop until he exposes you," said Georgina.

"Expose me? How?" Anna was in shock.

"It's obvious, isn't it? He's going to find Seán and bring him back to Armstrong House to admit the truth," said Georgina.

Anna felt herself wobble and her head felt light as she desperately searched to hold on to something to stop herself from falling. Georgina quickly seized her and held her tightly to prevent her from collapsing. She gently led her over to a bench in the garden and sat her down, before sitting down beside her.

Anna had a glazed look in her eyes as she stared out into the distance.

"Anna?" asked Georgina eventually. "Anna, shall I fetch you a drink from the house? Do you need a doctor?"

"No," Anna said, not taking her eyes from a fountain in the distance. Her mind was whirling with confusion and fear. She steadfastly refused to look at Georgina. What if all this was a trap? Georgina, who she hadn't seen in nearly two decades, suddenly showing up and expecting her to believe and trust her.

"I don't blame you for not trusting me," said Georgina. "Why should you? We are practically strangers now, regardless of how close we were in the past. But Sinclair wanted me to confirm it was true. And I denied it."

Anna managed to look at her.

"Yes, Anna, I can still read your thoughts. I always could. But there was a time I didn't need to. When you spoke your thoughts to me as they came into your mind. That is how much you trusted me. That is why I was so hurt after – that night." It was Georgina's turn to get a faraway look in her eyes as she thought back through the years. "Do you remember? We planned it so meticulously. We waited until Edward was away and there was a fair in Castlewest."

"Please don't, Georgina," whispered Anna.

"I stole one of the servant's clothes and we dressed you up as a peasant. I drove you into town with the plan you were to go with a random stranger at the fair and hopefully become pregnant. But, when I went back that night, there had been a faction fight in the town, and you were not where you were supposed to be. I fretted all night, thinking you had been killed, and then you turned up at Armstrong House the next morning, telling me you had been caught up in a faction fight, and that your servant – Seán – had been following you the whole night, curious and concerned as to what you were doing, and he had rescued you and brought you back to his cottage to safety. And that next day everything changed between us. It was as if you blamed me for coming up with the plan that had failed and put you in danger. But it hadn't failed, had it, Anna?"

"I never knew for sure that Seán was the father. It could have been Edward," whispered Anna.

"You convinced yourself Lawrence was Edward's, I'm sure of it. At the christening I asked you was Seán the real father and you denied it and banished me from the house and your life forever."

"I had no choice. The fact you even suspected it meant I could not have you near us any more."

"That was your mistake, Anna. You were never a schemer, you needed me in your life to concoct the schemes and keep you safe. If I had been part of your life, I would have made sure you were never in the danger that you now are in."

Anna's eyes blurred with tears. "Is that what you think, Georgina? That I unable to scheme? Then you never really knew me as you think you did. Oh, I schemed plenty after you had left, to my shame and regret. After – that night – Seán was the perfect gentleman – he left working for us in the house, and went to work in the stables. We agreed to keep out of each other's way and for the night never to be mentioned again. But after Lawrence was born, he came back to Armstrong House and insisted on meeting me. He said he had stolen into the house and went to see Lawrence in the nursery and knew he was his son." Anna's voice became panicky and stressed at the memory. "He was speaking like someone insane. He was suggesting and pleading that I leave Edward and take Baby Lawrence and leave with him to start a new life in America as a family."

Georgina's eyes opened wide with amazement. "He clearly was insane! How could he ever possibly think that Lady Armstrong would –"

"I didn't know what to do! He said he would expose what happened between us and that he was the baby's father!"

"But surely he knew nobody would believe the word of a peasant!" Georgina was shocked.

"I feared that if he did what he threatened, that you would back up his story and we would all be destroyed," said Anna.

"But – but how could you think I would betray you in such a way?"

"I didn't know anything any more! You had become so bitter and we had fallen out, so I felt you could do such a thing. I couldn't take the risk. So I," Anna's voice became quiet, "framed Seán for stealing a locket in order for him to be thrown off the estate and away from us. But then I learned he was to stand trial and be shipped to Van Diemen's land, where he would face life imprisonment with hard labour!"

"And was he? Was he shipped to Van Diemen's land?"

"No. I pleaded with Edward to have mercy on the man and that to be thrown off the estate was punishment enough. And that was what happened and that was the last we ever saw of him."

"And whatever did become of him, I wonder?"

"I don't know!" Anna's voice became desperate. "The Famine had started and thousands were dying around the country. And I realised that I had driven Seán away from the safety of the estate into the terror of the Famine."

Georgina saw that her cousin's face was immersed in pain.

"I became consumed with guilt. I couldn't look at Lawrence without seeing Seán, and to think – to think – I was responsible for his death was unbearable. So, I set out to find him."

"Find him? But how?"

"I threw myself into charity work for the Famine in order to visit the workhouses to find him. I spent every hour of every day desperately going through the workhouses, distributing food and medicine, to search for him. I visited every port and looked through every passenger booking to see if he had emigrated. You don't know the lengths I went to, Georgina, to undo what I had done and save Seán from the ravages of the Famine. I left no stone unturned, no workhouse unvisited. Every ditch and hedge where I saw starving people I searched, looking into the faces of the dying and sick, hoping – just hoping I could find Seán and save my baby's father from death." Anna's voice broke and she began crying.

Georgina put her arm around her. "But you found nothing?"

"It was as if he vanished into thin air," said Anna. "He wouldn't have had much when he was thrown off the estate. And the country was besieged with destruction – how could he survive that?"

"You would be surprised what these peasants can survive when their back is against the wall. They would rob, beg and kill to survive."

"Not Seán – don't you remember how he was?"

186

Georgian nodded sadly. "Yes, I do."

She continued to comfort Anna as so much made sense to her now. Anna's tireless work during the Famine that everyone said had caused fits of depression afterwards. There was another reason for it all: Anna was haunted by the most terrible guilty conscience. And each day Lawrence was an inescapable reminder of what she had done.

Georgina put her hands on Anna's shoulders and turned her towards her.

"The reality is, Anna, that Seán may have perished in the Famine like a million others, but may very well not have as well. And if he is alive and Sinclair finds him, then your whole world will be destroyed. Or if Sinclair finds any other evidence that Seán is Lawrence's father. Does Lawrence really look like Seán, as Sinclair claims?"

"I have never giving it any thought – his temperament is very like Edward's," said Anna.

"I don't believe you! Do they physically look alike?"

Anna nodded. "Yes, they do, but are yet so different. Seán was a peasant, Lawrence is a gentleman."

"If Seán had been given the background and education Lawrence had, then I'm sure he would look like a gentleman too. Has anyone ever remarked on it before Sinclair?"

"No, not a soul. But there's nobody left at Armstrong House who would even remember Seán this many a year. All the servants from that time have long since gone. And, as for our friends, who ever looks in the face of a servant and remembers what they look like? Who from back then could possibly remember Seán? I'm shocked Sinclair even recalls what he looked like."

"Well, you made a fatal mistake, when you were framing Seán, in having Sinclair involved in the investigation and arrest. It has made Seán stand out in his memory."

"You're right. A mistake that has come back to haunt me."

"Your second mistake was coming back to Armstrong House at all! You should have all stayed in London!"

"I couldn't keep Edward and Lawrence away any more," said

Anna. "It never dawned on me that Sinclair would put two and two together."

"And that was your third mistake. It struck Sinclair when he saw Seán again after such a long absence. If he had seen Lawrence grow up without a gap, he might never have noticed." Georgina patted her own grey hair. "Do you suppose anyone at Tullydere has noticed me age from day to day and week to week, in the way it struck you when you saw me today after eighteen years? And don't bother trying to deny it – this is no time for kindness."

Anna stared at Georgina in bewilderment and awe. It was like they had gone back to the way they had been in their youth. With Georgina being determined and pointing out facts and taking control. It was how Georgina had been when she concocted the plan that Anna have sexual congress with a peasant and pass the resultant child off as Edward's.

"Edward has never shown any suspicion or hinted at the boy not being his?" questioned Georgina.

Anna was horrified. "Of course not! He worships Lawrence."

"And if Sinclair ever revealed or could prove the truth, how would Edward react?"

Anna spoke quietly. "It would kill him."

Georgina became impatient. "What I am asking is this: if Sinclair went to Edward and told him his suspicions, as he did to me, how would Edward react? If he pointed out the resemblance between Lawrence and Seán, brought up the locket story, would Edward believe him?"

"No! Edward thinks I am the perfect wife who has never even looked at another man. He would be furious that Sinclair was trying to cast aspersions on both me and Lawrence."

"That is good. And Sinclair knows that too. Sinclair will not risk his own position on the estate by bringing his suspicions to Edward without proof to back them up."

"But what if he gets firm proof? What then? Where will it leave us?"

"Sinclair won't rest until he gets Lawrence exposed as a fraud and tries to claim the Armstrong estate for himself," said Georgina.

"I think it is wise to find out where you stand legally on the matter, in case the truth ever does come out."

"But how could I do that?" Anna was terrified. "How could I discuss this with an outsider without risking everything?"

Georgina sat in thought for a while. "A solicitor would be bound by confidence."

"I can't, Georgina! I can't tell anybody what I have done. The risk is too great – it would destroy me!"

"I could speak to one on your behalf. Not mention your name, and say I was enquiring on behalf of a friend."

"It's too risky, Georgina. I forbid it!"

"So what do we do in that case? Wait like sitting ducks for Sinclair to make his next move?"

"I need time to think – I need to figure out what to do," said Anna.

Georgina nodded. "I shall think as well – I shall try to think of something that could save you and Lawrence from this danger."

Anna and Georgina walked back to the house in silence until they reached the forecourt.

"Can you arrange a carriage for me to go back to the town?" asked Georgina.

"Georgina, please stay the night here – I really don't want you to stay at an inn."

Georgina shook her head. "No, Anna, I want to be gone before Edward and Lawrence arrive back, and you must not tell them I was here today. Edward will think it most unusual that I just turned up out of the blue – he'll be suspicious. What's more, Sinclair will find out I was here and we do not want him to know we are once again in cahoots."

Anna smiled. "In cahoots? Isn't that what got us into trouble in the first place?"

"Just think, Anna – if we didn't plan what we did all those years ago, then you wouldn't have Lawrence today."

Anna saw a gardener coming up from one of the terraced gardens and called over to him. "Please go around to the stables and tell them to bring a carriage to the front of the house as quickly as possible."

"Yes, my lady," said the gardener as he raced out of the forecourt to the back of the house.

Georgina looked up at the house. "In a way I've missed this place, and you."

"I don't know why you're helping me after the way I treated you through the years," said Anna.

"I was always there for you, you just didn't realise it," said Georgina. "And now I better understand the pressures you were under."

A carriage came into the forecourt and drew to a halt beside them. The driver leapt down and opened the door for Georgina.

She stepped inside. Sitting down, she leaned out the window and whispered, "I'll be in touch. Any letter you get from me, burn it straight after reading it."

Anna nodded as she took her hand and impulsively kissed it. "Have a safe journey home," she said, adding fervently in a whisper. "And *thank* you."

Georgina smiled and whispered, "Try not to fret too much. I'll find a solution."

Anna stepped back and called up to the driver, "Take the lady to Castlewest."

"Very good, my lady," said the driver. He shook the reins and drove out of the forecourt.

Anna watched the carriage go down the driveway and along by the lake before she slowly turned and went inside the house.

Georgina sat in the carriage, deep in thought. How strange it was after so long to be back in Anna's life. And it felt right. It was where she was meant to be.

Then suddenly she noticed two men on horseback riding through the parklands, laughing and chatting as they rode. She discreetly leaned forward to get a better look and recognised Edward as one of the men. She looked at the man on the other horse and gasped. She realised Sinclair was right.

For a split second she was sure the other man was Seán, Anna's long-lost servant, before she realised that it must be Lawrence.

CHAPTER 26

Anna was in a daze as she made her way into the house and back into the drawing room. How her life had been turned upside down within a couple of hours! Damn Sinclair and his meddling! He had been a thorn in her side since the day she arrived at Armstrong House. She was furious with herself that she had allowed them to return from London. They should have stayed there, where they were safe from all of this. It had never occurred to her, never dawned on her, that anybody would even remember Seán, let alone what he had looked like. It was nearly two decades ago!

And yet her past had come back to haunt her. And worse, to destroy her. She couldn't think what to do.

She heard activity in the forecourt and saw Edward and Lawrence ride in and dismount. She looked out the window. As the horses were led away by stable boys, she saw her husband and son laughing and joking as they came towards the house. She quickly went to her desk and pretended to be writing the letter she had left off when Georgina had arrived.

A minute later the men came into the room.

"Did you have a good day?" asked Anna, smiling over at them.

"Oh, yes," said Lawrence. "We rode all the way over to Knockmore today."

"It is lovely there, isn't it?" said Anna.

"The scenery is breath-taking," said Lawrence.

"Writing your letters?" said Edward as he came over and kissed her.

"Yes, I'm writing to the Countess of Mountdare accepting the invitation for Lawrence to stay with them next week. You are still sure you want to go, Lawrence?"

"Of course I am!" said Lawrence enthusiastically.

"Which is just as well as otherwise there would be a very upset young lady in Kildare," said Edward, winking over at Lawrence who began to blush.

"You will be careful, Lawrence, while you're there, won't you?" said Anna, her face serious.

"Of course I will, why would I not?" said Lawrence as he turned to go. "I'd better change out of these riding clothes before dinner."

Anna watched him as he left the room.

Edward chuckled. "You are funny, Anna. He is adult now. There is no need to fuss over him like you used to. He will not be thrown from a horse, or fall down some stairs or nearly drown in a lake. I've never seen such a strong swimmer as Lawrence is now."

"I wasn't thinking of that kind of trouble," said Anna ruefully. "I was more thinking of the kind of trouble the Prince of Wales got into when he was in Kildare."

"Anna!" said Edward, horrified. "How could you even think such a thing? This is our Lawrence we are talking about, not the playboy Prince of Wales. Our son is a gentleman."

"And the Prince of Wales isn't?" Anna asked wryly.

Edward made no answer, nonplussed.

Anna stood up, went to the window and looked out. "What if he did though? If he became embroiled in a scandal. Would you be horrified?"

Edward looked confused. "What father wouldn't?"

"But – but you would stand by him?"

"I never gave such an eventuality any thought. But yes, I would stand by him, I am his father after all. He is my responsibility by virtue of the fact he is my son."

His words didn't offer Anna any comfort. Edward was saying he would stand by Lawrence during a scandal because he was his son, but what if the scandal was that Lawrence was proven not to be his son?

Edward came over and put his arms around her. "Enough of this silly talk. We are blessed with Lawrence. He will never disgrace or dishonour us."

She smiled up at him. "Of course he won't."

Lawrence was in the bathroom that led from his bedroom, changing out of his riding clothes. He heard somebody come into the room.

"Is that you, Tommy?" he asked, coming out of the bathroom wearing a towel, thinking it was one of the footmen.

"Oh! Sorry, Master Lawrence!" cried Gertie who was standing there, holding a pile of towels.

Lawrence quickly grabbed his dressing gown and put it on.

"I thought you were still out riding," she said. "I was just putting some clean towels in your bathroom."

"Oh, eh, you can leave them on the bed," he said.

She went over to the bed and placed them on it. He watched her, full of curiosity. Then she turned to him, smiled, gave a little bob of a curtsy and left the room. He still could not believe Harry when he had implied he had been with Gertie. Surely he had just been jesting with him? But the girl did have a twinkle in her eye, he thought.

CHAPTER 27

As Sinclair Armstrong sat down opposite him across his desk, Jeffrey Fetherston got an unnerving feeling about the man. He had been a barrister for forty years, which made a person a good judge of character. There was something in the man's black eyes that was almost threatening. He did not recognise him. Fetherston knew and had dealt with most of the merchants and aristocracy in the country through the years and guessed this man was of some breeding but not wealthy or that important. A member of gentry in one of the counties, Fetherston guessed.

"And how can I help you, Mr. Armstrong?"

"I have a matter to discuss that is somewhat delicate," said Sinclair, surveying the barrister who was a man in his sixties, bespectacled, with grey hair combed back. Sinclair had just arrived from the train station to the Fetherston offices in Parliament Square.

Fetherston smirked. "By the time most matters come to my ears, they are usually delicate. Pray continue."

"I have a friend," said Sinclair.

Fetherston smirked again. If he had a penny for all the times a consultation started with the 'I have a friend' phrase he would be a far richer man than he was. By the end of a consultation the client had often admitted the 'friend' was the client himself.

"Yes?"

"And my friend suspects his wife was unfaithful in the early years of their marriage and that his son is in fact not sired by him."

194

"I see," said Fetherston, sitting back. "And your friend wants to know if this is grounds for divorce?"

"No, my friend wants to know if this is grounds for disinheritance – of his son."

"Well, a man doesn't need any grounds to disinherit a son, Mr. Armstrong. If only grounds for a marriage annulment was as simple!"

"So there is nothing preventing my friend from disinheriting the child?"

"Nothing at all! Even if the child was his actual son, there is nothing preventing him from cutting him off without a penny. It is called free will, and free will to make his will in any way he sees best!" Fetherston chuckled as he made this old much-used joke.

Sinclair leaned forward, excited at the barrister's words. "And what about the law of primogeniture? That the eldest son inherits?"

"Primogeniture only exists in the absence of any will being made. Then the estate of the deceased passes through to the eldest son without objection. If it is intended that the eldest son will inherit the estate then a will is of no consequence as that is what will happen in any case. If, however, it is not a person's wish for this to happen, then a will should be made to prevent it from happening."

Sinclair sat deep in thought for a while.

"Is that all?" asked Fetherston.

"What if there is a title in the matter?"

"A title?"

"Yes, an aristocratic title?" said Sinclair.

Fetherston's face turned from smug to serious as his mind began whirling as to who this man was.

After a pause, he spoke. "Well, an aristocratic title will pass to the eldest son born in a legally binding marriage regardless of who the actual biological father is. The son is not illegitimate, at least in the eyes of the law, and so will inherit the title. That matter is closed."

"So – am I understanding you correctly? – an Earl may disinherit his eldest son of his estate, but not his title?"

"That is correct. Although one could argue what use is a title without an estate to support an Earl in the manner to which he is accustomed?"

"Very true, Mr. Fetherston," Sinclair said, standing up. "Thank you for your time."

"I'm glad I have been of some assistance," said Fetherston, looking a little disgruntled as Sinclair left the room. He was craving to know who the earl in question might be.

He called his clerk in.

"What is the address given of the man who just came to see me?"

The clerk rushed out and brought in his appointment book. "County Mayo, sir, was all he wrote as his address."

"County Mayo," mused Fetherston, as he matched Sinclair's surname with the county. He could scarcely believe the matter was in some way related to Lord Armstrong of Armstrong House.

The next day Diana stayed out riding for hours. It was the only thing she could do to clear her head with all that was going on. Sinclair was expected back from Dublin that evening and she was burning with curiosity as to what the barrister had said. As she rode through the Armstrong Estate, she could barely allow herself to think that they could be the natural inheritors of so much. She dared not raise her hopes. She had been in that position before, in the years before Anna gave birth, and everyone had assumed Sinclair and Harry would be Edward's successors. It had been shattering for her when Lawrence had been born and they had been displaced. To think now, after all these years, that the child was a fraud and they were being cheated! But she was frightened also, and she didn't frighten easily. The game Sinclair was playing was very dangerous and could leave them destitute if it backfired.

By the time she arrived back at Hunter's Farm, Sinclair had arrived home and was looking joyous.

"What did Fetherston say?" asked Diana.

"He said that Lawrence could be easily disinherited from the estate, but not the title," said Sinclair. "It is just a matter of Edward making a will to make it so."

Diana clasped her hands together. "But would he, Sinclair? Would he change the will if we proved Lawrence wasn't his?"

"I can't see why not. Lawrence is an imposter. The Armstrongs

196

have been on this estate for three centuries, and are one of the proudest names in the country. Edward would not see our legacy pass to the son of a peasant. We are his blood relatives, Harry and I. This is our estate by rights, and Edward will have to see it that way."

"It will destroy him when he learns the truth – it will destroy Edward," warned Diana.

"Then he should have had the good sense not to have married a harlot in the first place."

"But what if Edward, on learning the truth, divorces Anna and marries again. He still has plenty of time – he is only in his forties. What if he produces new heirs by a new wife?"

Sinclair guffawed. "He can marry as many wives as he wants but Edward will not produce any heirs. He is clearly incapable of doing so. Anna, for all her faults, would have been the last person in the world to end up in a peasant's bed but for her desperation to beget an heir. She clearly is not infertile, and Edward clearly is. Also, divorces are very hard to come by and I would say Edward would not put himself or the family name through the disgrace of making Anna's adultery public."

"We must be very careful, Sinclair. We can't let our ambition trip us up now. We have to be very careful before we can prove the truth beyond all doubt. Fetherston is trustworthy? He won't repeat anything you said?"

"As I told you, it's said that if Fetherston ever spoke of all he knows, then three quarters of the aristocracy of Ireland would be destroyed!"

"So what is the next step for us to take, now that we have learned it is legally possible to disinherit Lawrence?"

"I need to find out more about this Seán. Where he was from and who his people were. I don't even know his surname."

"And how can you find that out?"

Sinclair sat on the sofa, lost in thought. "There was a head groom who worked in the stables the same time Seán worked there. I believe he's still living on the estate in a house provided by Edward. I think I need to pay him a visit."

CHAPTER 28

Lawrence had left to stay with the Mountdares at their estate. Anna thought the house was very lonely without him and was counting the days until he returned. She had received a letter from the Countess informing her Lawrence had arrived safely and that he was a pleasure to have as their house guest. She had also received a letter from Lawrence confirming he was having an excellent time. She had then received a further letter from the Countess, effectively 'inviting' herself, her husband and Margaret to stay with them the following month at Armstrong House.

Each day, Anna sat in the small parlour sifting quickly through her post to see if Georgina had sent her a letter. Then, at last, one came.

She recognised Georgina's handwriting on the envelope. Even after all these years, Georgina's handwriting was so recognisable to her.

She tore open the seal and began to read.

> *River Cottage*
> *Tullydere Estate*

> *My Dear Anna,*
> *I can't tell you how elated I am to have been in your company again after so long. My dearest friend has come back to me, even if it is under such dangerous circumstances. Anything that has passed between us in the past, any thoughts of betrayal, please let us put it all behind us – it is*

forgotten. My only concern now is for you and your son's welfare. As promised I have given the situation much thought. And I believe your best course of events is to attack Sinclair before he attacks you. You must think of a way to discredit him, to destroy his reputation with Edward before he gets the chance to do you harm. In the same way you discredited Seán when you needed to, when he became a threat. I know this will not be easy, as I know the love Edward has for his cousin Sinclair. But I can see no other way for you to protect yourself.

I will be in contact with you soon. Burn this letter once you have read it.

I remain your closest friend and ally,
Georgina

Anna quickly reread the letter before crumpling it up in her hands. How could she do what Georgina was suggesting? What possible way could she discredit Sinclair so much that Edward would disown and have him sent away from the estate? Sinclair was a dangerous and clever foe, one she had always tried to avoid. And now Georgina was saying to frame him, a man like that?

She stood up quickly and walked to the fireplace. Taking the box of matches on the mantelpiece, she set fire to the letter and flung it into the grate.

She watched it burn then picked up the poker and mashed up the burnt paper.

Then the door opened behind her.

She swung around guiltily.

"Is everything all right?" Edward asked as she stared at him in confusion.

"Oh, yes," she said and forced a smile.

"What are you burning?"

"Oh!" She felt herself flush as she replaced the poker. "A – a letter from Lady Fitzherbert."

He smirked at her. "Is her style so bad it warrants burning on reading?"

She crossed quickly over to the sofa, sat down and laughed lightly. "A letter from Lady Fitzherbert always warrants burning on reading! She writes such drivel! And always manages to insult me in the most polite way!"

"Yes, she is the mistress of a backhanded compliment, I give you that. She told me at the last dinner she attended here that I was aging most handsomely for a man in my fifties! I responded by reminding her that I had not yet reached that decade!"

Anna laughed and continued to riffle through her letters. "I received a letter from the Countess of Mountdare who said the ball went wonderfully. And that Lawrence is the most charming guest they have ever received, and they were quite reluctant to let him come back to us."

Edward laughed. "He's due back tomorrow, is he not?"

"Yes. She has also invited herself, her husband and Margaret to come and stay at Armstrong House next month!"

"I see! Rather forward of her, don't you think?"

"She's a mother with a daughter to marry off – there's no such thing as being too forward in her position," Anna said with a laugh.

"I wouldn't have thought she would have too much trouble marrying Margaret off," said Edward.

"Neither do I. But she clearly is keen that Lawrence be the groom!" Anna became serious. "I don't know if we were wise in allowing him to go to Mountdare at all. Are we not only giving the Countess and Margaret encouragement and false hope?"

Edward smiled. "It is Lawrence who is giving them encouragement, my dear. He is clearly smitten with Margaret."

"But he hardly even knows her!"

"Ah, when a young man's fancy lightly turns to thoughts of love!" said Edward with a laugh.

"Please don't start quoting Tennyson at me!" said Anna who was spotting an opportunity to remove them from the dangerous situation they were in. "You see, this is exactly what I feared would happen!"

She stood up and began to pace angrily up and down.

"Whatever are you talking about?"

"Coming back to Armstrong House! Isolating Lawrence down here so that he thinks he's fallen in love with the first girl he meets!"

"Hardly the first girl he's met, and hardly love – yet!"

"You said it, not I! The Countess and her daughter are going to get their hooks into him before he knows what's happened and he'll be marched up the aisle before he knows where he is."

"They haven't even started a courtship, my dear," said Edward.

"No, but it won't be long till they do! Can't you see how unfair we are being on Lawrence, bringing him home here?"

"It was he that insisted!"

"He is limiting himself so much, when he could have the world at his feet. He should be in London at dinners and balls every night, meeting hundreds of young ladies and then deciding who he wishes to fall in love with!"

"He's been to plenty of balls and dinners since he arrived back in Ireland. And you don't choose who you fall in love with, Anna – it just happens, one would hope!"

"Perhaps for a naïve young man like Lawrence, but not for a crafty young woman like Margaret. Can't you see she's just after him for the money and the estate, no thought for him whatsoever?"

"You are being utterly ridiculous, Anna! Margaret is not some desperate young woman, but a highly cherished and loved daughter of one of this country's finest families, who I have been told comes with an enormous dowry. Lawrence would be doing very well in marrying her."

Anna rushed over to him and sank to her knees as she grabbed his hands. "Oh, please, Edward, let's leave this place! Let's take Lawrence back to London, where he can have a full life. He'll never find happiness here!"

Amazed, Edward looked down at his wife and saw tears were threatening to spill down her cheeks. This excess of emotion was alarming. He took her hands and pulled her to her feet.

"I can understand this might have come as a bit of a shock to you," he said. "No mother likes to see her child grow up and be independent from her. But it is the natural course of things.

Lawrence is old enough to decide what life he wants. He has chosen his life to be Armstrong House, and if he chooses Margaret as his wife that's his decision, not ours."

He leaned forward and kissed her forehead, before he left her.

The tears that were threatening began to fall silently down Anna's cheeks.

CHAPTER 29

Sinclair was in the library for his weekly meeting with Edward, going through the business of the estate. He sat on the other side of Edward's desk as Edward pored over the accounts books.

"It looks like this is going to be a very profitable year," said Edward happily.

"The harvests are very good. The rents are coming in on time, and I think we are doing very well," said Sinclair.

"Very good," said Edward, closing over the books and sitting back.

Sinclair was silent for a minute before saying, "Edward, with Lawrence being back, have you given any thoughts to the future?"

"The future?"

"When you aren't here any more," said Sinclair.

Edward looked confused, then he smiled. "I am still quite young, Sinclair. I wasn't planning on going anywhere for a while."

"I know that, of course. It's just, if anything ever happened, it's important that there is a smooth transition of power to Lawrence, without any disruption to the running of the estate. In short, have you made a will?"

Edward looked quite shocked at the question. "As a matter of fact, I have, Sinclair. Although there is no need under primogeniture, as Lawrence as my eldest and only son and will inherit the estate regardless. But I have put in place that this be the course of action, in case there is any doubt. And I also have made my other wishes known."

"I see," said Sinclair, nodding.

"You are quite safe, Sinclair, if that is the purpose of your question. I have requested that yourself and Diana should remain as tenants at Hunter's Farm. Although I doubt that Lawrence would ever want you gone from there, in any case."

Sinclair stood up and smiled. "Thank you, Edward. It's reassuring to know what your plans are."

Edward nodded. "I don't blame you for wanting to know that your future is in safe hands."

Anna had spent the day racking her brains, going over Georgina's letter in her head. She was desperately trying to come up with a way that she could discredit Sinclair, but could not think of anything so substantial that it would cause a permanent falling out with Edward. Goodness knows, she had tried enough during the years to get Sinclair out of their lives, to no avail.

She now thought that her emotional outburst with Edward was most ill-advised. It might arouse Edward's suspicions and work against her should the truth about Lawrence come out. She must make every effort to keep control of her emotions and consider her actions.

She decided she needed a lie-down to give her head some peace and left the drawing room to go upstairs. As she walked across the hallway she got a fright as she came face to face with Sinclair who had come from the library.

They stared at each other for a moment silently, his dark eyes boring into hers.

"Good afternoon, Sinclair."

"Anna." He nodded at her.

"You are looking for Edward?"

"No, I've just left him in the library – we are finished our meeting."

She found herself shaking and was unable to stop.

"Are you all right, Anna?"

"Yes, I just think I might have caught a chill," she said.

"A summer's chill, there is nothing worse," he said. "Unable to enjoy the fine weather because of a cold. There is something unnatural about it being at the wrong time of year, something unnatural about it being in the wrong place."

She nodded.

"When is Lawrence due back?" asked Sinclair.

"Tomorrow," she answered.

"Well, I look forward to seeing him." Sinclair nodded at her and continued to the front door.

Once he had gone, she clung onto the bannisters for support, her heart beating wildly. She rubbed her temples, and continued up the stairs.

Edward sat pondering at his desk in the library. Everyone was acting so strangely, he thought. Sinclair asking about wills, Anna despairing that Lawrence might be starting to court a girl. He shook his head, and stood up and left the library.

He walked down the hallway and into the small parlour where he took his pipe from the mantelpiece. He filled it with tobacco and, taking the box of matches, lit it up before flinging the match into the grate. He spotted the letter Anna had burned from Lady Fitzherbert in the grate and spotted a small piece of it that had failed to burn. Curious, he reached down and picked up the scorched fragment. In small precise handwriting, it read: '*main your closest friend and ally, Georgina*'

Edward nearly choked on his pipe. *Georgina!* What was she doing writing to Anna after all these years?

And what did it mean? How strange to use the word 'ally'! The half-burnt word 'main' obviously had to be 'remain'. He whispered to himself: "*I remain your closest friend and ally.*"

He folded the piece of paper up and put it in his pocket.

CHAPTER 30

Lawrence and Margaret were strolling through the long gardens at Kilternan House while the Countess and other members of the family sat on the terrace at the back of the house, having tea and keeping a watchful eye on them.

Kilternan House was so different to Armstrong House, Lawrence thought. It was a Palladian mansion, quite unlike the baronial style of Armstrong House. In fact, everything was different at the Kilternan Estate, from Margaret's loud noisy siblings to the flat countryside.

"Everything here is so – neat!" said Lawrence as they reached the end of the gardens and he looked down the rolling fields that seemed to go on for miles.

"It might be pretty here but it cannot compare to the majestic beauty of the Armstrong Estate," said Margaret.

He smiled at this compliment. "It's certainly different. Not a lake or a hill, let alone a mountain in sight. It reminds me quite of southern England."

"Yes, it is not dissimilar. I much prefer the wildness of your county. It must be amazing to live there. I can't wait to go back next month – that is, if your mother agrees to our proposed visit."

"Of course she will! It is the only consolation I have – that I will see you soon again. I can't believe I have to leave tomorrow."

"I'll be counting the days until I see you next," she said and stopped walking to look at him.

Lawrence suddenly went bright red. "Margaret – there is

something I have been meaning to ask you."

"Yes?"

"Could you – would you – might you – ever consider accepting a marriage proposal from me should I ever proffer it?"

Her eyes opened wide as she looked at him.

"Should you ever proffer a marriage proposal, I should not need to consider it in the least and would be delighted to accept," she said, her heart thumping from excitement.

"Oh!" He clasped her hands. "But we don't know each other that long. You may need time to reflect on it and discuss it with your parents."

"I have no need to reflect on it and my parents, I am sure, would be overjoyed at the prospect. My mother is so fond of you she would marry you herself if she had the opportunity!"

"Then . . . you are accepting my proposal?"

"I can't . . ."

"What?" His face dropped and he looked at her in confusion. "You just said you would!"

"Yes, I did," she said, smiling, "but you haven't made a proposal yet!"

"Oh! Oh, yes. Margaret – will you do me the honour of becoming my wife?"

"Yes!" she said, jumping into his arms, and he kissed her.

"*Margaret! Margaret!*" called the Countess, jumping up from her seat on the terrace, alarmed at the couple's intimate embrace.

"We had better let them know!" said Margaret and hand in hand they walked back to the terrace.

"Oh, what news! What wonderful news!" said the Countess, embracing her daughter as soon as the two of them were alone in her bedroom at Kilternan House.

"I can hardly believe it!" said Margaret. "I know we have fallen in love, but I never thought he would ask me to marry him so soon."

"You are very fortunate. I have always thought it an unexpected bonus when love is also included in a marriage." The Countess then shrugged. "Although its absence from my own marriage to your father never hindered us in any way."

"He is to ask Papa for permission to marry me this evening," said Margaret.

"Oh!" said the Countess. "I had better make sure I am present at that meeting. Between Lawrence's dithering and your father's dathering, the deal will never be struck! And what of his own family? When does he propose to tell them?"

"I presume when he goes home," said Margaret.

"*Hmm*, I might give young Lawrence a word of advice on how to handle that. He should concentrate on telling his father, and not tell his mother until he has his father's approval and it's too late to undo! Lady Anna can be so unpredictable."

That evening Lawrence stood in the drawing room at Kilternan House, his hands clasped behind his back, his face red, as he spoke to Margaret's parents.

"I have asked Margaret, and she has kindly agreed to . . ." began Lawrence. "That's if you don't have any objections . . . or concerns . . . that is, after I have asked . . ."

"For goodness' sake, spit it out, boy!" cried the Countess.

"Objections that I may ask, sir, and ask you, madam, for . . ." began Lawrence before stopping again.

"That you may ask for Margaret's hand in marriage!" the Countess finished for him before rising quickly. "And the answer is yes! Yes, yes and yes again!"

The Countess went to Lawrence and embraced him.

"We are so delighted to be welcoming you into our family," said the Countess, kissing both his cheeks. "Aren't we, Grover!"

"Absolutely thrilled," agreed the Earl as he headed to the drinks cabinet and, lifting a decanter of port, said, "In fact, I think this calls for a drink to celebrate."

"Put that *down*!" warned the Countess. "You know the new rule – no drinking until after nine at night!"

Disappointed, the Earl replaced the decanter.

"Now, Lawrence," said the Countess, linking her arm through his and leading him to sit beside her. "A cautionary note on how to break the news to your parents . . ."

CHAPTER 31

Sinclair rode into the estate village. Edward was so proud of the village he had built with its beautiful Victorian cottages around the green, and the church standing at its top. Edward had built the village at the same time as he had Armstrong House built. He had used the same English architect to design both, and they were both made from the same granite. Unlike many of the villages on the great estates of Ireland that had been thrown up or casually expanded, this village had been built with great precision, with fairy-tale gabled arches and latticed windows on the cottages.

Sinclair dismounted outside one of the cottages, tying his horse to the gate before he strode up the short garden path and knocked loudly on the door. A minute later a man in his seventies opened the door and looked quite shocked to see Sinclair.

"Good afternoon, Davis. I hope you are enjoying your retirement?" said Sinclair.

"Yes, very much, Mr. Sinclair," said Davis, who stood at the door trying not to look scared.

Like most people who had worked on the Armstrong Estate he feared Sinclair and seen many examples of his cruelty. Now he feared what had brought Sinclair to his door. Edward had been very good to Davis and provided him with the cottage on the green rent-free when he had retired. He now feared Sinclair was there to tell him the arrangement was over.

"May I come in?" asked Sinclair.

"Of course," said Davis, stepping out of the way and allowing him in before closing the door.

Sinclair glanced around the small parlour. Why Edward allowed ex-servants to live in the village rent-free was beyond him. He had tried to talk Edward into at least charging a nominal rent, to no avail.

"Can I get you tea, sir, or anything else?" asked Davis.

"No, nothing," said Sinclair, sitting down in a chair and gesturing to Davis to sit down as well.

They sat in silence for a minute with Sinclair smiling fondly at the man.

"I often tell Edward that you were the best head groomsman Armstrong House ever had," said Sinclair.

"Oh!" said Davis, surprised. "Thank you, sir. I tried to do my work as best I could."

"Do you miss it?"

"I do, surely," said Davis, thinking back to his working life up at the Big House. But, suddenly fearing he was going to be put back to work, he hastily said, "But not that much!"

"You oversaw many a stable boy in your years as head groom."

"That I did. I remember them all. The cheeky ones, the lazy ones, the hardworking ones, and the downright bad ones!"

Sinclair smiled even more at the man's claim that his memory was so acute.

"Cast your mind back, Davis – oh, I'm talking nearly twenty years ago. Do you remember a stable boy called Seán?"

Davis scratched his head. "Half the stable boys we had over the years were called Seán, Mr. Sinclair!"

"Yes, but this one was different. He had been working as a house servant first, before he got transferred down to the stables. Do you remember him?"

"Ah, sure, a lot of the servants were swapped between the Big House and the stables, sir! Hard to remember a fella by that!"

Sinclair found himself becoming impatient. "He was Lady Anna's servant before he went to the stables? Ring any bells?"

Davis searched his memory but his face remained blank.

Sinclair didn't bother hiding his irritation on having to be so specific. He had not wanted to alert Davis to anything. He knew how servants and ex-servants gossiped.

"He stole Lady Anna's locket. I arrested him and we locked him up in the stables for the night, but released him the next day and threw him off the estate – now do you remember who I am talking about!"

Davis's eyes flashed with the memory. "Ah, that Seán! Ah, I surely do remember him. I couldn't believe him to be a thief. He seemed such a nice honest lad. But then you never know with people, do you?"

"No, you certainly don't. Do you know what became of him?"

Davis shrugged his shoulders. "No, why would I? Not after he was escorted off the estate. Sure, he wouldn't come back here for fear he might be arrested. Lord Armstrong showed quite a kindness to him, as I remember, not forcing him to stand trial for the theft."

"He certainly did. Do you know anything else about him?"

"I know he rented a few acres on the estate over at Knockmore – that's where he lived. He never lived up at the Big House, even when he was in service there."

"I remember the cottage, that's where I found the locket when I carried out a search of it. Go on," encouraged Sinclair.

"He was hardworking, and helpful, though always had a cheeky side to him."

"Do you remember him having any girlfriends. Was he courting?"

"Ah, there was always girls interested in that fella, and he gave them attention back as I remember!" laughed Davis.

"But nobody in particular?"

"Not from what I remember, no."

"What was his surname?"

"His surname?" repeated Davis, searching his memory. "Oh, I can't remember."

"Think, man, think!" ordered Sinclair.

Davis's face creased with stress as he tried to think of Seán's surname. "It began with a 'H', I think. Seán H–h–"

"Think! Was it Hurley?"

211

"No – Hegarty! Seán Hegarty, that was his name!" Davis was relieved to have remembered as he saw Sinclair relax.

"And I know he wasn't from the estate here," said Sinclair. "Because, when there was that trouble about the locket, it turned out he wasn't related to anybody on the estate. Where did he come from originally?"

"He was from Galway," said Davis, now very proud of his recall. "His people came from the Hamilton Estate. I remember that because he was always saying what horrible landlords they were and that he wanted to get away from their estate as soon as he was old enough, and that's what brought him here."

Sinclair looked very happy as he stood up. "Thank you, Davis – you have been most helpful."

"Glad I could be, sir," said Davis, smiling as he showed him to the door.

Sinclair opened the door and walked out, then turned to Davis, his face serious and threatening.

"Oh, and Davis?"

"Yes, sir?"

"I wasn't here today and we did not have this conversation. If I find out you discussed my visit with anybody, you will suffer the same fate as Seán Hegarty and be thrown out of this cottage which Lord Armstrong is only giving you out of the kindness of his heart. Do you understand?"

Davis's eyes widened in horror as he nodded quickly and said, "Yes, sir."

David watched Sinclair walk down the path, mount his horse and gallop away.

Then he quickly closed the door and went to sit down and steady his nerves.

CHAPTER 32

It was evening and Lawrence was due back from his visit to the Mountdares. Edward was sitting on an armchair beside the fire reading a book, while Anna was sitting on the sofa doing tapestry. As he looked over his book at his wife, he saw that she was doing her needlework in an almost frantic way, the needle darting in and out with ridiculous haste. She had been incredibly agitated over the last few days. Distracted, short-tempered, irritated. She had not brought up the fact that she had received a letter from Georgina and he could not help but think that the letter was the reason for her agitation. He wondered why she had not mentioned the letter, and he of course could not bring it up as it would make him look as if he was spying on her, finding the remnants of a burnt letter in the grate. He sincerely hoped that the letter was just a random one, and they had not entered into regular correspondence with each other. The last thing Anna needed was Georgina back in her life. He had been delighted when they seemed to have got rid of her.

A carriage drew up in the forecourt and Anna threw down her tapestry and ran to the window.

"He's back!" she cried.

A minute later, Lawrence came bounding into the room, looking very happy.

"Hello!" he said.

Anna rushed to him and enveloped him in a hug – it seemed she would never let him go.

"I've only been gone a week!" said Lawrence, gently pushing her away.

"It seemed like forever," said Anna.

Edward put down his book and rose up to shake his son's hand and give him a clap on the back.

"Did you have a good time?" he asked.

"Oh, I had a capital time. The ball was excellent, the parties before the ball were excellent and the parties afterwards were excellent. It was one big party!"

"Yes, the Mountdares certainly know how to enjoy themselves," said Edward as he retook his seat.

Anna led Lawrence over to the sofa and pulled him down to sit beside her.

"Did you get a letter from the Countess?" asked Lawrence excitedly.

"Yes," said Anna. "Did she not tell you I responded?"

"Yes, she did," said Lawrence. "They are coming to stay in two weeks' time. That's all right, isn't it, Mama? Isn't it, Papa?" He looked over anxiously at Edward.

"Of course it is," he replied. "We are very much looking forward to having them here to stay. I've always found Clementina amusing."

"The Countess must in that case be an acquired taste," said Anna cynically.

"You mother has been planning a full itinerary to keep them occupied," said Edward

Lawrence was happy and satisfied on hearing this.

"I thought you might have had enough of the Mountdares for a while, having just come back from staying with them for a week," said Anna.

"Oh, no, they are lovely people. Very hard to get enough of lovely people, I always think," said Lawrence.

Edward smiled as he spoke. "I think your mother is a little anxious that you might be spending a little bit too much time, too soon, with Margaret."

Lawrence looked at Anna, concerned. "But why would you think that?"

214

Anna glared at Edward. "Your father is talking nonsense – I think no such thing."

"Your mother thinks that you should cast your net far and wide before you decide which fish to catch," mocked Edward.

"Edward! I think no such thing!"

"Really?" smirked Edward. "Then I must be mistaken, or perhaps misunderstood you."

"Yes, you must have!" snapped Anna. "Don't irritate me, Edward! I'm not in the mood!"

Lawrence looked on in confusion at his parents who seemed to be harbouring some unspoken hostility. But if what his father was saying was correct, then the Countess's warning was also true. And he realised it might not be the wisest thing to announce his intention to marry Margaret straight away, at least until Margaret's father had a chance to speak to Edward when they visited and the opportunity to seal the deal and discuss the dowry.

Anna stood up and bent down to kiss Lawrence. "It's wonderful to have you home but I have a headache, so I am retiring to bed early."

"Goodnight, Mama," said Lawrence, taken aback.

Anna walked out of the room without saying anything to Edward.

Edward sighed and closed over his book.

"Is everything all right?" asked Lawrence.

"Everything is fine, my boy," said Edward, gazing into the fire. "I do hope when you are choosing your wife that you pay attention to the girl's temperament. A beautiful wife is a wonderful thing, but behind many a beautiful wife is a complicated character – sometimes unfathomable."

"Oh, if you are talking about Margaret, she's the least complicated person I've ever met. She couldn't hold a secret to save her life!"

"Then she's a find, my boy," Edward said, smiling at him.

CHAPTER 33

Sinclair brooded as he rode out to the Hamilton Estate. He didn't know the Hamiltons or have any connection with them. Although known to be wealthy, they weren't part of Edward and Anna's aristocratic circle, and so were not known to them personally. He knew their estate was huge, running to several thousand acres, nearly as big as the Armstrongs'. Which meant there would be many hundreds of tenant farmers living on it. And he would be trying to find one family, the Hegartys. It would be like trying to find a needle in a haystack and so he would need some assistance. He would find the Hamiltons' estate manager and, with the persuasion of a bribe, he hoped the manager would be able to assist him in his search.

He reached the entrance to the drive that led up to the Hamiltons' manor and saw there was a large gatehouse there. He dismounted and knocked on the door.

A middle-aged man emerged.

"Can I help you, sir?"

"I'm looking for the estate manager?" enquired Sinclair.

"You have just found him," answered the man, looking at Sinclair suspiciously.

Sinclair smiled broadly. "My name is Sinclair Armstrong – what would be yours?"

"Balfour," answered the man.

"You might be able to help me find a family who live on the estate here. Hegarty is the family's name?"

"Are they in some kind of trouble?"

"Not in the least. I'm here to do them a favour and hope they are in the position to do me the same," said Sinclair.

"Mr. Hamilton wouldn't like strangers visiting his tenants without his knowing. I suggest you continue up to the Big House and ask the butler to announce you to Mr. Hamilton and see if he will receive you."

"I'll make it worth your while if you help me, and we could keep this private," said Sinclair as he reached into his inside pocket, took out a wad of notes and held it temptingly out to Balfour.

Balfour stared at the money and Sinclair saw the look on his face change.

"You had better come in," said Balfour, beckoning him inside.

As Sinclair went into the gatehouse, Balfour checked to see nobody had spotted them and then closed the door.

Balfour led Sinclair into a large study stacked with shelves of ledgers and gestured to him to take a seat.

"I don't want any trouble on this estate," warned Balfour. "If you've come to cause trouble then no amount of money you offer me is worth me losing my position here."

"There will be no trouble, that I promise. I just want to speak with them," said Sinclair.

"And what kind of business would a gentleman such as yourself have with a poor tenant family?"

"It's of a private nature, if you don't mind."

"Oh," said Balfour, with a sudden look of realisation on his face. "One of their daughters working on another estate has gone and got herself pregnant, has she?"

"Something like that," said Sinclair.

"Silly bitch! We had a scullery maid up at the Big House here and the same thing happened last summer. Mrs. Hamilton was disgusted by it all. She said, instead of doing her job washing dishes, the girl had been fornicating with the postman! I don't know what became of the girl – she came from King's County and Mrs. Hamilton had her returned to her own people to deal with it themselves."

Sinclair nodded sympathetically. "That kind of thing can be a dreadful smear on the reputation of a Big House."

"It certainly can. I'm glad now I brought you in here and didn't send you up to the house – that kind of thing is not for Mrs. Hamilton's ears," smirked Balfour. "Sure, most of the peasants know better. The local priest tries to keep them in line, but when half of them are sleeping with pigs in the parlour in their hovels of cottages, how are they supposed to know how to behave properly if they manage to get a job in the Big House? The butler and cook try to civilise them when they arrive in to work first, but you can't polish shit!"

"Most true," said Sinclair, thinking that this estate manager might actually treat the tenant farmers worse and hold them in lower regard than even he did himself.

"Mrs. Hamilton said she would only employ staff that come through an agency in Dublin in future. Properly trained with references – that way she hopes to avoid any more scullery-maid scandals!"

"Probably wise," said Sinclair.

Balfour rose from his desk and began to check the spines of the ledgers on his shelves. "But that doesn't help you in your predicament, Mr. Armstrong, in trying to get your problem off your hands and get the wretched creature working in your house back to her family before the story gets out." He stopped at a ledger. "Hegarty – you said the name was?"

"Yes," said Sinclair, sitting forward as Balfour returned to his desk with a huge ledger marked 'H'.

Balfour looked at Sinclair and smiled. "If I could have the money first?"

"Of, course," said Sinclair. He reached into his pocket, took out the wad of money and handed it over to the man.

Balfour opened a drawer in his desk with a key and put the money in before locking it again.

"Haughey, Healy – Hegarty!" said Balfour as he ran his finger down the pages in the ledger. "There are quite a number of Hegarty families on the estate. Do you have any idea which one the girl is from?"

Sinclair shook his head. "The girl wouldn't say."

"Trying to keep the truth from her family – they'll know soon enough when she arrives back to them as big as a house! *Hmmm*, could be any of these in that case."

"If you gave me directions I could visit them and make enquiries?" asked Sinclair.

"Probably your only option. Poor bastards, the last thing they need is a pregnant daughter dumped back on them – more mouths to feed," laughed Balfour.

A worry had been racing through Sinclair's mind. "Would any of the families named Hegarty have been evicted in the Famine?"

"Mr. Hamilton ordered a lot of evictions here, but I don't remember any Hegarty families being thrown out." Balfour managed to look a little sad. "I remember each eviction we did as if it was yesterday, don't remember having any trouble with any family called Hegarty. I think they managed to keep up with their rent payments."

Sinclair felt relieved.

"Why did you ask that?" asked Balfour then, confused. "The girl couldn't be so old that she left her family here during the Famine, could she?"

"No," laughed Sinclair. "Of course not. Just making sure they are in a position to take her back and not in rent arrears going back years."

"Well, they might still not accept her back," warned Balfour. "I don't know what will happen to her then. But I'll write down the directions to all the Hegarty farms and you can do your own investigation from here."

"Thank you, Mr. Balfour," said Sinclair.

Sinclair covered many miles on the Hamilton Estate that day, following the directions that Balfour had given him. As he travelled he realised the land was quite barren and rocky in comparison to the Armstrong Estate. The Hamilton Estate was on the wild Atlantic coast, with views stretching for miles across the ocean. Beautiful to look at, Sinclair thought, but a harsh environment for the farmers to try to earn a living. It was no surprise to Sinclair that Seán had left there as a very young man to try and get a better life elsewhere.

Sinclair visited Hegarty family after Hegarty family to enquire if they were related to Seán. The locals treated him with suspicion and curiosity as he made his enquiries. He found bribery helped oil their mouths.

After he had turned his horse from a dozen families that failed to know or be related to Seán, he was beginning to despair. Perhaps they were lying, he thought – but they had no reason to lie. He had told the families he was offering a big reward to find Seán, and was in a position to give him a large amount of money if he found him. Besides, Sinclair had also become an excellent judge of character, having managed tenants for so many years. He could sense when they were lying, or hiding the truth, and he sensed none of that as he interviewed these people.

He hoped Davis hadn't got the name of the estate wrong. Or perhaps only said he came from the Hamilton Estate to appease him. Sinclair sighed as he rode along the coastline, the sea crashing against the cliffs below him. He checked Balfour's directions and continued on till he reached another cluster of small farmhouses and rode down the drive to the first one. He dismounted and saw some unwashed children playing in the dirt in the yard in front of a small thatched cottage. To think that Lawrence was descended from such people, thought Sinclair as he approached the cottage door. He knocked loudly and peered inside.

"Hello?" he called.

As he continued to peer inside, his eyes widened in shock as he saw a figure come out of the shadows.

Lawrence was walking down the stairs, whistling happily to himself at the thought of seeing Margaret again soon when he spotted Harry in the corner of the hallway whispering to Gertie. He slowed his step as he watched them and then they suddenly became aware of his presence.

Gertie went red in the face and rushed past him to the back of the stairs and down to the servants' quarters.

"Hello, Lawrence," smiled Harry. "Just here to drop this rent money to your father."

"I think he's in the library," said Lawrence.

"Indeed. I hear the Mountdares are coming to stay?"

"That's correct."

"I believe my mother received some invitations for us for events here during their stay. It will be nice to see Lady Margaret again," said Harry with a wink.

"Yes, it will," said Lawrence.

Harry leaned near to Lawrence and spoke conspiratorially. "Have you had any luck with the maids yet?"

Lawrence shook his head. "No, I haven't."

"I told you to try Gertie – she's a goer!" said Harry with another wink.

"Yes, indeed," said Lawrence.

"Anyway – you and I have hardly done anything since you arrived. Let's go for a ride to Knockmore tomorrow and we can do some fishing while we're there."

"I'm actually quite busy tomorrow. Perhaps another time?"

Harry shrugged. "Suit yourself. I'd better deliver this money to your father."

With that, he walked past Lawrence and went to the library door which he knocked on before entering. Lawrence looked after him. Ever since Harry had implied that he had been having a liaison with Gertie and whatever other members of the household staff, Lawrence had tried to keep a distance from him. He found it deplorable that Harry should, first of all, take advantage of somebody in a subservient position as he claimed he had. But he found it equally deplorable that an Armstrong, albeit an untitled one, would lower themselves to bed a maid. His mother had always warned him to keep a distance from Harry and said they were not of the same class even though they shared the same blood and surname. Lawrence was beginning to think that his mother, on this one, was right. Even if Harry was at best gentry, he should not be messing around with maids and it said everything about him and his character. What's more, if this liaison were ever to become public Harry would bring shame on the House of Armstrong and was risking his own future on the estate if the truth ever came out. Lawrence was sure a man of his own father's moral compass would have Harry fired from the estate if he found out, relative or not.

Lawrence thought back to that day he nearly drowned on the lake in Harry's company. It was so long ago and the memory had become hazy over the years, so that sometimes he wondered if he had imagined that Harry had deliberately overturned the boat. He was just a child at the time, after all, with a child's vivid imagination. But he'd always had a bad feeling about Harry since that day. When he returned to live at Armstrong House he had wanted to forget that bad feeling and become friends with Harry again, as when they were children. But now everything he was learning about Harry as an adult was warning him to stay away from him.

CHAPTER 34

Present Day

Kate sat at her computer at her desk in the library. She needed to find out more about the shooting party the week of the assault. If she could find out who was there it could help narrow down who might have been the woman who was attacked and who was the guilty party. From the local paper it sounded as if it was a glamorous affair and there were important guests staying at Armstrong House that week. She reasoned Lord and Lady Armstrong were prominent people, friends of the Prince and Princess of Wales, so their activities and social events might be reported in the press the same way those of celebrities were today. If so, it might have made the national press as well.

She began to do a search through the newspapers' archives. She decided to start with the *Times* as it was the leading newspaper of the day. She typed the year 1865 into the *Times* search engine and put in the name 'Armstrong'. She then narrowed it down by putting in 'Lord Armstrong estate'. To her surprise an announcement came up on the screen in the announcements section.

'*The Earl and Countess of Mountdare of Kilternan Manor, County Kildare, are delighted to announce the engagement of their daughter Lady Margaret to Viscount Lawrence Armstrong, son of Lord and Lady Armstrong of Armstrong House, County Mayo.*'

She looked at the date the article was published and saw it was the 13th of August 1865.

"The same day as the assault," she said to herself. So, not only was the week of the assault one of the most important weeks of the year for Armstrong House with the Glorious 12th but also Edward and Anna's son had become engaged to Lady Margaret Mountdare. She imagined there must have been a fever of excitement and festivity in the house.

And then in the middle of all this there had been a violent assault. As she looked around the library she imagined how the atmosphere must have changed in an instant from joy to horror.

Kate sat in silence for a while and then stood up. A tour was in process and Valerie had offered to assist in showing the tourists around. Kate decided to go and check on how Valerie was doing.

Two weeks had gone by since Valerie had come to stay. Kate really didn't mind her being there. It was the height of the tourist season and so Valerie was more than coming in handy helping out with Cian and, as she was doing that day, helping with the tourists who seemed to really like her and warm to her.

Kate entered the hall and, standing at a discreet distance, watched as Valerie conducted the tour.

"And this is Lady Hilda Bagswagon Armstrong who eloped to the Caribbean where she found herself engaged in a torrid love affair with a native," said Valerie, pointing to the portrait of Lady Anna and Lord Edward to a group of tourists.

Kate waited until the tourist group had gone and cornered Valerie in the drawing room.

"Valerie!" said Kate angrily. "If you're going to help with the tours then stick to the script! Stop making up rubbish!"

"They were Japanese! They hadn't a word of English between them. I could tell them she was Hitler's love child and they wouldn't understand what I was saying!"

"Enough, Valerie!" snapped Kate. "If you want to continue to help then stick to the script I gave you."

"Sorry, darling! It won't happen again!" promised Valerie, looking suitably contrite.

"This might be a bit of fun for you, but the tours provide the income that we need to run this place!"

"I know, darling, I promise it won't happen again."

"Thank you!"

Kate sat down and, taking out her diary, looked at the tours for the rest of the week.

"It's not that I don't appreciate your help," she said as she did so.

"No need to say another word, Kate – I totally understand," said Valerie as she walked around the room, inspecting the antique furniture and the paintings on the walls. "I shouldn't have been so flippant. Hey, are all these real antiques?"

"Yes."

"They must have cost a fortune."

"Yes, they did. They were bought when I was married to Tony and money was no object."

"But the frames on these paintings alone must be priceless. Why don't you just sell a few antiques and solve all your money problems? Then you wouldn't have to waste your time with bus tours."

Kate looked up from her diary. "I couldn't do that! Some of them are originals that we had painstakingly restored and the rest are exact replicas that cost a fortune to commission. They are as much a part of Armstrong House as the bricks or the views of the lake."

"Just saying!"

"Also, that's very short-term thinking. If we start selling off the family silver, what will we have then?" said Kate.

"True. I wish I could be more practical-thinking like you, Kate," sighed Valerie.

Later that day Kate read and reread the police report from Sergeant Bourke from the night of the assault in 1865. If only he had pushed for more information to include in his report. But she realised Lord Edward was a very important man and the Sergeant didn't want to push him further if he did not want to cooperate. Besides, the Sergeant probably even saw the Armstrong estate as outside his jurisdiction and under the complete authority of Lord Edward.

"What were you hiding? What were you covering up?" she asked as she looked up at the portrait of Edward and Anna one evening.

"Talking to yourself? First sign of madness," said Nico as he came down the stairs behind Cian.

"Then I must be completely mad – I'm always talking to myself," said Kate as she went and hugged Cian.

"Have you got any further with your – 'investigation'?" Nico said the last word sarcastically.

"No, I've hit a brick wall," she said.

"Oh, well. Never mind," he said.

"Mummy, come on!" Cian tugged at her hand. "We're going to watch a movie downstairs before I go to bed."

"Sweetheart, I have something to do first – I'll be down to you in a short while and I'll make some popcorn! How about that?"

"Yay! My fav'rit!"

Nico threw her a cynical look. "Right – suit yourself." He took Cian's hand and they continued to the back of the stairs and down to the basement.

Kate watched them go. If Nico's lack of interest in her film was beginning to annoy her, his implied criticism of her reaction to Cian infuriated her.

She went back into the library and read the police report again. She read out the line from Sergeant Bourke's report: *"Lord Armstrong said the woman in question was being attended to by a doctor."*

She suddenly wondered who the doctor was. She assumed he would have had his practice in Castlewest and there couldn't have been that many doctors in Castlewest at the time – perhaps only one. But she knew the nearest census to 1865 would have been in 1861 and those records hadn't survived. Incredibly, they were intentionally destroyed by the government after statistical information had been extracted from them – it was unclear why – some issue to do with a promise of confidentiality on one of the forms was the suggested reason.

She wondered if Daniel might have any information on the local doctors from the work he was doing at the famine grave.

The next day Kate walked through the gates onto the excavation site and saw the team of experts working painstakingly on the site. She spotted Daniel who was supervising a dig and walked over to him.

"Hello there," he said cheerily.

"How is everything going?"

"We are making great progress. We've transferred some of the bodies to the labs and already started to do autopsies."

"Well done!"

"How is your own project going?" he asked.

"Well, I was wondering if you could help me. I'm trying to find out who the doctor was who was mentioned on the police report the night of that assault. Do you have any information on the doctor who attended here at the workhouse? I know that would have been years before the assault but I was wondering if it could be the same man?"

"Unfortunately, no, Kate. The doctor who attended here was the District Doctor, a man called Atkins. When I say the word 'attended', I use it in the loosest possible way. Although he is down as the official doctor he rarely visited. What faced him was far too overwhelming for him to deal with, as we can see from this mass grave. Anyway, it couldn't be Atkins who attended the night of the assault."

"Why?"

"He eventually caught typhus, probably from visiting here, and died at the end of the famine period in 1850," said Daniel.

"So he was long dead by 1865. I wonder who replaced him?"

"Follow me into my office," said Daniel and he led her into the building.

There he began a search on his computer.

"My father is a doctor and, from what I know, all doctors in Ireland have had to register with the Medical Directory, and that's been since the beginning of time." He pointed at the screen. "Yes, all doctors have had to register since 1858 in what was then the United Kingdom of Great Britain and Ireland. The records of the Irish doctors since then are kept in Dublin at the Irish Medical Directory." He wrote down the address and phone number of the institute on a Post-it and handed it to her.

"That's wonderful, Daniel," she said.

He pulled a face. "Even if you find out who the local doctor was, Kate, I doubt they have any records from way back then. It would have been just a country practice, and those records wouldn't have been archived."

"Well, this is a start," she said, smiling at him.

That night as they were going to bed, Nico asked, "Kate, has Valerie mentioned at all when she is leaving?"

"No."

"Well, then, she mustn't have bought a return ticket to New York."

"I don't know."

"Well, don't you think it would be good for us to know how long she plans to stay?"

His voice was even and so Kate didn't deduce that Valerie had done anything in particular to drive him mad that day.

"Well, she isn't getting in the way that much, is she? In fact, she's only too eager to help out all the time," she said.

"Well, no, she's like a veritable Mary Poppins around the place, if one can ignore the constant chattering and keep filling her with wine."

"She's on her holidays, Nico, she's entitled to a few drinks!"

"I'm not saying she isn't. It's just this is beginning to feel a little more than just a holiday. She doesn't discuss any plans she has, any work she's waiting for, anything about the future. All she talks about is her past, which usually involves men. I just think there might be something else going on, something she's not saying."

"Maybe you're right, I don't know. She seems really happy so I don't think there is anything troubling her. But I'll try to have a word with her and see if there is anything else going on. It won't be tomorrow though."

"Why not?"

"I'm in Dublin tomorrow."

"Something to do with your film?"

"Yes – I've made an appointment at the Medical Directory office in Dublin. I'm trying to find out who the local doctor was here, at the time of the attack on that woman."

"I see. If you had given me a bit f notice I could have arranged my schedule and worked from home to mind Cian," said Nico.

"It's not a problem – Valerie is minding him."

Nico wanted to comment that it seemed to suit Kate very well having Valerie stay. It gave her more freedom to do her research on her film. She also seemed to be so preoccupied with the film that she didn't give Cian the time he needed. It worried him. He wasn't just a jealous husband, resentful of his wife's work, and looking for all her attention. He always worried that perhaps she wasn't truly satisfied with her life with him and being a mother to Cian. That maybe they weren't enough for her. He knew how much she loved him and Cian, but he also knew she was formerly a successful actress with a wealthy husband, who had lived a very exciting life, receiving a lot of attention. He worried that making this film would entice her back into that world and away from Cian and him.

But he decided to say nothing as he didn't want it to lead to another argument.

CHAPTER 35

At the Medical Directory office in Dublin, Kate sat with the friendly warm administrator in her office.

"I read about the new film you're doing – is this in connection with it?"

"It is actually," said Kate with a smile.

"I saw your last film – the one you made on your house. Such an interesting place to live!"

"Yes, I'm very lucky."

As the woman continued to grin at her, Kate realised she might be a fan.

"I used to watch you in your films years ago – I used to love them."

"Oh, thank you," said Kate, hoping her fascination might make her go the extra mile to help her with her research.

"Now, you were looking to see who was the doctor in Castlewest, County Mayo, in – what year?"

"1865. I understand you keep records from 1858?"

"That's correct," said the administrator as she began a search on her computer.

"There might have been more than one doctor in the locality?"

"Perhaps."

Kate waited, trying to possess herself in patience, as her eager helper tapped on keys and frowned at the screen.

"Actually, no," the woman said at last. "There was just one according to the register at the time. And his name was Doctor

Barry Davitt, and his practice was at Manor Street in Castlewest up until 1870. Then he moved to the hospital in Castlewest which was established in that year."

"So he worked at the hospital from then on?"

"Yes, doctors were few and far between back then so he was probably appointed to head the hospital as he was the only one in the vicinity."

"Can I ask if there is any way you could check if there were any records kept from Doctor Davitt's practice before he left for the hospital?"

"No, we don't keep the actual records from the doctors, only their details."

"I wonder what became of the records?"

"I imagine a country doctor's records from the nineteenth century would have been destroyed, Kate," the administrator said sympathetically

Kate left the offices of the Medical Directory feeling excited and deflated all at once. She now knew who the doctor was who had attended the victim on that night. It had to be Doctor Davitt as there was no other doctor within twenty miles. She had an idea and a hope regarding his records but it was a slim chance.

She took out her phone and rang Daniel.

"Any luck?" he asked.

"Yes, I got the name, a Doctor Davitt who was the local doctor in the 1860s. But as you had warned no records were kept. But I found out that he was made head of the hospital when it opened in Castlewest. And I know that all hospital records are kept at the National Archives."

"Okay . . ."

"But they are notoriously hard to access. I know, I dealt with them for my last docudrama and the obstacles were many. I suppose people's medical records are still considered private even a century and a half later. I was just wondering, hoping, that with you doing the work in Castlewest and it being government-funded, you might be able to arrange for me to have access?" She held her breath, as she knew it was a huge favour.

"Leave it with me and I'll see what I can do," he said. "I'll ring you back."

Kate spent the next hour waiting anxiously before Daniel got back to her.

"Okay, I got you an appointment on Friday at two in the afternoon at the National Archives," he said. "I've said it's in connection with the famine-grave work, so don't say anything to contradict that or I'll be in trouble."

"Oh, Daniel, I don't know how to thank you!"

"You already have. If you hadn't given me Hunter's Farm, I'd still be in a hotel room in the Castletown Arms!"

Kate and Valerie lay on sun loungers out in the terraced garden while Cian played beside them.

"Where's Nico today?" asked Valerie.

"He has a meeting in Dublin," she said. "He won't be back till late. Speaking of Dublin, I have to go there on Friday. Any chance you could look after Cian again?"

"Of course. You know I love spending time with him. What are you doing in Dublin – shopping?"

"I wish! No, Daniel organised an appointment for me at the National Archives – I'm just trying to dig up some information for my film."

"Daniel organised it? You seem to be getting on very well with him?"

"Yes, we do get on very well actually. I find the work he is doing at the famine grave fascinating, and he is really interested in my film. Which is more than Nico ever is."

"He does seem to be resentful of you working. Maybe he wants a little housewife at home. What did his first wife do?"

"She's a journalist, so I don't think Nico expects a wife to be a stay-at-home mum," said Kate. "No, Nico certainly doesn't mind me working – I think he just doesn't like the work I do. He's quite protective over his family's privacy and history and he's inclined to think I prostitute it out to earn a crust!"

"Well, at the end of the day you're from a very different

background and have led a very different life from Nico, Kate. I remember as a child before we emigrated to America, his family used to come down on holidays here from Dublin. They seemed a right lot of toffee-nosed twits. And then being a well-known actress, you're used to and love dealing with the public. All Nico seems to like to deal with is his architect's board! To be honest, I don't know how you two ever got it together! Unless it was a case of opposites attract?"

"Well, I suppose we bonded when we worked together restoring Armstrong House. As you know, he was the architect Tony and I employed when we bought the house and were restoring it."

"Oh – I see!" said Valerie, knowingly.

Kate quickly lifted her sunglasses and looked over at Valerie. "Nico and I didn't have an affair, if that's what you're thinking. Both our marriages were well and truly over by the time we got together."

"Oh, I wasn't implying anything," Valerie said innocently. "But you must miss it all, Kate? The life you used to have with Tony? The parties, the glamour, all his money, you being a famous actress back then? It must be hard to try and get used to a normal life after all that. Perhaps that's why you relentlessly pursue making films about the house, to keep you somewhat back in that world?"

"No, I don't miss any of it," said Kate, irritated. "Looking back on it, it was all false and superficial. I've never been happier than I have been these last years with Nico. My life is now Nico, Cian and Armstrong House."

"If you say so," said Valerie. "Though making this film seems to be taking priority over everything else for you at the moment."

"Does it?" said Kate, thinking that clearly Nico thought that too. But she felt her life with Nico was under scrutiny from her sister and felt the need to defend it and him. "And say what you want about Nico, but he's the most sincere person I've ever met – he's genuine and kind. What you see is what you get with Nico. There are no secrets or unpleasant surprises with him . . . he doesn't try to be something he's not and couldn't lie to save his life. And that is something I adore, especially after life with Tony."

"Yes, those are all very commendable qualities. But a gal needs a bit of fun too!"

"Nico is fun," protested Kate.

"*Hmmm*," said Valerie.

"As you said, we're just from a different background than Nico – you just don't understand him."

They sunbathed in silence for a while.

"Ah, this is the life!" said Valerie. "So much nicer than the hustle and bustle of New York."

Cian came over with some flowers he had uprooted rather than picked from a flower bed and handed them to Kate.

"Oh, are they for me?" she said.

"Yes, specially for you," said Cian, giving her a hug.

"What about me? I'm feeling jealous," said Valerie.

"I'll pick you some too," said Cian and he ran back to the flower bed.

Kate pulled a face. "Let's just hope the gardener doesn't catch him rooting up his precious flowers!"

Valerie giggled. "I'll take the blame," she said.

"He'll hound you back to New York!" Then Kate seized this opening of the subject. She settled back on her sun lounger and said, "Actually, don't you have any commitments back in New York, Valerie? Won't your employers be missing you?"

"Oh no, you know the club business in New York, Kate. I'll just pick up where I left off when I get back."

"When are you planning on going back?" Kate asked, making sure to keep her voice light.

"Oh, I'm not so sure."

"Did you not buy a return ticket?" asked Kate.

"No, I just got a single."

"I see," said Kate.

Valerie suddenly sat up and took off her sunglasses. "Oh! You want me gone!"

Kate also sat up quickly. "No, of course not!"

"Well, Nico does then." Valerie reached for her cardigan and draped it over her shoulders "You know I had a French boyfriend once who said that house guests were like fish – they start to go off and smell after three days! I've obviously gone very stale at Armstrong House at this stage! I always thought Nico didn't like me! Well, I'll be gone in the morning."

Valerie stood up and walked over to the steps up to the forecourt.

"Valerie! Will you wait!" said Kate, struggling off the sun bed and running after her. "I said nothing about you not being welcome here. We love you being here. Cian absolutely adores you and I can't tell you how much help you've been to me!"

"That's all very well, but Nico wants me gone! I should have known he didn't want me here!"

"Valerie!" exclaimed Kate, shocked by Valerie's outburst. "Nico loves you being here!"

"Liar!" cried Valerie, and began to sob. "He *hates* me!"

"He does no such thing!" said Kate, reaching out and embracing her.

"I've tried to stay out of his way as much as possible. I try not to be a nuisance. I try my best to cook every day and mind Cian and I even did dusting yesterday!"

"I know! And we so much appreciate it. Valerie, you are being absurd! Please calm down!" pleaded Kate.

"Aunty Valerie, what's the matter?" Cian was looking up at his aunt in dismay, his fist full of flowers. "Look! I brought you flowers!" He looked in danger of bursting out crying as well at seeing Valerie so upset.

Valerie began to wipe her eyes. "Oh, so you did! You're a good boy!" She took the flowers with their earthy roots from him and smiled.

"Why don't you get some more, love?" said Kate. "And Aunty Valerie can put them in her room?"

Cian nodded enthusiastically and rushed off.

"I'm sorry, Kate," said Valerie. "I just get so emotional when I suffer rejection."

"But we're not rejecting you, Valerie. You're my sister, I love you!"

"A sister you haven't seen in years, and then I just show up and start freeloading and annoying her husband!"

"That's just nonsense, Valerie. If the truth be told, Nico only asked was everything all right in your life. He just got a feeling everything might not be as good as you've made out."

Valerie bit her lip. "Nico is a wise man, Kate."

"Are you in some kind of trouble, Valerie?"

Valerie nodded. "Well, not me exactly – my boyfriend is."

"And who is your boyfriend?" asked Kate, becoming alarmed.

"A guy from Spain – Carlos. We've only been going out a few months. And it turned out he owed money to some people and then he went into hiding and then the people he owed money to came hassling me, threatening all sorts. And I didn't know what to do and so I just got on a plane to Ireland!"

"Oh, Valerie! Why didn't you just go to the police?"

"They're not the kind of people you go to the police about, unless you want to get yourself into a whole lot more trouble."

"And who is this guy? This Carlos?"

"Well, he just seemed to be the sweetest kindest man I ever met. But – he got involved in something to do with gambling."

"Oh, Valerie!" Kate was horrified.

"And casinos – that's how I met him – I was singing in a casino in New Jersey." Valerie suddenly burst into sobs again.

"*Shhh – shhh* . . ." Kate tried to soothe her. "You'll upset Cian again."

"I didn't know what to do, Kate. Those men were really threatening, and I couldn't get hold of Carlos, so I just fled."

"You did the right thing, Valerie. Of *course* you should have come to me – I just wish you'd told me everything from the beginning."

"I was too ashamed to! You with your perfect husband and child and life – and me *on the run from the mob!*" Valerie wailed.

"And what are you going to do about those people?"

"I just thought I'd lie low here for a while, and then go back when the coast was clear."

"But surely they would understand that this debt is nothing to do with you?"

"They don't care – they think by putting pressure on me that Carlos will come out of hiding and give them what they want."

As Kate looked at Valerie, her heart went out to her. Although it was very different from the situation Valerie was in, she remembered being held accountable for Tony's business dealings in the past and the terrible feeling of being held responsible for something you didn't know about. Maybe she was more like her sister than she ever realised.

"Look, you can stay here at Armstrong House as long as you want," she said. "I don't want you going back to New York until you are comfortable and, most important, safe to do it."

"But I can't stay, if Nico wants me gone."

"Nico doesn't want you gone, Valerie – get that idea out of your head. Leave Nico to me and I really don't want you to worry about anything any more. I want you to feel safe and protected here." Kate hugged her sister tightly.

"Mummy, is Aunty Valerie crying again?" asked Cian and he hugged their legs.

"She just felt a little sad, but now she's happy again, love," said Kate, stroking his tousled hair.

That night in their bedroom Kate explained to Nico the situation Valerie was in. She wasn't sure how he would react. He had never even got a parking fine in all his life and here she was telling him her sister was on the run from the mob.

"And who is this guy?" asked Nico, trying to digest the information.

"A Spanish guy called Carlos," said Kate.

"Valerie is like the United Nations she's been out with that many nationalities!"

"She's never been a wise chooser of men."

"You can say that again. It's all so – seedy, Kate."

"It's not seedy," objected Kate.

"Really? Being on the run from the mob? It's not exactly Teddy Bears' Picnic stuff, is it?"

"She's just had a bit of bad luck. And she's taking time out to pick herself up and dust herself down."

"So we're stuck with her until who knows when?" he said, despairing.

"It won't be that long, I'm sure," said Kate.

"Well, I'm not so sure. And what if these people come looking for her here, Kate? We have to think of Cian and put his safety first."

"They aren't going to find her here. They don't know anything about her and the west of Ireland is the last place they'll look. My guess is these guys aren't the Mafia, they are just small-time hoodlums who will move on very quickly. I grew up in New York, remember – there are lots of guys like that, all mouth and no trousers."

"Well, I hope you're right," he said.

"I would have thought, I would have hoped, that you might have shown some sympathy here in this situation, Nico. I know all this is very alien to you and your world, but at the same time I would have hoped for some compassion from you. I guess I was wrong." She was more disappointed than angry. "Maybe I just need to accept that we are very different people and just get on with it. Maybe I should stop expecting you to be someone you're not and you stop expecting me to be someone I'm not."

He looked at her and saw the disappointment in her face. He didn't know why they were at each other's throats recently. He wasn't sure if it was being caused by Valerie's presence, or Kate's new film and the knowledge of the upheaval it would cause in their lives, or her preoccupation with the excavation with the famine grave and this Daniel character. But he did feel ashamed that his initial reaction to Valerie's problems was annoyance rather than sympathy.

He went over to Kate and put his arms around her. "Look, of course she can stay. Valerie is your sister and Cian's aunt so of course I don't want any harm to come to her."

"And will you try to be nice to her, Nico? Less of the sarcastic comments?"

"It's she makes the sarcastic comments!"

"Nico!" she pleaded.

"Okay! I'll be nice as pie to her. I'll even order in more crates of wine for her. And if any mobsters come around here looking for trouble, I'll throw my architect's board at them – that should see them off!"

"Thanks," she said, managing to dredge up a smile.

CHAPTER 36

1865

Armstrong House was being prepared for the visit of the Mountdares which was scheduled for the following week. Anna was sitting in the drawing room, going through menus with Taylor.

"Yes, these all look excellent, Taylor," she said as she quickly read through them.

"Thank you, my lady," said Taylor, chuffed with himself. He had spent hours going through the menus with the cook.

"All is prepared for the garden party during their stay?"

"Everything will be ready for the day. And I posted your invitations myself yesterday."

"Please impress on all the staff how important the Mountdares' visit is. The Countess is known for her impeccable taste and eye for detail. If anything is out of place, she will mentally note it, and it will reflect badly on us." To put it more accurately, the Countess was renowned for her snobbery and nobody could compete with her social graces. Anna did think Lawrence was rushing in too fast with his feelings for Margaret, but she did not want to let him down in any way.

"Is that all for now, my lady?" asked Taylor.

"Yes," said Anna with a smile.

He took the menus, bowed and left the room.

Anna bit her lip. The last thing she needed was a visit from the Mountdares. Not with so much going on in her mind since Georgina's visit that she could hardly sleep at night with worry. But she had no choice. The Mountdares were coming, whether she liked it or not, and she would have to disguise the utter fear in her heart while they were there. She wished Georgina was there with her. At least then she would have somebody to discuss her predicament with. And Georgina had always been so clever, and often ruthless with her plotting. As much as she racked her brains, Anna could not think of anything that could discredit Sinclair to such an extent that he would be removed from their lives forever. Even when she was convinced that Harry was trying to kill Lawrence when he was a child, Edward did not take her seriously enough to get rid of Sinclair and his family. She knew deep down he had never believed her theory about Harry being behind the accidents that had befallen Lawrence, and had only agreed to move to London as an act of appeasing her. Now, all she could think of was what Sinclair was up to, what he was planning to accomplish her and Lawrence's downfall. She tried to convince herself that Georgina was always a Cassandra who looked on the worst scenario of a situation. How could Sinclair possibly expose her? Her only Achilles' Heel through the years had been Georgina because she had been privy to what she had done. But now Georgina had assured her she was her friend and not her enemy.

She got up and walked out of the drawing room and down the hallway to the library. She opened the door and entered.

Edward was working at his desk and she saw he was counting a large amount of money.

"Is everything all right?" he asked.

"Yes!" She smiled at him as she sat down. "Everything is on course for a wonderful stay for the Mountdares."

"Lawrence will be pleased to hear that," he said.

"I think we couldn't have put in better preparations if it actually was the Prince and Princess of Wales coming to stay!"

"Good." Edward sat back and looked at her seriously. "Anna?"

"Yes?" she said, nervous at his tone.

"You know, I suspect that Margaret's father will request a private conversation with me where he will bring up the prospect of an engagement between Lawrence and his daughter."

"Oh!" she said, shocked. "Whatever makes you say that?"

"Oh, from Lawrence's demeanour and a few hints."

"I have noticed no such hints! And if he had anything to say about a courtship he would obviously tell me, his mother!"

"Anna, you would be the last person Lawrence would drop hints to! You have been far from encouraging about the relationship!"

Anna felt wounded at the very idea of Lawrence not confiding in her and alarmed at the notion the Earl might open a matchmaking discussion with Edward. "But, in any case, what would the Earl want to discuss at this very early stage of proceedings?"

"He would wish to discuss Margaret's dowry – and Lawrence's financial situation. He might want to encourage the engagement with the dowry and also get an assurance from us that we are financially comfortable enough for Margaret to marry into."

"And are we?" asked Anna. She left all business details to Edward, and actually had no idea what they worth, apart from what they owned in property.

"Quite comfortable enough, I should think, to impress the Earl that his daughter – and her dowry – are going to a safe home!" Edward chuckled.

Anna looked at Edward, and wondered how he was always so relaxed and good-humoured and never took anything too seriously. Then she realised he was quite protected from the world. If he carried the secrets she did, he would be a very different man from who he was.

Anna watched as he gathered the stacks of money from the desk and carried them over to a sideboard on which he placed them. He pulled back the heavy sideboard and opened the safe that was behind it with the key he always kept in his breast pocket. She watched as he knelt and put the money in the safe to join the rest of the rent collection for the month. He then locked the safe and pushed the sideboard back into place. The monthly rent was always kept in the safe until it was brought to the bank at the end of each month to be deposited. Anna knew the routine well over the years. Edward was the only person who had a key to the safe, except for Sinclair who had been given a spare key for the years that they were in London.

242

An idea flashed through her mind. She remembered Edward telling her when they had arrived back from London that he was leaving the spare key with Sinclair in case of an emergency. She remembered being irritated when he told her, but it had made sense in case anything did happen to Edward and the key was lost, denying them access to the safe.

She continued to stare at the sideboard.

"I think it's going to be a nice evening," mused Edward as he looked out the window. "Shall we take in a walk down by the lake before dinner?"

"Eh – yes." She smiled at him and took the hand he was offering her to assist her from her chair.

CHAPTER 37

That night Anna lay in bed awake, staring at the ceiling. Edward lay fast asleep beside her. She glanced at him as he slept silently. He was the most silent sleeper, she thought. He never made a sound and hardly stirred while he slept. She remembered Lady Fitzherbert divulging once that she and her husband never shared a room. That she could simply not bear his snoring and so insisted on separate rooms. So unlike Edward, Anna thought. He slept as he lived his life in waking hours, with impeccable decorum. No guilty secrets to keep him awake at night, no fear of being exposed for past sins. As she watched him sleep, and with the real fear that she could lose him if she was exposed, she felt she had never loved him more. Not even when they first met in her father's house in Dublin when he was visiting and she had fallen instantly in love with him.

The curtains were open and she could see the full moon in the sky outside. She sighed, slipped out of the four-poster bed and walked over to the window. She looked out across the lake spread out into the distance, the moon weaving its ghostly light across the water's surface.

Then she glanced below to the forecourt and saw a figure standing in the centre of the forecourt, looking up at the house.

"Who on earth is that?" she whispered to herself, as she stepped nearer the window pane to get a better view. As she stared down, she could see that it was Lawrence in the courtyard.

"Lawrence?" she whispered to herself in confusion and worry as to why he was out there alone at this time of night.

She went to open the window to call down to him, but as she looked again she realised it wasn't Lawrence. Her heart began to throb in her chest.

"*Seán!*" she gasped.

She stood in terror for a moment and then closed her eyes – and when she opened them again he was gone.

She eyes anxiously searched the forecourt but she couldn't see him. She quickly opened the window and leaned out, but nobody was there. She frantically looked all around and could neither see nor hear anybody.

She quickly closed the window and her head began to ache. Was her mind playing tricks on her? With all the recent stress? It couldn't be Seán! He had disappeared twenty years ago. Suddenly she was terrified that her mind was playing tricks on her and it *had* actually been Lawrence standing out there, and she had mistaken him for Seán with everything going on. She started to panic.

"*Edward!*" cried Anna loudly as she ran to the bed and shook Edward.

"W-w-what is it?" asked Edward, struggling awake.

"It's Lawrence! Quick, get up! He's outside the house! He must be sleepwalking or something! Wake Taylor and the servants! Before he falls into the lake or something!" She ran to the bell-pull and tugged it.

"What are you talking about?" said Edward, sitting up.

"Lawrence is outside the house, wandering around. He must be sleepwalking!"

Edward got out of bed and pulled on his dressing gown.

"I saw Lawrence out in the forecourt, Edward! I don't know what he'd be doing out there – he must be in a trance or something. We must find him!" She raced from the bedroom and down the corridor to the top of the steps where a dazed Taylor was coming up the stairs in his nightgown and nightcap.

"Did you call, my lady?" asked Taylor, confused. It was three in the morning.

"Yes, Taylor. We must wake all the servants and find Master Lawrence. He is out in the gardens, and I fear in some danger!"

Edward stood behind Anna, wondering what on earth was going on. Lawrence had never been subject to sleepwalking. As far as Edward was aware, Lawrence was as sound a sleeper as he was. As Anna continued to issue instructions to a confused Taylor, Edward walked quickly down the corridor to Lawrence's room. He swung open the door and saw the room was lit up dimly from the dying fire.

In the large bed was the sleeping form of Lawrence.

"*Anna*!" shouted Edward down the corridor.

"What?"

"Come here!"

"We don't have time!"

"*Now*!" shouted Edward.

Anna quickly walked down to him.

Edward pointed to the bed.

Lawrence was beginning to sit up and rub his eyes. "What's happening? What's the matter?" he said, alarmed.

Edward stared at Anna in fury as she stood stock still.

"Nothing, Lawrence. Nothing's the matter. Go back to sleep," said Edward as he closed the door.

Anna watched as Edward marched angrily down the corridor to the stairs.

"I apologise for the disturbance, Taylor," he said. "Please go back to bed."

"Yes, my lord," said Taylor who quickly turned and left.

Anna walked down the corridor back to their bedroom and followed Edward inside. She saw that the fury on his face was not dissipating.

"I'm sorry – I thought I saw Lawrence outside," she mumbled.

"*What is wrong with you?* You nearly woke the whole house!"

"I must have mistaken somebody else for Lawrence and I just feared –"

"You feared Lawrence was going to be killed! I know! I've heard it so many times before! This had to *stop now*, Anna!" shouted Edward. "I thought we had left all this behind us! When you thought he was in danger here as a child. When you were accusing

Harry of trying to kill him! And now you are starting again! Because the problem is, Anna, the problem is *you*! You don't want to be here. You don't want to be at Armstrong House. And you forced us to leave last time by lying to me, lying to yourself that Lawrence wasn't safe here. And now, because I won't go back to London as you want, you are starting the whole thing again!"

"No! I'm not! I did see –"

"Enough, Anna, enough! I will not go through all this again with you like I did before. I will not listen to your fantasies this time! This time – *you will not get your way*! I'm happy here, Lawrence is happy here, and I really don't care any more if you're not happy here. I've had enough. Now I'm going back to bed."

Edward shrugged off his dressing gown and threw himself back into bed.

Anna stood still as she watched him become still again. Then she went over to the armchair beside the fire and sat down, sinking her face into her hands.

CHAPTER 38

There was a coolness between Edward and Anna after that night. On the afternoon of the Mountdares' arrival, as her maid helped her change, she thought of that night and how she had woken the whole house in near hysterics. Edward, in typical fashion, had not mentioned the night since. She cringed at the thought of it, and what he must think of her. All she could think was that she had been hallucinating when she thought she saw Seán out in the forecourt. That the pressure of Sinclair knowing the truth and her risk of being exposed had made her see the figure in the moonlight. Perhaps she had been half asleep when she looked out the window. And then thinking she had seen Seán jolted her out of her half-sleep and, fully conscious, she knew it couldn't be Seán and had then reasoned it must be Lawrence due to their physical similarity. And Edward had thought it was all a ploy. Did he really think her so manipulative? Did he really have so little faith in her after all these years?

Anna and Lawrence were to be driven into Castlewest to meet the Mountdares from the train. Lawrence had insisted they go meet their guests instead of just sending a carriage for them.

"They did it for me when I visited them at Kilternan House. They were all at the station to greet me – Margaret, her parents, her sisters and brothers."

"I'm sure they were," said Anna cynically.

As she came down the stairs that morning she saw Taylor in the hall and said, "Taylor, is Lawrence around?"

248

"He's in the library with His Lordship, my lady."

At that moment the library door opened and Lawrence and Edward came out. Edward's hand was on Lawrence's shoulder as he said, "You don't worry about a thing, leave everything to me."

"Thank you, Papa," said Lawrence.

As Anna viewed them she wondered what they had been speaking about – obviously conspiring over something that she was being excluded from.

"Lawrence, if we don't leave soon," she said, "we'll not be there on time and the Mountdares will be left sitting on the platform. You don't want that, do you?"

"No – eh, Taylor, is the carriage ready?" asked Lawrence.

"It is waiting in the forecourt," said Taylor.

"Excellent!" said Lawrence, offering Anna his arm. "In that case, Mama, shall we go?"

Anna took her son's arm and nodded. As she walked past Edward, they didn't acknowledge each other.

Anna and Lawrence were waiting in the carriage outside the train station. Lawrence was excited and kept looking for a sign that the train was coming.

"The train is late!" he declared impatiently.

"For goodness' sake, Lawrence, calm down! You're like a child waiting for Christmas."

"That train is always running bloody late. It's a bore!"

"I'm just grateful we have a train at all!" said Anna, remembering back to the days when they had to make the long journeys cross-country by carriage.

Anna glanced around the street which was teeming with people. It was market day, and so Castlewest was full of farmers selling their goods, their wives selling their wares. As people passed the carriage, they nodded and took off their hats as a mark of respect for the Armstrongs.

Lawrence suddenly stood up. "I'm going to wait on the platform – at least I'll be able to see the train approach from there."

"You do that, dear, if you feel the need," said Anna.

Lawrence climbed down from of the carriage and left.

Anna sat back and sighed. In her present state of mind this visit was going to be an ordeal. She really wasn't up to it and she prayed she would have the strength to put on the kind of show that would be demanded of her.

Time passed and at last she heard the whistle of the approaching train. She stirred and leant out the window to call the driver to help her dismount. Then she sank back in her seat, feeling unable to make the effort. She would just wait for them where she was.

She glanced out the window at the crowded street. The farmers will be happy, she mused. She saw a young girl walk past the carriage smiling up at her, and she smiled warmly back. Then she idly looked across the street to see if the drapery was doing much business.

She suddenly froze. Across the street was a figure staring straight over at her. She blinked a few times and looked again. But the figure was still there, staring at her.

As she stared back, there was no denying who it was.

"*Seán*," she whispered. She felt her whole body go cold.

She flung open the door of the carriage and stumbled out.

Seán had turned and begun to walk away.

"*Wait!*" she called.

"My lady, is everything all right?" asked the driver in alarm, looking back at her from the front of the carriage.

She strained to look through the busy crowd, but the figure of Seán had disappeared

"Here we are!" came the happy voice of Lawrence.

Anna ignored him as her eyes continued to search the crowd.

"Mother!" said Lawrence. "Our guests are here!"

Anna remained standing like a statue staring down the street, as white as a ghost.

"Good afternoon, Lady Anna," said the Countess loudly.

Anna didn't respond.

"Mama?" said Lawrence, putting a hand on her arm.

Anna swung around, startled, and was confounded to see the Mountdares right there staring at her, a porter with their luggage behind them.

"Oh, excuse me! I – I thought I saw an old acquaintance . . . welcome . . . welcome to Mayo!"

"It is wonderful to see you again, Lady Armstrong," said Margaret.

"And you," said Anna.

She shook hands and kissed her guests as the driver and porter loaded the luggage onto the back of the carriage and secured it.

Lawrence assisted Margaret and her mother in, then his mother, before the Earl and he climbed in. He slammed the door shut then leaned out the window. "Drive on!" he ordered the driver and the carriage took off down the street.

"I hope you had a nice journey?" Anna enquired.

"Most comfortable. Most kind of your husband to reserve a carriage on the train for us," said the Countess.

"Yes, he is very kind," said Anna.

The Countess smiled at Lawrence, while trying not to show concern that Anna seemed so pale and distracted.

As Anna eyes continued to search the streets they passed, the Countess looked at her husband and raised an eyebrow.

CHAPTER 39

The Mountdares were shown to their rooms by Taylor. Anna went to her room and lay down straight away. She knew she was being a bad hostess by not being downstairs, waiting for the Mountdares to descend. But she couldn't face them. Nor could she face the rest of the guests who were coming to dinner in a couple of hours.

She knew she had seen Seán, and now she knew she had not been hallucinating the other night when she had seen him in the forecourt. She had managed to get a much better look at him today in the daylight, though it was across the street. He looked older of course – the last time she had seen him was twenty years ago, so he would be in his forties now. He was dressed respectably – not like a gentleman but not like a peasant farmer either. What was he doing back here? Her mind was tumbling with emotions that were going from extreme to extreme. Had he come to exact revenge on her? Had he come to expose her? Had he come to forgive her? She remembered the tender, kind young man he had been. She couldn't imagine he could become as vengeful as that. And yet she had wronged him so badly, more than any man could take.

And then she sat up and whispered, "He's alive! Seán is alive!"

She thought back to the time when she had framed him for the theft and banished him from the estate and then, when the Famine took hold, the years of guilt she had suffered fearing she had sentenced him to certain death. The years of trying to find him and to get him to safety.

And there he was today. Somehow, he had survived the Famine.

She felt relief as the years of guilt lifted, mixed with the fear of what was he would do now. There was a knock on the door and the maid Gertie entered.

"Sorry, my lady, but His Lordship asked me to tell you that dinner is being served in half an hour and that the other guests have arrived and are all in the drawing room with the Mountdares, that's what he said for me to tell you," Gertie said all in one breath as she curtsied.

Anna sat up in bed. "Gertie, can you tell His Lordship that I have a headache and – and I shan't be able to face dinner tonight."

Gertie looked surprised as she knew the amount of work that had gone into the Mountdares' visit and how Taylor kept telling all the servants how important it was.

"All right, my lady," said Gertie as she curtsied again and exited the room, closing the door behind her.

Anna lay back in bed, her mind still swirling with thoughts of Seán.

Five minutes later, the bedroom door swung open and slammed loudly shut. Startled, she opened her eyes and saw an angry Edward in the room.

"Edward, did Gertie not tell you –"

"Yes, she did! You have a headache and can't possibly attend your own dinner tonight!"

She touched her temples. "I don't know where it came from. Just a splitting headache that has quite overwhelmed me –"

"Get out of that bed now and get dressed!" said Edward, storming over to her dressing room.

"Edward!" she cried, shocked. She had never seen him so angry before.

He marched out of the dressing room, carrying a bundle of her ball gowns, and threw them on the floor.

"Edward, did you not hear me! I have a headache!"

"I don't care if you have the black plague! You are getting out of that bed, getting dressed and going to entertain your guests if it kills you!"

"*I will not!*" She was horrified by his forcefulness.

"You *shall*! I will not have you ruin Lawrence's big night. Do you realise that Margaret's father has asked to speak to me privately after dinner? Clearly, Lawrence and Margaret are about to announce their courtship and inevitable engagement."

"*What?*" Anna was stunned. "And he did not think to discuss this with me – his own mother!"

"Not a mother who overreacts to everything and is negative about most things. If Lawrence felt he could not confide in you, then you have nobody to blame but yourself. But make no mistake, the Earl is here to discuss the serious monetary arrangements of the marriage before it can go any further. And *you* will not let Lawrence down in front of his future in-laws! I'm not having you ruin such an important night for him." He started riffling through the gowns that he had thrown on the floor. He picked out a dark-blue gown that had tiny diamantes sewn on it likes stars in a night sky.

He threw the gown at her. "Get dressed."

"You don't scare me, Edward! I will not be bullied by you!"

He marched over to her and grabbed her arms. "There isn't a doubt in my mind that I don't scare you, nor could I ever bully you! I have loved you and put up with your moods for years, because – because I loved you! But when your behaviour now threatens our son's happiness, then I draw the line, and you would be very foolish to cross it. Now are you going to get dressed, or will I do it for you?"

There was something about him in the moment that did scare her. Something she had never seen before in Edward. She shook off his grip and got out of the bed.

With some help from him, she struggled out of the gown she was wearing and into the one he had chosen for her. He helped her to do it up.

She then went to the bell-pull.

"What are you doing?" he asked, halting as he was going to fetch her shoes.

"I need to call my maid," she said. "I need her help to fix my hair."

"There is no time. Just fix it."

Anna returned to the dressing table and did her best to tidy her hair, which luckily had been dressed that morning. She then put on her jewellery.

"Are you ready?" he asked impatiently.

"I'm a *mess*," she said vehemently. "I shall disgrace myself and you and Lawrence!"

"You'll do," he said.

He took her arm and walked her out of the room. He continued to hold her arm tightly, as if he was scared she was going to run away, as they walked down the corridor and began to descend the stairs.

"The man I married would have never behaved like this to me," she hissed at him.

"And the woman I married would never have behaved so selfishly as you are doing tonight," he hissed back.

She stared ahead and didn't answer.

He said, "I know you have been in contact with Georgina. I don't know what is going on between you, but all I know is whenever Georgina has been in our lives there is trouble in our marriage."

She shot a look at him, scared. How did he know about Georgina? Had Georgina betrayed her after all? Why hadn't he said anything before? She felt her world was closing in on her as they reached the bottom of the stairs and saw Taylor was leading the guests across the hallway to the dining room.

She saw Margaret and Lawrence walk in together, engrossed in each other. She felt a pang of hurt that Lawrence had not told her things had progressed so far with Margaret. It was like a betrayal from him.

"Ah, Lady Anna, we were getting worried about you!" said Countess Mountdare.

Anna smiled broadly. "You must forgive me, Countess. I lay down for a nap, and fell into such a slumber that I forgot what time it was."

"Ah, these things happen," said the Countess, wondering if the woman had no maid to rouse her. "Lucky for you that you have

Edward to wake you!"

"Yes, lucky for me," said Anna, avoiding looking at Edward.

Throughout the dinner Anna remained quiet, hardly speaking at all as the others chatted away merrily. Try as she might, she was just too overcome with worry and stress to put on a jovial act. Was it possible that Georgina had told Edward about her secret? How else would he know about their renewed correspondence? The thought he might know – and indeed the thought her friend had cruelly deceived her – made her feel so ill she could hardly eat.

As pudding was being served, Taylor came to Edward and said, "I'm sorry to disturb, Your Lordship, but Sergeant Bourke is here and would like to speak with you."

"Well, damn his timing," muttered Edward irritably. "Did he say what it was about?"

"No, your lordship."

Edward stood up and said to the company in general, "If you'll excuse me momentarily, a member of the local constabulary is here to see me. Probably about poaching on the estate or one of our tenant farmers involved in some fracas in the town."

Edward found Sergeant Bourke in the hallway with a young officer.

"Sorry to interrupt your evening, Lord Armstrong," said the Sergeant.

"Yes, we are at dinner. What is the problem, Sergeant Bourke?"

"Not concerning yourself directly, your lordship. But I thought I should make you aware that it had been reported to us by the police in Westport that there was a break-in at Frampton Manor last night and Colonel Frampton was found dead in his bed this morning by his butler. Knifed through the heart by the intruder."

"How dreadful! Has the murderer been caught?" asked Edward. Although he didn't know Colonel Frampton well, he had met him at social events over the years.

"The police in Westport have no idea. But there have been reports of break-ins at a number of manor houses in the west of the country and we suspect this is the same person. I imagine Colonel

Frampton awoke during the robbery and ended up being killed. We are warning all the manor houses to take extra precautions with security and make sure all doors and windows are locked at night."

"Yes, yes, indeed. Thank you, Sergeant," said Edward.

"Good night, Your Lordship," said the Sergeant and he and his officer bowed and left.

Edward turned and walked slowly back into the dining room where he regained his seat.

"Anything the matter?" asked Lawrence.

"Colonel Frampton at Frampton Manor was murdered in his bed last night. A theft apparently," said Edward.

"The poor man! Shocking!" said the Countess. "What times we live in!"

"Seemingly there have been a number of break-ins and thefts at manors. They believe it's the same person." Edward turned to Taylor who was standing by. "Taylor, make sure you and the staff are extra vigilant. Check all windows and doors are locked at night."

"I always do, my lord," said Taylor.

"Well, be doubly vigilant. In fact, for the present, you might appoint a pair of nightguards to patrol the house for the protection of our guests."

"Certainly, my lord."

"Well," said the Countess, "whoever this thief is, he had better not try and break into *my* room, or he'll find he is on the receiving end of a hairpin being rammed up his –"

"*Mama*!" Margaret cried.

CHAPTER 40

After dinner Anna led the guests from the dining room across the hall into the drawing room. She spotted the Earl and Edward breaking off from the group and heading towards the library, and her heart sank. Surely Edward's prediction couldn't be true? It seemed too precipitate to be likely.

As the Countess and Margaret sat down together on a sofa, the Countess whispered to her daughter, "I do sincerely hope your father doesn't mess up the negotiation with Lord Armstrong. I should really have attended that meeting myself to make sure there are no hiccups."

"You can't, Mama! That is men's business, not for you to interfere in!"

The Countess raised her eyes to heaven. "Men's business! My dear, if men's business was left in the sole hands of your father, this family would be in dire straits long ago! It is *I* who have kept a steady hand on this family's rudder through the years."

"I'm sure Papa will manage it just fine. And, let us be honest, he is not up against a hard and ruthless negotiator. I'm sure Lord Armstrong will be kind and reach a reasonable agreement with Papa."

"As long as they reach the agreement, I don't care the terms! At least I limited your father's intake of alcohol to one glass of wine over dinner and he will have a clear head for his talk with Edward!"

As the guests chatted, the Countess saw Anna taking a seat in an

258

armchair opposite them by the fireplace.

"My high praise to your cook, Lady Anna," said the Countess.

Anna smiled. "Yes, she is a find. Though I don't know where we found her. Edward did all the hiring of the staff while we were in London."

Just then Taylor approached with a tray of drinks.

"Where did we find the cook, Taylor?" Anna asked.

"I believe her previous position was at Westport House, my lady."

"Ah, then she really is a find!" said the Countess.

"Oh, Edward probably poached her from there, offered her more money – he's rather good at that kind of thing," said Anna.

The Countess smiled across at her. "Everyone has their price."

"Don't they just?" said Anna.

Margaret excused herself and went to join Lawrence, and Mrs. Foxe quickly took her place on the sofa beside the Countess and engaged her in conversation.

Anna sat sipping her port, looking over at Lawrence and Margaret.

As the guests continued chatting, on subjects as diverse as the hunting season to racing to gossip to the weather, Anna watched as the young couple talked quietly to each other, lost in each other's company as if nobody else was there. She felt a pang as she remembered what that had felt like in the early years with Edward. It was love devoid of complications, devoid of everything but simplicity.

After an hour Edward and the Earl walked into the drawing room, looking merry.

"Ah, gentlemen, it is so good of you to join us!" said Anna with a smile as the men approached. She beckoned to Lawrence. "Lawrence, do come here!"

Lawrence and Margaret smilingly approached.

Anna turned her attention to Edward. "Have you had a satisfactory meeting?" she asked loudly.

"Eh . . . yes," Edward said uncomfortably.

"Have you managed to get everything down to the last pound,

shilling and penny?" she continued.

The Earl looked at the Countess, embarrassed.

"Anna," whispered Edward as the whole room fell quiet.

"Well, I just hope we know exactly what we are getting, and the Mountdares know exactly what the Mountdares are getting. We don't want a mismatch in any way, do we? A marriage of unequals can be quite tragic for all concerned."

"*Mother*," said Lawrence urgently.

Anna ignored him and smiled at Margaret who was looking at her as if she couldn't believe her ears. "My dear girl, you have no idea of the machinations that go on behind a young couple's back. How a simple love story can be turned into a grubby affair by the hands of others, mostly under the guise of concerned parents, of course."

"*Anna!*" warned Edward.

"Tell me, Edward, did you have a similar conversation with my father when you asked for my hand? I never thought to ask before and am now rather curious, having seen what the whole business is really about. What exactly did you get for my hand in marriage? I do hope it was enough because, let us be honest, I have never been the easiest of wives to live with or deal with."

Lawrence and Margaret were clutching each other's hands, their faces full of horror.

"Well," asked Anna with a sharp smile. "What was my dowry worth?"

Edward stared at her, deep into her eyes, and she could see the hurt she had caused.

His voice was low. "I received no dowry when I married you. Your father did offer, but I refused to take it. In the same way that I have told the Earl tonight, having discussed it earlier with Lawrence, that he will refuse to take a dowry if and when a marriage takes place between him and Margaret."

Anna's eyes filled with tears as she quickly looked away into the fire.

The uncomfortable silence continued for a while. No one in the room spoke.

"I always feel guilty when I have eaten too much," said Anna eventually as she looked from the fire to around the room. "Still, after all these years – all these years after the Famine . . . I feel guilty if I eat too much, and more guilty if I leave food behind on my plate."

"Anna, don't," whispered Edward.

Ann turned and stared back into the fire. "The memories never leave me – of what I saw during those years. The workhouses, the tiny children separated from their parents. And they were the lucky ones, compared to those outside the workhouses . . . the sight of mothers cradling their infants, on the side of roads, in ditches, unable to feed them, knowing that they would soon die . . . their lives being thrown away, because nobody cared enough to save them."

Edward saw his wife's eyes fill with tears and one spill down her cheek. He reached over and placed a gentle hand on her arm.

She turned to look at him and she felt as if there was nobody there but them.

The Countess coughed loudly and turned her attention to Mrs. Foxe.

"Do you play lawn tennis, Mrs. Foxe?" she asked. "It's becoming all the rage."

"No, I'm afraid, I don't. I am simply not agile enough to attempt the sport."

"Quite right. I think there is something unfitting about a woman playing tennis in any case," said the Countess.

Anna could no longer hold Edward's gaze, and turned to look into the fire.

When the night was finished, everyone who was staying at Armstrong House retired to their rooms, while the others left by carriage. In their bedroom, Anna watched silently as Edward went to his dressing room and changed into his night attire. She went to her dressing table and began to remove her jewellery.

When Edward emerged he said, "Goodnight" and went to sleep without saying another word.

The Countess was unhooking her corset in her bedroom as the Earl got ready to go to bed.

"What a strange woman Lady Anna can be," she said. "Whatever is the matter with her? Trying to embarrass us all talking about dowries so openly and then that tirade about the Famine!"

"Most strange," said the Earl as he lifted the decanter of sherry that had been left in the room and went to pour himself a glass.

"Put that *down*!" shouted the Countess abruptly and the Earl put down the decanter irritably. "Do you know, I think her problem is that her mother died young. She didn't have a firm female hand to guide and direct her when she was going through her formative years."

"Perhaps," said the Earl, not sounding that interested.

"And then she married Edward who, being the lovely man that he is, gave her too much of a free rein. A wife needs to know clear boundaries in marriage and never overstep the line. Grover – come here and undo the rest of my corset!"

Sighing, the Earl went over to his wife and began to unclip her.

"I mean gallivanting around the country during the Famine doing all those 'good works', and the letters she sent to parliament and newspapers. Politics is no place for a woman! I'd like to have seen your reaction if I had abandoned you and gone off doing good works during the Famine, Grover!"

"I'd have given you my blessing as I waved you off, Clementina," the Earl said sarcastically.

"*Hmmm*, and I wonder what kind of state Kilternan House would have been in if I'd ever left it in your hands for too long!" said the Countess who, finally free of her corset, turned to face her husband. "So, is this true what Edward was saying – that they will not accept a penny as a dowry for Margaret?"

"That's what he said. He said if Lawrence didn't marry for love then he shouldn't marry at all, and refused to take any money on behalf of his son."

"Well, that is a coup for us. Although I suppose he only has one child and so really feels a dowry is not necessary. I can bet you if he had a few daughters to provide dowries for, he'd be anxious enough to demand a dowry from us!"

"Hmmm . . . I wonder . . . I wonder . . ."

"Oh, spit it out, Grover!" said the Countess.

"I wonder are we wise to allow Margaret to continue with this marriage?"

"Whatever makes you say that?" The Countess was aghast.

"Well, I'm just wondering, considering Lady Anna's display tonight, if there might not be an element of insanity running through the family? Do we wish for Margaret to be married into a family tainted with insanity?"

"Anna isn't insane, Grover – she's just selfish and spoilt in my opinion. And even if she is a tad mad, then Edward has enough sanity for the both of them – and thankfully Lawrence takes after his father in totality and not his mother."

"But –"

"Shut up, Grover! The marriage will go ahead, mad mother-in-law or not! Thousands of acres, a mansion like this, a townhouse in London as well as one of the most respected titles in the realm – a mad mother-in-law is a small price to pay for Margaret in exchange for all that!"

And she climbed into bed.

CHAPTER 41

The next morning, Anna heard Edward get out of bed. She had spent another sleepless night. She began to prepare herself for the day ahead. The garden party was due to start at two in the afternoon.

Edward came out of his dressing room, dressed in a dark-grey suit. He looked at her as she was brushing her hair at her dressing table.

"Edward?" she said, turning to him.

"Yes?"

"I'm – I don't know happened last night –"

"I'll tell you what happened last night – you made a show of us! You were a disgrace! Poor Lawrence! What must the Mountdares think?"

"Well, I told you I wasn't feeling well!" she defended herself.

"How could you behave in such a dreadful manner? Could you not have just held your tongue and spoken to me later!"

"It is all your fault, Edward! I was quite happy to stay in bed for the night. You forced me down to meet those people –"

"*Those people*!" His voice rose. "*Those people* are to be our in-laws and you had a duty to behave in a respectful and respectable fashion!"

"You speak so cruelly!"

"*You act so cruelly!*" he shot back.

"Keep your voice down! The Mountdares may hear you!" she hissed.

"Does it matter if they do? Could it colour their opinion of us any worse after your behaviour last night? I can barely face seeing them today. How will they react?"

Anna took up her brush and began to brush her hair furiously. "They will act as the Mountdares always act – as if nothing happened. I suggest we play along with them."

He calmed down, walked over and sank to his knees beside her.

"Anna – I can see something is troubling you greatly. Why don't you tell me, whatever it is?"

"There's nothing wrong with me, Edward. Besides, what is the point in talking to you? Any time I try to, you dismiss me as being irrational and paranoid."

"I am sorry if you feel that, but it's how you come across sometimes. I want to help you, if you could just trust in me. Has it something to do with Georgina?"

"There is nothing wrong, Edward."

"Why have you been back in contact with Georgina after all these years?"

"And how do you know that I have been?"

"Does it matter?"

"It does. Have you been spying on me?"

"Look, I can't really say," he said awkwardly.

"Or did she contact you?"

"No, she did not," he answered.

He said it with such conviction that she believed him and felt a degree of relief. She should not have doubted her friend.

"I can't dictate who you are in contact with, Anna," he went on. "But I imagine Georgina is the source of your anxiety? Is she not?"

Anna stood up and walked over to the bell-pull and tugged it. "You'll have to excuse me, Edward. My maid is waiting to dress me for the day, and our guests are awaiting me."

Edward sighed heavily as he stood up and went to leave the room. "All right. I have tried, but if you want to keep your secrets that is your choice."

She watched him leave, and wished with all her heart she could keep her secrets forever, but she felt they were about to come tumbling out and destroy them all.

That morning Anna put on an act as if she was a different person from the night before. Over the breakfast table she chatted and charmed the Mountdares, paying particular attention to Margaret. She had let Lawrence down the previous night, and was determined not to do the same again.

"I must thank you for your hospitality and all the events you have set up for us during our stay, Lady Armstrong," said the Countess.

"It's an absolute pleasure to be your hostess. I do hope you enjoy the garden party this afternoon."

"That will be nothing compared to tomorrow – the Glorious 12th!" said Lawrence excitedly, as he smiled at Margaret who was seated beside him.

The next day was the twelve of August, and the start of the official grouse-hunting season.

"I believe you have some of the best grouse-shooting in Ireland here on the Armstrong estate," said the Earl enthusiastically.

"I can promise you an excellent day of shooting," said Edward, aware of the Earl's reputation as a fine shot.

"I've never been on a shoot before," said Margaret.

"Oh, it's exciting! You'll love it," said Lawrence. "Though Mama doesn't enjoy it."

"I'm afraid I don't," said Anna. "I find it a little disturbing watching the prey being shot."

Edward smiled at his guests, anxious that her non-attendance should not be seen as a continuation of her odd behaviour the previous night. "My wife is a city girl at heart, having been brought up in Dublin, so she never attended shoots growing up, hence her reluctance."

Anna nodded at Edward in appreciation of his supporting her on the topic. "When I was growing up it was all politics, with my father being a Member of Parliament. I was far more likely to be found sitting at my father's political rallies than attending shoots."

"But your mother's family were from the Tullydere estate in the midlands, were they not? Did you not attend shoots while visiting there?" asked the Countess.

Anna glanced awkwardly at Edward at the mention of Tullydere

266

and its association with Georgina. "As my mother died when I was quite young, my visits to Tullydere were sporadic," she said. She was telling the truth about her mother dying when she was young, but not about the frequency of visits to Tullydere.

She quickly moved the conversation on to fashion.

Taylor and his footmen had set out the upper terraced garden with a series of round tables that had been impeccably dressed in white linen tablecloths for the garden party.

Anna led the party from the house, across the forecourt and down the steps into the garden as other guests arrived. The main conversation seemed to be the murder of Colonel Frampton. Though he lived many miles away, an attack on one of their own class in his own home had sent shockwaves through their community.

"Isn't it dreadful, Anna?" said Mrs. Foxe as they went. "Poor Colonel Frampton! I only met him a couple of times but he was so sweet. They say it's a thief targeting all the big houses. Mr. Foxe is now sleeping with the shotgun by our bed!"

"I shouldn't worry too much, Mrs. Foxe – I'm sure the police will catch the culprit soon," said Anna.

"I'm wouldn't be too sure of that, Anna. They can't catch the poachers on our estate, let alone a murdering thief!"

When Anna spotted Margaret standing on her own admiring the view, she seized the opportunity to engage her in conversation. She went out of her way to be polite and warm, fully aware of how rude she had been the previous night. She was impressed by Margaret's composure. She chatted back cheerfully and politely, as if nothing had happened. Anna had met many young daughters of the aristocracy in London and many of them were petulant and would have taken great delight in gossiping about Anna's behaviour the previous night. Margaret did not seem like that in the least. As the other guests continued to mill around admiring the view and the recently installed tennis court which was to the right of the garden, Anna decided to try to make amends.

"Margaret, I was so extraordinarily insensitive and impolite last night. I'm quite embarrassed over my behaviour – asking what your father was offering as a dowry! I really don't know what came over me. I do hope you will not hold my behaviour against me, although I can think of no reason why you should not."

Margaret looked surprised at Anna's apology. Her mother had reared her to always ignore any social faux pas that occurred and pretend as if it had never happened. She had taught her that this was the best way to deal with any unpleasantness in life.

"Oh, no, Lady Armstrong, I took no offense! Don't concern yourself in the least!" she said.

"That's very kind of you – your discretion is very kind indeed. I do hope you can forgive me as I would like us to be friends. If the truth be told, the seriousness of your relationship with Lawrence has taken me by surprise. I never imagined he would enter into a commitment so young. I feared he was making a mistake. I do think he's too young for an engagement. But, as I said, I would like us to be friends, if for no other reason than that Lawrence cares about you greatly and I care greatly about him."

Margaret reached out and took Anna's hand. "It would be a great honour for me to be your friend. I heard so much about you growing up, it was an honour to finally meet you."

"Did you?" asked Anna surprised.

"Yes, of course! The good works you did during the Famine – the relief programmes you established. Not to mention how you pushed your father so relentlessly to speak about the Famine in Parliament. Not to mention all the letters you wrote to the newspapers highlighting the devastation – quite unheard of from a woman! We were always told as women not to even mention politics, and there you were at the core of it."

Anna was impressed by Margaret's knowledge of such affairs. "I think you are being too kind now, Margaret," she said. "I did no more than many others. But I'm glad my son feels so strongly about you. And I can see what attracts him to you so much."

"*Margaret!*" called the Countess from across the gardens. "Come and look at these geraniums! They are so pretty!"

Margaret smiled at Anna and went to join her mother.

Anna looked over at the Countess and froze as she saw that Sinclair, Diana and Harry were with her.

Sinclair smiled over to her and Diana waved.

As the guests enjoyed afternoon tea with sandwiches and cakes, Harry spotted Margaret speaking with Lawrence at the end of the garden. He made a beeline for them.

"Well, hello, there!" he said cheerily. "Remember me?"

"Yes, of course, Harry, how are you?" said Margaret.

"Just 'capital', to use Lawrence's expression. You do look well, Margaret."

"Thank you."

"So, I hear Lawrence paid you a visit in Mountdare," said Harry.

"Yes, we had a wonderful ball, and Lawrence attended," said Margaret.

"I hope his dancing has improved somewhat?" said Harry, glancing at Lawrence dismissively.

"Yes, I'm glad to report his dancing has much improved," she said, smiling at Lawrence.

"I'm glad to hear it! Let's face it, it couldn't have got any worse!" Harry moved in between Lawrence and Margaret, gently elbowing Lawrence aside. "I've tried to take Lawrence in hand since he came back from London. Tried to teach him about being a country gentleman, but some people are just slow learners! Poor Lawrence – it is rarely I have seen a man as unable to manage a horse as Lawrence."

As Harry continued in this vein, Margaret saw Lawrence's face was getting redder – not from anger but embarrassment. She wondered why he didn't defend himself against Harry, but realised he seemed to be intimidated by him. But she knew for sure she was not going to waste the entire afternoon listening to Harry's boasting and self-congratulation.

"I wonder if you could excuse us, Harry, but Lawrence promised to show me the flowers in the lower terraces. I have a great interest in flowers."

With that, Margaret took Lawrence's arm and led him away, leaving Harry staring after them with a mixture of shock and anger.

Lawrence and Margaret went down the steps leading to the next terraced garden and made their way across it.

"How can you listen to such drivel from Harry all the time?" Margaret asked. "I have never met a man so full of himself and so full of nonsense!"

"Well, I actually haven't had too much to do with him since arriving back at Armstrong House," said Lawrence.

"I'm glad to hear it!"

"We used to be so close as children, but coming back I've realised we have really nothing in common." Lawrence was thinking of Gertie.

"You are right, you have nothing in common. Your personalities are completely different. And may I warn you, Lawrence, Harry is not the friend he pretends to be to you. He is always putting you down and you let him get away with it."

"Let's not talk about Harry any longer. The day is too nice to waste it talking about him," he said, embarrassed that Margaret seemed to be chiding him for not being able to defend himself against Harry.

"We shouldn't go much further – people will talk if we go out of sight," said Margaret, glancing back to the top terrace where she could see people looking over the balustrade.

"Oh, let them talk! We will be official soon!" said Lawrence, leading her down the next flight of steps.

"Well, until we are, I have my reputation to think of!" Margaret said laughingly.

"Very well – we'll go back." Lawrence stopped as they reached the lower garden. He turned to her and gazed at her seriously. "But, wait a moment, Margaret – there's something I want to say."

She looked at him in slight trepidation.

"I am so sorry about my mother's words last night. She embarrassed me beyond measure. And in front of your parents!"

"Oh, don't you apologise as well, Lawrence! I've already

listened to your mother's apology!"

"Mama apologised?" Lawrence was amazed.

Margaret thought quickly. Although she found Anna's outburst shocking she did not want to alienate Lawrence by criticising his mother. They weren't married yet!

"Yes, she did. Quite profoundly – and quite unnecessarily. In a way, it was refreshing to hear somebody speak as she did last night, careless of the social constraints that confine the rest of us."

"My mother is a complex woman," said Lawrence. "She's often seems so – complex is the only word I can use to describe her!"

"I was struck by what she said about the things she saw in the Famine. It would haunt a person, I should think, change them."

"Oh, for goodness' sake! She was not the only person who witnessed the Famine! Sometimes she speaks as if she was the only one there!"

"She probably was one of the few of our class who was in the very furnace of it."

"Well, sometimes I don't know how my father puts up with her," he said.

"You should never speak like that about her, Lawrence. She loves you very much, probably too much, if such a thing can be. Your welfare is her only concern, hence why she was so suspicious of me."

"But you won her over," he said with a smile.

"I can understand her fears about losing the one thing that means the most to her. She fears losing you to somebody who is not worthy of you."

"Don't put me on a pedestal, Margaret – I might just fall off!"

"And what is all this about you not accepting a dowry from my father? Do you think that's wise?"

"My father suggested it and, when he did, I completely agreed. I don't want to marry you for your money, but for you."

"I hope you won't regret it in years to come. When I am a cantankerous old crone, and you will think that you didn't even get a farthing for me!" she teased.

"I still shall not regret it," he said, leading her over to some trees. He checked they were out of view from the upper terraces and then put his arms around her and kissed her.

"Shall we go back and announce the news officially that we are engaged?" he asked.

"I think we'll disappoint all of them if we don't," beamed Margaret.

Harry was reaching for a cake from one of the tables when he spotted Gertie walking around collecting empty cups and placing them on a tray. She came over to the table he was standing beside and started to clear cups away from it.

She looked up at him and smiled. "I can make it out of the house tonight again, if that suits you?" she whispered.

"Yes, that suits – what time?"

"The usual? Two o'clock out at the stables?"

"I'll see you there."

She winked at him and walked off, carrying the tray.

Afternoon tea devoured, most of the guests were now looking at a tennis match being played out between Edward and the Earl. The guests had gathered around the tennis court that was positioned to the right of the tables at the end of the first terraced garden.

Anna sat alone at her table, looking out across the lake, wondering where Seán was.

"May I sit?" asked a voice.

Looking up, she saw it was Sinclair.

She nodded nervously and he sat down.

"Congratulations, a wonderful day," he said.

"Thank you."

"Are you going on the shoot tomorrow?"

"No." She shook her head.

"I didn't think you would be – you never liked country pursuits, did you?"

"I wouldn't say that – just not the hunting."

"You never really belonged here," he said.

Her voice became stern. "This is my home, Sinclair. Edward

built this house for me when we were engaged."

"Oh, I know that," he said. "Well, not exactly true. He didn't actually build it. He spent a lot of time looking over architects' plans but it was actually I who oversaw the building of Armstrong House and made sure it got built and to budget. Were you ever aware of that?"

"I knew you had a hand in it, yes," conceded Anna.

Sinclair sighed. "It's like everything else around here. I do all the work while Edward gets all the credit."

Anna became angry. "Well, if you don't like it why don't you just go? Leave the estate and go and live somewhere else – preferably far away!"

His eyes flashed. "You'd like that, wouldn't you?"

Anna's nerves were at breaking point and she could not take Sinclair's game-playing any further. "I should like for nothing more! It has been my dearest wish since I came to live here over quarter of a century ago!"

"I'll never leave here, Anna. This land has been in my family for three hundred years. Passed down from father to son, the way it should be."

"And the way it is now," said Anna.

He leaned forward and whispered, "But it's not, is it, Anna? That is not happening now with Lawrence."

Her face paled. "I don't know what you're talking about – nonsense, as usual."

He nodded towards the end of the terraced garden and said, "Take a look over there."

Anna looked over to the opposite end of the garden from the tennis court. There was a workman there pruning the trees.

"What am I supposed to be looking at exactly?" she demanded.

The workman stopped pruning and turned around. Her heart began to palpitate as she saw the same man – the man who had been in the forecourt that night, the man who had been standing across the street from the train station when they were collecting the Mountdares.

"Seán," she whispered.

The man was staring at Anna and waved over to her. Then he turned and disappeared into the trees.

She stood up abruptly and said "*Seán!*" and began to move after him.

Sinclair grabbed her arm and pulled her back to her seat.

"Be careful, Anna, act normally," he cautioned as he spotted the Countess noticing Anna's behaviour from the side-line of the tennis match.

"Where did you find him?" gasped Anna.

"I found him, that's all you need to know," Sinclair said. "I need to speak to you in private. I will not be attending the shoot tomorrow either. I'll meet you down by the lake at the boathouse, at noon. Understood?"

Anna was trembling and unable to speak.

"*Understood?*" he hissed at her.

She nodded quickly.

"Game, set and match to Lord Armstrong!" called the umpire and the crowd began to applaud around the tennis court.

"Good show!" called a guest.

Just then Lawrence and Margaret came up the steps from the lower garden. They made their way across the lawn towards the tennis court.

Lawrence had thought about bringing his and Margaret's parents to their side before he made the announcement to the guests, but after his mother's behaviour the previous night he had decided not to, in case she started another scene.

"*Everyone, if I could have your attention for a moment!*" called Lawrence.

The guests sauntered over to the young couple.

"*Come along, everyone!*" Lawrence called, wishing he had a bell. "*I have an announcement to make!*"

Now there was a murmur from the guests as they whispered and speculated about what this announcement might be.

Lawrence waited until the majority of the guests were standing before him and Margaret.

"I would like to announce that I have asked Margaret . . ."

Lawrence smiled down at her before continuing, "and she has kindly agreed – to marry me!"

There was a loud cheer from the crowd as they all descended on the couple and started to congratulate them.

"You had better go and offer your best wishes," said Sinclair whose face had darkened.

Anna stood up and slowly made her way through the guests to Lawrence.

"Mama!" Lawrence greeted her happily.

"Congratulations, I'm very happy for you," she said and she embraced Lawrence, not letting him go for ages.

He finally gently pushed her away.

"For both of you," said Anna as she leaned forward and kissed Margaret.

"Thank you, Lady Armstrong," said Margaret, squeezing Anna's hand.

"Taylor!" called an overexcited Edward. "Fetch the best champagne from the cellars to celebrate!"

Anna turned and walked away from the crowd which was still cheering the happy couple. She walked slowly back to her table and saw that Sinclair was no longer there. As she reached the table she felt her head go light and she began to stumble. She reached out for the table for support. But as she did, she collapsed, dragging the table down with her.

There was a soft knock on the door and the doctor opened it. After a whispered exchange he let the Countess and Earl in.

Edward rose to greet them as Anna tried to sit up in her bed.

"Now, now, Lady Armstrong, you must rest," said the doctor as he gently pushed her back against the pillows.

Lawrence and Margaret were already seated beside the bed, their anxious eyes fixed on Anna.

"How are you feeling, Anna?" asked the Countess and, without waiting for an answer, turned to the doctor. "Was it the heat?"

"Probably, and also an element of exhaustion I suspect," he said.

"Mama, you should have said if you weren't feeling well.

Forcing yourself to continue with the garden party!" said Lawrence.

Edward looked shamefacedly at his wife. "Your mother did say she was feeling unwell last night, but I ignored it."

The doctor nodded. "I'll leave these tablets and if she continues to take them throughout the day and rests for the next day or two, she'll be right as rain. And she'll need plenty of liquids."

"Thank you, doctor," said Edward.

"I am so sorry for fainting and ruining everything," said Anna to the Countess. "The garden party *and* Lawrence's announcement."

"Nonsense, you poor woman!" said the Countess. "You're as pale as a ghost – you shouldn't have been in that heat when you're unwell."

"I think she should be allowed to sleep now," the doctor said as he packed his bag.

"Of course," said the Countess. "Come along, everybody!"

And she ushered the others out, leaving Edward to say goodbye to the doctor.

As the door closed on the doctor, Anna said, "Oh, Edward, how can Lawrence ever forgive me? Announcing his engagement and I collapse in a heap in front of everybody. I am so ashamed."

"Anna, there is no shame on your part. It is I who feel ashamed. You told me you weren't well and I demanded you continue being a hostess."

"I don't know what came over me."

"You have been doing too much. And it is all my fault."

Anna sat up, threw her arms around Edward and held him tightly. "Edward, none of this is your fault. None of it at all!"

She held on to him tightly as tears streamed down her face.

That night, Gertie crept out of the house as she had many times before. Unlocking the back door, she ran out to the stables for her rendezvous with Harry. She could hardly contain her excitement at the thought of seeing him.

The minutes ticked by as she kept a lookout for him.

After she had waited for what felt like a very long time she started to become anxious. She waited on, shivering with nerves and cold. At last she realised that Harry wasn't coming and she had better make her way back indoors for fear of being caught.

Slowly and despondently she walked away from the stables and went back inside the house.

Harry lay awake in his bed at Hunter's Farm, thinking of the day's events. He couldn't get Margaret out of his mind. She looked so lovely and was so pleasant, everything he dreamed of in a woman. And there she was announcing her engagement to Lawrence. *Lawrence!* Who was wet behind the ears and knew nothing about anything! What could she possibly see in him?

"A title, a manor house and thousands of acres, that's what she sees in him," he whispered to himself.

He was fully confident that Margaret wouldn't even look at Lawrence were he not the heir to a vast fortune. He knew, from how she had interacted with him and danced with him at the ball at Armstrong House, that it was really him that she was interested in. It was so unfair. He looked at the time and saw it was nearly half past two in the morning. He pictured Gertie waiting anxiously for him at the stables. He had no intention of going to meet her that night. Why should he make do with a servant girl when Lawrence had Margaret? Besides, with that killing of Colonel Frampton he wasn't going to risk walking through the parklands up to Armstrong House in case he was mistaken for a thief and got shot at by some overzealous night watchman. A roll in the hay with Gertie was not worth the risk of being shot.

CHAPTER 42

The next morning Anna opened her eyes and blinked at the sunshine streaming through the windows.

"How are you this morning, Anna?" asked Edward and she turned around to see him sitting on the bed, dressed in his hunting tweeds, smiling at her.

"What time is it?" she asked.

"It's half past nine," he said.

She began to sit up. "But I've missed breakfast – what will the Mountdares think of me?"

He gently pushed her back down against her pillows. "Breakfast has been and gone and everyone is getting ready for the shoot. We'll be all gone for the day and so you just rest in bed – there will be nobody here to disturb you."

"I slept right through the night. It must have been the tablets the doctor gave me."

He bent over and kissed her. "I'd better go – the rest will be waiting for me."

He rose from the bed and left the room.

She waited for a few moments, then slipped out of the bed and went to the window. In the forecourt below she could see the shooting party had gathered and there was much excitement. She saw the Foxes and Fitzherberts and other neighbours there. Some of the men were on horseback already and the women were in carriages. Men were examining their guns and dogs ran around excitedly while Taylor went around offering whiskies from a tray.

She saw Lawrence was on his horse beside a carriage Margaret and the Countess were seated in. He was animated as he spoke to them. She saw Edward bound down the steps from the house and a stable boy bring his horse which he mounted.

"*Ladies and gentlemen, if you are ready, we shall proceed!*" called Edward.

"*The Glorious Twelfth!*" shouted Lawrence excitedly.

The party began to move out of the forecourt, led by Edward, and she watched as it made its way down the driveway. She closed her eyes and thought about her meeting with Sinclair at the boathouse at noon with dread and fear. With a heavy heart, she walked towards her dressing room.

It was the Glorious Twelfth – the busiest day of the season with shooting parties setting off all around the country. Anna felt sorry for their prey, they didn't stand a chance. She knew how they felt as she prepared to meet Sinclair. She knew what it felt like to be hunted.

"*Fetch! Good boy!*" called Lawrence to a gun dog.

The dog raced through the undergrowth to collect the grouse and bring it back to his master.

"Good shot!" called Edward to his son.

The shooting party had only shortly before started their walk through the heather and ferns of the moorland the grouse frequented and already shots were being fired and the dogs were racing off to retrieve their prey. The beaters were moving along in front of the party to scare the birds from the ground into the air to make them a target.

"Isn't this fun?" cried Lawrence to Margaret.

"Is it?" asked Margaret doubtfully.

He tried to hand his gun to her. "Here, you have a go!"

"Lawrence, I have never handled a gun in my life, and I do not want to start now," said Margaret. "Killing defenceless creatures has never appealed to me."

"My strong-minded fiancée!" said Lawrence with a chuckle. "I applaud the fact you know your own mind! But, look, your mother seems to be enjoying herself . . ." He nodded over to the Countess.

Margaret looked over at her mother who was aiming a gun and apparently being advised by Edward.

"Step back – I'm about to fire!" warned the Countess and Edward hastily jumped out of her way.

The Countess fired and there was a loud squawk as she hit her target.

"*I got him! I got him! I got the bastard!*" cried the Countess, so excited that she had forgotten any semblance of decorum.

"Well done!" said Edward, surprised and impressed.

"*Fetch*!" shrilled the Countess to a nearby dog and it went bounding across the moor as ordered.

"I say – where did she learn to shoot like that!" said Lawrence.

"She has handled guns since she was a girl and was always an excellent shot," said Margaret. "She's probably a better shot than any of the men here."

"I'd never have guessed!" exclaimed Lawrence, looking at his future mother-in-law with new eyes.

"Mama has always had a fondness for blood sports – that's how she manoeuvres the society scene so well," said Margaret cynically.

"Margaret!" Lawrence protested, but with a grin. He was impressed – his bride-to-be had a cutting wit.

She laughed in response and shrugged her shoulders. "Lawrence, I'm really not going to enjoy spending the day watching my mother slaughtering harmless birds and showing off – I shouldn't have come – would you mind if I returned to Armstrong House?"

"But surely you're at least enjoying being out in this beautiful place on such a lovely day?" he protested.

"I only came because I wanted to be with you. But I see no fun in these shoots. Would you mind terribly if I went back?"

"But – but it would mean we'd miss the rest of the shoot!" Lawrence said, looking like a child who has been told Christmas has been cancelled.

"I don't mean for *you* to come back, dearest. I'll walk back to the carriages and get one of the servants to drive me back to the house."

"Are you sure?"

"Quite sure," she said, looking over at her mother who was trying to pull the grouse she had shot from the retriever's mouth, who was stubbornly refusing to relinquish it.

"*Let go, you bitch*!" the Countess shouted at the dog, as their battle continued.

Margaret reached up and kissed Lawrence's cheek. "Enjoy the rest of the day."

"Wait – I'd better escort you back to the carriages," he said.

"Not at all! It's a short walk." She pointed. "It's just over there beyond that copse of trees. You continue with your shooting!"

With a little wave and a smile, she walked off.

"You have more in common with my mother than I thought!" called Lawrence after her.

"And a little less in common than you thought with my own mother!" answered Margaret, pointing back at where the Countess gave the dog she had been battling a swift kick, causing it to yelp, drop the grouse and run away. The Countess reached down for the grouse and swung it in the air with pride.

"*Hurray for the Glorious Twelfth!*" yelled the Countess.

"I'll see you this evening!" Margaret called to Lawrence as she walked off through the heather.

Harry observed Margaret leave the party and set off in the direction of the carriages. He held back as the others in the shooting party stalked onwards. Once the hunting party were out of view, he headed quickly after Margaret.

Margaret entered the copse of trees beyond which were the carriages.

"Margaret?" said a voice behind her, giving her a start. She turned to see Harry there, holding a shotgun by his side.

"Harry!" she said. "Are you leaving the shoot?"

"No, I wanted to speak with you."

"What about?" she said nervously.

"Why did you leave the shooting party?" he asked.

"It wasn't to my liking."

"Even though Lawrence was there?"

"Harry, what do you want?" she demanded.

"Margaret, I know you are only marrying Lawrence because of the money. I know you don't really want to marry him. It's not fair on him or you to continue with this – this farce!"

Her eyes widened in amazement. "Harry, I love Lawrence very much."

"But you wouldn't if he wasn't the heir to Armstrong Estate – admit it!"

"I don't like your tone, Harry. And I don't really see what any of this has to do with you."

"No? I knew from the moment you met me that you had feelings for me," he said.

"*What?*"

"Don't deny it. The way you danced with me the whole night at the ball in Armstrong House. How you flirted with me. You didn't agree to corresponding with me the next day but only because your parents insisted you should give your attention to Lawrence as he was a good catch in their eyes."

"Harry, you're deluded! Yes, I danced with you, out of politeness, nothing more. And I most certainly did not flirt with you!"

"It's only the two of us here now, Margaret – you can be honest with me. We can be honest with each other. I think you are the most beautiful girl I have ever met." He came closer.

"I don't want to hear any more of this, Harry!" she insisted, becoming angry. "I have never had any interest in you. You are so full of yourself that you clearly think a woman only has to only say hello to you and she has feelings for you. That is not the case for me!" She was so angry at his audacity that she didn't care about his feelings. "As if I would ever even consider you! Harry, you need to take a good look at yourself and your life and stop with your delusions. I am engaged to Lawrence. I love Lawrence. You are merely an employee on his father's estate. Now, goodbye!" She turned to go.

Harry reached out and grabbed her arm, holding it in a vice-like squeeze.

She looked at his face and saw that a cloud had descended over it. He looked so angry and vicious. She glanced around and there was nobody in sight. She doubted that the drivers at the carriages would even hear her if she screamed for help. Her heart began to pound in fear – she was trapped with this man with no-one to come to her rescue.

Harry saw the fear on her face and then suddenly the red mist that had descended over him lifted. He quickly let go of her arm.

She looked at him for a moment and then turned and hurried through the trees towards the carriages.

CHAPTER 43

The carriage drove into the forecourt and the driver opened the door for Margaret to climb out. Her arm felt bruised where Harry had gripped her so hard. She was trying to figure out what had possessed him to act like that. Maybe she had only herself to blame. Her mother had told her she had danced too much with Harry the night of the ball and perhaps she had given him the wrong impression. But did he seriously think that he could stand a chance with her? Putting aside the fact that she was madly in love with Lawrence and that she actually disliked Harry, what life did he think he could offer the daughter of the Earl of Mountdare?

"Thank you," said Margaret, as the driver climbed back on the front seat of the carriage to drive back out of the forecourt.

She looked up at the house and wondered what to do for the rest of the day. The house would be empty except for Anna, who she was sure would be in bed resting all day after her faint. Perhaps she too should go to her room and rest – she still felt shaken after the encounter with Harry. She walked over to the balustrade at the edge of the forecourt and looked out at the view across the lake. She looked down at the terraced gardens and saw a woman walking across the bottom terrace. As she squinted in the sun, it looked like it was Anna.

"*Anna!*" Margaret called, but she appeared not to hear as she walked towards the steps that led onto the lakeshore.

Margaret was concerned. Anna was supposed to be resting that day – what on earth was she doing down at the lake? What if she fainted again? The doctor had given Anna some tablets – who knew how they might affect her?

She hurried down the series of steps that led to the lakeshore. Reaching the shingled shore, she saw Anna walking onwards toward the boathouse.

Margaret continued down the lakeshore after her as quickly as she could. She watched as Anna slowed down as she reached the boathouse and stood like a statue for a while. Margaret was going to call out to her again, but suddenly Anna moved forward and walked into the boathouse.

"Hello?" Anna called.

Sinclair stepped out of the shadows.

They stared at each other for a while.

"I wasn't sure you would come," he said eventually.

"Did I have a choice?"

"No."

"Is he here?"

"No."

"Where is he?"

"He's safe. You don't need to know his whereabouts."

She stepped towards him, her face creased in desperation. "*Where* did you find him?"

"It wasn't too hard to find him, if you looked in the right place," said Sinclair.

"But I looked *everywhere* for him. I was sure he was dead, killed in the Famine."

"Maybe he didn't want to be found then?"

"But he does now?" asked Anna. "He's come back after all these years? For what?"

"Because I brought him back. I found him and brought him back."

Anna glared at him. "To destroy me."

"You've been playing a long poker game, Anna, and your luck has run out."

"What's . . ." she found it had to say his name, "Seán like now?"

She wondered whether his looks might have changed with time.

"Same as he ever was," said Sinclair nonchalantly, reading her mind all too easily. "He looks like a peasant. More weathered than he did – twenty years will do that to a man. But, other than that, remarkably the same. And – very much like Lawrence."

"Georgina told me about your visit and your accusation," said Anna.

"Did she? Old friends die hard, I suppose. And it wasn't an accusation, it was a suspicion, a very strongly founded suspicion."

Anna still trod very carefully even though she knew, as Sinclair had said, her game was up. "And what has Seán told you?"

"He's told me everything. How you fornicated with him, and then framed him over stealing that locket to get him away from you after you had got what you wanted – a baby that Edward was unable to provide you with. And how lucky you were! A son!"

Anna's face went red and she stared down at the floor. She felt naked with shame, her worst, darkest secret being spoken aloud by the man she hated most.

"And what do you expect to do with this information? To expose me, to ruin me? Do you hate me so much that you would disgrace the whole Armstrong dynasty forever?"

"You were always an irritant, Anna, a nuisance in my way. But I haven't been driven to find Seán and expose him as Lawrence's father just to destroy you. You aren't that important to me."

"*Well, what do you want then*?" Anna cried in desperation.

"I want the Armstrong Estate, or the greater part of it at least," said Sinclair.

"What are you talking about? How can you have the Armstrong Estate – it is Edward's and Lawrence's after him!"

"It can quite easily be done. I have checked it all with my barrister. The title Lord Armstrong can't be changed as Lawrence was born in wedlock to Edward, despite being the bastard child of a peasant in reality. But the estate can be willed to me and Harry. Edward must change his will and leave the majority of the Armstrong Estate to Harry and me, as his natural heirs, as his closest male relatives. This is what must be done."

286

Anna began to tremble. "You are insane! Edward would never do that. Edward loves Lawrence more than life itself!"

"Not when he is told that he is not his real son. He will be horrified and disgusted that he has been fooled all these years, and I imagine will want to disown him. I know I certainly would. And I'd divorce you."

"But you are a very different man from Edward, Sinclair!"

"I doubt we are as dissimilar as you think. The Armstrong Estate has been in our family for three hundred years and I will not see it pass to the son of an uneducated, uncouth peasant. Edward will not either. But if there is any doubt that he will not do as I bid and change his will, then I will expose you and your bastard of a son as what you are. I shall take Seán to every drawing room of every mansion in this country and he will tell them he is Lawrence's real father. When the good people of those houses meet Seán, they will have no doubt he is telling the truth, as he looks so like him. I will not stop there. I will go to the newspapers and introduce Seán Hegarty to every editor and tell them the story of how Lady Armstrong fucked a peasant and Viscount Lawrence is not who he pretends to be. I will destroy your name, all your names, and destroy your son's life."

"But you will be destroying the Armstrong name that you claim to care so much about as well!"

"I do not care about that if I am to be cheated of my rightful legacy. Better for the name of Armstrong to be destroyed than for it to pass to this son of a peasant and for my son and I to be mere servants to him for the rest of our lives."

"You would destroy us all for your own greed? This will kill Edward if he learns the truth – do you not care about him? The man who has been like a brother to you all your life?"

"It is you who will be destroying him – I will merely be revealing your folly, a folly created out of your greed to remain in the position of Lady of the Manor by begetting an heir by any means you could."

"It is *you* who are possessed by greed!" she wept.

"You should be grateful to me," said Sinclair.

"Grateful? How? How on earth should I be grateful to you – *Cousin* Sinclair?"

"Because I am giving you an opportunity to save yourself and your family from utter destruction. If this comes out, then do you think Margaret will marry Lawrence, do you think any lady of any respectable family will even look at him? He will be ostracised. He will be a joke that no family will receive. He will be shunned by society. By telling Edward and getting him to change his will, Lawrence will be safe for the rest of his life. He will have the connections and the title to make a new life for himself. And I am not greedy, Anna – I do not ask for all of Edward's estate, just most of it. But I want what is rightfully mine and my son's. And I want it now. The choice is yours."

"You are presenting me with an impossible choice. Either we lose the estate or we lose our name and standing in society," she said.

"And the choice will ultimately be Edward's. If he cares as much about Lawrence as you claim, then he will not want the boy's name ruined."

"And what if Edward rejects Lawrence as you claim you would?" said Anna.

"That is his choice. If he rejects him then he will disinherit him anyway – he will shut him out of his will, as he is legally entitled to do."

As she looked at him she knew that if it was anybody else she could plead, beg for mercy. But she knew it was pointless with Sinclair. He had no heart.

"I need time to think about all this," said Anna.

"You've had twenty years to think about it. I want you to tell Edward the truth tomorrow."

"*Tomorrow!*"

"The Mountdares are leaving Armstrong House the following day, are they not?"

"Yes."

"Then I want this all done and decided before they leave. I want Edward to decide what he is going to do. If he refuses to do as I request, then I will tell the Mountdares the truth before they leave."

"Oh, your heart is stone!" she said, as the devastation that was about to unfold and engulf them overwhelmed her. "And what if I refuse to tell him?"

"Then I shall tell him and introduce him to Seán Hegarty to confirm the truth. When he sees Seán again, he will know the truth himself, from his resemblance to Lawrence."

Sinclair moved away from her towards the door.

"There is a drinks party being held at Armstrong House tomorrow evening to mark the end of the Mountdares' visit . . ."

"Yes."

"Diana and I have been invited by Edward. If you have not told Edward the truth by then, I will tell him." And he walked out the door.

Behind the boathouse, Margaret remained hidden. She had put her hands over her mouth to stop her from screaming at what she had heard. Now she could hear Anna sobbing loudly inside.

CHAPTER 44

That evening Anna heard the shooting party arrive back in the forecourt outside with much merriment. They would stay briefly for drinks and then depart with their spoils.

An hour later the bedroom door opened and Edward came into the bedroom.

Anna was sitting in a trance at her dressing table, staring at her reflection.

"Ah, you are up! How do you feel now?" he asked as he went to her and kissed her neck.

She nodded and smiled at him.

"Better?"

She nodded silently again.

"Best that you don't come down for dinner tonight though, my love, and rest up as the doctor ordered," he said as he threw off his tweed shooting jacket. "We had a wonderful day! One of the best August Twelfths ever, I would say. My gosh – you should see the Countess with a gun! She's like a different person once you put a gun in her hands! What a shot! And her ladylike demeanour and righteous etiquette goes straight out the window when she has a grouse in her sights!"

As Edward continued to praise the Countess's shooting skills, Anna tuned off and began to stare at her reflection again.

Margaret sat on her bed in her guest room, thinking over what she had overheard that day. If she had not heard what had passed between Anna and Sinclair for herself, she would never have believed it. It was unimaginable that a woman of Anna's background, breeding and reputation would have – could have – committed adultery. Many women did, of course, but not those of Anna's calibre. And then for her to have committed it with a peasant, a servant! And yet Anna had denied none of it to Sinclair. It was the truth. Lawrence had said his mother was complex, but even he could never guess or think how complicated she was and how her whole life was built on a foundation of lies.

Her darling, wonderful Lawrence was not Lord Armstrong's son, but the son of this Seán Hegarty, who had now come back to destroy them all with Sinclair's assistance. Margaret broke out in a hot sweat. Grabbing a fan, she went to the window and opened it up to get some air. She didn't know what to do. There was nobody she could confide in. If she spoke to her mother about it, her parents would cancel the engagement in a fit of horror and disgust.

But did this revelation change how she thought of Lawrence, how she felt about him? She closed her eyes as she stood at the window and looked deep into her heart to find the answer. The truth was that, no, it did not. It certainly made her look at him in a completely different light, but it did not change her love for him. In fact, in the strangest of ways, it made her love him even more. Lawrence was about to have his life destroyed and there was nothing she could do to protect him. He was either going to have his name destroyed or be disinherited. If Sinclair revealed the truth to the public as he had threatened, then there was no way her parents would allow the marriage to take place. And if Lawrence was disinherited, the only other outcome, then what would they live on? What would their future be like without his legacy? She couldn't imagine not living in a manor house and not having the trappings of wealth. She'd had that all her life. What's more, Lawrence had it all his life, and was completely unequipped to earn a living or deal with life without the legacy of being the heir to the vast Armstrong Estate.

There was a knock on the door.

"Margaret?" called her mother as she opened the door and

looked in. "Are you ready to come down to dinner? Your father and I are about to go down."

"Eh, yes, Mama," answered Margaret as she closed the window and walked across to the door.

"You missed the most excellent day's shooting!" said the Countess as they walked down the corridor.

"Yes?" asked Margaret.

"Your mother was like an execution squad with that gun!" said the Earl.

"I had a jolly good time! It's been a few years since I went on a shoot and I'd forgotten how exhilarating it could be. How did you spend the day, Margaret?"

"Oh, mostly walking in the grounds," said Margaret as they turned to go down the stairs.

"Tut, tut!" said the Countess. "One day you will be Lady Armstrong, and so I suggest you embrace country life with all your heart. Being the Lady of a Manor like this isn't just about parties and balls. To earn true respect, you need to be an excellent horsewoman and no harm in being a good shot as well! It will earn you extra respect."

"Although Lady Anna is not good at either, from what we can see," said the Earl.

"Well, Lady Anna might not be the best example for Margaret to follow," said the Countess with a raised eyebrow.

They reached the bottom of the stairs and walked over to the dining room where they found Edward and Lawrence already seated.

"Ah, there you are," said Edward as he rose to greet them.

"Lady Anna won't be joining us?" the Countess enquired.

"No, she's feeling much better, but has spent the day in bed and hopefully will be back to normal by tomorrow."

"That is good to hear," said the Countess.

As Margaret stared at Lawrence who was across the table from her, everything felt unreal. She sincerely doubted that Lady Anna would ever be back to normal again.

"Are you all right, Margaret?" asked Lawrence, snapping her out of her thoughts.

"Oh, yes," she said and managed to smile.

"We really missed you on the shoot today – pity you left," said Lawrence.

"Yes, I've been telling her she needs to take more of an interest in the estate – now that one day she will be Lady Armstrong," said the Countess.

Edward smiled at her. "I think Margaret will need no encouragement to take an interest in the Armstrong Estate. I don't think Lawrence could have chosen a better bride."

"Thank you, Lord Armstrong," said Margaret meekly.

As she studied her fiancé, she wondered if one could ever tell he was fathered by a peasant. But she couldn't see any sign of it whatsoever. He was a gentleman through and through. She looked at Edward. Now she could plainly see there was no physical resemblance between him and Lawrence at all, right down to their colouring being so different. And Lawrence didn't look like Anna either. And yet this total stranger called Seán Hegarty was supposed to have a striking resemblance to him.

As the others at the table chatted on about the hunt, Margaret watched. They all seemed so happy and merry, and yet they were on the verge of a disaster that would change all their lives forever.

Lawrence walked Margaret down the corridor that night to her room.

"Are you all right, Margaret? You are very quiet tonight," he commented.

"Oh, yes, I'm fine," she said, reaching her door.

"I can't believe you will be leaving for home the day after tomorrow – I will hardly be able to bear it until I see you next," he said.

"Well, it won't be that long. I'll be seeing you in a couple of weeks at the State Ball in Dublin."

He smiled at her. "That's a long time away!"

She studied him intently for a moment and then put her arms around him and held him tightly. "Whatever happens, Lawrence, I want you to know that I will always love you."

He hugged her tightly back. "What's all this about?"

She let him and go and smiled before saying, "Nothing, nothing at all."

She could hear her parents chattering, coming up the stairs.

"I'll see you in the morning," she said and went into her room.

CHAPTER 45

Harry sat at the window in his room at Hunter's Farm, smoking a cigar as he looked out at the countryside which was shrouded in darkness. Margaret's cruel words were playing over and over again in his mind. Her derogatory words, dismissing him as a nobody. Professing to love Lawrence, when it was so clear the reason she was marrying him was because of who he was. If Harry was the heir to the Armstrong Estate, would she dare speak to him as she had? He knew she would be falling at his feet if he was the heir and Lawrence wasn't. She wouldn't even have given Lawrence a second look.

"Damn Lawrence!" hissed Harry.

It was all Lawrence's fault. It had always been Lawrence's fault. The trouble was that Lawrence would no doubt be having children soon, pushing him further and further away from the seat of power. Harry had always known that Lawrence stood in his way to great wealth. Even as a young child he knew that. From their earliest childhood he had tried to lead Lawrence into danger – to ride that wild horse, cross that wild river, anything that could have caused Lawrence's death and get him out of the way. And Lawrence, the fool, never suspected. But Anna had and that's why she had taken Lawrence to London and safety away from him. When Lawrence came back, Harry had hoped to have further such opportunities but, after Anna had taken him aside and issued a warning, he couldn't do anything obvious. And besides, the sway he once had over Lawrence seemed to have disappeared and Lawrence did not seek his company any more.

And so here he was, so near a vast fortune and a different kind of life to the one he was condemned to lead.

He put his face in his hands. He couldn't face that life, a life of being nothing, when everything he ever wanted was almost in his grasp. If only Lawrence was out of the way!

He realised it was now or never. He could either act now and finally get rid of Lawrence or Lawrence would be married to Margaret soon with offspring and new heirs, and he would never inherit the estate. He didn't have much time.

But, as he sat there, a plan came to his mind.

It was the middle of the night and Anna lay awake. She thought of the plan she had devised earlier. Of taking Edward's key to the safe and taking the money that was stored there before replacing the key. With Sinclair being the only other person with a key, she'd hoped Edward would automatically assume Sinclair had taken it and would banish him from the estate. But she knew now that it was too late for that plan to work. Now that Sinclair had found Seán, he would just bring Seán forward and expose Anna even if she did try to frame him. Edward would realise it was a ploy by her to save herself. It would also be the same trick she had planned to frame Seán all those years ago, to have him banished from the estate.

As she looked at Edward's sleeping form she couldn't face what was going to come the next day. She had thought that evening of everything from running away to killing herself. But she realised none of it would stop Sinclair from exposing the truth to Edward about Lawrence not being his son. As Sinclair had made clear to her, this wasn't a personal vendetta against her. It was about him getting the Armstrong Estate and disinheriting Lawrence.

CHAPTER 46

Present Day

The following Friday, Kate was at the appointment at the National Archives that Daniel had arranged for her. She walked down through corridors stacked with files with a rather bored young civil servant called Roger. He seemed disinterested and she wasn't sure if she was happy or unhappy about that. Roger's disinterest suggested he wasn't going to be too bothered to ask too many questions.

"What hospital are you looking for again?" he asked.

"Castlewest in County Mayo and a doctor called Barry Davitt. It's specifically Doctor Davitt's files I'm looking for," she said.

Roger seemed to take ages running his fingers along the shelves of files before he struck gold.

"Doctor Barry Davitt, Castlewest, County Mayo," he said, pulling out a huge file. He brought it over to a table and placed it there. Then he put on white gloves and opened it.

Kate was nearly frightened to ask the question. "What year do his files start from in Castlewest?"

Roger checked the beginning of the file. "1858."

Kate's heart jumped for joy. This is what she had hoped for: that when Doctor Davitt transferred to the new hospital in Castlewest he had brought files from his own practice with him. And so he had, it seemed. And this had saved them from being destroyed and had led to them being eventually transferred to posterity here at the National Archives.

"What exactly are you looking for?" asked Roger, looking dismayed at the size of Doctor Davitt's file and not wishing to spend hours going through it looking for some general information.

"I'm looking for something very specific. His record of the 13th of August 1865," she said.

She sat down and waited patiently as Roger sifted through the file.

He seemed to take forever.

"These are the records from that day," said Roger eventually as he took out some sheets of paper from the file.

"May I see them?" asked Kate.

"You'll have to put on gloves, it's policy," he said.

"That's no problem," she said.

He sighed loudly. "I'll have to go upstairs to get you a pair of gloves. Don't touch anything!"

Kate waited until Roger was gone before getting up quickly and going to look at the sheets of paper he had left out. She read through Doctor Davitt's diary for the day. It was filled with a lot of mundane matters. A Mrs. O'Hara had a chest infection, a Mr. Hopkins had cut his hand. As she continued reading she saw an entry for that night.

"House call. 10'clock. Was asked to attend Armstrong House by a footman from the estate. Was met by Lord Edward who brought me quickly upstairs to one of the bedrooms. I attended to a young woman who was in a severely distressed state, crying and shaking. She had been sexually assaulted, had suffered severe bruises and her clothes were ripped. I tried calming her down and gave her a sedative. Spent one hour with the patient. Have been informed that the police are arriving. Patient's name: Lady Margaret Mountdare.

Kate picked up the piece of paper, stunned, as she stared at the name of the victim. Lady Margaret Mountdare: Lawrence Armstrong's fiancée.

As Kate drove back to Armstrong House that evening she was reeling from what had been revealed to her that day. She tried to picture the events in the house that night of August 13th, 1865. For a woman to have been assaulted would have thrown the house into chaos, but to now discover that the woman was Lady Margaret, the future wife of Lawrence and a lady of the realm! She began to understand why the charges weren't pressed. It would have buried all the parties involved in a scandal that they would never have recovered from. And in Victorian society Lady Margaret, the innocent victim, would have had her name destroyed by scandal through no fault of her own. How sad it was that Lady Margaret and her family, as important as they were, felt it was better to keep quiet over what happened than let the guilty be charged. But who was the culprit? Who had committed this terrible crime against this defenceless young woman who Kate imagined, given the times, was innocent to the ways of the world? Kate needed to find out.

As Kate sat in her drawing room that night, she was trying to think of how she could discover who the perpetrator was. She knew there was no reference to the event in any of the diaries or journals that had survived the fire at Armstrong House. But then she thought of Lady Margaret's family. She got up quickly, left the room and hurried across to the library.

Sitting down at her computer, she did a search on the Mountdares. She saw the Mountdares had been landowners of an enormous amount of land in Kildare and had lived at Kilternan House. She quickly discovered that Kilternan House was now being run as a hotel.

"Another great house that has succumbed to the pressures of commerce," she said cynically. As she continued to look into the Mountdare family, she read that when Kilternan House was sold on the death of the last of the Mountdares, a Lady Florence Mountdare, she had bequeathed the papers of the estate to Trinity College.

Kate looked up the Trinity College website and saw their library contained records of the Mountdare estate from the eighteenth century to 1956, including everything from receipts, invoices, correspondence and diaries. Although the Armstrongs kept what happened that night under a cloak of secrecy, Kate wondered if the Mountdares had been equally discreet?

CHAPTER 47

Kate made an appointment with an archivist called Martina at Trinity College and drove up to Dublin where she met her in the library. Martina ushered her into a side room and sat down at a desk with a computer. Kate sat opposite her.

"I read in the newspaper that you were planning a new film about Armstrong House during the Famine," said Martina excitedly. "Is this what this is connection with?"

"It is in connection with my film, yes. But I'm here today about something specific. I understand that the Mountdare family were guests there in the year 1865, and that you have all the records from their estate?"

"Yes, we were lucky to get them as most of the papers from the 'landed gentry' are donated to the National Archives or kept by the families themselves. But the last of the Mountdares, a Lady Florence, left the papers to the university when she died in the fifties. Rumour says that she had been in love with a professor here at the university all her life, but he refused to marry her. So she left the estate's papers to the college as a gesture of undying love for him!" Martina chuckled. "So what exactly are you looking for?"

"What I'm really looking for is information on the daughter of the house at that time, a Lady Margaret Mountdare. Specifically, any medical records she might have from the time. Or if she kept a diary?"

"Come over to this side of the desk, Kate, and sit beside me." Martina reached out and pulled another chair up to the desk and

Kate sat down.

Martina turned her attention to the computer.

"Luckily, all the papers from the estate have been uploaded onto a database. Otherwise I wouldn't like to have to go through two centuries of the Mountdares papers on library shelves, shifting through everything as mundane as grocery invoices to recipes!"

"It all gives a brilliant insight into the life they led, though, doesn't it?" said Kate.

"Yes, indeed. Have you many papers at Armstrong House from the centuries past?"

"There are a lot, yes, and I've tried to archive as much as possible. The trouble with Armstrong House is the fire in 1919 which destroyed a lot of papers. Presumably diaries and personal correspondence were destroyed in that – or else they were just never very good at keeping personal writings. In any case, I'm trying to fill in the gaps."

"Perhaps they had a lot to hide?" suggested Martina.

"Well, if you saw my last film on them, you'll realise you are probably right!" said Kate.

"I did see it, yes!" Martina squinted at the screen. "*Hmmm*, we don't seem have any writings or correspondence to or from Lady Margaret Mountdare. I imagine she took all her personal things with her when she married, so they were no longer part of the legacy we received."

"Oh, that is a pity," said Kate, thinking quickly. "What about her parents? Did they keep writings or correspondence?"

Martina continued searching through the database. "Lady Margaret's parents were Earl Grover and Countess Clementina Mountdare. From what I can see, the Earl was not a great writer or correspondent. Clementina, however, seems to have been – we have quite a considerable amount of writings and letters she received. She also did keep a social diary. They would have been big socialites."

Kate became excited. "Would she have kept a diary in 1865?"

Martina scrolled down the database. "Yes, she did. Would you like me to bring it up on the screen for you?"

"Yes, please!" said Kate.

Martina brought the Countess's diary up on the screen and left Kate alone so she could read through it.

Kate started scrolling down the pages of the diary starting in January of that year.

She could see that Clementina had beautiful handwriting and a clear concise approach. As she read the entries, Kate decided she liked this woman a lot. Clementina seemed witty and had a healthy sarcasm and occasional fruity language.

Kate's interest was piqued when she saw the first entry referring to Armstrong House. She read that Clementina and her husband had been invited to a ball at Armstrong House to celebrate the return of the Armstrongs to live there after their son Lawrence had finished school at Eton. Kate jotted down all this information about Anna and Edward in her notebook. She hadn't realised they had ever left Armstrong House to live anywhere else and now found out they had left the estate for a considerable period of time. She quickly continued through the diary to May of that year and the Mountdares' first visit to Armstrong House. Kate was bedazzled at Clementina's description of the house and the ball they attended there and of Edward, Anna and their son.

'Lord Edward and Lady Anna could not have been more gracious hosts. We arrived the night of the ball and were presented to Edward and Anna. We have missed them on the social scene in Ireland and are glad to have them back. Edward was as gracious and pleasant as ever, Anna as polite and warm – but yet she still had that distracted manner I had become accustomed to whenever we met on the social scene in Ireland before they left to live in London. But it was their son that struck us all the most! What a fine young man Lawrence has grown into since we saw him last. And manners to beat the band! We were all quite taken with him, but particularly Margaret. And as a mother with a daughter who will soon be in need of a husband, I'm delighted to say Lawrence returned Margaret's interest in full measure!'

Excited at the details she was learning, Kate read on. She learned from Clementina's diary that a correspondence had begun between Lawrence and Margaret. She then read that Lawrence had been invited to stay at the Mountdares' home for a week.

'One just could not wish or hope for a better guest than young Lawrence. He has entertained and charmed us all, his primary interest always being Margaret. If the way to a young girl's heart is through her parents, then in the case of Lawrence, I say – tally-ho!'

Kate giggled to herself at Clementina's wording and read on. According to Clementina, the friendship between her daughter and Lawrence quickly turned into a romance – which Clementina was not only giving her blessing to but was actively encouraging.

'I understand the Armstrong Estate runs to several thousand acres. As well as the impressive Armstrong House, the family own a house in London. Along with the impressive title, one wonders whether Margaret could do much better than that? But, aside from this, the icing on the cake is that Margaret seems madly in love with Lawrence and vice versa. Dare I hope there will no upsets? I worry about Lady Anna's opinion on the matter – that she will feel Lawrence too young to settle down. Sometimes one can never really know what Anna is thinking. She plays her cards close to her chest while putting on a gracious front. If there is any threat to this impending union between my daughter and her son, I suspect it will be Lady Anna.'

Kate anxiously read on, Clementina's insightfulness on Anna intriguing her, and giving her a whole new perspective on her. She skipped on to August and the Mountdares arriving at Armstrong House for their stay. Clementina wrote they arrived on August 11th and that there was a dinner that night to welcome them. Unfortunately for Kate, Clementina did not go into too much detail about the guests – not enough to give her possible clues as to who the potential culprits might have been in the lead-up to the assault. Clementina was too busy writing about Lawrence and Margaret's romance and worrying about Anna's mental health.

'We are all on tenterhooks on our first day at Armstrong House. After Lawrence asked for Margaret's hand in marriage, to which Grover readily agreed, we were waiting for Grover and Lord Edward to have their discussion to work out the details of the engagement and marriage. As we waited for dinner, it looked like

Anna wasn't going to join us. Finally, Edward stormed angrily upstairs, arriving back down some fifteen minutes later with a distinctly unhappy-looking Anna. We jollied our way through dinner and then Edward and Grover slipped away to have THE conversation about the engagement. When they returned, Lady Anna behaved in the most appalling fashion I have ever seen from a lady. She seemed very angry and started trying to humiliate Edward (successfully!) and embarrass us (unsuccessfully!) before she launched into a slow maudlin speech about the tragedies she saw during the Famine. We chose to ignore the episode and continued the night with joviality.'

Kate was intrigued at what she learned. Clementina was building a completely different picture of Anna than the one she had before. She seemed to be a very unhappy woman. Kate read on about the next day when there was a garden party on the terraced lawn and the announcement of their engagement by Lawrence and Margaret. And then Clementina wrote that Anna had fainted and had to be taken to bed. Kate began to understand that the week she was investigating at Armstrong House was a pressure-cooker of emotion between excitement and unhappiness, for whatever reason.

Kate read the next day's entry by Clementina.

'The Glorious 12th! Tally-ho! What a day! Never enjoyed myself so much. We walked miles through the moors on the Armstrong Estate. Excellent shoot! Best grouse in the country. It was Margaret's first shoot and she did not enjoy it so went back to the house on her own before the shoot had hardly begun.'

Kate reread the passage. Why had Margaret gone home on her own? Who was back at the house? Had somebody been watching her? Was somebody planning the attack on her that would happen the next day?

Kate held her breath as she went to scroll down to the next day's entry, hoping that it would finally reveal what exactly had happened to Margaret and who was the perpetrator.

Kate's heart sank as she saw the next day in Clementina's diary was blank. As was the next day and the next day and the following

THE LEGACY OF ARMSTRONG HOUSE

day after that. Clearly the trauma of what had happened to
Margaret had affected them all so badly that Clementina could not
even bring herself to write in her diary. The following week was
blank in Clementina's diary as well, as was the following week. At
last, three weeks later, Clementina made an entry.

'*What happened at Armstrong House that last night before we
left has affected me so badly that I have only been able to turn my
attention to my diary now. The events of that awful night will be
etched in my memory forever. Far worse for our precious Margaret
who will, I daresay, never be able to recover from an attack of that
sort.*

*I shall never know if we did the right thing not pressing charges
against that man. We did risk having Margaret's name reduced to
tatters had it gone to court, as Lord Edward said.*

*I don't know if banishment from the Armstrong Estate, to lose
one's home and position, is enough of a punishment for this brute
who did this to our darling daughter. But, even if the punishment
does not fit the crime, we still had no other choice.*'

Kate heart went out to Clementina. She tried to imagine what
she was going through as a parent coping with what had happened
to her child. She also was filled with frustration that Clementina
had not said in her diary who had done this terrible thing to
Margaret. She scrolled on throughout the rest of the year in the
diary, but there was no mention of the incident again. She then
checked Clementina's diary for the following year and again there
was no mention. Instead, Clementina's diary became filled with the
impending wedding arrangements for Margaret and Lawrence.
Kate thought it strange when she read that the wedding reception
was to take place at Armstrong House in the ballroom. Kate would
have imagined that Margaret wouldn't have wanted the most
important event of her life to take place in the house where she had
been so viciously attacked the previous year. But then she reasoned,
by marrying Lawrence Armstrong House would have been her
home for the rest of her life and she would just have had to get on
with it.

As she sat back, she thought of her own wedding reception to

Nico which had also taken place in the ballroom at Armstrong House. She felt a special connection with Margaret, thinking that their weddings had taken place in the exact same ballroom separated by one hundred and fifty years. As she thought back to her wedding day, she imagined guests on the day might also have thought it strange that she had chosen to get married and live in Armstrong House, after the tragic death of her first husband Tony there. And yet that had never occurred to her. She loved Armstrong House so much that the past could never change her opinion of it. And Kate felt the same had probably been true for Lady Margaret.

CHAPTER 48

1865

Taylor brought in the *Times* newspaper to the breakfast table the next morning.

"Pardon me, my lord, but I think there is something in today's paper that may interest you," he said, smiling as he handed over the paper.

"Oh?" said Edward, taking the paper and looking at what Taylor was pointing out.

"What is it, Papa?" asked Lawrence.

"*The Earl and Countess of Mountdare of Kilternan Manor are delighted to announce the engagement of their daughter Margaret to Viscount Lawrence Armstrong, son of Lord and Lady Armstrong of Armstrong House, County Mayo,*" read Edward loudly.

"Oh, excellent!" said the Countess, clapping her hands excitedly.

"I didn't realise you were putting it in the newspaper so soon!" said Margaret.

"Well, there was no point in waiting around," said the Countess.

"Show me!" said Lawrence excitedly as he took the newspaper and looked at the notice.

"Well! There's no getting out of it now, Margaret! We are official!"

Margaret looked at all the delighted faces and tried to look pleased. Her only thought was that, now that their engagement was in the newspaper, they would be all doomed when the truth came out.

Margaret's nerves were shattered as the day progressed, waiting for

Anna to appear. But she didn't leave her room and come downstairs. Edward set off after breakfast on business to the other side of the estate, and Margaret could tell from his cheerful and normal demeanour that Anna has obviously had not told him anything yet. Margaret could only imagine the heartbreak and pain Anna must be going through upstairs in her room, waiting for the inevitable time when she would have to reveal the truth to her husband.

In the afternoon Margaret and Lawrence went for a walk in the gardens.

"When is your father due back to the house?" asked Margaret.

"He said he would be gone most of the day. Why?"

"No reason," she said.

"The guests are due to arrive for the drinks party at seven, so I imagine he will be back in plenty of time to change into his white tie for that."

"Yes."

"I was thinking – after we are married, where should we live? Although Armstrong House is big enough for us to live with my parents, I don't think that would be an ideal situation for us, do you?"

"I hadn't given it any thought."

"There's a small manor on the estate on the other side of the village. It's in dreadful repair – I don't know when it was last lived in. But I was speaking to my father about us repairing it and making it our first home."

"*Hmmm* . . ." Margaret was hardly listening to him.

"I know it's not in any way comparable to Armstrong House or indeed to your own Kilternan House, but I think it might be a nice place for us to start our married life?"

"Perhaps," she said.

"I'm sure we'll be spending plenty of time at Armstrong House in any case as I'm sure you'll want to learn the running of the house for when you become Lady Armstrong one day."

Margaret didn't answer as they continued to walk along the paths.

"Margaret! Are you even listening to me?" Lawrence had become annoyed by her vagueness.

"Oh, for goodness' sake, Lawrence! We are only just engaged," said Margaret angrily. "It will an age before we are married. It's a bit early to think about what wallpaper to put up, isn't it?"

Lawrence was aghast and stopped walking as he looked at her. "I thought you would be excited about our first home."

"I am, but it's still quite a while off. Anything could happen in the meantime!"

"You're not – you're not regretting our engagement, are you? Are you having second thoughts?"

She sighed and held out her hand to take his. "Of course not, Lawrence. It's just, as I said, we have plenty of time to think about it."

He smiled at her. "Of course we do. Sorry – I have always been a little impetuous. And I apologise for speaking to my father about where we should live, before I discussed it with you."

"It's I who should be sorry. I'm just not in good form today, Lawrence, forgive me."

"Would you like to go back to the house?" he asked.

"No, not yet. I would like to walk for another while, but perhaps in silence?"

He nodded and smiled as they began to stroll on. "As you wish, my love."

CHAPTER 49

Harry was shoeing a horse in the courtyard behind Hunter's Farm when he heard somebody call his name. He turned around and saw Gertie at the side of the stables, calling him over. He sighed and walked over to her.

"What are you doing here?" he asked.

"I sneaked out and down here to see you. I was worried about you. You didn't show up the last night we were to meet at the stables and I haven't heard from you since."

"I've been busy."

"I waited for hours for you that night," she protested.

"More fool you!"

"I've missed you so much," she said, reaching her hands around the back of his neck and pulling him towards her to kiss him.

He took hold of her hands and shoved them away from him roughly.

"Harry?" she said, confused.

"I don't ever want to see your miserable face around me again," he said. "If I am at Armstrong House in future, you don't look at me or talk to me, do you understand me?"

"But, Harry, why are you being like this? You love me, don't you?"

"Love you! How could I love you? You're just a servant. I am an Armstrong! You're not fit to clean my boots!"

Shocked tears filled her eyes. "You said you loved me!"

"Well, let that be a lesson to you. Don't lift your skirts for the next man who tells you he loves you. Now clear off from here, get back to your work and leave me alone!" snarled Harry and he swung his arm in a gesture for her to go.

He returned to shoeing the horse.

Crying, Gertie ran away and back to Armstrong House.

All day Harry formulated his plan in his head. He knew now what he must do to secure his future and save himself from a life of drudgery.

That evening he walked into the parlour of Hunter's Farm where his parents were ready to leave for the drinks reception at Armstrong House.

"Harry! You aren't dressed for the drinks party? We are about to leave!" admonished Diana.

"I'm feeling unwell, so I'm not going tonight."

"What's the matter with you?" she asked.

"Oh, nothing to worry about – feel a bit shivery – maybe coming down with a cold."

"You'd better get to bed early if you're not well," said Sinclair. "I need you over at Toormore first thing in the morning."

"Yes, do go to bed and keep warm," said his mother as she pulled on her gloves. "Have a few hot whiskeys – that should help."

Harry nodded as they left. He looked out the window as their carriage drove away.

Then he walked out of the parlour and saw their cook coming out of the kitchen down the corridor.

"Cook, I'm going to bed early as I'm unwell. I do not wish to be disturbed for the rest of the night," he said.

"As you wish, Master Harry," she nodded as she went about her business.

Harry climbed the stairs and went to his bedroom. He opened a drawer and reached under the clothes inside, taking out a knife from under them. He held the knife tightly in his hand.

CHAPTER 50

Anna had changed into her ball gown for the evening and was in her bedroom, sitting beside the fireplace deep in thought. She had not ventured from her room all day. She had felt relieved that Edward had gone off on estate business for the day. It had allowed her time to put off telling him about their life being a lie. And had also given her time to think how to tell him.

She saw it was after six o'clock and there was still no sign of Edward. She imagined the Mountdares were already down in the drawing room with Lawrence, and the guests would be arriving soon – including Sinclair who would expect her to have told Edward.

Another half hour passed and she heard a horse pull up outside. She went to the window and saw it was Edward returning. She watched him jump down from his horse and hand it over to a stable boy before bounding across the forecourt to the house. She felt a cramp in her stomach and her mouth go dry as she steadied her nerves. She would have to tell him now. It was the last opportunity before Sinclair would arrive.

She stood looking at the door, waiting for it to open, and a few minutes later Edward came flying in.

"What a day I've had! I was delayed over at Vrayton. I couldn't get away and I'm running very late!" He stopped in his rush to look at her dressed in her ball gown and was pleased she had gone to considerable effort. "You look beautiful this evening, my dear!"

"Thank you, Edward."

He made for his dressing room.

"Edward!" she called.

"What?"

"Can I speak to you? I need to discuss something with you."

"It will have to wait, Anna. I barely have enough time to get ready before the guests arrive," Edward called from the dressing room.

"It is important – quite important," she insisted.

"Well, pray continue, I'm listening to your every word!" he called.

"Edward, I'd prefer if we were sitting down while we talked," she said.

The sound of carriages drawing up in the forecourt could be heard.

"Damn! They're arriving already. Anna, go downstairs and greet the guests and I will be down shortly."

"*Edward!*" she cried. "*This can't wait!*"

He popped his head around the door. "Well, it will have to, Anna. We can't leave the Mountdares to greet our guests! What will people think?"

"But –"

"Off you go, and I'll follow you down as soon as I can – I shan't be too long." Edward's head disappeared behind the door and he closed it.

She looked at the closed door, not knowing what to do. Then she walked over to the main door, out of the room and down the corridor. She steadied herself as she reached the top of the stairs and then began to descend.

From the drawing room came much chatter and laughter. She reached the door and halted. The Mountdares were there, as were the Foxes and Fitzherberts. Thankfully Sinclair hadn't arrived yet.

"Good evening, everybody. My apologies for being late," said Anna.

"Oh, you look much better, Anna," said the Countess. "Those couple of days of rest after the garden-party fiasco did you the world of good."

"Thank you," said Anna.

"Are you feeling much better, dear?" asked Mrs. Foxe, her face full of concern.

"Yes, much better – there really is no need to fuss," said Anna, embarrassed by the attention.

"A faint can happen to the best of us," said the Countess. "I remember going into the most frightful swoon at a ball in the Viceregal Lodge once. I remember I was dancing with a Turkish gentleman at the time – he was part of their diplomatic services, as I recall. I think it was the overbearing odour of garlic that was lingering on his breath that did me in! I cannot abide the odour of garlic."

"The incident nearly caused a diplomatic outcry," said the Earl.

"To give him his due, he was a wonderful dancer, as I recall, before I passed out in his arms!"

As her mother wittered on, Margaret observed Anna intently. She had put a lot of effort into dressing that evening, and looked well. But she could see she was pale, despite her glitzy gown and jewellery, and her eyes looked haunted. And there was no sign of Edward. Margaret had seen him arrive back not long ago and wondered had Anna told him. Was he broken in his room on hearing what Anna had said? Would he arrive into the room any second shouting and disowning his wife and son? Or was he too emotionally destroyed to even move?

At that moment the door opened and Edward came in, dressed in his white tie, smiling and looking as if he did not have a care in the world.

"I am so sorry I'm late! Estate business detained me. Has my wife been catering to your needs?" he said, putting an arm around Anna's waist.

"She certainly has, Edward – good to see her back to herself," said Mrs. Foxe.

"The Armstrong women are built of sturdier stuff than to allow a little faint from afternoon heat to put them out of action for long," said Edward, smiling warmly at Anna.

As Margaret looked on, she realised that Anna had not told

Edward anything. She had not followed Sinclair's instructions. She wondered if Anna had not been able to bring herself to tell him – or had she just not had the opportunity, with him away all day? Part of her felt relieved, but she knew Sinclair was due to arrive soon and when he found out she had failed to act, he would do it for her.

The door of the room opened and Taylor walked in.

"Mr. Sinclair and Mrs. Diana Armstrong," announced Taylor.

Sinclair walked in first, followed by Diana.

"Sinclair! Welcome!" said Edward, shaking Sinclair's hand before kissing Diana on the cheek. "I'm afraid I had a spot of trouble with some tenants over at the Vrayton part of the estate today. I'll discuss it later with you, Sinclair, if we get the chance."

Margaret saw Sinclair look anxiously at Edward's smiling face before he looked at Anna who steadfastly avoided his angry stare.

Diana stepped forward and kissed Edward on the cheek before turning to Anna and kissing her cheek.

"Thank you for the invitation, Cousin Anna," said Diana.

Anna said nothing and looked away.

Margaret could see Diana looked nervous and uncomfortable. Diana had struck Margaret as a cool calculating woman, but she wondered if the enormity of what was about to happen had dawned on her.

CHAPTER 51

Harry left his bedroom at nine and locked the door behind him, pocketing the key, in case of the unlikely event the cook or somebody else should look in on him. Although they would know better than to do that. He trod carefully down the stairs, making sure the cook wasn't around, and then nipped out the front door. Checking the coast was clear, he ran quickly over to the trees beside the house.

He then made his way carefully cross-country and up into the parklands that surrounded Armstrong House. His eyes darting everywhere, he made his way up to the stables behind the house. He knew there would be two night watchmen patrolling the house as they had done every night since the news of the murder of Colonel Frampton, so he moved with caution.

It was ten o'clock and nearly dark when he sidled up to one of the windows that looked into the kitchen. Religiously, the household staff at Armstrong House had tea at ten o'clock at the long table. Dinner had always been served upstairs by then and cleared away and the staff had their night tea before doing late-night chores and then going to bed. He saw them all there except Taylor and the footmen who he knew would be busy upstairs in the drawing room, serving drinks to the guests.

He walked around to the side of the house and moved stealthily along it till he found the small side door that led to the servants' stairs. He took a key out of his pocket and unlocked the door. He had the key from when he and his parents had lived at Armstrong House. Darting in, he locked the door behind him. He knew this was the only time he could safely gain access unnoticed into the house. An hour later all the doors would be bolted from the inside and windows locked. Listening for any sound, he began to ascend the servants' stairs as quiet as a mouse. He made his way up to the bedrooms on the first floor.

"What's wrong with you at all tonight, Gertie? You haven't said a word all evening and you look terrible," said the cook who was sitting at the top of the table.

"I'm not feeling very well," said Gertie.

The cook looked at Gertie. The girl was never ill and was always incredibly cheery. She was one of the best maids in the house and, if she was complaining about being ill, the cook realised she was not faking it.

"You get yourself up to bed then in that case, Gertie, and have yourself an early night. Hopefully, you'll feel better in the morning."

"Thank you," said Gertie as she made her way quickly from the table for fear she might burst out crying any moment in front of the rest of the staff.

Gertie walked to the back of the kitchen and through the maze of corridors that led to different storage rooms. She began to walk up the servants' stairs, which was a winding narrow stairway tucked away at the end of the corridor. It twisted up from the kitchens to each floor till it reached the attic. She couldn't wait to get to her bedroom in the attic where she would sob her heart out after the cruel words Harry had said to her that afternoon. How could he have been so cruel? How could she have been so stupid?

She reached the turn of the stairs on the first floor and was about to keep going up the stairs to the attic rooms when she saw somebody move at the bottom of the corridor. To her amazement she saw it was Harry. She hid behind the turn in the wall to watch him and she saw him stop at Lawrence's bedroom. Then she saw him carefully open the door and slip into the room, closing the door behind him.

Inside Lawrence's room, Harry looked quickly around. This had been his room for three years before they had been forced to move back to Hunter's Farm and he knew it like the back of his hand. The bathroom that led off to the left, the dressing room that led off to the right. He quickly went over to the drawers and looked through them. Yes, there was considerable money there, and expensive watches and gold coins. Enough to warrant a robbery. He went to the dressing room, opened the door and went in, closing the door behind him. There were wardrobes full of Lawrence's clothes, an array of formal suits and hunting and casual clothes. He ignored them all and went to the end where there was a large walk-in chamber. He knew that this was where the maids stored blankets, pillows and linen for the room. He knew it was a place that Lawrence would never look into. Opening the door to this chamber he walked inside and hid himself at the back behind the end of a shelf. He took a pillow and held it tight. It was now just a case of a long waiting game.

He imagined the drinks party would finish around one in the morning. Lawrence would come up to bed, probably slightly inebriated. After Lawrence had gone to bed, he would steal out of the wardrobe and dressing room. He would creep over to Lawrence's bed and cover his face with the pillow, before burying his knife into his heart. He would then take the valuables from the drawers and, safe in the knowledge that everyone had gone to bed, creep down to the library and unlock the window from the inside and escape. He would leave the window ajar and the next morning it would look like the footmen didn't lock that window and the intruder got in through it. And when Lawrence's dead body was found in his bed, knifed through the heart, everyone would think he was the victim of the thief that was going around breaking into manor houses, the one that knifed Colonel Frampton. It would be the perfect crime, Harry congratulated himself in advance.

CHAPTER 52

Present Day

Driving back from Dublin that evening, Kate phoned Daniel to tell him what she had found and he invited her to drop by to chat about it. So she turned her Land Cruiser into the driveway at Hunter's Farm before going home to Armstrong House.

Daniel opened a bottle of wine and poured himself and Kate a glass each.

Then he sat on the armchair opposite the couch where she had settled herself.

"I got so close to finding out the truth, but then hit another brick wall," said Kate.

He studied the copy of the page from Clementina's diary the week after the attack.

"And there was no reference to the attack in any other diaries or correspondence from the Mountdares' estate?" he asked.

"Nothing we could find," she said. "The trail has gone cold."

He studied the diary entry. "Well, let's see what you've learned from your different sources. You learned that Sergeant Bourke was called to the house and was told there was an assault but was then told by Lord Edward that charges wouldn't be pressed. So, between Lady Margaret being assaulted and the police arriving, Lady Margaret and her parents decided not to press charges, obviously to avoid scandal. You learned Doctor Davitt attended to Margaret, confirming there was an assault. Let's think about what Clementina wrote in her diary . . . and about who we know or suspect was in the house the night of the attack."

"Go on," said Kate, taking a sip of her wine and listening intently.

"Lord Edward couldn't be the culprit as he called for the police – no, that's not true – calling them could in fact cover his own guilt."

"Or somebody else might have called for the police when they found out Lady Margaret was attacked and then Lord Edward sent them away to protect himself."

"How could he take such a risk?" said Daniel. "That would incriminate him if the Mountdares tried to follow it up the next day."

"True."

"Sergeant Bourke did say Edward was shook," said Kate, trying to look at all angles.

"Of course he was – after what had happened in his house," said Daniel. "And I doubt Lady Margaret would have come and lived in Armstrong House after she got married with a father-in-law like that around if he had been the guilty one!"

"Besides, Clementina goes by Edward's advice in her diary," said Kate. "Again, she would not do that if he was the culprit."

"So, we've cleared Lord Edward then," said Daniel with a touch of irony.

"Seems so," said Kate, pulling a face.

"Right! We can also rule out Lawrence as the attacker, under the assumption that one would hope Margaret wouldn't have consented to marry him if he had attacked her!"

"Absolutely. And I can tell how much Margaret adored Lawrence from correspondence in the house from much later in their marriage."

"So, it could have been one of the guests who was attending the engagement party that night?" suggested Daniel.

"I thought of that first. But then look again at what Clementina writes in her diary – she says that she didn't know if being banished from the Armstrong Estate and losing one's home and position was enough punishment for the man who was the attacker. This wasn't a guest attending the party that night. This was somebody who lived there."

"But that could mean a servant. Or a tenant farmer on the estate."

"You're right. In fact, Clementina said that Margaret had not stayed with the shoot on the Glorious 12th two days before the attack but had made her way back to the house on her own. She might have been watched by somebody on the estate – somebody might have followed her. And not getting the chance to pounce that day, it could have put it in his head to attack her."

"That would be more likely. It's hard to think a servant in the house would have taken the chance to attack Margaret as she could so easily identify him. But maybe a tenant farmer, or a stable boy, broke into the house, hoping she wouldn't be able to identify him."

"But how can I ever identify that person?"

"Do the records survive of the running of the estate from that era? The rent collections from the tenant farmers and the payments to servants?" he asked.

"Yes, they do. I mean there's boxes of files in the attic of the house from then. I have managed to file personal items and stuff like the different cooks' menus and recipes over the decades but I never got a chance to put the financial statements into any order. It all looked like boring stuff to me, of no interest to anybody."

"Well, if you find out if from those records if somebody was dismissed from the house or estate in the week of this attack, then I think you might just have found your man." Kate stared at him. "Brilliant! You're absolutely right!"

"Yes, I am – both brilliant and right!" he chuckled.

Kate sat in thought and took a sip of her wine. Then she said, "But it will take me ages to go through all that, and my producer Brian is waiting on a full proposal by the end of the week to save my film from being rejected by all and sundry."

"I'll help you."

"But you have enough to do with your own work," she said.

"It's not a problem. Now I'm dying to find out who did it myself!" he said with a grin.

Nico looked at his watch. It was nearly eleven. He was concerned about Kate. She should have been back from Dublin hours before.

He had tried phoning and texting her and there was no response.

He came down to the kitchen, having just put Cian to bed. Valerie was drinking wine and chatted away incessantly about her time when she was a singer on a cruise ship. Mindful of the promise he had given Kate, he nodded and smiled and consciously tried to be polite. He had to admit, for a woman on the run from the mob Valerie was either a very good actress or wasn't experiencing too much concern or fear.

"The great thing about being a singer on a cruise ship is that you are seeing a new city every couple of days. We were in Miami one day and then San Juan in Puerto Rico the next. Where else can you get an experience like that? I remember I met the most gorgeous Swedish guy while working the cruise liner. It was a kind of whirlwind romance. Unfortunately, he left the cruise in Cuba and it was the last I ever heard of him."

"Did Kate give you any indication of what time she was supposed to be home? She's very late."

"She didn't say. You know Kate, she's a bit like me in that regard, a free spirit at heart."

"*Hmmm*," said Nico.

"I think it comes from having emigrated when we were kids," mused Valerie, in what was one of the few pieces of wisdom Nico had heard from her.

Then he heard Kate's high heels come clicking down the stairs.

"Sorry I'm so late!" said Kate as she came into the kitchen. She hurried over to Nico and gave him a kiss.

"Kate, I phoned and texted you and was getting very worried," said Nico.

"I know, I'm sorry, I left my phone in the car when I dropped into Hunter's Farm." She quickly put on the kettle for a cup of tea.

"What were you doing there?" asked Nico.

"Well, I found the most interesting information today at Trinity College and wanted to get Daniel's opinion on it."

"I see!" said Nico, looking more surprised than angry.

"I think we are finally narrowing down the possible attackers of Lady Margaret."

"We?" repeated Nico, arching his eyebrow.

She ignored his comment. "I just need to go through the records of employees and farmers on the estate and see if anyone was thrown off the estate the week of the attack!"

Nico realised that in her excitement she hadn't a clue that he had no idea what she was talking about. "You haven't really been filling me in on what you've been discovering, so this is all news to me," he said.

"Well, you haven't really been interested, have you?" she retorted.

He had to admit to himself that this was the truth. He remembered, when she was doing the research for her last film, she did tell him what she was finding out as she went along, even if he hadn't been supportive. This time she obviously wasn't going to bother wasting her time involving him, when she had a willing and enthusiastic pair of ears in Daniel.

"Do you want help going through the estate records here?" Nico asked.

"Oh, no, Nico. You wouldn't have the patience for that – you'd only get in my way. Daniel's offered to lend a helping hand."

"Oh, right." Nico felt deflated.

"Yes, with his experience in research he'll know exactly what we should be looking for."

Valerie didn't show it on her face, but she looked at the two of them with concern. Kate and Nico might not be realising what was happening in their marriage, but Valerie had been around the block too many times not to be able to spot the glaring danger signs.

CHAPTER 53

Kate and Daniel sat in the one of attic rooms on the third floor of Armstrong House. These used to be rooms where the servants lived. They were small rooms with dormer windows jutting out from under the roof. There was still a back stairway that led from the attics all the way down to the kitchens in the basement. That was the stairway the servants used. It was here in the attics that boxes of papers from previous centuries were kept.

Daniel got up from the chair he was sitting on and went to the small window. He looked out at the view across the lake.

"You know, if you ever turned this place into a hotel you could turn these rooms into bedrooms," he suggested.

"Don't, Daniel! If I ever suggested a hotel here it would be a certain divorce between me and Nico. Things are bad enough as they are."

"Oh?" He looked at her curiously. "What do you mean?"

"Oh, he's just unnerved with Valerie being here and the thought of me doing another film at the house. When we shot *The Secrets of Armstrong House*, our home was turned into a film set for six months. There was production staff telling Nico to move all the time and that he was getting in the way!"

"I suppose that could be difficult to live with. He was kind of surplus to requirement as regards his own home and family history," Daniel observed.

"In a way he was," she sighed. "I think he feels I've hijacked his ancestral home and his family history . . . maybe I have."

"I couldn't imagine anything more exciting, a film being made about my family's past and me there seeing it being made," said Daniel.

"Well, that's because you're an archaeologist, Daniel – you dig to find out what happened in the past. Nico is an architect – he builds for what will happen in the future."

"Nicely put," he said.

She ran fingers down columns in a ledger.

"I wish we had all this stuff on data base. It would make finding things so much easier. You should have seen the speed that the archivist in Trinity found what we were looking for."

He smiled and went to sit down again to study the ledger he had been previously examining.

"Well, that's all the household servants, gardeners and stable boys accounted for," she said. "Their payments for the year show nearly all were still working here at the end of the year. There was one dismissal of a scullery maid in the March of that year, the reason given as insolence. So, it wasn't a member of the household staff."

"It must have been a tenant farmer in that case," said Daniel. "Although I can't come across any tenant farmers that had been evicted or thrown off the estate so far that year. 1865 was a relatively prosperous time – things had recovered from the Famine, so there wouldn't have been evictions as a rule."

"Which is good for our purposes. If we find a tenant farmer who was evicted in August 1865, he may very well be the culprit," said Kate as she took up another ledger which read: 'Armstrong Estate – Tenancies of Fifty Acres or More.'

She knew that most of the tenant farms only stretched to less than five acres. So these would have been well-off tenants, and maybe even members of the gentry amongst them.

She opened the ledger which was organised alphabetically and the first name she saw was 'Armstrong – Sinclair – Hunter's Farm – Eighty Acres – rent £5 annually'.

Kate then read across the payments for Hunter's Farm for each month and saw the rent was paid on the first day of the month. She suddenly stopped when she saw the last month was August 1st. The rest of the months were blank.

"*Daniel, look at this!*" she said, pointing to the ledger entry. "It's for Sinclair Armstrong who was Lord Edward's cousin and the estate manager. He lived in Hunter's Farm. The last payment was for the first of August."

Daniel took the ledger and examined it.

"I read about this man from the police file you gave me," said Kate excitedly. "He sounded like a bit of a brute. He was always making complaints to the police, and there were even some complaints about him from peasants that he had hit them. The police did nothing as he was Lord Edward's cousin. He had been the estate manager here for years. The police file for the Famine that you gave me stretched back twenty years before this."

"And he was family," said Daniel. "And a member of the gentry. It would make perfect sense that he would have been invited to the engagement party that night at Armstrong House."

"It has to be him! It would make sense from Clementina's diary – Lord Edward would banish him from the estate and his position. Not just from Hunter's Farm, but from his very prominent position as estate manager."

Kate went scrabbling through the ledgers and found the next one for tenant farmers of holdings of more than fifty acres. She opened the front page and saw there was no Sinclair Armstrong listed under the 'A's'. She ran a finger down the pages until she found an entry.

'*John Dillon – Hunter's Farm – rent £5 annually (new estate manager).*'

"Look!" said Kate excitedly, showing him the entry. "Hunter's Farm was then leased out to this new man John Dillon and he was the new estate manager. Sinclair must be Margaret's attacker! There is no other reason why he would leave this place in the previous August – leave his home and the job he had for well over twenty years."

CHAPTER 54

1865

The drinks party at Armstrong House was in full swing. Some of the guests took turns playing the piano while others played card games. As Taylor continued serving drinks, the chatter and laughter grew louder. Margaret was sitting on a sofa beside Lawrence. As he chatted away happily to the others, she was a silent observer. Sinclair did not take his eyes off Anna the whole time, his black eyes glaring at her while she avoided even glancing in his direction. Margaret saw that Sinclair made several attempts to engage Anna in conversation but she always managed to draw somebody in to join them, much to Sinclair's fury. As the clock struck ten, Margaret saw that Anna had been cornered by Sinclair beside the fireplace and this time there was nobody at hand to rescue her. She saw Anna's face fill with fear and dread.

"You have not told Edward!" Sinclair accused Anna, his voice a vicious whisper.

"I did not get chance, Sinclair. You heard him yourself – he was detained on estate business all day," said Anna, blinking several times. "I saw him for barely two minutes when he got back!"

"I told you if you did not tell him today, then I would tell him," said Sinclair.

"Oh, please Sinclair! I promise I will tell him tomorrow."

"I've waited long enough for what is mine. The Mountdares will be going tomorrow and I told you this needed to be done before they went."

Anna looked over at Edward who was laughing as he spoke to the Countess.

"Just one more day, Sinclair!" she pleaded with him.

"No! You've had your chance and you have no intention of telling him so it must fall to me. I'll take him outside and tell him now," said Sinclair, and he made to move away from her.

"*No!*" she begged. "I will tell him. I will tell him now."

Gertie waited at the servants' stairs a long while for Harry to reappear from Lawrence's room. But as time went on and there was no sign of him, she became curious and worried. Why wasn't Harry down at the drinks party with the rest of them? What was he doing in Master Lawrence's room? Curiosity finally got the better of her. And she really needed to speak with Harry. Perhaps she had caught him in a bad mood earlier, and he would be different now. She walked down the corridor and knocked lightly on Lawrence's door but there was no answer. She opened the door and peeped in, but she could see nobody there. As she looked around the room, she wondered where Harry had got to. He had definitely not come back out of the bedroom onto the corridor. She decided he must be in the bathroom and went over to the door leading into it.

"Harry?" she whispered as she opened the door carefully and looked in. But Harry wasn't there either.

She was flummoxed as she came back into the main bedroom and looked around. She looked under the bed to no avail, although she had no idea why she did that as why would Harry be there?

Looking at the door leading into the dressing room, she decided it was the only place Harry could be. Although, again, she had no idea why he would be there unless he had spilled drink on his clothes and Master Lawrence had told him to go up and borrow some of his clothes and change into them. Yes, that's what it must be, she thought, as she went over to the dressing room, preparing herself to apologise to Harry for whatever she had done to upset him earlier. She opened the door and looked in. But again, there was no sign of Harry. She walked inside. Unless she was going mad, this was the only place Harry could possibly be. Was he hiding on her? Her head muddled as to what was going on, but determined to find out, she began opening the wardrobes but could see nothing except Lawrence's clothes.

She reached the end of the dressing room and the linen chamber. She pulled back its doors and peered in. She could hear something move and she went further in.

And to her horror she saw Harry crouched there.

"*Harry!*" she cried in shock. "What are you doing here?"

"What the *fuck* are *you* doing here?" he retorted, standing up and walking out of the linen chamber, his face contorted with anger.

"I saw you coming into Master Lawrence's room and came to see what you were doing," she gulped and, now nervous, she scuttled back out of the dressing room into the main bedroom.

He followed her. "*You nosy fucking bitch!*" he spat at her. "*Spying on me!*"

"I wasn't spying, I –" she continued, backing away from him, but as she saw the disgust on his face she became angry too. "*What are you doing here, Harry?*"

"It's none of your business," he said.

"I'm going straight down to Lord Armstrong and I'm going to tell him I found you hiding in Master Lawrence's room!" she threatened. "And, while I'm at it, I'm going to tell him that you've been riding me for months! We'll see how clever you are then, *Master* Harry!"

"*You'll do no such thing!*"

"*I will, I will, I tell you!*" she said furiously. "And Lord Armstrong will know what to do with the likes of you when he finds out all about you! Taking advantage of a poor maid and then breaking into his son's room to steal! That'll teach you to mind your manners in the future and you won't mess with me or my likes again!"

Harry looked at her, his rage growing as a hundred thoughts passed through his head. Everything from the fact that Lawrence could confirm he had been having a fling with Gertie because he had confided in him, to fury that this little tramp was threatening him, to the consequences for him if she did go to Edward and exposed him. To the fact that his plan to kill Lawrence was now in tatters. All because of this stupid interfering girl!

"I'm going now to tell Lord Armstrong everything!" she said as she turned to leave.

Harry reached out and grabbed her arm, pulling her back.

"*Let me go!*" she demanded and she tried to shake him off her.

Suddenly, she saw what he had in his other hand which he had been holding behind his back. A knife.

Gertie looked down at the knife and looked up quickly at Harry's murderous eyes. She opened her mouth to scream at the top of her voice for help, but he slapped his hand over it, silencing her.

Margaret took in every detail of the scene between Sinclair and Anna in the drawing room. She saw their rushed whispered conversation and Anna pulling Sinclair back as she pleaded with him. She was filled with alarm and terror as she saw Anna stand for a while blinking back tears before she walked slowly over to Edward.

Margaret found herself trembling. She looked at Sinclair, looking pleased with himself as he took a cigar out of his pocket and sauntered over to a window to look out.

She got up and walked over to him.

"Good evening, Mr. Armstrong," she said.

Sinclair turned and was surprised to see Margaret was addressing him. He had only ever said two words to her – hello and goodbye. To him, she was just another spoilt child of an earl.

"Good evening, Lady Margaret," he said.

"I – I – should like to speak to you in private," she said.

"What about?" he asked.

"It is of a private nature, but it is very important and quite urgent," she said.

He thought of Anna speaking with Edward and didn't want any distractions from this silly girl.

"Whatever you have to say, you can say to me here," he said.

"What I have to say must be said in privacy, and not with spying eyes and the risk of being overheard," she said quietly, indicating

330

the others in the room who were laughing and chatting close by.

"It will have to wait, whatever you need to speak to me about," he said, going to turn away from her.

"If you won't speak to me, then I shall have to go to Lord Armstrong immediately and discuss the matter with him. It is of such an urgent and serious nature."

Sinclair looked at her, perplexed, and decided whatever she had to discuss must concern Harry, and God only knew what his son had done now. Most importantly, he didn't want this girl to go and interrupt Edward, not now when Anna was finally about to reveal the truth about Lawrence to him.

"All right, let us leave and find a private place to speak!" he said, irritated.

"No!" she said. "I can't be seen to leave the room with you. My mother will follow us immediately and will want to know what we are discussing. And what I have to say is not for her ears, I can assure you."

Sinclair was beginning to get nervous as he looked at the girl – she seemed so stressed and was trembling. If Harry had done anything to upset the apple-cart, just when everything they wanted was within their grasp, he would kill him.

"All right, where shall we talk?" asked Sinclair.

"I can't speak to you downstairs as the servants might see us. I'm staying in the Red Room – do you know it?"

"Of course – I lived here for three years, you do realise," he said.

"Good. I shall leave now and go there. You follow me. You cannot delay, or I shall go to find Lord Armstrong." And before giving Sinclair a chance to say another word, she turned and discreetly left the room.

Sinclair became agitated. He really didn't want to meet this girl, but whatever it was obviously concerned Harry. Perhaps something had passed between them and that was the real reason Harry hadn't come to the drinks party that evening. He needed to find out and silence whatever had happened before the girl brought it out in the open. He left the room. Outside there was no sign of Margaret and he walked to the main staircase and went up it. He walked down the long corridor and took the first left down a small passage until he reached the Red Room and knocked on the door.

"Come in," came Margaret's voice from inside.

He walked in and saw she was sitting at the dressing table on the other side of the room.

"Well – what is it?" he asked impatiently.

Anna stood beside Edward and the Countess in the drawing room, trembling as she tried to get the words out of her mouth to request to speak to Edward alone.

"Anna! This port you are serving is delicious – wherever did you get it from?" asked the Countess.

"A wine merchant's in Dublin," said Anna.

"You must give me their name," said the Countess.

"Edward, may I speak with you?" asked Anna abruptly.

"Eh, yes, of course," said Edward.

"Privately," she insisted, glancing at the Countess.

"Is anything the matter, dear?" asked the Countess.

"Edward – *please* – it cannot wait."

Edward shrugged and smiled at the Countess, feeling slightly embarrassed. "If you'll excuse me."

He put down his drink on a table and followed Anna out of the room.

"It's probably something to do with scullery maids – it's always something to do with scullery maids!" said the Countess as she finished off her port.

Edward followed Anna across the hallway and into the small parlour.

"Whatever is this about, Anna?" he demanded.

"Please close the door," she asked and he did as she bid.

She sat down on the sofa and buried her face into her hands.

"Anna?" he said, approaching her.

As she started sobbing he sat and put his arms around her.

"Anna!" pleaded Edward as he held her sobbing body. "Please tell me what is wrong with you."

"It's so difficult to tell you, Edward," she said between sobs.

"The hardest thing I've ever had to do."

"You are scaring me now, Anna. Please tell me what is the matter with you," pleaded Edward.

She drew back from him and wiped away her tears. "I want you to know, I need you to know, that I have always loved you. Always. Anything I have ever done is because of the love I have for you."

"I know you've loved me, Anna. I've never doubted it for a moment. As I have loved you."

"But can you love me when you find out what I've done?"

"What could you ever have done that could stop me from loving you?" he said with a smile.

In her room Margaret stared at Sinclair.

"Well!" he said. "What did you want to speak to me about?"

Suddenly Margaret burst out crying.

"Whatever is the matter with you?" asked Sinclair, walking up to her and looking down at her for an explanation.

"It's just – I just – we are just –"

"Out with it, girl!" demanded Sinclair.

Margaret stood up and walked quickly away from him to the door. Then she turned the key in the lock and, taking it out, slipped it down inside her corset.

"In case a servant walks in and hears us," she said.

"What is all this about, girl?" demanded Sinclair, becoming even more angry. Poor Lawrence, he thought, not only was he about to be disinherited but he was obviously getting married to a girl who was not the full shilling!

She walked quickly over to him and, to his astonishment, pressed herself against him. Then she put her hand around the back of his neck and pulled him towards her, kissing him passionately on the lips.

"What on earth do you think you're doing?" he asked, shocked, as she pulled him closer and put his hand on her breast.

"*Stop, Sinclair, please don't!*" she cried as she struggled against him.

"*It's you that must stop! I am doing nothing!*" Sinclair yelled as he tried to push her away.

She pulled back. Suddenly she reached for the top of her dress with both hands and, with all her strength, tore it open down the front. Pulling the hairpins out of one side of her hair, she dragged it down to her shoulder.

Then, to Sinclair's shock, Margaret suddenly started screaming at the top of her voice.

In the parlour Edward continued to hold Anna in his arms as her sobs subsided.

"Anna?" he gently questioned, trying to get her to speak.

She sat back from him and wiped her eyes. "Edward, do you remember when we first got married?"

"Yes, of course I do," he said.

"Do you remember we had a servant who worked in the house here?" Anna's voice was trembling.

"Anna, whatever is this about? Surely this isn't the time –" He stopped abruptly.

"It *is*," she said. "It *has* to be. Edward –"

"Hush a moment," he said, raising a hand to stop her.

"Edward –"

"*Shhh!*" said Edward as he heard a commotion outside the parlour.

Then a loud knocking sounded on the door.

"My lord! My lord!" cried Taylor as he opened the door and rushed in.

"What is it, Taylor? What is going on?"

"My lord, a woman is screaming somewhere in the house," said Taylor.

"What are you talking about? Who the blazes is screaming?" demanded Edward as he rushed out into the hall.

"*Edward!*" cried Anna after him.

Inside Margaret's bedroom Sinclair was staring at Margaret in horror as she continued screaming and tearing at her face and clothes.

"*Stop it, you mad bitch!*" he shouted at her before racing to the door.

Finding it locked, he turned and raced back to her.

"*Give me the fucking key!*" he yelled.

As she continued to scream, he grabbed her shoulders roughly but she began to fight him, tearing at his face with her fingernails. He pushed her to the ground and held her down as he struggled to get the door-key from her corset.

Edward moved through the guests who had begun to come out of the drawing room and gather in the hallway. They were all looking around trying to decipher where the woman's screams were coming from.

"What is it, Papa?" Lawrence cried.

"It sounds like a banshee!" said the Countess.

"Shut up everybody and let me hear!" demanded Edward and the crowd fell silent.

"*Help me! Help me!*" came a woman's cries between the screams coming from upstairs.

"*That's Margaret screaming!*" shrieked the Countess and, hauling up her skirts, she rushed up the stairs.

Edward, Lawrence and the footmen followed her, the Earl panting in their wake.

The Countess went racing down the corridor to Margaret's room, her huge crinoline preventing the men from passing her.

"*Margaret! Margaret!*" she screeched as she tried to open the door and found it locked. She began pounding on the door.

Edward pushed her out of the way and started to throw his weight against it to break it in. Lawrence began to barge at the door as well. Suddenly it burst open and Edward and Lawrence rushed in to see Sinclair and Margaret struggling on the ground together.

Edward halted, stunned, as Lawrence raced forward and pulled Sinclair from Margaret.

"*Margaret!*" screamed the Countess as she pushed a stunned Edward out of the way. Throwing herself on the ground, she embraced her sobbing daughter.

"Mama!" sobbed Margaret.

"What the blazes is going on?" demanded Edward.

"*Can't you see what's going on!*" screeched the Countess.

"*He attacked me!*" cried Margaret through her sobs. "I came up to my room and then he followed me up and came in and tried to kiss me and when I refused he tried to force himself on me!"

Everyone stared at Sinclair who was dishevelled, with his face scratched.

"*The girl is clearly insane!*" he spluttered. "It is *she* who attacked *me!*"

"He forced his mouth down on mine, and forced his tongue – *ohhh!*" Margaret began to wail.

"Sir – what have you done to my daughter?" demanded the Earl, stepping forward.

"*Fetch me a gun!*" shrilled the Countess. "*Fetch me a gun and I'll shoot the bastard!*"

Edward stared at his cousin in shock.

"The girl is mad, I tell you! It is she who jumped on me!"

"*You bastard!*" shouted Lawrence. He ran at Sinclair, knocked him to the ground and began to punch him.

"*Lawrence!*" Edward dragged his son off Sinclair.

"*If he won't kill him – then I will!*" shouted the Countess as she went to throw herself on Sinclair, but her husband grabbed her and held her back.

Sinclair struggled up off the ground and saw Diana was now in the room.

"*It's not true!*" he yelled at her.

"What were you doing in her room?" Edward demanded.

"I – I – she asked me to come! She said she needed to talk to me!"

"Lord Armstrong, your cousin has attacked and molested my daughter. I insist the police are called forthwith," said the Earl.

"Edward!" pleaded Sinclair. "This is me! Am I capable of such a thing?"

Edward stared at his cousin and the hundreds of times he showed cruelty to the peasant farmers flashed through his mind. He looked over at Margaret, in her torn dress and dishevelled state, now sobbing in Lawrence's arms.

Edward turned to Taylor and the footmen. "The facts speak for themselves. Take him and lock him in the wine cellar until the police arrive."

Taylor and a footman marched forward and grabbed Sinclair by either arm.

"*Let go of me!*" demanded Sinclair as he tried to shake them off.

"If you don't go peacefully, I'll escort you down to the cellar at gunpoint!" said Edward.

"*Edward!*" cried Sinclair as he was marched out of the room.

At the top of the stairs, Anna stepped out of the way as Sinclair was marched past her and down the stairs.

"Could you all please just leave us and send a footman to get a doctor and the police," said Edward.

"As quick as you can!" cried the Countess and she and Lawrence lifted Margaret to her feet and laid her on the bed.

Everyone began to chatter loudly as they made their way downstairs.

"I know he's a bit of a thug, but I never thought he would be capable of this!" said Mrs. Foxe to her husband.

"It's in the blood!" said Lady Fitzherbert. "Remember his father was Bad Black Jamie Armstrong, a notorious womaniser! He broke Sinclair's mother's heart and was a frequent visitor to the brothels of Dublin."

"Yes, although there's never been any of that kind of scandal associated with Sinclair," said Lord Fitzherbert.

Harry had held a terrified Gertie at knifepoint while he thought furiously. What could he do with her? Tying her up and gagging her would do no good. She would live to destroy him if he went ahead and killed Lawrence.

Suddenly, as he brooded, she threw herself backwards away from the knife and fell to the floor. In a second he was on her and grasped her by the throat as she opened her mouth to scream.

His hands tightened in his fear and fury and Gertie felt herself blacking out when suddenly a woman's screaming could be heard.

Jolted back to reality, Harry removed his hands from her throat and raised his head to listen. Gertie began to cough and splutter as she gasped for air. Harry listened intently as the woman's screams continued. Then there was much running and talking in the corridor outside.

Gertie looked up at Harry.

"If you make a sound I'll knife you!" Harry hissed at her.

Terrified for her life, Gertie did not make a sound as Harry got off her and went to the door. She quickly scampered to the corner of the room and huddled there, putting her head in her hands as she tried to recover.

Harry opened the door a fraction and peeped out. He could see much commotion down the corridor. And then, to his horror, he saw his father being led down the corridor by Taylor and the footmen. He quickly closed the door and tried to figure out what had gone on. He waited a while until the commotion had died down and then opened the door cautiously and saw the corridor was empty. He glanced at Gertie who was still huddled in the corner, staring at him petrified.

"If you say anything about me being here," he snarled at her, brandishing the knife, "I will come back sooner or later and cut your throat. Do you hear me?"

She nodded dumbly.

With a final warning look, he disappeared out the door.

Gertie struggled to her feet and then slowly made her way from Lawrence's room and down the corridor to the servants' stairs. Then she stumbled up the stairway until she reached her room in the attics and locked the door behind her.

Diana walked down the stairs alone after the others had left. She saw the drawing-room door was closed, shutting her out. Whether intentionally or not, it didn't matter, she realised. She had spent her life trying to get through the front door of this damned house. She didn't know what else was going to happen that night, but she didn't want to be there to see it.

She turned and walked to the door.

"My cloak," she said to the footman standing there.

She waited still as a statue until he brought it to her with her gloves and hat.

Then she left the house and walked slowly back to Hunter's Farm.

CHAPTER 55

Anna sat in the drawing room in a state of disbelief. One moment she was about to divulge her worst secrets to her husband – secrets that would engulf her family in the worst scandal imaginable. The next moment her son's fiancée had been viciously assaulted by her husband's cousin, throwing the family into an equally horrendous scandal.

The doctor was upstairs with Margaret as were her parents. Edward looked ashen-faced as he stood by the fireplace. The Foxes and Fitzherberts were present in the drawing room also, looking equally shocked. In the distance Sinclair could be heard, locked in the wine cellar, shouting to be released.

"With all Sinclair's faults, I always thought he was quite devoted to Diana. I never saw him even look at another woman," said Mrs. Foxe.

"Whatever possessed him?" said Lord Fitzherbert.

"He's a vain man," said Lady Fitzherbert. "I imagine he made a pass at Margaret, with the full belief she would fall at his feet, and then became violent when she rejected him."

Edward looked irritated at their conversation. "I am very sorry," he said, "but I'm afraid I'm going to have to cut the night short for obvious reasons and ask you to return to your homes. I do apologise."

"Oh!" said Lady Fitzherbert, looking very disappointed that she was to be excluded from what would be happening next.

"Of course," said Mrs. Foxe as she stood up.

"I also ask you, as our closest and dearest friends, to keep what has happened here tonight to yourselves – until we establish exactly what has happened and what has to be done," said Edward.

"That goes without saying, Edward. We fully understand that gossip and rumours must be avoided at all cost," said Mr. Foxe, looking pointedly at his wife.

Anna rose from her seat and tugged the bell-pull. When Taylor arrived a few seconds later she said, "Have the Foxes' and Fitzherberts' carriages brought to the front, Taylor. They are going home."

"Yes, my lady," said Taylor, quickly exiting.

"A word, Taylor!" Edward said and followed him out into the hall where he cautioned him to ensure that none of the servants spoke about what had just happened.

"Not a word, sir," Taylor promised solemnly. "Leave them to me."

Edward returned to the drawing room and his departing guests.

"My poor dear!" said Lady Fitzherbert, embracing Anna. "I can't imagine what Lawrence is going through. Give him our love and tell him he is in our thoughts – along with Lady Margaret of course."

"Thank you," said Anna. She kissed the ladies goodnight and they bade farewell to Edward and left.

Edward was standing by the fireplace and looked so lost in thought that Anna was frightened to say anything to interrupt him. Sinclair was still shouting in the distance, a muffled sound echoing through the house. Anna hoped Margaret could not hear him upstairs in her room.

Then the door opened and Doctor Davitt walked in, followed by the Countess and the Earl.

The doctor closed over the door.

"How is she?" asked Edward.

"*How is she?*" repeated the Countess, her face a mask of fury. "How do you think she is after being attacked by that brute?"

"Doctor?" asked Edward.

"Lady Margaret has had a very upsetting experience –" began Doctor Davitt.

"*Upsetting!*" shrieked the Countess.

"A *shocking* experience," the doctor corrected himself. "I have spoken to her and the injuries she has received correspond to the attack she says she suffered. Bruising to the upper arms, bruising to her bosom, bruising to her mouth – her dress has been quite badly ripped. It is fortunate that she managed to scream and get your attention – or goodness know what might have happened."

"*To think!*" cried the Countess.

"She is extremely distraught, as one can imagine," said Doctor Davitt.

"How did it happen?" asked Anna. "What was Sinclair doing in her room?"

"He followed her up!" said the Countess. "That – *beast of a man* – grabbed her and tried to ravage her!"

Edward looked down to the ground, overwhelmed with shame and shock.

"I've recommended that Lady Margaret should rest and I've given her a sedative," said the doctor. "I think the shock of what has happened has affected her more than the actual injuries she received."

"How can you say that? She has been assaulted," snapped the Countess.

"If there is nothing else?" said the doctor. "I will call on Lady Margaret tomorrow to see how she is."

"Thank you, doctor," nodded Edward and the doctor left the room.

The Countess could hear Sinclair's muffled shouting coming from afar.

"I'm going to shoot that bastard! Where is the nearest gun?" she demanded.

"Please, let us speak reasonably. We can't take justice into our own hands," urged Edward.

"Why ever not? It's the quickest, shortest form of justice!" said the Countess.

"Edward is right, Countess," cautioned Anna. "I understand how you feel, but all that shooting Sinclair will do is bring a murder charge against you."

"Then let them hang me!" declared the Countess, defiantly.

Taylor knocked and entered the room. "The police have arrived, my lord."

"About time!" said the Countess.

"I shall speak to them," said Edward. "And see what needs to be done."

"I can tell you what needs to be done! He must be hanged from the gallows!" said the Countess.

"Clementina! Please calm down," begged the Earl. "As Anna says, we need to think rationally."

"You were always weak in a crisis!" the Countess accused her husband. "Always a ditherer!"

"Where are the police?" Edward asked Taylor.

"I showed them into the parlour, my lord."

"They will no doubt want to speak to Margaret before they arrest Sinclair," said Edward.

"But –" began the Countess.

"Leave it to Edward!" demanded the Earl, silencing his wife.

Edward closed the door of the drawing room behind him and stood thinking for a moment. Thankfully Sinclair had gone silent for now. He then walked across the hallway and into the parlour where Bourke from Castlewest was waiting with a young police officer.

"Good evening, Lord Armstrong," said Sergeant Bourke.

"Good evening, gentlemen, I apologise for calling you out so late," said Edward.

"Your footman reported there has been an incident at the house?" asked Bourke.

"Yes." Edward searched for what to say. "Yes – there has been an attack on a young woman here at the house tonight."

"An attack?"

"Of a sexual nature," explained Edward.

"I see. Has the woman identified the culprit?"

Edward could hardly bring himself to speak. "Yes, she has."

"Is the culprit a member of staff at the house here as well?" asked Bourke.

Edward looked at Burke, confused for a moment, and then realised that Bourke assumed the young woman who was assaulted was a member of the household staff.

"Eh, yes," said Edward, thinking that Sinclair was officially a member of staff due to him being the estate manager. He could not bring himself to utter the words that the culprit was his cousin. "What is the procedure?"

"Well, if the young woman wishes to press charges then we will arrest the man and he will stand trial. Did intercourse take place?"

"No, the woman has been examined by a doctor," said Edward.

"Then we will charge him with assault with the intention of rape," said Bourke.

"We will have to interview the woman, and of course she will have to give evidence at the trial," said the Sergeant.

Edward closed his eyes and wished he could wake up from this nightmare.

CHAPTER 56

Anna, the Countess and the Earl sat in silence in the drawing room, waiting for Edward's return.

The door opened and to their surprise they saw Margaret being led in by Lawrence.

"Margaret! What are you doing out of bed? The doctor said you were to rest!" said the Countess, hastily standing up and leading her daughter to the sofa where she sat down beside her.

"I couldn't stay in my room any longer," said Margaret.

"How are you feeling?" asked Anna.

"How do you think she feels?" snapped the Countess angrily.

"Thank you for asking," said Margaret, looking around, frightened. "Where is Sinclair?"

"He is locked in the cellar and that is where he will stay until the police arrest him," said the Countess.

"Police?" said Margaret, becoming agitated.

"Yes, Edward is with them now," said Anna. "In the parlour."

"But – you should have spoken to me before you fetched them," said Margaret.

The door opened and Edward walked in.

"Margaret! How are you feeling, my dear?" he asked.

"I wish everyone would stop asking her that! How is one who has just been defiled expected to feel?" snapped the Countess.

"Lord Armstrong, are the police here?" asked Margaret, panicked.

"Yes, I've just spoken to them in the parlour. They will need to speak to you before they arrest Sinclair."

"No! I don't wish to speak to them!" said Margaret.

"But you must, my dear, in order for them to arrest Sinclair and for him to stand trial," said the Earl.

"I do not wish for him to stand trial!" insisted Margaret.

"But *of course* he must stand trial and face the consequences of his actions!" cried the Countess.

Edward studied Margaret's panicked face and said, "You do understand what all this means, Margaret? Sinclair will stand trial and you will have to give evidence in court – explain to the judge what Sinclair did to you."

"But I can't face that! I can't do that! I will be ruined! My name will be destroyed!"

"It's he who will be ruined and destroyed, not you!" said the Countess.

"But the scandal will ruin me! And you! You know that as much as anybody, Mama!" cried Margaret.

"She's right, Clementina," said the Earl. "Margaret's name will be always associated with a filthy humiliation and disgrace if this goes to trial."

"But –" began the Countess.

"And not just Margaret's," cautioned Edward. "But your family name, and of course the Armstrong name will be dishonoured beyond repair."

"*You* are only trying to protect your family and your disgusting cousin who committed this heinous crime!" the Countess accused him.

"I don't give a damn about Sinclair after what he did tonight – you can throw him to the wolves for all I care. But I'm thinking about my son Lawrence and his fiancée's good name and the ruination of both."

"I don't care about Margaret's name. I'll marry her and love her no matter what!" Lawrence declared.

"You're too young to understand the consequences of this, Lawrence," said Edward. "Your wife will be known as being assaulted by a member of your own family. The wedding could not proceed."

"*Not proceed!*" shouted the Earl. "Why should Margaret suffer – she is the innocent party! And who – who else would marry her once she gives evidence at the trial and it is all in the newspapers that she was sexually assaulted!"

"I think I'm going to faint!" said the Countess.

Lawrence stood up angrily to face his father. "My marriage is going ahead with Margaret no matter what. I will not abandon her, come what may!"

"Can't you see, you stupid boy, that the scandal will be too much – it will break you and Margaret," insisted Edward.

Anna suddenly jumped to her feet and shouted, "*Will you all be quiet!*"

Everyone turned to look at her.

"I think –" she began, "I think the decision about what is to be done is for one and only one person to decide and that is Margaret. Margaret is fully aware of the consequences of what she decides to do. And I think the rest of us should, indeed have to, step back and let her to decide what she wants to do."

Everyone turned to look at Margaret.

Lawrence went to her and knelt on one knee in front of her.

"Margaret?" he said. "Whatever you want, I will stand by what you decide and by you."

Margaret bit her lip. "I do not want to have charges pressed against Sinclair. I will not put myself, my fiancé or my family through the trauma of a trial, which none of us will ever recover from, as Lord Armstrong said."

Edward looked noticeably relieved.

"But – but he can't just get away with it," insisted the Countess.

"Oh, Sinclair will not get away with what he did tonight!" said Edward. "And Margaret will never have to see him again. I can assure you of that."

"Thank you," whispered Margaret.

"I shall go tell the police that charges are not being pressed. I haven't revealed as yet that Margaret was the victim and I will not."

Edward hastily left the room.

"He never even told them you were the victim!" scoffed the

Countess. "Nor did he tell them his cousin was the culprit, I can tell you. I fear Lord Armstrong is covering this crime up to protect his family."

"He's trying to protect us all," said Margaret as she reached out and took Lawrence's hand. "And most importantly us, Lawrence, and our future happiness."

Anna sat down and stared over at Margaret and Lawrence who were gazing at each other with deep love.

"The young woman in question does not wish to press charges," Edward informed Sergeant Bourke.

"I understand," said Bourke. "Which is probably just as well for you. This kind of thing can reflect badly on a Big House and its reputation."

"Yes," said Edward, thinking the Sergeant would collapse in shock if he knew the victim was his son's fiancée, the daughter of an Earl, and the assailant his own cousin.

"You will take care of the man in question yourself?" the Sergeant checked as Edward showed him and the other policeman to the front door.

"I most definitely will, have no fear of that," confirmed Edward solemnly. "Goodnight, gentlemen."

Edward closed the front door after them and turned to find Taylor waiting in the hallway.

"Taylor, you and the footmen are to take Sinclair Armstrong from the cellar and have him locked in a stable for the night. Make sure he cannot escape."

"Yes, my lord," said Taylor and he rushed off to obey orders.

Harry opened the front door of Hunter's Farm and walked down the corridor to the parlour. He needed a strong whiskey after what he had been through that night. He had gone for a walk by the lake to clear his mind before coming home. It was as if a red mist had descended on him when Gertie had interrupted him and all he could think to do to silence her was to kill her. He fretted that she would report what had happened. But he concluded that she would be ruining herself if the truth came out.

But now he was worried at why his father had been escorted away by Taylor and the footmen. What on earth had been going on?

He walked into the parlour and saw his mother seated on the sofa and to his shock saw she had been crying. He had never seen her cry before.

"Where have you been?" she demanded.

"Just out for a walk," he said. "Where's father?"

Diana looked like she was about to burst out crying again. "I don't know! Something terrible has happened."

"What's happened?" he demanded.

"I don't know . . . I can't explain . . . your father has been accused of the most terrible thing!"

"What thing?" said Harry. "What has father been accused of? Who would dare accuse him of anything?"

Diana struggled to answer but the tears that had been threatening tumbled down her face.

It was nearly two in the morning when Anna and Edward went to their bedroom. Everyone else had gone to bed by then. Edward sat down on the bed and put his face in his hands.

"I just – I just would never have believed it of Sinclair," he said eventually. "We grew up together, we were like brothers."

"Oh, come on, Edward! I know how you always idolised Sinclair, but you have to have known how cruel he could be and how he treated people so badly on so many occasions. I pointed it out to you enough times over the years."

"Of course I knew he could be ruthless . . . but I always thought that he acted so to protect me. He always thought I was soft and so stepped in to deal with situations ruthlessly to protect my interests. But to attack my son's fiancée!" Edward shook his head in confusion and horror.

Anna had to admit she could not fathom the events of the night herself. As only she knew, Sinclair had everything in his grasp. He was about to expose the truth about Lawrence's father and could only come out the winner in the situation. Why would he throw all that away? Why would he destroy himself when he was about to take everything that he believed was rightfully his? It made no sense.

"Perhaps it's as Lady Fitzherbert said, that he was vain enough to think Margaret was attracted to him and reacted violently when she rejected him," she suggested.

"Poor Diana – how could he treat her like that?"

"Poor *Margaret*! *She* is the one who was attacked." She paused. "What are you going to do, Edward? With Sinclair?"

"I'm going to throw him out of Hunter's Farm and off the estate. Fire him from his job with no reference."

"Is that punishment enough for what he did tonight?"

"He'll be left with nothing and lose everything he holds dear. You should be happy – Sinclair will finally be out of our lives – isn't that what you always wanted?"

"Not like this," answered Anna.

But Edward was right. It was what she had always wanted. What's more, the events of the night had saved her, Lawrence and Edward from losing everything. Because of what had happened with Margaret, she would never have to reveal the truth to Edward about Lawrence's true father. And if Sinclair tried to tell Edward or anyone else the truth now, he would not be believed. He would be seen as just a bitter man trying to make up a lie to get revenge. Her only fear now was that Seán could step forward and tell the truth. But she hoped, desperately hoped, with Sinclair now destroyed, Seán would slip away, back to where he had been hiding all these years.

CHAPTER 57

Present Day

Kate and Daniel both stared at the ledger showing Sinclair had left the Armstrong Estate and that a new estate manager had been appointed.

"But there might be another reason the payments stopped," said Daniel. "He might have got ill and died. Or been offered another position?"

"Follow me!" said Kate and, ledger still in hand, she went racing out the room.

Daniel followed her down the stairs to the floor below and down the main stairs to the ground floor where she raced to her desk and sat at her computer.

"What are you doing?" he asked.

"I'm going on to Burke's Peerage to see when he died," she explained.

She punched in Sinclair's name and he came up on the Armstrong family tree as he had the last time.

"Sinclair Armstrong, born at the Armstrong estate 1798 – married Diana Hunter 1841 – lived at Hunter's Farm. Died 1885 – East London." She looked up at Daniel. "There is no way a member of the gentry would have left his comfortable home and life at Hunter's Farm and job here to go to live in the slums of the East End of London. He lived for a further twenty years after leaving the Armstrong Estate. And obviously was no longer able to secure a position as he had been shunned by Edward after what he had done to Margaret. He was then left to a life where nobody knew him in

351

the East End of London."

Daniel bent over Kate's shoulder, reading the entry on the peerage site.

He then stood up straight and offered her his hand. She looked at it, confused.

He smiled at her and said, "You've found your man. It has to be Sinclair Armstrong who attacked Margaret."

Kate felt a little dazed and elated as she shook his hand. Then laughing, she stood up and gave him a hug.

"I wonder what possessed Sinclair Armstrong?" said Kate as she and Daniel shared a bottle of wine in the library. "Did he honestly think he could get away with it?"

"Well, in a way he did. He didn't get a prison sentence or stand trial."

"But at what cost? He went from a life of extreme comfort and power to nothing."

"Who knows why he did what he did. He certainly had plenty of time to regret it in the following years."

"Thank goodness for Clementina and her diary!" said Kate.

He looked at her in awe. "You've done an amazing job, Kate. Piecing it all together as you did."

"Well, I couldn't have done it without you. You've helped me every step of the way. And now, hopefully, I will be able to make my film."

He picked up his glass and clinked it against hers.

Kate anxiously paced up and down the drawing room while talking on the phone to Brian, pitching her full proposal for the film, now centred on the attack on Lady Margaret and everything she had found out during her investigative work.

Valerie sat on the couch looking at Kate pace, clasping her hands together in anticipation.

"So we are changing the focus of the film from Lady Anna's charity work to Lady Margaret's attack with all the new information you have found," checked Brian as he listened intently to her.

"Exactly!" said Kate.

"Right – I love it!" said Brian.

"Really?" gasped Kate.

Nico walked into the room at that moment. "Kate, have you seen Cian's –"

Kate made a quick gesture to him to be quiet and he stopped talking and stood there waiting.

"You really like it?" Kate asked Brian.

"Yes, it has all the ingredients investors love and, more importantly, audiences love. I'll pitch the new concept to the original investors of our last film and I'm confident they will all want to get on board again."

"That's brilliant news, Brian. I'll start working on the script straight away."

"Great, I'll give you a call later," said Brian.

Kate turned off her phone and, clenching her hands, punched the air. "Brian says the film is a certainty. He says the investors will be lining up to get involved."

Valerie jumped up from the couch and hugged her. "That's great news, Kate. Well done!"

Kate ran over to Nico and embraced him. "I can hardly believe it, I thought the project would never get off the ground."

Nico's voice was calm as he spoke. "Congratulations, Kate. I never doubted for a second that you would pull it together."

Kate turned and began to pace again. "Now the hard work really starts. I have to pull the whole script together. And then there is all the production staff, and the casting for the roles."

"Is there any singing part for me?" asked Valerie.

"It's not a musical, Valerie!"

"Just saying!" said Valerie.

"It's going to be busy!" said Kate, full of excitement.

"Any idea when the filming will start and the house will be turned into a film set again?" asked Nico, trying to keep any annoyance from his voice.

"No idea yet. Pre-production will take a while. I'd better ring some of the casting agencies and see what they think about actors and actresses suitable. It's hard to get availability if we don't give plenty of notice."

Kate went rushing out of the room.

"I was trying to ask – have you seen Cian's green jacket anywhere?" Nico called after her but she was gone.

He looked down at the floor, lost in thought, forgetting that Valerie was even there.

"You have to understand this is who Kate is," said Valerie, studying the lost look on his face. "She's always had this side to her, the need to be busy. And that show business part of her, well, it never really leaves anybody who has worked in it."

Nico looked up at Valerie and was surprised to see her face was filled with sympathy for him.

"You should just accept her as she is, Nico. You know what they say – a happy wife means a happy life!"

He nodded at her and turned to leave.

"Cian's green jacket is in the utility room downstairs," she said.

"Thanks, Valerie," said Nico and he left the room.

Kate had been in the library for the rest of the day, making phone calls to all her old friends from the entertainment world, enquiring about everything from production staff to actors to scriptwriters.

Valerie was in attendance, writing down details for Kate as she got them from her calls.

"I'd love to get the same scriptwriter that we had for *The Secrets of Armstrong House*, but his agent says he's very busy and can't guarantee him for me," said Kate, hanging up the phone.

Valerie looked around the library curiously. "Does the whole house actually become a film set, like Nico says?"

"Well, more or less, yes. There are camera crews everywhere and production staff during the filming."

"It must be hard to live in that environment when it's your home as well?"

"It never bothered me," said Kate. "We still have downstairs as our private space, although the production team do use it occasionally, admittedly."

"I can see how a man like Nico might not like it though."

"Well, he didn't complain when we got paid for the last film. And this new film is really going to secure our future financially."

"But last time you were making the film you didn't have Cian," Valerie pointed out. "It might be much harder with a child in the house."

"I'll come up with a plan so that Cian isn't disturbed. Besides, it will be exciting for him with all the activity."

"Hopefully it won't be too unsettling for him." Valerie then put her hand on her heart as she said, "Kate, I'm the last person to be giving marriage counselling with my car crash of a history with relationships . . . but I do think you should include Nico in this more than you have done."

"What's the point? He just so negative about everything I try to do all the time. It becomes wearing after a while."

"Well, maybe that's just his way. But I think he's feeling excluded and, well, quite frankly for the sake of your marriage, you need to get him on board with this film. Otherwise, there's going to be disaster ahead for the both of you."

Kate looked at Valerie, taken aback by her words.

CHAPTER 58

The next day Kate drove down to the excavation site and walked in through the main gates.

"Hi, Kate!" called one of the team.

She had been down enough times to the site to have become a familiar face.

"Hi there. Where's Daniel?"

"He's in the labs."

"Thanks!" said Kate as she walked towards the building.

As she looked at the work being done she could see they had made amazing progress and the dig had gone deep into the earth.

As she walked through the building down to Daniel's office, she bumped into him coming out of a lab dressed in a white coat.

"Hi!" he said. "Wasn't expecting you today."

"Oh, Daniel, I've got great news. I got the go-ahead to make the film. My producer Brian rang me this morning confirming he has all the investors lined up," she said excitedly.

"That is good news! Well done, Kate!" said Daniel and he gave her a big hug.

"Thanks, Daniel. You know I really couldn't have got this done without you."

"Nonsense, I did nothing."

"You know you did more than that. It was you who gave me the police file in the first place and kept coming up with suggestions on how to get to the bottom of the mystery of who attacked Lady Margaret. Without this new angle and the investigative work you

356

did with me, this project would have been dead in the water."

"Well, I was only too delighted to be involved. It will make a great film. But, hey, I've actually made a bit of an exciting discovery today myself."

"Oh?"

"Yes – a body that we took from the mass grave – it's not like the others."

"In what way?" Kate asked, intrigued.

"Well, why don't you come into the lab and I'll show you what I mean?"

"Okay," said Kate, becoming excited at the thought.

Daniel fetched her a white coat and then took her into the lab where the skeletal frame of a body had been laid out on a table. The frame was clothed in dilapidated clothes.

"It's an adult male," started Daniel. "It struck us at once that it's very very different from the others we have exhumed from the grave."

"In what way?" asked Kate.

"Well, we can always see that the bones of the bodies we have exhumed are severely damaged before death, due to starvation, malnourishment and the diseases that brings on, for example scurvy or typhus. But the bones of this man show no sign of either malnutrition or disease. He wasn't a victim of the Famine."

"So what was he doing buried in the famine grave with the others?"

"Well, that's the mystery. But if you look here," said Daniel, pointing to the skull, "you'll see there is a large indentation to the side of the skull. Which indicates that this man was killed by a severe blow to the head."

"An accident?" asked Kate.

"I doubt it from the injury he suffered and the angle of the indentation. This man was struck by somebody else."

"Gosh!" said Kate, taking a closer look.

"Also, from the clothes he was wearing, he wasn't an inmate in the workhouse or a victim of the Famine from outside the workhouse who was thrown into the grave as often happened. The victims of the Famine were literally wearing rags. This man not only had a full set of clothes and shoes, but was also wearing an overcoat."

Kate was impressed by Daniel's ability to tie the smallest details together to produce facts.

"I guess if he could afford an overcoat, he could afford food," she said.

"Absolutely," said Daniel.

"Would it have been a robbery? Some desperate victims of the Famine killing him for his money?"

"I thought that initially," said Daniel before pointing to some items on a table in the corner of the lab. "But we found a wallet on him and coins amounting to some value. So it can't have been a robbery."

"What on earth could have happened?" asked Kate.

"He was murdered, it seems, because whoever put him in the grave didn't want him found – indicating that it was not an accident. The famine grave was the perfect place to hide this body. There were nameless victims of the Famine being thrown in there every day and this body was hidden there, the perpetrator safe in the knowledge that nobody cared about the people being buried there."

"The perfect crime," said Kate.

"Absolutely. I'm going to trawl through the police file from the time again to see if there were any reports of missing men. But to be honest, I don't hold out much hope. I've studied the file already in detail, and I don't remember any reports in the Castlewest area of that type."

"Perhaps the murderer brought him here from another place to avoid detection?" said Kate.

"Doubtful. Remember the country was teeming with police trying to keep order at the time. I don't think the murderer would have risked moving the body that far. No, this murder was committed locally and the body disposed of at the nearest famine grave, which was here."

"And that's where he's been all these years, until you found him," said Kate, mesmerised by the whole development.

CHAPTER 59

Conscious of what Valerie had said about her and Nico, Kate made a determined effort to try and include Nico in the film project as it developed. But, as she had always said, he was less than enthusiastic about it.

"The public's thirst for salaciousness never ceases to amaze me," he said to her as she went into detail about how they were now focusing the film around the attack on Lady Margaret.

Kate and Nico were in the small parlour at the front of the house. She had asked Valerie that evening to put Cian to bed so she could spend some quality time with Nico. She had opened a bottle of wine and was enjoying it with him.

"I wouldn't call it salacious," she said.

"Really? You only managed to sell the project on the promise of sex and violence. Shouldn't surprise me, that's how you got the last film made," said Nico.

"Aren't you interested that Margaret was attacked? Don't you think that it should be revealed that the guilty person was Sinclair Armstrong?"

"Well, no. If Lady Margaret did not want it to be revealed that she was attacked by Sinclair Armstrong in 1865 and it was covered up, as you say, then what right have you to reveal it now?"

"Who says Margaret didn't want it exposed? She was probably pressurised into keeping it quiet to avoid scandal and the ruination of her name," said Kate.

"But you see no problem with ruining it now?"

"You're being ridiculous, Nico. Social conventions have completely changed since the nineteenth century. If it was now, one would hope and expect, there would not be a cover-up. I feel we are giving Lady Margaret the justice she was denied in 1865."

"Nonsense! Even now the majority of sexual assaults are not reported and, even if they are, don't make it to court. For the same reasons that existed in 1865!"

"Yes, and that is not right! I want justice for Lady Margaret."

"*You* want to make a successful film!"

"Is that what you think of me?" Kate demanded angrily, though what he'd said had a ring of truth.

"Kate – Lady Margaret was my great-great-grandmother. Don't you think I should be the one who decides whether this all becomes public?" asked Nico.

"You've always used that as an excuse in the past to override my opinions. That the Armstrongs are *your* family and that I was an outsider who didn't have a right or a say in how the family should be represented!"

"Not that that ever stopped you!" said Nico, reaching for his wineglass and taking a gulp.

"But you know that doesn't work any more, since Cian was born. Margaret is Cian's great-great-great-grandmother, and I as Cian's mother am as much a part of this family and its history as you are!"

"Okay, so you've listened to my concerns and now you're just going to ignore them anyway?"

Kate found herself bubbling with frustration as she found that despite her best efforts she was at loggerheads with Nico again.

Then she heard the doorbell ring and was grateful for the distraction.

"*I'll get it*!" Valerie could be heard calling from the hallway.

"Are you expecting anyone?" asked Nico.

"No," answered Kate, taking a sip of wine and trying to hide her irritation with Nico.

A few moments later Valerie came into the parlour, accompanied by Daniel.

"Sorry for arriving in unannounced," said Daniel.

"That's no problem. Is everything all right with Hunter's Farm?" asked Kate, smiling.

"Everything is absolutely fine, thanks. Hello, Nico."

"Daniel," nodded Nico, outwardly warm, but inwardly vexed that Daniel was once again at the house, and would no doubt be staying for the rest of the evening as he babbled on about the excavation site with Kate.

"Glass of wine?" Kate offered, holding up the bottle.

"Eh, no thanks, I can't stay too long," said Daniel, sitting down on an armchair beside the fireplace.

That makes a change, thought Nico.

Valerie sat down too. She was hoping for once that Daniel wouldn't be staying too long. As much as she liked him, she had been hoping that Kate and Nico would have had the opportunity to mend some bridges that night.

"I just called because I have some news about the excavation site," said Daniel.

Here we go, thought Nico.

"Oh?" Kate asked, excited.

"You know the odd body I showed you earlier in the week, Kate?"

"Odd?" asked Nico.

"Daniel and his team found a body amongst the famine victims, but the signs are that this man was murdered and dumped there at the time," explained Kate quickly. "Go on, Daniel!"

"Well, we have been carrying out further tests. He was a man between the ages of twenty and twenty-five. And my suspicions were correct – the man was bludgeoned to death with a heavy object."

"How grim!" said Valerie.

"Yes, but an exciting piece of historical discovery," said Daniel.

As Nico looked at Daniel, he realised how similar he was to Kate. They could both experience excitement from the discovery of tragic events. Nico wondered if Daniel was having an effect on Kate.

Daniel looked at Kate and then Nico, a sparkle in his eye. "The thing is, in trying to identify who this man was, we did a DNA test and tried to match it with all the people in the locality who gave DNA examples to see if he was related to anyone locally."

"And was he?" asked Kate, holding her breath.

"He's not one of ours, is he?" asked Valerie excitedly. "Was our lot associating with murderers and thieves?"

"No, the man has no DNA connection with your family." Daniel then turned to look directly at Nico. "But he is related to you, Nico."

Nico head jerked up abruptly. "Me?"

"Yes, it's a hundred-per-cent match. This man was related to you from the DNA sample you gave me."

"But how could that be?" Kate was amazed. "An ancestor of Nico's couldn't have ended up in a famine grave! They were aristocrats – it's just not possible!"

"But remember I told you this man wasn't a famine victim, Kate – he had been murdered and placed there," said Daniel.

"Kate knows much more about my family than I ever could, Daniel," said Nico, "but as far as I'm aware all my ancestors are fully accounted for and buried in mausoleums."

"Nico is right, Daniel. I know the Armstrong family tree inside and out – there's nobody missing who this man could possibly be. In fact, the Armstrong family in the 1840s when the famine grave was in operation was very small – there was only Lord Edward, his wife Anna and their son Lawrence. All of whom lived long healthy lives for many decades after that time."

"Could it be a cousin?" ventured Valerie.

"There was only one cousin during the 1840s and that was Sinclair Armstrong who lived till the 1880s and died in England as I discovered," said Kate.

"That makes no odds as it couldn't be a cousin," said Daniel. "As the DNA indicates, Nico is a direct descendent from the man we found in the grave. You see, we used Autosomal DNA from the sample Nico gave us and this DNA is inherited equally from parents and this is traced back to three great-grandparents."

"But it doesn't make sense," said Kate. "All Nico's ancestors are accounted for since the Napoleonic wars and even before that. They are all buried in the local village graveyard, as Nico says, in mausoleums and under tombstones. Right up to when Armstrong House was vacated after the fire in 1919. You can check the graveyard yourself – everyone from Nico's great-grandfather Lord Charles to Lawrence to his father Edward to his father and so on."

"Could it be an illegitimate relative?" asked Valerie. "Perhaps one of those lords were poking the scullery maid and this man is the offspring."

"Oh, shut up, Valerie!" snapped Nico. "You always have to be so crass."

"Sorry!" said Valerie, making a contrite face.

"A good point, Valerie," said Daniel, throwing a reproving look at Nico. "But, as in the cousin scenario, that can't be. Nico is directly descended from this man."

Nico was trying to take it all in. It was unnerving for him to be told that an ancestor of his had been murdered and thrown into a mass grave without the dignity of a proper funeral. And it just didn't make sense.

"You must have made a mistake," said Nico.

"I really don't think so, but I'd like to take a second DNA sample from you to make sure," said Daniel.

"Yes, I think you should do another test, because you obviously got the first one wrong!" said Nico.

Daniel didn't stay long after taking another sample from Daniel. Kate was relieved at that, as Nico was clearly confused and upset by what he had said. He was very quiet for the rest of the evening.

In the course of the evening it dawned on Kate why the news was affecting Nico so much. Nico had never been that interested in his family's history because he was fully confident in it. She realised that Nico had been born and lived with the full knowledge of who his family were. That was probably why he was so quietly confident in himself – he always believed he had nothing to prove. He took his breeding for granted. But this news had come out and hit him like a bombshell.

As they went to bed that night, she found herself in the unusual position of *her* being intensely quizzed by Nico about his family.

"In all the research you've done, you've never found any anomalies in the Armstrongs' lineage, isn't that so?" Nico asked.

"No, none at all," said Kate, perplexed. "I've found plenty of strange behaviour but no anomalies. In fact, that's what made the Armstrong family so easy to investigate – there has always been a direct line of inheritance. In most aristocratic families, a line of the family dies out and the title and estate goes to a cousin, or a nephew or in the case of the Arbuthnots in Scotland, a distant relative. But that was never the case with the Armstrongs."

"Then who on earth is this man Daniel found?" asked Nico.

"I don't know," said Kate.

Kate found it strange that for the first time ever it was Nico who needed an answer for the past and was looking to her for the answer. And this time she couldn't give that answer and, judging by how this was affecting Nico, she wasn't sure if she wanted to. As she had said to Daniel that evening, she knew the history of the Armstrong family inside out. If this man had been killed in the late 1840s and was in the age bracket of twenty to twenty-five, Nico *couldn't* be descended from this man. Lord Edward and Lady Anna were Nico's ancestors at this time and they had one child, Lawrence, who would have been a just a baby then. This man, whoever he was, did not fit into the equation.

CHAPTER 60

Kate wanted to check the dates of death of Nico's ancestors. She already knew them but she needed to confirm she hadn't missed anything. Or it might be that the records were incorrect. The easiest way to check was to visit the graves of Nico's ancestors that were in the Protestant graveyard on what used to be the Armstrong Estate. She drove down to the local village and parked there.

The village had a similar architecture to Armstrong House and had been built by Lord Edward for estate workers at the same time as the house, work being completed in 1840 just in time for Edward's marriage to Anna. As she walked about the village which was set around a village green, she thought of what a progressive man Edward had been. Most of the villages of the great estates at the time had been just casually thrown up without thought of consequences. And yet Edward had employed an architect to build this village and put as much thought and detail into it as he had into Armstrong House. The result still shone through history, and it was one of the most beautiful villages in Ireland. The only difference between it now and during Lord Edward's time was that most of the houses in the village were now owned by professionals in Dublin and used as holiday and weekend homes, instead of being occupied by housing estate workers as they were back then.

She opened the gate into the old church grounds. The church was mainly closed now and only held services at Christmas and Easter or for a special occasion like a wedding. Kate hoped that it wouldn't close down altogether and be bought and turned into somebody's stylish house or restaurant, which had become all the fashion with these old churches. She continued walking behind the church onto the old graveyard. The graveyard was now quite neglected and overrun. Kate had been there before as she researched the Armstrong family history and knew exactly where the Armstrong graves were as she made her way through the paths that criss-crossed the graveyard. It had been a Protestant graveyard for the gentry and, as Kate looked at the gravestones, she realised that nobody had been buried there since the 1920s. Looking at the graves, she saw there was a surge of burials during the period of the First World War, young officers who had been sent off gallantly by their families to fight only to be returned here. And Kate knew from her knowledge of history that many more hadn't been returned but had been buried in France. She continued, making her way to the huge tombstones that towered at the end of the graveyard. No Armstrong had been buried there since they had fled the house and the area during the War of Independence and so the last Armstrong buried there was Nico's great-grandfather Lord Charles, that decadent degenerate who had brought this great family to their knees. As she already knew, the grave confirmed he died in 1903. He was buried next to his long-suffering wife Arabella who died a couple of years later. Then she saw Charles' father Lawrence's grave, stating he was born in January 1845 and died 1899. He was buried beside his beloved Lady Margaret. Kate moved on to the next gravestone and saw it was Lord Edward, born in 1818 and deceased in 1880. And then there was Edward's father, Frederick, who she knew little about as Armstrong House hadn't been built in his time, but she saw he had died in 1832. All of Nico's male ancestors were accounted for and were here in graves before her. There was no possibility that Nico could be descended from this man Daniel had found in the famine grave who died in his early twenties in 1846.

She stood there looking down at the graves. It was so quiet and she could hear an owl hoot. It was hard to believe that the people whose lives she brought to the screen were lying here in front of her. It suddenly struck her that there was truth in what Nico was always saying: would they like it if they knew she had aired their lives and all the secrets they kept? What would they make of her? It was hard for Kate to think her son was also descended from these people. Looking at their towering tombstones, these people suddenly felt very real to her. A sudden wind rustled through the leaves of the trees and she shivered. To use that expression, she felt a goose had walked over her grave, but as she looked down at the Armstrongs trying to rest in peace she realised it was she who was walking over their graves. Suddenly she jumped as she felt somebody touch her arm. But when she turned around there was nobody there. Another gust of wind rustled through the trees and it was like she could hear her name being called in the wind – *Kate.*

She suddenly started to feel frightened and, turning quickly, made her way through the graveyard and out through the church grounds back to her car.

CHAPTER 61

Kate waited anxiously for Daniel to contact her and when he phoned three days later he sounded very excited and said there had been a development. He asked if he could call and see her. Nico was away with work for the day and so Kate agreed. She thought it was best she should meet with Daniel on her own with whatever information he had, so she could hear it first before Nico did.

When he arrived, she brought him into the library where he handed her the results of the second DNA test.

"It confirms what the first test said: this man is a direct ancestor of Nico's," said Daniel, looked very excited and pleased with himself. "What's more – we found a name – we know who he is."

"How?" she asked, perplexed.

"In the man's inside pockets he was carrying papers that identified him – a payment slip and letters. They were in fairly bad condition as you can imagine, but we used the latest technology to highlight the writing. The man's name was Seán Hegarty, and . . ." Daniel paused, savouring the moment, "his address was the Armstrong Estate. He lived here on the Armstrong Estate, Kate!"

"But who was he and why had he got Nico's genes?" Kate asked in confusion.

"I don't know yet, but I'm hoping to find out. Hegarty is normally an Irish Catholic name, so he probably wasn't aristocracy or gentry. I reckon he worked on the estate. We have to check the records of the employees and tenant farmers on the estate at the time to see if there was a Seán Hegarty living here."

"Do you want to do it now?" asked Kate. She suddenly felt very nervous. She didn't know what all this was about, but she felt Daniel had an idea formed already of what had happened in the 1840s with this Seán Hegarty.

Kate and Daniel went up to the attic rooms and Kate found the ledgers for the household staff in 1846 and the ledgers for the payments of the tenant farmers.

Kate watched as Daniel fingered through the household staff at Armstrong House first.

His face lit up as he exclaimed, *"There he is – Seán Hegarty!"*

Kate anxiously looked at the entry he was pointing to and read it out: *"Seán Hegarty – stable boy – pay three shillings a week."*

"And look at the last entry for him," said Daniel. "Last entry was in May 1846 – there were no further payments made to him or explanation why he was gone. We *know* why he was gone! He had been murdered! Quick – get the previous year's household staff ledger."

Kate looked along the shelves of files and found it. She handed it to Daniel.

"Look at this!" he said. "He was transferred to the stables in the summer of the previous year. The year before that he worked here actually in Armstrong House itself as – Lady Anna's servant!"

Kate read the entry from the earlier part of the previous year: *"Seán Hegarty – household servant – position – in service as driver to Lady Armstrong – three shillings a week."*

"So – what are you implying?" she asked.

"I'm not implying anything. The facts speak for themselves. This Seán Hegarty was a direct ancestor of Nico's, which means the only time he could fit into that equation was when he worked here at Armstrong House, in the service of Lady Anna Armstrong." Daniel stared directly in Kate's eyes. "They had an affair and the result was Lawrence. It's the only way Nico could have the same genes as Seán Hegarty."

Kate looked at him, horrified. "What you're suggesting is outrageous!"

"Outrageous or not, I'm a scientist and scientists only work with facts, and the fact is Nico is descended from Seán Hegarty. I bet you now if we exhume the body of Lord Edward Armstrong we will categorically prove by DNA that Nico is *not* descended from him."

"*Daniel!*" Kate was dismayed.

"*Kate!*" came a shout from somewhere downstairs.

"It's Nico, he's home – he said he wouldn't be back until later," said Kate, quickly taking the ledgers and putting them away. "Daniel, please don't say anything about this to Nico yet. I need to think about this."

"But, Kate, this could be sensational," said Daniel. "Think of your film!"

"Are you at Hunter's Farm this evening?" she asked.

"Sure."

"I'll come by about nine and we can discuss it further."

Daniel nodded.

Kate could hardly think straight for the rest of the afternoon as she digested what Daniel was saying. If the DNA results were correct, then there was no other plausible explanation. But this meant the Armstrong family had been living a lie for over a century and a half.

"You're quiet this evening," commented Valerie to Kate over dinner.

"Just a bit tired," she said.

"Is everything all right?" asked Nico.

"Of course," she said. "It's just my mind is a bit overworked from the film project." She looked up at the clock and saw it was past eight o'clock. "In fact, I might go for a walk. Some fresh air will do me good."

"Do you want me to join you?" he asked.

"No. You stay here, I just need a little time to think my project through."

Kate went down the long drive and out the main gates onto the road. She walked along the road, soon reaching Hunter's Farm.

She walked up to the door and rang the doorbell.

"Hi!" said Daniel, beckoning her in.

She smiled at him and walked down the corridor and into the parlour where he had a bottle of wine open and two glasses.

"I could do with a drink after what I learned today," she said.

He poured her a glass and sat down on the couch beside her.

"Are you absolutely sure of the DNA test, absolutely sure of what you're saying?" she asked earnestly.

"One-hundred-per-cent sure. The test can be rechecked by anyone you want – they'll only come up with the same results."

"It's like finding out you were adopted or something," said Kate.

"Well, it certainly will be a surprise for Nico. You didn't tell him yet?"

Kate shook her head as she drank her wine. "I don't know how to tell him. I mean, it will be like taking away his identity. He's thought all his life he is descended from this mighty Armstrong dynasty and then to find out he's the descendent of a lowly servant! A stable boy!"

"Like most of the rest of us!" said Daniel. "But it doesn't just affect Nico. The Armstrong family in Ireland lost any power and influence a century ago with Irish Independence. But Lawrence had six children and most of them went on to marry dukes in England and even into the fabulously wealthy Van Hoevan family in America. When this comes out there's going to be a lot of important people who will be shocked and affected."

"Yes. Those people are only distant relatives of Nico and he's never met any of them, so I hadn't thought of that. It will have far-reaching implications."

"Do you think Nico will consent to Edward's grave being exhumed for us to confirm once and for all he can't be descended from him?"

"Of course he won't! He'd never allow such a thing!"

"*Hmmm* . . . in that case we have to check where we stand legally on this. I'm sure you could give consent as guardian of Cian who is an Armstrong descendent as well."

"Daniel! Do you understand what you are saying? Nico is my husband and you're suggesting I take legal advice to override him?"

"Why not?" he smirked. "You override him on everything else.

371

You're going ahead and making the film which he is vehemently against, aren't you?"

Kate downed her drink, reached for the bottle and refilled her glass.

"And how *did* Seán Hegarty end up with his head smashed in a famine grave?" she asked.

"I don't know how he was murdered, but it was the perfect murder. Nobody was going to exhume a famine grave looking for a missing person."

"So where do we go with this from here?"

"Well, as far as I'm concerned it's the most sensational discovery that has come out of our excavation. I was expecting that the sum of my discoveries would be stuff we already knew about the desperate deaths and treatment of the famine victims. What we have discovered about Seán Hegarty is a whole new dimension. It's the type of story we archaeologists can only dream of as a once-in-a-lifetime discovery during our digs. A significant revelation about one of the most important families in the country at the time."

"Yes, I can see why you're excited," said Kate.

"But just think – if you thought investors were lining up before for your film about Lady Anna and Lord Edward with the revelation about Lady Margaret, just think of the effect this will have! So we need to get to work straight away. If you won't face Nico with a legal challenge, you'll need to tell him, somehow get him on board and get his permission to exhume Lord Edward's grave."

Kate stared down into her glass of wine before taking another gulp. "If I tell him the truth about being descended from Seán Hegarty, it will really destroy him."

"For goodness' sake, he needs to toughen up! Those events happened one hundred and fifty years ago!"

"Yes, but he feels a certain pride, an unspoken understanding, a belief they are a link in the chain from the past to the future. That's why he loves Armstrong House so much – he feels he's only the custodian of the place to pass it on to the future."

"He always struck me as somebody not that interested in the past," said Daniel. "You said that yourself."

"I've come to realise it's not that he's not interested, it's just that he's *sure* of the past. The past can't change, or at least that's as it should be, he thinks. That's why he hates what I do with my research and work – it upsets his whole equilibrium. And I think this revelation will be one too much for him. And the fact that I'm going to make financial gain out of it, without any thought to the memory of those people, he will think that despicable."

"And what of Seán Hegarty? This poor unfortunate man who sired a child that he never knew and ended up murdered and thrown into a pauper's grave? Does he not deserve for this to come out? Does he not deserve justice? Or just like back then, is his life unimportant as long as the Armstrong name is protected?"

"I'm not saying he doesn't deserve recognition," she said. "If the truth be told, Daniel. I'm really worried about the effect this will have on my marriage."

"How so?"

"I don't think Nico and I will survive together if I reveal this in my film. All we do recently is fight. It has come to the stage where we don't even enjoy each other's company, because we just make snide comments at each other all the time."

"Maybe . . . maybe you've just come to the end of the road with each other," said Daniel.

"We can't have come to the end of the road! We have our beautiful small child, our beautiful home and –" Kate stopped as the tears spilled down her face.

"And it looks like you are looking for excuses to stay together," said Daniel as he reached over and took the glass from her hand. He then leaned towards her and gently kissed her mouth. He pulled back a second and looked into her eyes before leaning in and kissing her again.

She began to kiss him back. Then she stopped abruptly and gently pushed him away.

"I'm sorry, Daniel," she whispered. "I don't know what just happened, but I'd better go."

She stood up quickly and walked to the door.

"Kate!" he called.

She turned around at the door, looked at him and said, "The

third reason I was going to give you as to why Nico and I could not have reached the end of the road is – I love him."

She walked out the door, leaving Daniel staring after her.

Kate walked quickly to the end of the drive of Hunter's Farm, then stopped for a moment to catch her breath. She put her hand to her mouth, feeling dazed and confused. She then quickly walked up the road. The sun was beginning to set and she just felt the need to be home in Armstrong House as quickly as possible and with Nico. She turned into the gates and walked up the drive, seeing the welcoming light of Armstrong House come closer to her. The walk seemed to last forever but she finally got to the forecourt and hurried up the steps to the front door.

She steadied herself as she took out her door-key and waited to calm down before letting herself in and closing and locking the door behind her. As she looked down the long hallway she was overcome with a feeling of safety to be in her home. She could see a light on in the drawing room. She walked over and, opening the door, saw Nico was on the couch reading a book. She walked into the room.

"Did you have a nice walk?" he asked, looking up from his book for a moment before continuing to read.

She said nothing but walked further into the room.

As she hadn't answered, he looked up again. "You were a while – did you go down to the lake?"

He noticed her expression was upset.

"Is anything the matter?" he asked.

She looked at him and then she burst out crying.

"Kate!" he said, flinging down his book and standing up quickly. "Whatever is wrong with you?"

She said nothing but continued crying. Nico was shocked as Kate so rarely cried. He couldn't remember the last time.

"Oh, love!" he said, rushing over to her. "What's wrong?"

He put his arms around her and she grabbed on to him and held him tightly.

"Has something happened to you?" he asked, full of concern.

"Just hold me, Nico," she managed to say through her tears.

CHAPTER 62

1865

Anna did not get any sleep the night after the drinks party as the events of the evening whirled through her mind. Poor Margaret being attacked by Sinclair. But the events that unfolded had saved her from exposing the truth to Edward. Sinclair, who was about to force Anna's destruction was now locked in a stable, disgraced and waiting to be banished from the estate forever.

Anna watched Edward as he quickly got ready the next morning.

"I'm going down to the stables to confront Sinclair before I throw him off the estate," he said.

"Is that really necessary, Edward? We know what happened – what use is there discussing it with him?" she asked in panic, fearing that Sinclair would still be given the opportunity to tell Edward the truth.

"I want to know why he did it. Why did he attack Margaret? I couldn't sleep all night from thinking about it."

"Will it make any difference, knowing why he did it?" she asked.

"I need to know for myself."

"Oh, please, Edward, just let it go! Have Taylor and the men escort him from the estate and –"

"No, Anna!" said Edward angrily. "He didn't have to answer to the police, but he still has to answer to me."

Before Anna had the opportunity to say another word, Edward stormed out.

Anna felt a splitting headache seize her.

"Unbolt the door," ordered Edward at the stables and the head groomsman did as he was bid.

Edward walked into the stable and found Sinclair sitting on a stack of hay, looking dishevelled and angry. He stood up abruptly on seeing Edward.

"Leave us," Edward ordered the groomsman and the stable boys and they quickly departed, closing over the door, leaving Edward and Sinclair alone.

"Has she admitted the truth?" demanded Sinclair.

"Margaret has fully reported what happened, yes."

"The girl is mad! It's better Lawrence finds out now she has a mental illness than after he marries her." He went to march past Edward to the door. "How dare you keep me locked up here for the night? What must Diana think?"

Edward stood in front of him, halting him from going any further.

"Margaret has told us everything. How you grabbed her and forced yourself on her and tried to silence her by covering her mouth but, luckily, she managed to scream, or goodness knows what would have happened."

"I tell you, that did not happen, Edward! She pounced on me like a cat on a mouse. It was she who tried to seduce me, and then started ripping her dress and screaming like a madwoman."

"Do you honestly expect me to believe that?" asked Edward cynically.

"Yes!"

"But why were you in her room?" demanded Edward.

"She said she needed to speak to me urgently."

"But what could Margaret possibly need to speak to you urgently about?"

"Ask her! Why I would attack her is the more important question!"

"I've been asking myself that all night. Lust? Envy? Anger at seeing Lawrence finding happiness with such a beautiful sweet girl, so you tried to somehow defile their love?"

"Sweet! There's nothing sweet about that girl! *She's a heinous creature, a witch, a bitch and a whore!*" shouted Sinclair.

"*That's enough*!" roared Edward. "You are very lucky that you are not in a jail right now. Margaret has decided not to press charges against you."

"That's because it wouldn't stand up in court!"

"Of course it would! You were caught in the act! There were enough witnesses! She is not pressing charges because she will not put her good name through such a filthy trial, and humiliate herself and our family publicly. I, for one, am very grateful to her for that."

"I don't know what game she is playing or why she is playing it, but bring her here to me. Let me speak to her and the truth will come out quick enough!"

"I will not bring her anywhere near you. You will never see her again. I've made my decision and you are to leave the Armstrong Estate today. You'll be escorted back to Hunter's Farm where you, Diana and Harry will pack your things and leave and you are never to return here." Edward's voice was filled with determination.

"You can't do that! You can't run this place without me!"

"I shall have to try. There is no other option. You can no longer stay here."

Sinclair's face filled with disbelief. "You are putting the word of that little tart you hardly know before me? Your cousin who you have known and loved all your life as your brother?"

"I believe her, Sinclair. I really didn't want to, but it's plain to see what happened last night. And, I must admit, it's in keeping with your character." Edward sighed. "I've thought about all the times you showed such cruelty over the years. The amount of times you've hit a tenant farmer, struck a stable boy over a minor demeanour, threatened to use violence to somebody who got in your way."

"But – that was the peasants! I've never done anything to somebody from our own class!"

"That I know of – until last night. But you have an uncontrollable temper which can lead to violence. There's no doubt in my mind you did what Margaret accuses you of. And I am horrified by you. That you would do that to my son's fiancée – that you would insult my son –"

"Your son!" guffawed Sinclair. "Your darling precious son Lawrence!"

"Insulting him is the greatest insult you could throw at me," said Edward.

Sinclair stood back and his face twisted into a nasty grin. "You are so stupid, Edward. I don't think I've ever met anybody as stupid as you in all my life."

"Your opinion no longer matters to me," said Edward.

"Ha! I take Anna didn't tell you then?"

"Tell me what?"

Sinclair savoured the moment. "That Lawrence is not your son."

Even in the darkened stable, Sinclair could see Edward pale.

"What are you talking about?" he said.

"I gave Anna an ultimatum that either she was going to tell you or I would. Can't you see, Edward? Can't you see who he has grown up looking like? The *servant* you employed to look after Anna when she first came to live at Armstrong House. It's plain to see Lawrence is his son, and not yours. It's obvious Seán Hegarty was doing more with Anna than just driving her into town and back!"

Edward's temper was reaching boiling point. "Is it not enough for you that you defile my son's fiancée but now you insult my wife's honour?"

"Well, Lawrence is only marrying the same kind of woman that his mother is – a whore and –"

Edward swung his fist back and punched Sinclair in the face, sending him flying backwards.

Sinclair staggered in shock, his hand on his cheek where he had been struck. He had never seen Edward strike anybody or show any violence in all his life.

"She's admitted it to me, Edward. Anna admitted the truth to me when I confronted her. She admitted Lawrence is Seán Hegarty's bastard and she was going to tell you before I told you. She's played you for a fool all these years. Passing Lawrence off as yours. You fool! Doting on him all these years, when he is just a blow-in, has no more right to be here than the scullery maid. He's not an Armstrong, he's a bastard!"

"*Shut up! Shut up or I will kill you with my bare hands*!" Edward yelled.

"I am telling you the truth for your own sake and this is how you react?" said Sinclair. "I know this is a major shock to you, but you must see the truth now. For God's sake, man, what's wrong with you?"

Breathing deeply, Edward calmed and the fury left his face. "Nobody will ever believe what you are saying, Sinclair. It is just an attempt to deflect from what you did to Margaret. You will never prove that Lawrence is Seán's son –" He stopped abruptly as he realised what he had said.

Sinclair confusion suddenly lifted as his eyes widened in amazement. "You knew! You knew all along! You knew Lawrence wasn't yours, didn't you? When did you find out? Did you always know? Or did it dawn on you when Lawrence began to grow up and looked like Seán?"

"I will no longer listen to this mindless rubbish from you. I'll have you escorted to Hunter's Farm. Pack your things and get off this estate as soon as possible. I never want to see you again."

"But why did you put up with it? Why didn't you confront Anna if you knew the truth?" Sinclair demanded. "Why do you love Lawrence so much when he's not yours and the son a peasant?"

"You will never understand me, Sinclair, and I will never understand you," said Edward as he went to leave.

"Because you couldn't have your own child, you accepted his?"

"Goodbye, Sinclair."

"I've found him," Sinclair said, stopping Edward in his tracks. "I found Seán Hegarty and he's admitted everything to me. That's why Anna admitted the truth to me. She invented that story about him stealing the locket to get him away from the estate after Lawrence was born. She's seen him – Anna has seen him. I brought him up to the estate so that she could see him. I was going to bring him up to meet you and tell you everything if she didn't tell you."

Edward turned and stared at Sinclair.

"Where did you find him?" he asked.

"I tracked him down through his family."

"Where is he now?" demanded Edward.

"In a safe place," said Sinclair. "He's ready to come forward and tell the truth about his affair with Anna and that he is the true father of Lawrence Armstrong. You think you've got all the power here, Edward, but you have no power. Seán is willing to tell the world about what happened between him and Lady Armstrong and you will be ruined if you do not work with me and do as I say. I'll bring Armstrong House down like a house of cards if I do not get what I want. And what I want is this estate, as my rightful legacy. You change your will and make it mine."

Edward was lost in thought for a while and Sinclair waited.

"Bring him to me then, Sinclair. Bring Seán Hegarty to Armstrong House and let me speak to him. Let me ask him for myself."

"I will! I will bring him to you! Are you sure you really want me to bring him to Armstrong House and let everyone see him? For Anna to see and meet him again? And Lawrence to see a man who will look like his own mirror-image in twenty years? Do you really want to do that?"

"Yes, I would very much like to meet Seán Hegarty after all these years and for him to tell me he slept with my wife and fathered my son," said Edward.

"And the newspapers. I will take him to the newspapers and he will expose the tawdry affair he had with Lady Armstrong. This will bring down the House of Armstrong, Edward."

"Do it! Do it all!" goaded Edward.

Sinclair stared at Edward in confusion.

"Because whoever this man is that you have found and shown to Anna is not Seán Hegarty, Sinclair," said Edward.

"He is. You will see he is."

"He can't be. Who is he, Sinclair? A relative of Seán Hegarty's you found on the estate he came from? A brother, a cousin?

Someone who is the same age group that Seán should be with a strong resemblance. Let's face it, as you have already pointed out about Lawrence, there seems to be a strong family resemblance running through the Hegarty family. And you passed this man off as Seán to Anna, scaring her to death, blackmailing her to reveal the truth to me, thinking I would disown her and Lawrence. It's you who are the fool, Sinclair."

"It's Seán, I tell you, it's Seán Hegarty I have found!"

"It is not, Sinclair. It's an imposter. Somebody from his family who you are paying or threatening to pretend to be Seán."

"It is him, I tell you!"

"It can't be Seán, Sinclair . . . because Seán Hegarty is dead. He's been dead for many years."

Sinclair saw something in Edward's face that he never saw before as he spoke the last sentence. A cold stare in his blue eyes which were like ice. It chilled him throughout his body.

"He's dead, Sinclair, and so this man you are parading can't be him," said Edward.

Sinclair wanted to say more, but there was something in Edward's expression that made him fall silent. He had never thought it possible for him to be frightened of Edward, and yet this man standing before him frightened him greatly. To such an extent that he realised that, if he didn't follow his orders and leave the estate immediately, he himself would be in danger.

Edward pulled open the stable door.

"*Taylor!*" shouted Edward as he marched outside.

Taylor, the groomsman and the stable boys came rushing across from the other side of the yard.

"Escort Mr. Sinclair to Hunter's Farm and allow him some time to pack his belongings and then have him escorted off the estate. If he should ever come back, call for the police immediately."

"And what of the wife and boy?" asked Taylor.

"They all must leave," said Edward.

Sinclair came to the stable door and watched as Edward marched up home to Armstrong House.

CHAPTER 63

Anna waited with the Mountdares in the drawing room for Edward to return. Margaret had not come down from her room all morning while Lawrence had gone out for a ride. Lawrence was so angry Anna had suggested the ride to get him out of the house as he was only serving to agitate the Mountdares further.

"I still cannot believe what happened," said the Countess. "It is like a bad dream – nay, a nightmare, that I expect to wake up from any moment."

"I know," said Anna.

"To think our precious daughter should suffer such a horrific attack in her own fiancé's home," said the Countess.

"We all feel terrible about what happened," said Anna.

"And you should feel responsible as well, Lady Armstrong. To invite that – *creature* – to your house when there are ladies present," said the Countess.

"We do feel responsible," offered Anna. "But he has never shown that side to him before."

"From my understanding of what the Foxes and Fitzherberts were saying last night, Sinclair Armstrong always showed a violent nature," said the Earl.

"That is true – but to the peasants on the estate – never to a lady before," said Anna.

"A violent nature is a violent nature, Lady Armstrong, and you can't polish shit!" said the Countess, so enraged that all her decorum had vanished. "What was your husband thinking of

382

inviting him here if he has a violent nature? He put our daughter in danger and she suffered the consequences."

"Sinclair has always behaved as a gentleman when he attended events at Armstrong House over the years," said Anna, not believing herself she was speaking in Sinclair's defence.

"*We could have all been raped!*" shrieked the Countess.

"Clementina! Control yourself!" said the Earl, becoming irritated at her dramatics.

As the Countess continue speaking in a flurry of fury, Anna was on tenterhooks thinking about what was passing between Sinclair and Edward. She knew that Sinclair would have told Edward the truth about her and Seán as soon as he got the first opportunity. She was hoping that Edward would be so enraged that he would see it as a lie and an attempt to deflect from what he had done. But he would still be shocked by Sinclair's accusation and she was terrified of the consequences.

The door opened and Edward walked in. She held her breath as she studied his face. He looked agitated but didn't even look at her as he gave all his attention to the Mountdares.

"Rest assured I have dealt with the matter. Sinclair and his family are being removed from the estate and banished from our lives forever," said Edward.

Anna all but choked with the relief that flooded through her.

"But is that punishment enough?" the Countess demanded stridently.

Edward was exasperated. "Well, it is the only punishment we can administer other than we hand him over to the police, and I thought we had decided that that was not the course of action to be followed."

"Did he show any remorse?" asked the Earl.

"None at all. He denies the whole thing, and said it was Margaret who attacked him," said Edward.

"The man is clearly deluded and has mental issues," said the Countess.

"I believe you may be correct in that assertion," said Edward

"It must be a terrible shock to Diana," said Anna.

It was the first time since coming into the room that he looked at her. She didn't notice any change or peculiarity in his demeanour towards her.

"Yes, although my sympathies are with Margaret," he said, "I cannot help but feel sorry for Sinclair's wife and son, who must suffer too because of his actions."

"Well, I don't wish to come across as in any way ungrateful or discourteous, but I cannot wait to leave Armstrong House today and get back to safety of my own home," said the Countess.

"I do hope in time that you will get over this dreadful episode," said Edward, "and give us the chance to allow you to change your view of Armstrong House. It will be Margaret's home for the rest of her life once she marries Lawrence and she will be Lady of the Manor here one day."

"It is not my opinion of the house that matters, but Margaret's," said the Countess. "She is the one that must live here – if she chooses to continue with her engagement to Lawrence."

"Surely she would not allow this to alter her plans to marry Lawrence?" asked Anna, horrified.

"No, I most certainly will not!" said a voice, and Anna saw the speaker was Margaret who had come in quietly.

"My poor child!" said the Countess as she stood up quickly and ran to Margaret, enveloping her in an embrace. "How are you feeling today?"

"Much better, Mama. I slept well," said Margaret, gently pushing her away and walking further into the room. "May I make myself clear – I will certainly not let what happened interfere with my engagement to Lawrence. Nor will I let it colour my perception of Armstrong House. This will be my home as it is Lawrence's and I aim to love it and care for it as much as he does for the rest of my life."

"What a trooper!" sang the Countess. "I always said you took after my side of the family and not your father's!"

As Anna observed the girl while her parents fussed over her, she couldn't help but feel complete admiration for her. She seemed to have nerves like steel and was carrying on as if nothing had happened. She would make an amazing Lady Armstrong one day, Anna conceded.

Edward came over and sat down on the sofa beside Anna. Anna felt unnerved as she forced herself to look at him for any signs of Sinclair's revelation.

He turned to her and smiled before and taking her hand. She smiled back at him as she squeezed his hand tightly.

CHAPTER 64

Gertie had spent the night awake, sitting on her bed, shaking from her experience with Harry. She didn't know what to do. She didn't know whether she should report what had happened to Lord Armstrong. But this would mean her instant dismissal as it would come out that she had an affair with Harry. And also Harry had threatened to slit her throat. She shuddered every time she thought of that.

When morning came, she put on her highest collar to hide the red marks around her neck where Harry had gripped her. Something had been going on in the house the previous night but she didn't know yet what had happened. After that woman's screams Gertie had heard much comings and goings and loud talking and shouting. She had been too scared to come out of her room to investigate what was going on.

She made her way down to the kitchen where she found the servants all aflutter and talking in whispered conversations.

"What's going on?" Gertie asked Jessie, another maid.

"Mr. Sinclair attacked Master Lawrence's fiancée Lady Margaret last night!" said Jessie excitedly. "He . . ." Jessie leaned close to Gertie's ear as she gave the rest of the details.

"*No!*" said Gertie shocked.

"*Yes!*" answered Jessie, nodding enthusiastically. "Mr. Sinclair was locked in a stable all night and Mr. Taylor said Mr. Sinclair and all his family are to be thrown off the estate today!"

"Leaving Hunter's Farm?" Gertie was shocked further.

Jessie nodded again. "That's the last we'll see of them!"

"Master Harry is to leave too?"

"All of them, I tell you!" said Jessie.

"Get on with your work, your two, and less gossiping!" the cook called over to them.

Gertie and Jessie quickly made themselves busy.

As Gertie digested the information, she was overcome with relief. Harry would be thrown off the estate and she would never have to see him again. She now felt she didn't have to do anything and her job and position were safe. As she did her work, she realised that she had been taught a very valuable lesson, to stay away from sweet-talking cads. As she remembered Harry's hands around her neck, she thought of how it had nearly cost her life. And whatever had happened between Sinclair and Lady Margaret that was causing their departure, she realised that Lord Armstrong would never know how much danger his son's life had been in the previous night as Harry lay in wait for him with a knife.

Diana heard the front door open and slam and rose to her feet. She hadn't slept. She had been waiting anxiously all night.

The parlour door swung open and Sinclair stormed in.

"*The bastards!*" he shouted.

"What happened?" she demanded.

"They locked me in a stable for the night. *Me!* That Edward would do that to me!"

"But with the girl – what happened last night with the girl?"

"I haven't a clue! She told me she needed to speak to me privately and when I went to her room she tried to kiss me and then started tearing her clothes and screaming," said Sinclair.

"But why – why would she do such a thing?"

"I have no idea! And they called the police and they were going to arrest me and then she didn't want to press charges because it would muddy her name and so they locked me in the stable for the night. How dare they treat me like that?" Sinclair was speaking fast and furiously.

"But – did you give her any encouragement? Did you flatter her or make her think you were interested in her?" Diana was trying to understand.

"I never even looked at her since she arrived. She's just an insignificant wallflower as far as I'm concerned."

"But surely Edward does not believe this folly?"

"He does! He's furious with me and believes I attacked his son's fiancée. He says we are to leave Hunter's Farm today – pack our things and be escorted off the estate. Taylor and the others are waiting outside to make sure we leave!"

"Harry and I as well?" Diana was horrified.

"All of us!"

"Oh!" Diana felt she had been kicked in the stomach. "But this can't be!"

"I tried to reason with Edward, tried to tell him the girl was mentally unwell. But he was having none of it. He's – he's disowned me!" Sinclair's eyes filled with tears.

Diana had never seen him like that before. "And what of our plan? What of Lawrence being Seán Hegarty's son – did you tell him the truth?"

"Yes, I told him everything." He looked at her. "And he already knew from what I could tell."

"*What?*"

"He seems to have known all these years that Lawrence wasn't his and he doesn't care. He loves him as if he is his own. He knows everything."

Diana's mind was whizzing. "Did you threaten that we will expose the truth! That we have found Seán Hegarty and he will testify that he slept with Anna and fathered Lawrence?"

Sinclair sank down on the sofa. "It's no use, Diana. He knows the man we have been showing to Anna is not Seán Hegarty. He guessed he was a relative of his who just looked like him."

"But how would he know that?"

Sinclair looked up at her, his eyes fearful. "He said he knew it couldn't be Seán Hegarty – because Seán Hegarty is dead."

"Dead? How would Edward know that? Nobody knows what happened to Seán Hegarty after he was thrown from the estate all those years ago. Even his brother said he never returned to the Hamilton Estate and his family assumed he had died in the Famine!"

"I know. But there was something in the way he said it, Diana, something in the way he said Seán was dead that frightened me. And I didn't think Edward was capable of frightening a mouse. The game is up, Diana. We had better tell Seán Hegarty's brother to return to the Hamilton Estate and warn him to say nothing of this ruse, otherwise Edward will charge us with attempted blackmail as well. I will make it clear to him that it is dangerous for him to stay – in case he gets any ideas about blackmail himself. Even so, I'm afraid I'll have to pay him a hefty sum to secure his silence."

"But where will we go? This has been our home since before we were married," said Diana.

"I don't know. But Edward has finished with us and we do not have his protection any longer. We had better leave immediately as he says, or the consequences will be too dreadful to consider."

"But I can't pack in an afternoon! This has been my home for twenty-five years! I wouldn't know where to start," exclaimed Diana.

"We had better make a start quickly, or else we will be thrown off the estate without our possessions."

Diana flew into a rage. "This is all your fault! You have never been content with your place in life! You have always been envious and jealous of Edward and his family and trying to take what was theirs!"

"And you alongside me, encouraging me every step of the way! It was you who came up with the idea to pass Seán Hegarty's brother off as him to frighten Edward and Anna into signing the estate over to us!"

"*I didn't come up with the idea of you going to that girl's room last night and whatever happened between you!*" she shouted back. "*You've ruined our lives!*"

"I should have never even have married you! I could have done so much better. I could have married somebody with money. I was the grandson of a lord, you were a widow going nowhere when I married you!"

Outside Hunter's Farm, Taylor and the other men from Armstrong House could hear the shouting and screaming coming from inside the house. To a man they were hugely delighted at Sinclair's downfall.

Inside, Harry sat on the stairs listening to his parents screaming at each other. He could not hear everything being said between his parents but realised they were to be evicted from the estate. He felt crushed. He had been so close to finishing Lawrence off and inheriting everything. Now he faced an uncertain future.

As he looked out the window at Taylor and the other men ready to escort them from the estate he knew there was no point in objecting and causing a scene. His fate was sealed.

CHAPTER 65

That evening Edward and Anna were in the forecourt saying goodbye to the Mountdares as a carriage waited to take them to the train station in Castlewest.

"I do hope next time we meet it will be in more pleasant circumstances," said Anna.

"So do I!" said the Countess.

"We can only apologise again for what happened and hope Margaret recovers soon," said Edward.

"Can one ever recover from such an experience?" said the Countess.

"I think Margaret is made of stern stuff," said Anna as she looked over at her.

Margaret was already seated in the carriage as she spoke to Lawrence who was standing beside it holding her hand.

Taylor arrived into the forecourt and came up to Edward. "My lord, if I could speak a moment with you?"

"Certainly," said Edward and he walked away from the others to talk in private.

"Just to report to you that Mr. Sinclair and his family have left Hunter's Farm and been escorted off the estate," said Taylor.

"Very good. Has Hunter's Farm been secured?"

"Yes, my lord."

Edward nodded and rejoined the others.

"I don't know how I'll cope until I see you next," said Lawrence as he leaned into the carriage to Margaret.

"It will only be two weeks until we see each other again in Dublin," she said.

"It will feel like an eternity," he said. "Are you sure you're all right?"

"Yes, Lawrence, please don't worry about me any more. What happened is over, and I will certainly not want to dwell on it again. I am happy to know that Sinclair has been sent from the estate and we will never have to see him again."

"Oh, I can promise you that. And if I ever do see him again, I will kill him with my own bare hands!"

She leaned forward and kissed him.

"Right! Are we ready to go!" said the Countess as she arrived at the carriage.

The footman opened the door and she climbed in, followed by her husband.

"Goodbye, my love," said Margaret as the carriage took off out of the forecourt.

"Goodbye!" called the Countess, "And good riddance," she muttered sotto voce.

"Clementina!" said the Earl.

Anna, Edward and Lawrence stood in the forecourt, watching the carriage continue down the driveway and out of view. Lawrence waved until it had disappeared.

"Right!" said Edward, placing a hand on Lawrence's shoulder. "We have a lot of work to do! Now Sinclair is gone there's going to be a lot more for us to do running the estate. Are you ready for all this responsibility?"

"Of course, Papa – isn't that what I was born to do?" smiled Lawrence.

"Well, let's make a start. There's this month's accounts for us to go through, and then we have to order new stock for next month."

Edward and Lawrence walked across the forecourt together.

Anna watched them walk up the steps and into the house. She would never understand what had happened over the past twenty-four hours. One moment she was on the brink of destruction and then through a twist of faith she had been saved. Edward appeared to be acting normally with her and so Sinclair had not been given the opportunity to tell Edward the truth or Edward had simply dismissed what he had said as a ridiculous attempt to save himself. But here she was outside her beautiful home, at last free in the knowledge that she was safe, and her son was safe. Could she at last enjoy Armstrong House in peace? She turned and looked out at the lake.

But Seán was still somewhere out there. She had seen him with her own eyes in the forecourt that night, in Castlewest in the street and the day of the garden party. He had been brought back into their lives by Sinclair. Now Sinclair was gone would Seán slip away again? She felt deep down that Seán wasn't a danger to her. That, despite of what she had done to him all those years ago, he would not want to harm her or Lawrence. Perhaps Sinclair was blackmailing him to come back. And though Sinclair had eventually been able to find Seán and bring him back, perhaps Seán had not come back with any malice towards her. Perhaps he had just come back to see her and his son. To see his son grown into a man and to see they were all right. And maybe to let Anna know that he was all right. That he hadn't died in the Famine as she had always thought. That she hadn't sent him to his death. She felt the years of guilt and uncertainty lift from her and she felt free like she hadn't done in years. She turned and walked into the house, closing the door behind her.

CHAPTER 66

Present Day

Kate lay in bed, looking at the sun streaming through the windows, thinking about Daniel and what happened the previous evening when he had kissed her. She felt exhausted and emotionally drained. She hadn't told Nico the cause of her being so upset the previous night. How could she? Nor had he pressed her to say. They had spent some time in the drawing room with her being held by him and she had finally drifted off to sleep in his arms.

She didn't know nor could even explain to herself what had happened at Hunter's Farm. Daniel kissing her had come out of the blue, and yet she had responded to him when he did it. She had, albeit momentarily, kissed him back. There had obviously been a growing attraction and closeness developing between them that she hadn't even been aware of. And she hadn't even recognised or admitted to herself the danger signs. And, before she knew it, she had been in over her head. They had bonded over their work investigating the history of Armstrong House. She wasn't even sure why she should be surprised. Nico's and her feelings for each other had developed when they were working together restoring the house. It was like the house took over her heart and soul and she lost the run of herself, last time with Nico who she ended up marrying, and this time with Daniel. And by doing she so she had nearly thrown away everything she loved the most. Maybe she was having a mid-life crisis, she thought. But whatever the reason behind it, she knew that she had not put what should be the most important things in her life first: Nico and Cian. As she thought of the desperate tension between herself and Nico over the summer, she realised she had come close to losing everything, and maybe it was still too late to fix it.

The door opened and she saw Cian come rushing into the room, following by Nico who was holding a breakfast tray.

Cian jumped onto the bed and Kate sat up and hugged him close to her.

"We were cooking your breakfast all morning," said Cian with a big exaggerated sigh.

"Were you?" said Kate. "Aren't you the cleverest boy in the world?"

"Bacon, sausages, eyes sunny-side up just as you like them, black pudding, white pudding and tea! Oh, and toast!" said Nico as he placed the tray on the bedside table beside her.

"Nico, you shouldn't have done all this," said Kate, smiling at him appreciatively.

Nico sat on the side of the bed beside them.

"You must eat it before it gets cold!" Cian scolded.

"Yes, I will, sweetheart," she said, rolling her eyes at Nico who grinned and put the tray on her knees. "I can't remember last time I had breakfast in bed!"

"Our honeymoon?" said Nico.

"Yes, probably."

He sat again and took her hand as Cian helped himself to a slice of toast.

"How are you feeling this morning?" he asked.

"I slept like a baby all night. Thanks – for last night."

He shrugged. "I think you're just exhausted, love. Working too hard?"

She nodded. "Yes, you're right. I've just been pushing myself too hard."

Nico smiled and squeezed her hand. He didn't want to say any more. He didn't want Kate to think he was trying to dissuade her from her work.

Later Kate sat in the library and steadied herself as she picked up the phone and dialled Brian.

"Hi, Kate, great news. I've three more investors on board for the film. If we keep going like this we'll have a budget as big as *Titanic*!"

"Brian, I don't know how to tell you this, but I'm going to have to shelve the film for now."

"*What?*"

"I'm so sorry, Brian. It's for personal reasons. I just can't commit to the film right now."

"But, Kate, we have the finance all ready to go and you've put so much work into this already!" Brian couldn't believe what he was hearing.

"I know, Brian, and I'm sorry. But I just can't do this film right now and not for a long while, if ever," said Kate.

"Is everything all right?" asked Brian, concerned. He had known Kate for a long time. He knew how committed she was to a project and she never gave up. It was unsettling to hear her pull out of a project.

"I hope everything will be all right, Brian. But it's not at the moment and it will need all my time and effort to make it all right. I hope you understand?"

"Of course. I hope whatever it is works out for you."

"Thanks, Brian."

"Let's – keep in touch!"

"Yes," said Kate, smiling at his using the term she usually hated but didn't this time. "Let's definitely do that."

She hung up the phone and sat there thinking.

Valerie came in with the post.

"These are all your letters," she said, cheerily putting them on the desk.

"Thanks, Valerie," she said.

Looking down at the letters she saw the top envelope just had her name written across it and had no stamp.

"Where did this come from?" asked Kate.

"It was in the post-box along with the other letters. Hand-delivered by the look of it." Valerie left the room.

Kate picked up the envelope and it seemed bulky. Puzzled, she opened it up and saw there was a set of keys in it and a note. She unfolded the note.

Dear Kate,

Please find enclosed the keys for Hunter's Farm. I've found a new place to stay in town, much closer to work at the excavation site. Thanks for everything and apologies for any misunderstanding.

I wish you the very best in the future,

Daniel

Kate's forehead creased as she reread the note. The cold and clinical scientist side had come to the fore in Daniel by the tone of the note. She hoped he wasn't embarrassed or humiliated by what had occurred the previous night. She really held herself to blame but, along with a feeling of guilt, she also had a sense of relief that he had left Hunter's Farm and there was no need for them to be in contact with each other again. She put her head in her hands as she relived that moment of the kiss.

"Maybe in another life," she whispered. "But this is my life now, here with my family who I love."

She thought about the second DNA test that Nico did and wondered what Daniel would do with the information. She concluded that he would do nothing. He would need Nico's consent to make the results of the DNA public and she was sure he would not seek that after what had happened the previous night in Hunter's Farm. Daniel would just have to make do with what else he found at the famine grave, and keep Nico being descended from Seán Hegarty a secret. She was sure it would be infuriating for an archaeologist like Daniel to keep that information quiet, but he would have no choice.

CHAPTER 67

Nico and Kate were taking a walk that evening along the lakeshore. Nico kept the conversation light as he could see Kate was distracted and lost in her thoughts.

They turned back and as they reached the steps leading up to the terraced gardens, Nico asked, "Any more investors come through for the film?"

Kate came to a halt. It passed through her mind that it might be easier just to say that the investors had pulled out, but she decided she had hid truths from Nico for too long.

"I'm actually delaying making the film for now," she said.

"Oh?" he said surprised. "Why?"

"I just don't have the time to commit to it."

"But – you were all ready to go with it," he said, perplexed.

"Yes, and I've just been giving a lot of thought to it the last couple of days. You are right, Nico, it would just be too disruptive to our lives. Look what our lives were like during the last film, and we didn't have Cian then. It just wouldn't be fair on him, or you. Or me even. I don't have enough time to give to everything."

"And what brought on this huge change of mind?"

"I don't know – just going through everything in my mind, I suppose. I know I wouldn't have had the time to do all the research if Valerie hadn't been staying with us and stepping in to mind Cian and taking care of my other commitments. And Valerie, regardless what you might think, won't stay with us forever. She'll get a notion in her head and be gone as quickly as she arrived. That's Valerie."

"Well, I can't say I'm not happy about the film being shelved. But I don't want you to be unhappy either, Kate. If not making the film makes you unhappy, then I really don't want that."

"I've made my mind up, Nico, and you know what I'm like when I make my mind up," she smiled. "I'm looking forward now to spending more time with Cian and you."

He shrugged and smiled. "Okay, whatever you want."

They started walking up the steps and then he stopped abruptly.

"What?" Kate asked.

"And what about Daniel?"

Kate felt herself go cold. "What about him?"

His face was anxious and concerned. "What about the DNA test and all this stuff about me being descended from this Seán Hegarty? Have you heard anything back from him since?"

Kate felt her mouth go dry. Yes, she wanted to be honest and open Nico from now on, but she knew that if she told him Daniel had confirmed the truth from the second DNA test it would turn Nico's world upside down.

"Oh, yes, I meant to tell you. The results came back from the second test and confirmed that you are not related to Seán Hegarty," she lied.

"I see!" Nico's face visibly relaxed as if a weight was lifted from his shoulders.

"The first DNA test was proved completely wrong," said Kate.

"I was thinking . . . I was thinking it *had* to be wrong. It just didn't make any sense at all," said Nico.

"Sometimes life doesn't," she said as they continued up the steps.

That night Kate sat with Valerie at the table in the kitchen.

"Well, I for one am glad you're not going ahead with the film," said Valerie.

"Are you?" asked Kate.

"Sure I am. Sometimes you got to stop reaching for the stars and look around and appreciate what you've got on earth."

"Wise words, Valerie," said Kate. "In fact, I owe you a lot since you came to stay."

"Owe me?" Valerie was stupefied. "I think you'll find I owe you about five hundred bottles of Merlot at this stage not to mention eating you out of house and home."

"That's only material things," said Kate, reaching out and taking her hand. "You've been such support here with Cian and the tours and everything. But more than that, you've pointed out to me where I was going wrong in my life. Held a mirror up to me and stopped me from making some big mistakes and ruining my life."

"Well, if I have, then I'm glad!"

"I really enjoy having you here. We were never close, even as kids. And then we became adults and we went our own separate ways. This time is really giving us the chance to get to know each other again."

"It's been a ball!" said Valerie, squeezing her hand back.

Nico came into the kitchen and gave Kate a kiss on the top of her head.

"Kate's just been telling me how the film has been put on hold," said Valerie. "You know, now that you're going to have a bit of free time, why don't you head off on a little holiday?"

"Oh, I don't need a holiday," said Kate.

"Actually, that's not a bad idea, Kate," said Nico. "Just a short break even. A few days away could do you some good."

"And I can man the fort here for you . . . and you may as well take advantage of that while you can because I'm going to have to head back to New York soon." Valerie pulled a sad face.

"Back to New York!" Kate exclaimed. "But it's not safe for you!"

"Well, I've been keeping in contact with a few of my friends there and the word on the street is that Carlos has re-emerged from hiding and paid off his debt to those people."

"Well, that is a relief!" said Kate. "But you are not going back to him, are you?"

"Fuck – no!" said Valerie. "I ain't ever going near that fella again! A gal likes a little bit of excitement, but that guy doesn't know the difference between excitement and danger!"

"Well, I'm glad you won't be seeing him again," said Kate.

"You know, there's three billon men in the world. There's so many more to choose from than to get stuck with a loser like that!"

"And no doubt you'll keep looking for the right one." Nico winked at her

"Besides, I've a few job offers for singing in clubs and – and it's just time I get back to my life," she said.

"Well, we'll miss you," said Nico earnestly. "I kind of got used to you being around."

"Thanks, Nico!" Valerie smiled appreciatively. "So you should really take advantage of my offer and take a few days' break before I leave. I think you only have one bus tour next week, Kate? I could handle that no problem and look after the house till you're back."

Kate looked at Nico. "What do you think?"

"I think it's a great idea. It will do you the world of good and Cian as well," said Nico.

"Let's book it now!" said Valerie, reaching for the laptop sitting on the counter. "What do you think of Barcelona? Hear the clubs are great there."

"We won't be going clubbing with Cian!" said Kate as she became excited at the thought of a break away from everything.

CHAPTER 68

The following Monday Nico loaded their suitcases into the Land Cruiser and strapped Cian into the back seat.

Kate was talking to Valerie on the steps to the front door.

"Are you sure you'll be all right here on your own?" asked Kate. "You won't be lonely or scared?"

"Scared!" scoffed Valerie. "If I lived in the Bronx for two years without being scared then I think I'll manage a few days here on my own!"

"Okay. Phone me if there are any problems."

"There won't be! Now go or you'll miss your flight," urged Valerie.

"All right!" said Kate and gave her a hug.

Nico came back to the steps and gave Valerie a kiss on the cheek.

"Just don't worry about a thing and have a *good time*!" insisted Valerie as she watched Nico and Kate get into the front seats of the Land Cruiser.

Kate smiled at Valerie and waved at her as Nico started the car and they drove away. Valerie blew kisses after them as Kate continued to wave back at her.

Kate and Nico were sitting at a table on the pavement outside a café in Barcelona while Cian tucked into a bowl of different-flavoured ice cream as the sun beat down on them.

Kate had just made a call to Valerie.

"Is everything all right at home?" asked Nico.

"Just fine. She did the bus tour today and it all went well," said Kate.

"That's good."

"Nico, I was thinking about something. All the papers we have at Armstrong House from the centuries . . . the ledgers, the rent books, the cook books and recipes . . ."

"What about them?"

"Why don't we give them to the National Archives? A lot of the families from the great estates bequeathed their papers to them."

"But I thought you loved having them, and they were always there if you wanted to reference something."

"But I'd still have access to them in the National Archives, but it would be sharing them with other people as well. They will archive them properly and put them in a database. I think it would be good to share all this information with others who can read them as well. Armstrong House shows where your ancestors lived, but the papers show *how* they lived. It's really the true legacy of Armstrong House."

Nico nodded in agreement. "And they will be safe there in the archives for the future."

After their few days in Barcelona, Kate felt refreshed and relaxed as they landed at Dublin Airport and made their way down to Mayo. It had done them all the world of good to get away – just walking around the city, stopping off at cafés and taking time out to enjoy life. She couldn't remember the last time she had enjoyed herself so much – just being with Nico and Cian without any distractions was enjoyment enough for her.

It was ten o'clock at night as they pulled into the forecourt at Armstrong House and Kate saw the light shining brightly and warmly from the front hall. They got out of the car and Kate unstrapped Cian from the car seat as Nico took the luggage from the back. They walked up to the front door and Kate used her key to let them in.

"*Aunty Valerie! Aunty Valerie!*" called Cian excitedly, wide awake after his long sleep in the car, as he went racing down the hall and down the stairs to the kitchen.

Nico stood the two suitcases and other baggage inside the door, turned to Kate and asked, "Tea?"

"Oh, yes, please," she said and she leaned forward and kissed him.

Nico hurried off after Cian.

Kate looked around. It felt good to be home.

She was walking down the hall towards the back stairs when she stopped abruptly. She looked up at the wall and saw there was a blank space where the portrait of Lord Edward and Lady Anna usually hung.

She blinked a few times to make sure she wasn't seeing things. The portrait was definitely missing. She twirled around quickly and looking at the walls she saw there was another portrait missing – and then another!

She walked quickly across the hallway and into the drawing room and stared in horror as she saw the room was empty of all its contents. No couches, no cabinets, no sideboards, no ornaments.

"*Nico!*" she shrieked at the top of her voice, shaking from shock.

Nico came racing up the stairs from the kitchen.

"What's wrong?" he asked and then froze as he saw the empty drawing room.

"We've been robbed!" Kate cried.

Nico stood stock still, trying to take in what was happening.

Suddenly panic overtook Kate. "Oh, Nico, where's Valerie? She might be hurt or tied up by the thieves!"

Nico went pale at the thought. He turned and raced up the stairs, shouting, "*Valerie! Valerie!*"

Kate quickly came out of the drawing room and went to check the other rooms downstairs. As she hurried over to the dining room she spotted a note on a side-table in the hallway. She rushed over to it and picked it up. It was in Valerie's handwriting.

The note said simply said –

Sorry, darlings.

Kate stared at the note in disbelief.

Nico came racing down the stairs.

"I can't find her upstairs," Nico said.

"Nico – stop." She beckoned him over and handed him the note.

"What's this?" he asked.

"It's a note from Valerie," Kate said.

"I don't understand."

"She's robbed us! Robbed us blind!" said Kate.

"She wouldn't have!" said Nico.

"Oh, she would and she has," sighed Kate as she went and inspected the rest of the ground-floor rooms to see what had been stolen. Walking into the dining room she saw most of the furniture was still there, but the silver was all gone. The small parlour was stripped of everything. And some portraits from the ballroom had disappeared as well.

"But why would she do this to us, after all we did for her?" Nico was in shock.

"Why indeed?" said Kate as she stood in the hallway. "The bitch!"

At London's Heathrow Airport Valerie walked down the aisle of the plane, carrying a large bag, after everyone else was already seated.

"Could you take your seat quickly, miss?" urged an air steward.

"Sure I will, if I can just find it!" said Valerie.

The steward looked at her ticket and pointed to a seat by the window.

There were two seats together by the window and a man with well-groomed brown hair and an expensive-looking business suit was seated on the outside.

She smiled warmly down at him and then began to struggle to lift her bag into the overhead storage.

"Oh, would you mind?" she said, appealing to the man.

"Not at all," said the man, unbuckling his seat belt. He stood and took the bag and placed it in the compartment for her.

He smiled at her and allowed her to take her seat by the window before sitting back down.

"I nearly missed the flight!" she said to him as she fastened her seatbelt.

"That would have been a pity."

"It sure would! I've never been to Rio De Janeiro before. Have you?"

"No, it's my first time," he said.

"Two virgins together!" she giggled. "Are you going on business or pleasure?"

She was checking his finger and seeing no sign of a wedding ring.

"Business. I'm moving there with work."

"How interesting. I'm going for pleasure," she said. "But I might be staying a while."

"Lucky you!"

"I'm really looking forward to it. I wish this flight would take off and we could order a drink, don't you?"

"It won't be long now," he assured her.

The plane began to head away from the terminal and towards the runway.

"Oh, I'm such a bad flyer! I hate take-off! Do you mind if I hold your hand to settle my nerves?" she asked.

"Not at all," he said, offering his hand which she took and squeezed tightly as the plane gathered speed.

"I'm so glad that I ended up sitting beside you," said Valerie. "But then, I've always been lucky at landing on my feet."

Later that night, Nico and Kate sat in the kitchen in silence for what seemed like ages, trying to digest the fact they had been robbed.

"Well, I'd better call the police," said Kate, reaching for the mobile.

"What's the point? She'll be long gone out of the country by now, as will our antiques. Shipped to the continent and sold on the black market."

"We still have to report it," she said.

"Why? The insurance won't pay up. They'll say it was an inside job. They will want to know who was staying here and minding the house while we were away and we can hardly lie! They'll want to get a statement from her. So the truth will come out. We left the thief in charge of the house with a set of keys!"

Kate fought back angry tears, picking up the note that Valerie had left and waving it in the air. "We need to let the police know what has happened. She's even left an admission of guilt!"

"All that note says is – *sorry, darlings* – Valerie could be doing no more than just apologising for burning toast if the police see it. They won't be able to do anything. Valerie is gone, the furniture is gone. We should be just grateful she left us with what she did and didn't take everything."

"But she made sure to take all the expensive pieces! How will we ever be able to replace them? They cost a fortune."

Nico shook his head. "I'll talk to people I know in the furniture business. I'm sure they'll be able to make replicas."

"Cheap replicas instead of the originals and the expensive pieces that I had made." She shook her head. "Perhaps she was desperate. With that mob she was saying were after her in New York. Perhaps she had no choice but the raise the money any way she could."

"I think now you're just looking for excuses for her. That whole mob story was probably made up. Or if people in New York were after her for money, she had probably scammed them like she did us!"

Kate reached for her phone again. "She can't get away with this. I'm calling the police."

He took the phone off her. "Do you really want to see your sister's photo on *Crimewatch*? Do you really want this to come out?"

She thought hard. Nico was right. The insurance wouldn't pay and all they would be doing was bringing shame on themselves and becoming a laughing stock.

"So – we're just doing what your family has done for centuries in Armstrong House and just covering up a crime in order to save our reputations?" she said.

"The irony of it – but yes, it's the only way," said Nico.

"I thought you'd be more angry. I thought you'd be the one seething and I'd be trying to calm *you* down!"

He came and knelt by her chair. "Something happened this

summer, Kate. I'm not sure what was going on or why, but we stopped communicating. I think we nearly lost each other. And what's a few pieces of furniture compared to that?"

"It got that bad, didn't it?" she said as he embraced her.

"I thought I'd lost you," he said.

Kate held him tightly as she thought of Daniel and how near it had come to that.

"She even took Lord Edward and Lady Anna's portrait," said Kate. "She knew how much that meant to me."

"I nearly lost Lord Edward as my ancestor, and you know what that would have meant to me," he said.

Kate pulled back and looked at him, knowing that the furniture really didn't matter to Nico, but if he had learned the truth about Seán Hegarty it would have affected him deeply. She had never understood it before, but now she understood the importance of keeping secrets.

EPILOGUE

1866

Lawrence and Margaret's wedding day was a spectacular event, all the guests present agreed. They had been married in the church in the village on the estate and then the wedding party had made its way back to Armstrong House where the wedding banquet took place in the ballroom.

Edward and Anna sat happily side by side at the top table. It would soon be his turn to make a speech and he was much looking forward to doing so. It was such a day of pride for him and he would enthuse about all of Lawrence's qualities. He reminded himself that he must not forget to enthuse about Margaret as well and not make the speech all about Lawrence. The truth was, he reflected, he could not be any prouder of Lawrence being his son. Even if he wasn't his natural biological father. He had known that almost all of Lawrence's life.

He had been told the truth in the most shocking way. His smile left his face as he thought back to that fateful night when Lawrence was a baby sleeping in the nursery upstairs at Armstrong House. Seán Hegarty had been Anna's driver and general servant but had been thrown off the estate the previous year when Anna had accused him of stealing a locket of hers. Edward had been working late in the library and when he looked up he had got a shock to see Seán standing there. He had somehow managed to creep back into the estate and into the house. And then – and then – the memories came flooding back to Edward as he remembered what had occurred. Seán had declared to him that he had slept with Anna and

409

that Lawrence was his son. He had been horrified by the lie. But then, as he looked at Seán, he realised that he was speaking the truth. And it had all come together in his head. The fact that Anna had remained childless for years was in fact because he was unable to father a child. He realised that Anna had taken a desperate measure and slept with her servant Seán to beget a child and provide Edward and the Armstrong Estate with an heir. As Seán stood there telling him Lawrence was his and that he was going to tell everybody what had happened and claim the child, his voice had got louder and louder until he was shouting. Before Edward knew what he was doing he had picked up a poker and hit Seán across the head. He had never meant to kill the man. All he was trying to do was stop him from shouting such obscenities. He was terrified that somebody would hear. Edward had watched as Seán dropped to the floor, dead. Later he had taken the body and rolled it in a rug and had ridden in the dark of night to the local famine grave and put his body in there amongst all the other bodies. It was a perfect murder, he had always thought, and the perfect hiding place for a murdered body – nobody would ever find him there and find out what had happened.

Edward had decided after that night that he would never think about what had happened. It was as if it had never happened in his mind. He also allowed himself to forget that Lawrence was not his real son. But then Sinclair had brought it all home to him again, forcing him to relive what he had done.

He didn't forgive Anna for what she had done as he felt there was nothing to forgive. She had done what she had to do to give them a child. He could forgive Anna as he could forgive himself, because the most important thing was Lawrence and ensuring he had a happy life. And, as he looked at Lawrence beaming at Margaret on his wedding day, Edward congratulated himself and Anna for achieving just that.

"Are you alright, Edward?" asked Anna as she placed her hand on his.

He turned to look at her, beautiful in her wedding finery, and smiled.

"Of course," he said.

"You seem lost in your thoughts," she said.

"I was for a moment or two. Just thinking back through the years."

She blinked. "I haven't been the easiest wife to live with over the years, Edward. I'm sorry if I ever caused you hurt and pain, embarrassment or discomfort."

"On the contrary, I've told myself every day of my life how lucky I am to be married to you," he said.

"Really?" she said with a smile.

"Of course. As well as always being in love with you, you gave me the best son in the world, didn't you?"

Edward and Anna stared into each other's eyes as the smiles left their face faces for a moment.

"Anyway, it is time I made my speech!" said Edward, the smile back on his face as he stood up quickly and chinked a glass with a fork to bring silence to the room.

Anna sat listening as Edward praised his son and welcomed Margaret into the family. As she looked at Lawrence and Margaret she couldn't think of a couple who ever looked happier. She glanced at the long lines of tables filled with their guests.

"There are more titles in this room than in a library!" the Countess, who was seated on Anna's other side, whispered gleefully to Anna.

Anna nodded happily. There had also been a message of congratulations read out from the Prince and Princess of Wales.

As Edward spoke on, Anna was relieved that the Mountdares seemed to have got over the dreadful incident with Sinclair. They never mentioned it again, and she realised that was the way the Mountdares operated. They held their heads up and got on with things. Particularly Margaret. What a remarkable girl she was, thought Anna.

Thankfully Sinclair and Diana were out of their lives. They never made contact again after the day they were escorted from Hunter's Farm and off the estate. They never even heard of what became of them. Edward never mentioned them either. She knew what had happened had affected Edward deeply and so he never wanted to hear Sinclair's name mentioned again.

Anna never saw Seán again either. When she was in Castlewest she would often cast her eyes around the street to see if he was there like he had been before, looking at her. But she never did see him. Or, if he was there watching her, he kept himself hidden. Often, as she lay awake at night, she would creep out of her bed and over to the window and peer out, wondering if he was down in the forecourt looking up at her window, like he had been that other night. But he was never there. Sometimes she even hoped he would be there waving up at her, letting her know again he was all right. But deep down she knew she would never see him again.

She had given much thought to Sinclair's attack on Margaret over the year since it happened and she still could never fathom it. When he had everything in his grasp that his ambition and pride had always hungered for, for him to just ruin it in that very moment? She could never understand why he did it.

"How is the shooting season going for you this year, Anna?" asked the Countess, once the speeches were over and dessert was being served.

"I believe this season has been an excellent season so far," said Anna as she reached for her glass of white wine and sipped it.

"I might be lucky enough to have Edward organise a shoot while we are here? I did so enjoy the shoot here last year."

"I'm sure he would be delighted to do so. He still speaks of what an excellent shot you are!" said Anna.

"Oh, I try my best! You won't accompany us?"

"No, I'm afraid I still do not enjoy the sport," said Anna.

"Pity! Margaret is the same unfortunately," said the Countess.

"Oh? I thought she had enjoyed the day's shooting last year?"

"Enjoyed it? She hated it! She only spent an hour on the shoot and then abandoned us!"

Anna thought back to that day. It had been the first day of the shoot, the Glorious 12th.

"Where did she go?" she asked.

"She got a carriage back to the house here, idled her time away here – walking, as I recall," said the Countess.

Anna head was whirling as she thought about that week the previous year. The shoot had been on the Glorious 12th, the first day of the shooting season – she could never forget it as it was also the day she had met with Sinclair in the boathouse. The day he had revealed he knew the truth about Lawrence's father and was going to expose them. She had fainted at the garden party the previous day and so had spent all the time in her room, except for going to the boathouse to meet Sinclair. She had never known that Margaret had not been on the shoot. She had thought everybody was away from the house except for her during that day.

Anna thought of the Countess's words about Margaret: *'Idled her time here away here – walking, as I recall.'* Anna looked at Margaret who was laughing and joking with Lawrence as a realisation flashed through her mind. Had Margaret been out walking down by the lake in the afternoon when she met Sinclair in the boathouse? Had she seen Anna go into the boathouse and then followed her and heard her talking with Sinclair and listened in? It all started to make sense to Anna.

If Margaret had heard what Sinclair was saying then she would have known that Lawrence and the Armstrongs were about to be destroyed.

Anna stared at Margaret.

It had never made sense to her that Sinclair had attacked Margaret that night, not when he was about to be handed the Armstrong Estate. And now she realised that Sinclair had been speaking the truth. He never did attack Margaret. She had in some way laid a trap for him to go to her room and then faked an attack on herself. She had done this in order to save Lawrence and their future together. It all made sense to Anna in an instant. Margaret's cool demeanour the next day. Her happy face as she rode away from Armstrong House.

Margaret had staged the whole thing.

As Anna continued to stare at Margaret, the girl seemed to sense her stare. She looked over at Anna, then smiled and waved to her.

Anna waved back and Margaret continued laughing and

chatting with Lawrence.

"Lawrence has done very well for himself," said the Countess. "Margaret is an exceptional girl. So intelligent and loyal, she will be a great asset to him in the years to come."

"Yes," said Anna. "I do not doubt it for a moment."

On her other side, Edward said, "Ladies and gentlemen – raise your glasses in a toast to the happy couple – Lawrence and Margaret!"

"To the happy couple!" said the guests in chorus as they clinked wineglasses with each other.

Edward turned to Anna, holding his glass out to her while he smiled lovingly.

"To the happy couple," repeated Anna as she clinked her glass against her husband's.

The End

The House

Can a house keep secrets?

1840's – When Lord Edward Armstrong builds the house for his bride, Anna, the family is at the climax of its power. But its world is threatened when no heir is born. Anna could restore their fortunes, but it would mean the ultimate betrayal. Then the Great Famine grips the country.

1910's – Clara finds life as lady of the manor is not what she expected when she married Pierce Armstrong. As the First World War rages, she finds solace in artist Johnny Seymour's decadent circle. Then the War of Independence erupts and Clara is caught between two men, deceit and revenge.

Present Day – When Kate Fallon sees the house it is love at first sight. She and her tycoon husband Tony buy it and hire the last Armstrong owner, architect Nico, to oversee its restoration.

As Kate's fascination with the house grows, she and Nico begin to uncover its history and the fates of its occupants in centuries past. But then, as her husband's business empire faces ruin, Kate realises that she is in danger of losing everything.

Betrayal, deceit, revenge, obsession – one house, one family, three generations.

A. O'CONNOR

ISBN 978-184223-550-8

ALSO AVAILABLE

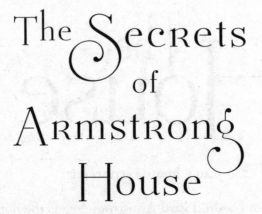

The Secrets of Armstrong House

Present day – Kate and Nico Collins are filming a docudrama about life in their home Armstrong House in Ireland during its golden age at the turn of the century. When they discover a cover-up of a terrible crime involving Nico's great-grandfather Lord Charles Armstrong, they set out to solve a mystery over a century old.

1888 – Arabella Tattinger arrives to attend a glittering ball at Armstrong House as the family's younger son Harrison's fiancée. Her head is turned by the glamorous aristocratic family, and most of all by the eldest son and heir, the exciting but dangerous Charles. A chain of events unfolds from that night which casts the family into years of a bitter feud.

1899 – When American heiress Victoria Van Hoeven marries into the family, she is determined bring peace at last to the Armstrongs. But everywhere dangers are circling and secrets are ready to emerge from the shadows. Not just from outside the house but from within their golden circle. Victoria is stepping into the firestorm.

Kate and Nico press on in their efforts to uncover the truth – but are some secrets best kept hidden?

A. O'CONNOR

ISBN 978-184223-626-0

THE
FOOTMAN

*From the country mansions of 1930s Ireland, to the decadence of
1940s wartime Paris to the courtrooms of
London in modern times.*

What the Footman saw . . .

In 1930s Ireland, Joe Grady becomes the footman at the stately
home Cliffenden, owned by the glamorous Fullerton family. Joe
is enthralled by the intrigue and scandal above stairs, and soon
becomes a favourite of the daughter of the house, Cassie. There is
mounting pressure on Cassie to marry American banker Wally
Stanton. But Cassie is having a secret affair with the unsuitable
Bowden Grey.

What the Footman did . . .

When Cassie and Bowden's affair is discovered in disgraceful
circumstances, the lovers are banned from seeing each other. Joe
risks his position at Cliffenden, becoming a messenger between
them, until he finds himself making a choice that will change the
lives of everyone at Cliffenden forever.

Decades later, Joe has achieved great success as a barrister. When
suddenly Cassie is arrested for a sensational crime, he sets out to
discover what happened to her in the intervening years. He
realises his actions at Cliffenden set off a chain of events that led
to murder. But is Cassie guilty? Innocent or guilty, can Joe ever
make amends for his part in her downfall?

A. O'CONNOR

ISBN 978-178199-904-2

The Left-Handed Marriage

Irish beauty Diana Cantwell meets Max Von Hoffsten, heir to a German count, and their romance blossoms in the carefree days before the First World War. But, when they become engaged, Max's father insists on a 'left-handed marriage', a custom among the German aristocracy in cases where the bride does not have the required pedigree. So, though Diana will be Max's lawful wife, neither she nor their children will have any claim to Max's eventual title or wealth.

Max and Diana agree to these terms and the newlyweds dazzle from Ascot to the Riviera. However, as the dark clouds of war gather across Europe, Diana becomes concerned by her husband's unpredictability and what she suspects are sinister secrets beneath his family's glamorous lifestyle.

When war is declared Diana finds herself caught between two sides, as her own Anglo-Irish family are fighting for the British and Max is an officer in the German army. When Max is reported missing presumed dead, Diana is rejected by his family. Widowed, penniless, she sets out to rebuild her life.

A.O'Connor once more spins an extraordinary tale that holds us spellbound, with the mixture of impeccable research and powerful storytelling that made *The House* and *The Secrets of Armstrong House* bestsellers.

A. O'CONNOR

ISBN 978-178199-9400

Talk Show

Joshua Green's talk show has stormed to the top in Irish TV, providing him and his beautiful wife Soraya with an enviable lifestyle. Soraya is blissfully happy with Joshua, two toddler children and her teenage stepson Lee. The flies in the ointment are her well-heeled parents' contempt for her husband, and Lee and Joshua's troubled relationship.

The show's researcher Brooke Radcliffe considers herself a moral person, so why is she having an affair with a married man? When the network's new boss, Guy Burton, takes an interest in her, she is flattered but cautious. Perhaps she is under selling herself?

The show's producer Kim Davenport feels no guilt about exploiting guests' emotions for higher ratings. That's what makes a talk show tick, after all. But then a whispering campaign starts, with accusations about the callous treatment of guests on the show. As the hate campaign gathers pace, details of Joshua's life that Soraya never knew emerge.

Kim realises that somebody is out to ruin everything she and Joshua have worked for. As her career and Joshua's idyllic life unravel, they struggle to identify their enemy. But time is running out.

A. O'CONNOR

ISBN 978-184223-499-0

Ambition

Franklyns – London's high-end store for the rich and famous – is being run into the ground by its egocentric owner Karl Furstin, who uses the store's bank account as his own personal trust fund.

In steps retail legend Stephanie Holden, a single mum with a real rags-to-riches story, to try and bring Franklyns back from the brink.

But not everyone is happy with the new management. HR director Nicola Newman, who's used to getting her own way, is determined that Stephanie will fail and sets out to sabotage her every move, while making a few moves herself on the man of her dreams.

Franklyns' general manager and the store's ladies' man, Paul Stewart, owes his success to Furstin, but will he play along with the new management or double-cross them on his way up the ladder?

As she tries to rebuild her fragile relationship with her wayward son Leo, will Stephanie be able to add Franklyns to her list of success stories? Just how far will the cold and calculating Nicola go to hold on to the control, and the man, she yearns for? Blinded by success, will Paul finally see the happiness that's standing right in front of him?

A. O'CONNOR

ISBN 978-184223-396-3

If you enjoyed this book from
Poolbeg why not visit our website:

www.poolbeg.com

and get another book delivered straight
to your home or to a friend's home.

All books despatched within 24 hours.

POOLBEG

Why not join our mailing list at
www.poolbeg.com and get some
fantastic offers, competitions,
author interviews and much more?

@PoolbegBooks